Love & Other Liabilities

FIONA McCANN

POOLBEG

This book is a work of fiction. References to real people, events, establishments, organisations, or locales are intended only to provide a sense of authenticity, and are used fictitiously. All other characters, and all incidents and dialogue, are drawn from the author's imagination and are not to be construed as real.

Published 2026

by Poolbeg Press Ltd., 123 Grange Hill, Baldoyle,

Dublin 13, Ireland

Email: poolbeg@poolbeg.com

A catalogue record for this book is available from the British Library.

ISBN 978-1-78199-654-6

www.poolbeg.com

About the Author

Fiona McCann lives in the foothills of the Dublin mountains with her husband, two children and one exceptionally placid Golden Retriever. Born in Cork but making her way to Dublin as a child via Coventry and London, her formative summers were all spent on a very special West Cork island that inspired the setting for this novel. Over the years she has worked in a non-creative capacity in the animation field, in a creative capacity in the accounts field and in both capacities in the motherhood field! This is her first novel (if you don't count the two gathering dust in a drawer).

Acknowledgements

I've been trying to figure out how to write a novel for many years. Over that time a lot of innocent people have been subjected to my efforts. On their behalf, I would especially like to thank Neasa Murphy for the many thousands of words she has read and for her early and wholly-biased praise which gave me the courage to keep going. I'd also like to thank my dad, Fin Breatnach, for his willingness to read draft after draft and his unerring eye for a typo – as well as the gift of life itself, obviously! And my mother Carmel for her steadfast belief that her quietest chick could have something to say that people might want to hear. (* See also for the gift of life).

To my siblings, who are in all my best memories of growing up. To doctors Cormac and Colm for being there to offer medical advice whenever I needed to put a character through the ringer (all mistakes my own) and to therapist Cara for emotional support of the author herself. I think my knee has finally stopped shaking!

I've been fortunate to cross paths with some very talented people whose feedback on early manuscripts helped me grow as a writer. Chief amongst these are Rebecca Horsfall and Becky Hunter whose knowledge, insights and encouragement were invaluable.

To Paula Campbell for her belief in this story and for her guidance which made it stronger. To Gaye Shortland for her formidable eye for detail and for so deftly steering me through edits. To David Prendergast for all his work on the layout and design and to all the team at Poolbeg Press.

To my children, Niamh and Seán, for just being their wonderful selves and last, but certainly not least, to my husband Stephen for, well, pretty much everything. I was so lucky to marry my best friend. If I've managed to write a good romance, I've had plenty of inspiration.

To everyone who has bought this book, thank you! I hope you'll love reading it as much as I loved writing it.

Fiona x

Dedication

To my grandparents Monica and Riobárd Breatnach

For the love, the magic and the stories.

x Fíóna Beag

Chapter One

Casual Inconspicuous

If Lily Barrett had ever imagined herself returning to this place, it wouldn't have been broke, in disguise or with an attention-attracting happy-head in tow.

Cassandra whooped to a halt beside her, forcing disembarking passengers to veer as she managed a low bounce under the weight of her overstuffed rucksack.

'*They have a bus, Lily! I knew there had to be one!*'

Dressed for the wilds in a flamingo-pink singlet and satin shorts, with hiking boots on her feet and a zebra-striped bandanna in her hair, Lily's flatmate had been preparing herself both mentally and stylistically for this ordeal since early morning.

Lily steered her down the pier before she could announce their arrival any louder. Casual Inconspicuous was her own look for the day and while the August heat had ruled out a trench coat and the sea breeze made hiding behind a newspaper hazardous, her top was shapeless, her baggy shorts unflattering and her distinctive mane of auburn hair tucked out of sight under a baseball cap. Head down, she could be any day-tripper to the island. That was how she wanted it. The fewer people who knew she was home – she corrected that thought sharply – who knew she was *here* the better.

'There's no bus,' she murmured. 'Everyone just walks.'

But Cassandra was still looking as though she'd won the lottery. 'But over there, though. See?'

Lily followed her line of sight as the milling crowds parted to reveal a rusting minibus into which bags and bodies were being unceremoniously thrown. A fair-haired man in jeans and a tight T-shirt was having an easy time hustling for business. He handed a middle-aged woman into the last empty seat and made promises to return 'in no time' for everyone else.

Lily bit on a chunk of cheek until it hurt. Thirty seconds on Inish Ruin and she was already off-kilter, unsure if it was the things that were different or the things that were the same that unsettled her most.

She pushed her mirrored shades further up the bridge of her nose as she cast a glance back to her only means of escape. The *West Cork Ferries* logo was the same but Seánie Murphy had got himself a bigger boat sometime in the last decade: metal instead of wood, two decks instead of one and the crossing from the mainland that had always taken twenty-four minutes now took just seventeen.

Seánie would recognise her as easily as any islander if he got a good look at her, but his attention was currently on his crew as they tossed trays of groceries onto the pier. Like his boat, he was now bigger round the middle too. But his face was exactly as Lily remembered it, weathered to a ruddy sheen with a tweed cap pushing down unruly tufts of white hair.

His gaze shifted in her direction and she snapped into motion to join Cassandra at the end of a rapidly forming queue.

'You really grew up here?' Cassandra's face was beaming as a sweep of her hand took in the small harbour, then back across the bay, all the way to the mainland town of Cúltrá with its necklace of gleaming yachts.

'It always looks good in the sunshine,' Lily admitted, 'but you wouldn't like it in winter with the sea spray hitting your window from half a mile away.'

'But you'd have cosy fires and be curled up in front of the telly while the wind howled.'

'With rubbish channels? No mobile coverage? No–'

Cassandra held up her phone and grinned. 'You can stop trying to wind me up about this place. Free Wi-Fi.'

Lily stared at the full bars of signal in disbelief. When had *that* happened? When she'd been here the frustration level from lack of signal was so high that no one was bothering with mobiles. If you needed to reach someone you used the landline or you got on your bike and pedalled. But, as everyone she'd loved then lived less than ten minutes away, it hadn't felt that much of a hardship.

Nothing had felt hard about living here, in truth. Except being sent away.

'First you tell me we've to walk when there's a bus,' said Cassandra. 'Next not to bother with my phone 'cause it won't work. Are you sure it's a cottage we'll be staying in? It's not going to turn out to be a hotel with a nice spa, is it? Seaweed wraps and sea-salt scrubs? Oh my God, I'm right, aren't I? It's a surprise to celebrate my new job. Ah, Lily, you shouldn't–'

'I didn't,' she said quickly, before expectations could run any wilder. 'Sure I didn't even know you were coming until yesterday, when you just announced you'd bought a ticket. It's just a cottage, I swear. Old. Small. Nothing to get excited about.'

But Cassandra's enthusiasm was undimmed. 'I just know it'll be gorgeous.' She turned away and started photographing a pile of old fishing nets that had been weighted down with a tractor tyre.

The words 'quaint' and 'cute' were uttered.

And Lily sought refuge in calculations. There were forty-two people ahead of them in this colourful queue, their clothes flapping in the breeze like oversized bunting. The minibus had rattled off full to capacity with nine souls aboard. The island boasted just 4 kilometres of road but the best of the beaches lay on the far side and speed was severely restricted – by the terrain as much as the faded speed-limit sign by the pier wall. They'd be here an hour.

A group of teenagers had apparently reached the same conclusion. They headed off at a marching pace, sleeping bags strapped to their rucksacks and plastic bags clinking from their wrists.

The queue moved forward a few metres.

A woman ahead of them, wearing a straw hat with a pink ribbon, gave a tired sigh as she shuffled. It was her daughter, though, who drew Lily's attention. She was around nine or ten, with hair the exact same hue as her own.

'Let's walk too, Cass,' Lily said. 'It'll be much faster.'

'We can't,' Cassandra whispered. 'I have a plan.'

The girl shot a curious glance their way and Lily saw her eyes were a blue so steely they were almost silver.

'What is it?' she asked, turning back to Cassandra.

'The plan,' Cassandra explained, as the ferry engine suddenly growled to life with a chug and belch of diesel fumes, 'is to wait for everyone else to give up.'

Lily chanced another glance behind her, in time to see the crew hauling in the ropes. Then the vessel slowly pulled away from the pier as Seánie reversed it, with practised ease, into the start of his turn.

No escape now.

'Could we *please* walk?' she said.

Cassandra reluctantly agreed to try what her legs might accomplish. The steep hill from the pier nearly finished her though. She clutched her stomach at the top and demanded to know which side her appendix was on.

The minibus tooted as it passed them on its way back down.

Cassandra held up her hand in a plea for mercy.

The driver acknowledged it with a friendly wave and carried on and only Lily's promise it was almost all downhill from here could move her on again.

Cassandra whipped off her bandanna and wiped her forehead with it, releasing a mass of golden curls. 'I suppose that means we're going south,' she surmised as the road dipped.

With the morning sun beating hard on their backs, Lily scrutinised Cassandra's face for comedy. Found none. '*Umm* ...'

'Thought as much.'

Small fields, pockmarked by cattle hooves, spread out to their left. To their right a scrub of weather-beaten evergreens clung to a rise of rock. Here the road forked by a wooden signpost into which letters had been carved and painted white. *O'Callaghan's Pub 500m* marked the uphill path, *Beaches* the other.

Cassandra turned a readily interpretable face to her.

'No,' said Lily. 'It's ten in the morning. And it's uphill.'

'I could manage five hundred metres if there was a drink at the end of it. You've dragged me to this wilderness. I'm gasping.'

'I dragged you? You booked yourself an airline ticket behind my back. Plus there's a full water bottle sticking out of your pocket. You won't die of thirst.'

'Ah, come on, Lily. Who goes on holiday by themselves?'

'I never said this was a holiday. I have ... *things* to get done while I'm here.'

'Ah, but a working holiday is still a holiday, though. Not much difference. Besides, a girl on the ferry said the barman in O'Callaghan's is a complete ride.'

Lily tripped over her own feet and had the fleeting sensation of being in waves too big for her, of holding her breath until she broke the surface. She forced an inhale. No. Whoever was working at O'Callaghan's right now couldn't be *him*. *He* was somewhere far, far away – fighting fires probably or rescuing mountain climbers or deactivating bombs. Any job where he could be dramatically helpful and get paid for it. On second thoughts, why be that generous? He was somewhere just pretending to be heroic while casually breaking hearts. Yes, that was a better fit. Luke the Pretender. He certainly wasn't still pulling pints in his family's pub. Even so, they wouldn't be going within five hundred metres of it.

'We're not going.'

'*At all?*' choked Cassandra. 'But it's the only pub on the island!'

'It's just for a few days. Think of it as a deep cleanse for your system. Even better than a spa break?' She strode on down the left fork: a single lane of weathered tarmac divided in the middle by a stubby line of grass.

Cassandra's dragging footsteps followed. 'It's fine for you but some of us have to work for our love lives. Keep our eyes peeled for opportunities. I'm tired of fellas at the club only talking to me to get your number.'

'They're talking to you because you're a gorgeous girl everyone wants to hang out with. If you could just try have a bit more self-confidence.'

'They're talking to me about you, Lily. I'm on the receiving end of it. I know what they're talking to me about.'

Well ... feck. Lily halted and waited for her to catch up. 'I'm really sorry if that happened. But what do I always say about nightclubs?'

'To never let you order tequila in one.'

'No. The other one.'

Cassandra's forehead scrunched in momentary concentration. Then she rolled her eyes and *tsk*ed. 'That they're not the place to find love.'

'And?'

'That love isn't worth the trouble. But you could still try to help me find it. I'm nearly twenty-four. I'll be over the moon soon.'

'Over the hill, you mean?'

'Both,' she said, her large, blue eyes watering plaintively.

Lily scratched her neck, wondering at what point Cassandra would remember Lily was four years her senior. 'You're a million miles from the moon – and the hill. You do know that, right?'

'Okay. Sure. But this could be our last chance to go out in ages.'

Their last chance in forever more like, as Cassandra had just secured her dream job at a woman's publication in Belfast and would be moving out of their pokey London flat in less than a fortnight. And Lily was as happy about that as Cassandra herself could be. Yes, happiness was the emotion tightening her chest every time she thought of living in that dingy place without her. But it would be so much easier not having anyone to care about again. And she'd never intended to become friends with Cassandra, she reminded herself. The girl had just proved impervious to all attempts to keep her at a distance.

She made to walk on but the long pause had left Cassandra looking uncomfortable. 'Lily?'

'Yeah.'

'Belfast is just a short flight from London. I could come back all the time.'

'That'd cost you a fortune. Besides, you'll be swamped at the weekends from now on. Networking and socialising with all those photographers and writers and beauticians you were so excited to meet. Don't feel you have to come back just to keep me company.'

But Cassandra looked so hurt Lily almost winced. 'But we're practically family. The big sister I never had.'

Lily swallowed hard. The sentiment was lovely but while she'd never been anyone's sibling she imagined the job description included giving younger chicks a push when they needed to fly. Besides, Cassandra already had two older sisters. A fact it felt timely to point out. So she did.

Cassandra however remained unfazed. 'The one I never had,' she repeated firmly and gave Lily's hand a quick squeeze. It was a curious gesture – half rebuke, half sympathy. 'No woman is an island.'

Lily felt sweat beading on her forehead and sought for a change of subject. 'Remind me again about the place where you'll be staying in Belfast. Did you say it was near the sea?'

But Cassandra's answer was cut short as a cheerful toot drove them into a dense bank of ferns to avoid being run over by the minibus. It bumped over a rut, its suspension squeaking, and disappeared round a bend.

Here a wall rose, waist-high, guarding the edge of a steep promontory. Below, sunlight bounced off the swollen waters of An Fáinne, the little inlet around which the hilly spine of the island curved. The tide was high but Lily could picture how it would look in six hours when the waters would have retreated, leaving a drab hunting ground for redshank and curlews, stirring the shallows for lugworms.

'Wow, that's some view!'

It was indeed and Lily's lung capacity seemed to double as she took the deepest breath. But she led them off again, following the road as it sloped gently to run level with the inlet. They passed the school – a two-roomed building with posters showing the insects of Inish Ruin – and then the shop/post office which was a grey Portakabin on blocks with a handwritten sign on the door that read "*Open at 2*".

After this came a tunnel of trees. Alder and sycamore cast heavy shade but the humidity here heavily outweighed any relief from the sun. It was oppressive. Not a leaf stirred which made the buzzing of insects sound all the louder. Lily pulled off her cap and shades and shook out her hair to cool herself as Cassandra flapped at them both with her bandanna.

At the end of the tunnel the air lightened once more as a magnificently planted garden came into view. The stone building at its heart looked as if it had taken root, tethered by trailing lines of jasmine. A wind chime tinkled and a profusion of scents filled the air.

Cassandra read the plaque. '*Rivers' Hostel.* What rivers?'

'There's none. It's run by a man called Jasper Rivers.'

'Oh. Well, it'd be lovely to stay here.' Cassandra was gazing past the rows of flowers to the meadow beyond which ran on back down to the shoreline of An Fáinne – and the focal point of a wicker bench, nestled in a patch of oxeye daisies.

'We can't,' Lily said. 'It's a retreat for recovering alcoholics. A place they can come on holiday and know temptation won't be put in front of them. Jasper does all the cooking, runs classes in painting and mindfulness. He's very talented.' Not to mention one of the three people she'd cared about most on Inish Ruin. Nana was dead. *He* was dead to her. What of Jasper?

'He doesn't seem to have any guests.'

'They must be on a day trip. Come on. Another five minutes and we're there.'

They reached another crossroads and another wooden sign: left and uphill for the church, right for the beaches. They turned right and heard the minibus long before they saw it this time. Emptied of passengers now, the driver gave a toot as he flashed past them. Then he hit the brakes.

'Here we go,' said Cassandra, with a nod to the cap and shades in Lily's hand. 'I suppose you don't want me to give him your number?'

Lily scrubbed her long fringe down over her eyes. 'Please don't even give him my name.'

The driver reversed as the exhaust pipe gave the grassy divide a few gentle whacks. He wound his window down the last few inches. 'Down for the weekend, are yez, girls?'

It was a Dublin accent and Lily hazarded a glance to find a pleasant, sun-kissed face staring back at her. A face not much older than Cassandra's. A face that seemed to expect good things were about to happen.

'We're here for a few days,' said Cassandra, sounding a little breathy beside her. 'Maybe longer.'

It was all the invitation he needed. He turned off the engine which spluttered before extinguishing itself with a judder. 'I came for a week once. Never left. Well, you've picked a good one. It's to stay fine for the Bank Holiday. Nice for camping.' His words included them both but his gaze was fixed on Lily, a coaxing look about him.

Cassandra cleared her throat and regained his attention. 'Oh, we're not camping. Never thought to bring the gear unfortunately.'

'Ah, that's a shame. It's great craic at the beach. There's a big crowd in this weekend too. Mostly lads though. Might be rowdy.'

'I could handle it,' said Cassandra. 'I was in the Brownies.'

Lily expected a snigger at this guileless confession but to her relief he gave Cassandra a megawatt smile instead.

'No way!' he said. 'I was in the Scouts but I couldn't tell you a slip knot from a square knot now. I've a pop-up tent these days. Burst its bag last summer in the back seat and nearly took out three passengers.'

Cassandra laughed.

The bus driver laughed.

Cassandra blushed.

The bus driver blushed.

And Lily experienced the lovely sensation of becoming invisible.

'I'm Eric.' He stuck his arm out the window and Cassandra shook the hand attached to it readily.

'Cassandra.'

'*Cas-san-dra*,' he tried it out slowly. 'That's a beautiful name. Suits you. Something Grecian about them curls.' He suddenly frowned. 'Have you taken a wrong turn then if you're not camping? The hotel is beside the pub. There's nowhere else to stay except the hostel ... you're not ...?'

'Not recovering alcoholics? No. Not yet anyway.'

Eric smiled again, seemingly charmed. 'I can give you a lift back?' He started up the engine and looked at Cassandra hopefully.

'Oh no. We're not booked into the hotel. We're staying at Barrett Cottage.'

His brows rose. 'Here for the wedding so? That's great. I'll get to see a lot of you.'

'Oh?'

'Because I'm helping out and everything.'

Cassandra blushed a darker shade. 'I'd like that.'

'You would?'

'Who's getting married?' asked Lily, loath to interrupt but unable to curb her curiosity.

'Betty McCarthy. But if ye're staying at Barrett Cottage then–'

'Oh my God! To whom?'

'Sorry?'

'Who is Betty getting married to?'

'Ned Dennehy, but aren't you–'

'I don't believe it! When's the wedding on?'

Eric was staring at her, his mouth open, before Lily remembered she wasn't supposed to be drawing any attention to herself.

'I must get them something,' she murmured, looking to the ground.

'Yes, we really must,' said Cassandra. 'Guess I'll see you around, Eric. Or not,' she added with a sigh. She adjusted her rucksack with a toss of her shoulders and set off.

Eric saluted them with a toot and drove on.

With a quick sprint Lily caught up to her. But Cassandra's expression was now glum. 'What's up?'

'You just have to smile at them.'

'Cassandra, stop.'

'Forget it, okay? I know it's not deliberate.'

'No really stop. This is the turnoff.' To their left was the start of Barrett Lane.

'Oh. Where's the cottage?'

'It's just over that ridge.'

Cassandra stared up the steep slope, her expression hardening from marshmallow-soft to marshmallow-determined. She took a deep breath in through her nose, her chest rising.

'I can do this.'

'Yes, you can,' Lily agreed as she slid her hand into her pocket. There it brushed crisply folded solicitors' stationery. She pictured the even crisper eviction notice printed on it. Her reminder there was *no choice* but to deal with her financial situation now. So, assuring herself she could do this too, Lily led them on.

Chapter Two

Heaven and Hell

Luke O'Callaghan was neither fighting fires, rescuing mountain climbers, nor deactivating bombs that morning. Instead he was leaning over a wooden picnic table in the beer garden of O'Callaghan's Pub, a sketch pad under one hand and a stick of charcoal balanced between the thumb and middle finger of the other. The muscles in his back and neck were tightly strained as he worked like lightning across the textured page, his attention locked on the building fifty feet away.

Speed was always of the essence when he sketched. If he thought about what he was doing too much he would invariably ruin it. The more he just *felt* his way through, the better a result he got – at least that's what his teacher had surmised way back when she first discovered his talent. As people had been paying good money for his work ever since, he was disinclined to question her logic at this stage. It was usually wild and discarded things that drew his eye: shells and fallen rocks, driftwood and tangled seaweed and bigger sketches of deserted beaches that sold almost as fast as he could produce them. The cheerful vista of his family's pub wouldn't ordinarily have drawn out his charcoals but as a farewell gift-cum-peace-offering to his dad, he was hoping it would be well received. With his eye on the building eight seconds out of every ten, he willed his fingers to translate what he saw into faithful line and shadow.

A quick glance through the window showed his dad puce with emotion, wiping the countertop with enough force to remove the varnish. The row between them that morning had been epic but since Luke had absconded from the field of battle to go sketch, Paudie was now venting his frustrations on the next available target and their trainee barman Mikey was being told to get his arse in gear, that the beer glasses wouldn't unload themselves from the dishwasher and that he'd get better value out of a head of cabbage.

Luke returned to his sketch and checked his progress on the page, softening a corner with a dancing shuffle of his ring finger.

There was a crash of glass from inside the bar followed by a roar.

The patio doors opened. Luke glanced up, expecting to see his dad but his mother stood there instead, looking as immaculate as any Golden Age film star in cashmere and silk. With a bracing smile, Eithne O'Callaghan closed the door behind her and crossed the lawn. Her smile dipped as she took in his face. He guessed there was a smudge of charcoal on there somewhere or other. He gave his unfinished drawing a rueful glance.

'I'll go talk to him again,' he said.

'Don't bother.' She sat beside him. 'I've been telling him for years I didn't want my sons stuck here when they could be out in the world. I told him that when Mark left and we had the same conversation about Conor *and* James. He'll get over it. He always does.'

'I'm the last though. He says he can't retire unless–'

'Retire? That man'll never retire. What would he do if he did? Only sit around the place trying to tell you how to run it. Don't mind him. He thrives on stress. No, I won't have you ending up like me.' She looked down at her outfit and picked a speck of fluff off the sleeve. 'All dressed up and nowhere to go. And my teachers forever saying how much potential I had? All wasted.'

'I'd just like his blessing, you know? It's not like I'm leaving to go rob banks.'

'I know, Luke. He was just really hoping one of ye would have your heart set on being a publican but I'm delighted you're moving to Cork full-time. A chance to settle down properly at long last.'

Settle down properly was code for 'be more like Mark'. The Golden Child, his eldest brother had become a doctor, a husband and a father by the time he was Luke's age. No pressure then. He was happy for Mark, truly he was, but it was hard for the rest of them not to feel like runners-up beside him. He looked away across the bay and spotted the returning ferry making the turn into Cúltrá Harbour and reminded himself that in a week he'd be on it himself to go start a job *he* was proud of at least.

'So, how's Gráinne doing?' she asked, pulling him from this thought.

'Fine, I'm sure. We're not dating anymore.'

'Ah, Luke. Why not? She's lovely.'

He raised a brow as he stared at her. 'You never even met her.'

'Maybe. But didn't you say she was Betty's grandniece?'

'So?'

'So good people. And she's a nurse, isn't she? So ye'll both be medical professionals. Just like Mark and Saoirse.'

'Saoirse's a clerical officer.'

'Who works at a hospital! And look how happy they are. Married. Two kids.'

'Mam, seriously?'

'Sure you might get back together when you're bringing all the emergency patients in for treatment. Watch *Grey's Anatomy*. Love blossoms in life and death circumstances.'

He was about to protest when she suddenly cocked her head towards the bar.

'It's gone very quiet.'

It had.

They exchanged a glance, rose together and went inside.

The decor in the bar reflected Luke's parents in so far as everything clashed. His mother had wanted cruise-liner glamour and his dad something that resembled the hold of a galleon. The result was lacquered wooden floors, polished white marble tabletops, mini-chandeliers and the contents of Blackbeard's attic draped all around the walls.

There was no sign of his dad but young Mikey was serving Donie, Pat and Luke's Grandad Tadhg at the bar. It was too early yet for the tourists. Lunchtime would be hectic but for now it was just the three retirees sitting in a row, their elbows resting on beer mats for comfort. Donie and Pat were deep in discussion while his grandad was nodding hard. At ninety-one, with a Dowager's Hump that had taken at least a foot off his height, he made the two eighty-year-olds beside him look positively sprightly.

Luke opened a packet of peanuts, poured them into a bowl and set them on the counter in front of Donie, who immediately leaned in and fixed him with a sly look.

'What have yeh been doing to Paudie, boy? He looks like he's about to burst a blood vessel.'

'Ah now,' said Eithne before he could answer. She'd want to be the one making the announcement he was leaving for good *only* when she was sure of getting maximum value for her news, precious commodity that it was. 'No one's bursting any blood vessels and if anyone *was* bursting blood vessels it would be me.'

Donie smiled, turning his pint clockwise a few degrees. 'Why would you be bursting a blood vessel, Eithne? Sure aren't you cool as a cucumber? Nothing flusters you.'

She tidied a lock of hair behind her ear, looking pleased. 'Well, be that as it may, I've a lot on this week with the wedding. We're almost completely booked and catering to big numbers is no easy task. I think the entire island is invited. It'll be all hands on deck. Any help in the run-up gratefully accepted.'

Donie was in quick with his usual excuse. 'You know I'd offer to help but for this dodgy back.'

'What dodgy back?' scoffed Pat. 'You know there's nothing wrong with his back, Eithne. He just doesn't want to miss a match.'

'And you do, I suppose?' said Donie, looking betrayed.

'No, but I can just say that and not make up a lame excuse about it. I can't help with the wedding preparations, Eithne, because there's likely a match on.' He shrugged, 'I'm just being straight with you, like.'

Rookie mistake. Luke watched with anticipation as his mother smiled sweetly. 'And I appreciate it, Pat. I know how the matches are very important to you.'

'See?' said Pat, turning to his friend. 'Women appreciate honesty.'

'I'll make sure we record them and you can watch them after.'

Donie guffawed as Pat gulped.

'Ah. Well, I'd have no problem only for the arthritis in my wrists. They can spasm without warning and I wouldn't want to drop a platter or anything with all the hard work that goes into them. Maybe you could get an apron on Tadhg here? His wrists are grand. A nice white hat and a frilly apron and he's your man.'

Tadhg wheezed and gave his chest a few bangs as though restarting himself.

'I don't think Grandad is up for helping either,' said Luke.

Tadhg shot him a grateful look as Eithne moved the peanuts down the counter to him – his reward, presumably, for being an innocent party. He grinned as he quickly secured himself a large handful before announcing, 'Luke's moving to Cork full-time.'

Eithne moved the bowl pointedly from Tadhg to Pat.

'Are you now, boy?' said Donie, looking delighted. 'Now *there's* a bit of news. No wonder Paudie's about to blow. Did you break it to him gently?'

The phone rang behind the bar. Luke knew better than to answer it, his mother being 'the voice' of O'Callaghan's.

Sure enough, she cleared her throat and picked up the receiver. 'O'Callaghan's Hotel and Bar, Eithne O'Callaghan speaking.' There was a moment's silence as she screwed up her face to listen. 'Hello? Seánie?

Ah, how are you? Keeping well? Good summer, yes. On the up again. Were you looking for Paudie? What's that?'

There was a long pause during which her eyes suddenly darted towards Luke. She turned away and dropped her voice but he could still hear her just fine.

'*Aha, aha*, sure, yes, yes, he'll be very glad. Someone's just coming in. I better go. Yes. I will. And you.'

She hung up and brushed her skirt down as everyone watched expectantly. 'I think I'll go find your dad.' And without another word she headed off across the lounge in the direction of the family quarters.

With a frown, Luke left his post and followed her.

'Did Seánie say something to upset you, Mam?'

'Nothing. No. Don't be daft. How would Seánie upset me?'

'I don't know. You just sounded eager to get rid of him.'

Her face flushed. 'I wasn't. He just goes on a bit and I don't have time to be chatting all day.'

'He's never rung for a chat before.'

She stopped abruptly and glared at him. 'If you *must* know, someone left a pair of sunglasses on the ferry. If anyone's looking for them he has them.'

'That's what he was ringing about? Lost property?'

'What else would he be ringing about?' she said sharply.

He held his hands up. 'Okay, okay. What type of glasses are they?'

'What type of glasses? Maybe it's the guards you should be going into, Luke. Make your grandad delighted to have you following in his footsteps and interrogating all the suspects.'

'I'm only asking.'

She'd reached the door, her face redder than ever. 'They were Ray-Bans. For a man. A man has lost his sunglasses. Call the newspapers!'

'Okay, relax.'

'And put some socks on, will you? You're not Hugh Hefner.' On this parting shot, she swung past him and he heard her heels clacking up the stairs.

Shaking his head, he went back to the bar as a family of six wandered in looking weary and sunburnt. They settled at a large table overlooking the beer garden. Luke rustled up a high chair and some colouring sheets. Mikey went into a fluster searching for a pen so Luke took their food order and went to get the chef away from the TV and into action.

When he returned to the bar, his dad and mam were there to greet him. Paudie's foul mood had entirely dissipated. He was beaming from ear to ear. It was Eithne who was wearing the dark cloud now and muttering. They beckoned him over to a quiet section by the fireplace.

'Y'all right?' he asked, glancing between them.

Eithne shot Paudie a warning look before turning to Luke with a smile so forced it looked painful. 'You know, I was thinking maybe you should go to Cork today, Luke, and not bother waiting any longer. We'll manage here without you just fine.'

He looked to see what his dad might say to this.

'But you wouldn't run out on us just before the wedding, would you, son?' It was more a statement than a question. Paudie already knew the answer and, by the look of him, he liked the answer.

'I wouldn't, no. Betty asked me to be an usher and wants me around for the rehearsal. And I have to arrange a rota for walking the dog.'

The beam on Paudie's face widened. 'See, Eithne? He'll be staying a little longer. No need to be rushing him off.'

Luke didn't know what new notion had got into his dad's head but he hadn't gone through the morning's abuse to back down now. 'I will be leaving after the wedding, though. I'm sorry but there it is.'

'Of course, Luke,' said his dad. 'Absolutely.'

Luke looked from one parent to the other, now at a complete loss.

More families arrived trailing sand. The subject was dropped as they sprang into action. Eithne played hostess and took orders, Paudie worked the bar with Luke, and Mikey delivered the food, the crockery rattling on the tray in his hands.

In the middle of this bustle, Eric arrived off the minibus and pulled up a stool next to the old timers. He gave Luke a wink.

'The usual, please. No wait,' he added, with a flourish, 'make it a double.'

Luke filled a beer glass with ice cubes and poured a double ginger ale into it. The next ferry was due in twenty minutes and Eric would be back in an hour and a half for another soft drink and chat. That was how he spent his days in the summer, staying busy and hydrated.

He took a large gulp and gasped in satisfaction.

'Lads,' he said, 'you're looking at a man who's just seen heaven and hell.'

No one said anything.

'Aren't you going to ask me how?' he demanded.

They looked at each other and grinned.

'No,' said Luke.

'Ah, yeh're no fun! I'm talking about women. Two that came in on the last ferry. The first one looks like a cherub. All dimples and curly blonde hair and big, big–'

'Boobs?' asked Donie, hopefully.

'Blue eyes. Sweet as an angel. *Heaven.*' He took another enormous gulp and banged the glass down on the counter, sending the ice cubes inside clattering. 'Go again,' he said.

Luke snapped the cap off two more little bottles.

'And the other woman was hell?' asked Pat. 'Not ... pretty?'

Eric's eyes twinkled as he regarded him over the rim of his glass. 'You've no imagination, Pat, if your idea of hell is a "not pretty" woman.'

'Go on so,' said Paudie, straightening suddenly, a grin stretching his lips as he cast a glance at Luke. 'What did she look like?'

'*Hmm.*' Eric's tongue ran over his top lip. 'She looked like ... *sin.*' He saw he had his audience hooked, pints held mid-air. 'Imagine hair the colour of whiskey, double-malt, long past the shoulders, lazy waves of it. A little pouty mouth that's begging to be kissed and eyes that can't decide if they're green or brown but would give up their secrets if you only knew the right question to ask.'

'Big boobs then,' concluded Donie, unmoved by the poetics.

'Couldn't say,' shrugged Eric. 'Too much the gentleman to look.'

'Yeah, right,' said Donie. 'As if you didn't.'

Eric held his hands up. 'I already told you she looked like sin. Decide for yourself on her measurements.'

'Just tell me, you fecker!'

'I swear I can't. No more than I could tell you the dimensions of heaven. You believe in my innocence, don't you, Luke?'

'Naturally,' he said, smiling. 'Did you get her name so?'

'I did indeed.' Eric fished out a small ice cube from the bottom of his glass and crunched on it. 'You're not dealing with an amateur here.' He made them wait while he swallowed the icy shards. '*Cassandra*. Isn't that perfect? And she's here for the wedding so you'll get to meet her – but remember I saw her first,' he added. 'Finders keepers.'

'Ah now,' said Donie. 'All's fair in love and war.'

'They're staying at Barrett Cottage,' continued Eric, 'so they must be friends of the family. Betty'll give us the inside track.'

Luke's heart did a sudden and uncomfortable extra beat. 'They're staying at the cottage? Just so I'm clear, Eric, which one was Cassandra?'

'Heaven, of course.'

His chest tightened. 'And the redhead. What was her name?'

'Didn't say. Seemed kind of reserved but, man, when she smiled ...'

Luke was gripping the edge of the counter as his mother arrived with a docket. He turned to her in disbelief. 'Lily's home, isn't she? That's what Seánie was ringing about. He saw her on the ferry.'

Her face crumpled. 'Oh, Luke. Just leave it. So what if she's back?'

'Will you shut it, woman?' hissed Paudie. 'If Lily's back to stay then he might too.'

'*And what good would that do him!*' she screeched.

'Ah, now, calm down, Eithne,' said Donie, clearly enjoying the show. 'Watch that blood vessel.'

Luke heard no more. He was already striding for the door.

'*Luke!*' His mother scurried after him as the diners turned to watch. She lowered her voice as she reached him. 'Please don't go over there. What's the point when it's all worked out for the best?'

He halted and stared at her. He'd often wondered how he'd react in this moment. How he'd feel when Lily Barrett finally came home. Now he knew.

'Ten years and not a word to me, Mam. Not a phone call. Not even a postcard. I just want to see she's really alive – and then I'm going to kill her.'

And with that he was gone.

Chapter Three

Off-duty Pirate

With its flowering red and purple fuchsia bushes and swathes of bright-orange montbretia, the stone walls either side of Barrett Lane were colourfully lined. But though it made the climb more cheerful, Lily's stomach still clenched as they finally crested the hill. From there, she could see down towards the dead-end of the lane and the steel farm gate which separated it from the grazing land beyond.

And just before the gate, its eastern gable showing, was Barrett Cottage, looking like the last house in the world. No other building lay between it and the westernmost tip of the island. And after that it was nothing but sea all the way to the horizon.

At some point in the last century, the access route to the cottage had been altered and the back of it had become the front with a long, sloping section added. This had allowed for a glassy porch entrance at the nearest end, a bigger kitchen in the middle as well as a scullery extension at the far end.

But Lily's gaze was on the gable right now, where she had a clear view of white paint peeling all the way up the chimney.

As she and Cassandra drew closer, more ravages revealed themselves. Black paint was flaking from the sills, a window in the scullery was missing a pane and the wisteria Nana had taken such pains to grow had fallen away from its brackets and was lying across the porch door, blocking it.

'Lily? What's that?'

There was a loop of rope hanging from a bedroom window with swatches of fabric attached. Lily's mind went to an image of Tibetan prayer flags blowing in the breeze.

'Are those ... knickers?' asked Cassandra.

Not Tibetan prayer flags then. Lily squeezed her eyes shut and opened them again in the faint hope she was imagining things – but no. Large women's underpants were swinging from the window. *What on earth?*

A low growl sounded from the farthest end of the cottage, followed by the rattle of a chain. Lily walked past the front windows to peer down the side passage – between the scullery and the brick coal bunker – and into the side yard. Where something large lunged, barking frantically.

'Is that your nana's dog?'

Lily shook her head as she backed up, eyes wide. 'We never had a dog. *Afraid. Me. Bitten twice.*'

'Someone *must* be living here.' Cassandra had her forehead pressed to the kitchen window, her hands cupping her face against the glass. 'Whatever about the knickers, there's a whole pile of boxes in there and a lot of jars of mixed pickles.'

Lily took another step back and stared up at the cottage anew. In her dreams it was always pristine, glowing pink in the last light of the day. The porch door would open with the barest touch and she'd go straight to the kitchen where Nana would embrace her and make everything right. She had known reality would be different, of course, but she'd been sure the place would still feel like home. It didn't though. Not even a bit. She might have been an invader come to assess its defences, for all the welcome she felt emanating from it. Maybe this should have come as a relief, considering why she was here. But her disappointment was acute.

Pride instantly pricked her for that weakness. As if to prove she was stronger than it, she whipped out her phone, took a photograph and tried to calculate how much the cottage might fetch at auction. But the numbers wouldn't come together in her head, scattering like husks at every attempt to gather them.

She walked back to the porch, tipped the old terracotta pot that still sat beside it, and found the key underneath. It was a struggle to fit it into the lock and then the door needed a series of hard shoves before she could finally step over the wisteria and get inside.

Dust swirled and the air was rich with the smell of baked carpet and desiccated geraniums.

'Hello? Anyone here?'

Silence.

Straight ahead, down a short stretch of hall, was the closed door to the study – as Nana had liked to call it. But Lily turned right, moving past the flight of stairs, and into the kitchen. The best views from the cottage – out over the lane and fields and towards the nearest beach – were to be had from the large window on the right here. But the view *inside* the kitchen was far from picturesque as a collection of wooden crates took up half the space. To one side of them, the sink was stacked high with unwashed teacups. To the other side the table was covered with cans of

Pedigree Chum, jars of mixed pickles and an enormous single-tier cake draped in white icing. Lily's gaze travelled the room in dismay. There were cobwebs in every corner, the walls were streaked with dust and no cupboard door was quite in line with its neighbour. Even the sound was wrong, for the pendulum clock on the wall no longer beat.

Lily removed a sandwich-maker from the nearest chair, sat and put her head in her hands.

'It must be hard,' said Cassandra, who hadn't yet made it further than the kitchen door. 'Coming back now. Having missed the funeral and everything. If you want to cry I won't mind. It does help – crying, you know?'

But Lily just shook her head. They'd argued the merits of crying between them more times than she could count. '*Better out than in*' was Cassandra's motto and it served as well for emotions as it did for socialising and that one tequila too many.

'What's in there?' Cassandra gave a nod to her left, towards another door which was ajar. Without waiting for Lily's answer, she crossed the kitchen, peeped through the gap, inhaled sharply, and closed the door gently. '*Lily*,' she whispered. '*There's a woman in there. I think she's dead*.'

Lily sprang to her feet and was in the sitting room the next instant to find Betty McCarthy filling an armchair beside the fireplace, her eyes closed and her mouth open. If the kitchen got the best views out the front of the cottage, the sitting room at the back got the best of the light and the beams of it pouring in now haloed Betty's white curls and glinted off the ladybird clips that were liberally sprinkled about them. On the table by her elbow was a set of dentures and a box of Turkish Delight, with just one cube left amongst a hillock of icing sugar. That explained the powdery residue around her lips. On her chest a wedding magazine rose and fell. Lily sagged with relief. Not only was Betty alive but exactly as – if not where – she'd always been. Her nana's closest friend, she had a snug and exceedingly messy house just a minute's walk from the church. What she was doing asleep in this sitting room was therefore a mystery.

The barking started up again. Betty smacked her lips together and turned her head away from it as Lily and Cassandra retreated to the kitchen.

'That's Betty McCarthy – the, *uh*, bride-to-be the minibus-driver mentioned.'

'Oh,' said Cassandra. 'Right.' Then she glanced at the tins on the table. 'So ... should we feed the dog, do you think? It might be hungry.'

Lily shivered. It didn't sound like the kind of animal that survived on dog food alone. 'I think we should wait for Betty to wake up. She'll know when it's supposed to eat.' She eyed the crates again. 'Must be her stuff, all of this?'

'What do you think it's barking at now?'

They moved to the other side of the kitchen and through a narrow open door that led straight into the scullery extension where an enormous chest freezer and washing machine sat side by side. The back door was to their left here and they peered through its glass pane into the side yard that spanned the length of the western gable. A hip-high wall separated it from the back garden beyond. To one side of it was a wooden shed looking the worse for wear. A washing line attached to a corner of it stretched back to the cottage. Underneath this lay a well-chewed *Welcome* mat, two ceramic bowls and a steel ring cemented into the concrete. A chain was linked to the ring and straining it taut was a hound of enormous proportions: a cross between an Alsatian and a bear. Its fur was wiry: black mixed with brown. Its paws were the size of a mountain lion's. And while one ear cocked sharply, the other languished with an unruly kink to the side. It was barking at a pair of magpies who evidently knew they were safe as they strutted along the wall, taunting it.

'How about a tour of the cottage?' said Cassandra as they both turned away.

Half afraid what other surprises they'd unearth, Lily agreed and led her back through the kitchen and into the hall before turning right past the stairs and on to the study. She opened the door here to reveal an island of furniture she didn't recognise. Topping its summit were suitcases leaking dressing gowns and the whole thing was encircled by an ankle-deep flotsam of old toys and foam alphabet letters.

Without a word they both reversed and headed upstairs.

'Bathroom and hot press straight ahead.' Lily turned left down the landing where there were two facing doors. 'Spare bedroom this side.' She pushed open the door to the left and was confronted with a riot of ladybird-themed accessories. She closed it swiftly and opened the one opposite. 'And this was my room.'

A neat, whitewashed room was revealed. It still had the sturdy wooden bunkbed Nana had once been gifted, along with a narrow wardrobe and a fully stacked bookcase. Lily's heart lightened a fraction. Something, at least, was the way she'd left it. Peering out the window to the back garden, though, her spirits sank once more. It was nothing but a quarter acre of hay. The lumpy fields around it looked manicured in comparison but the half-dozen cows lowering their heads over the fence to extract clumps seemed well pleased.

Cassandra tutted. 'Are they allowed to be doing that? Eating your grass?'

'I'd invite them in to finish off the job only they'd crap all over the place. I don't know how I'm going to get the mower over it.'

They returned to the landing where Cassandra stopped by a collection of photographs on the wall. 'Are you in this?'

It was a group shot of children standing to attention. Lily nodded.

'That's not you, is it?' Cassandra pointed to a head at the back.

'That's a boy.'

'With hair that long?' She peered along the faces again. 'I give up. Which one's you?'

'There,' said Lily and waited for the reaction she guessed was coming.

Cassandra's hand went to her mouth, her eyes crinkling. 'With the eye patch? And the crazy hair? Oh Lily!'

'I know.'

She squinted for a closer look. 'And that girl holding your hand? Was that your best friend?'

'That's a boy too.'

'Seriously? Were there no scissors back then?'

'It's not *that* long ago or that long a haircut. And he looks cute.'

'Why? Was he your *boyfriend*?'

'Worse. My husband. We got married in the playground one break-time. Hugh O'Driscoll's Action Man presided over the ceremony. The girls threw petals and the boys threw soil. Very moving.'

Cassandra turned to her, eyes shining. 'What was his name?'

'Luke O ...' Lily caught herself and bit back the rest. What the hell was she doing? Reminiscing? Fondly? About *him*?

'Luko?' mused Cassandra. 'That's an odd one? Foreign?'

'*M-huh.*'

'So where is he now, little Luko?'

'Don't know.' *Don't care.*

'I recognise you in this one without the patch. What age are you here?'

'Twelve. Making my Confirmation.'

'So that's your nana with you?'

Lily forced her eyes to take in the woman in the stylish blue dress. Silver hair curled around a heart-shaped face and, though the fading emulsion made the expression in her eyes hard to read, her smile was a mile wide.

'She looks sweet.'

Lily swallowed past the lump in her throat. 'She was.'

'But you said you hadn't been back in years. Why?'

'Because you don't go where you're not wanted.'

Cassandra frowned at that but let it go. 'And who's that next to her? Your grandad?'

'No. That's just Seánie the ferryman. He and Nana were friends.'

'Oh. Well, it was nice of him to be there for you.'

'I guess.' She'd never really thought about that, to be honest. How Seánie was always in the background, smiling, at any special occasion. But then he was a man of few words. So quiet you'd nearly forget him.

'So did your grandad die young then?' Cassandra asked next, scanning the rest of the photos.

Lily drew a deep breath. She had never talked about her grandad to Cassandra before. 'I don't know and honestly couldn't care less. He was just some asshole who slithered off after he got Nana pregnant. He left her to be disowned by her own parents and everything. Different times.'

'Stupid times.'

Lily agreed and looked back to the photographs but felt Cassandra studying her instead. 'What was your nana like, apart from being sweet?'

'She was ... determined.'

'Ah.'

She could hear the smile in Cassandra's voice.

'You must have looked up to her then.'

It wasn't really a question but the answer, still, was complicated. Yes, she'd looked up to Nana. Had adored everything about her from her quick mind, to the steadfastness of her beliefs, to her resourcefulness – until she'd found herself on the sharp end of them.

'I owed her for raising me, Cass, and supporting me until I could support myself. No doubt she had better plans for her retirement.'

They circled back to the top of the stairs, past the hotpress and reached the bathroom. Lily threw the door open for a quick glance inside. Everything seemed in order.

This left just one more room to see: Nana's bedroom.

Lily reached for the handle here too but, as she went to push, all the strength leached out of her. 'I'll leave this one till later. If you don't mind.'

'Of course,' said Cassandra. 'And if you want to cry ...?'

'I don't. Let's go back down.'

They'd just reached the kitchen when a whizzing sound came from the lane out front. A figure on a bicycle shot past the kitchen window, dismounted in one fluid motion, and turned out of sight into the side passage.

The bicycle was left to come to a halt by itself and did so by clanging into the farm gate and then keeling over onto the grass.

Lily knew only one person who parked a bike like that.

She tried to bolt back upstairs, reverting to some primal instinct to hide. Unfortunately, the kitchen door was swinging closed and she misjudged the remaining gap between it and the frame, colliding with its edge nose-first. She yelped and reeled.

'Oh Lily! Are you alright?'

Over delighted barks came the sound of knocking on the back door.

Betty emerged from the sitting room, her hair sticking up but for one strand swinging taut with the weight of a dislodged ladybird clip. She was trying to catch hold of it with one hand while the other worked the dentures back into her mouth. She shrieked when she saw them, the dentures hitting the floor. *'Jethus, Mary and Jotheph!'*

In the yard the barks turned to expectant whines.

There was another series of knocks, followed by a curse and the sound of keys dropping onto concrete.

Betty retreated to the sitting room while Cassandra armed herself with dog food, a tin in each hand, and took up a defensive position. 'Who is it, Lily?'

'The Pretender,' she rasped.

Cassandra shot her a look of confusion as Lily stepped back into a shaded corner, clutching her throbbing nose as she tried to see past streaming eyes.

The key slotted into the lock and turned.

The door opened and, in another instant, Luke O'Callaghan was in the kitchen and it felt like the seconds before a collision in a movie where all the details – velocity, remaining distance, obstacles and innocent bystanders – have time to register but make absolutely no difference to the outcome.

Cassandra just stared at him transfixed, her mouth open.

And if Lily herself could have looked away she would have. Instead her eyes devoured him, cataloguing the changes a decade had wrought. He was taller than the boy she remembered. His frame had filled out and the muscles that now girded his body were poorly concealed under a faded T-shirt and low-slung jeans. It was a man's body filling the doorway, no soft edges left. His jaw was stubbled. There was a scar crossing one eyebrow and streaks of black swiped his cheeks. Off-duty Pirate was the overwhelming impression. Hot Off-duty Pirate. *Look out!*

The beam of his gaze swept the room and found her in the shadows. Their eyes locked and the impact – that jolt of reconnection – left her weak.

That horrible confusion from the pier was back, only magnified a hundredfold, because Luke was different *and* the same. For all the changes to him, every fibre in her tingled in recognition and a feeling which in other circumstances she'd have called relief welled up inside her. Her legs moved of their own volition. She took two shaky steps towards him into a beam of sunlight.

He blinked. Once, twice. Then his hand went to his brow, shielding his eyes as though he couldn't bear the sight of her.

He backed away towards the exit as she waited for him to look at her again. To say something. Anything. The tension was almost unbearable.

Cassandra handed her a tin of Pedigree Chum.

In silence, she handed it back.

Then Luke turned on his heel and strode back outside.

'*Hey!*' Lily moved past Cassandra and was in the yard before she realised her mistake. The hound bounded forward as the door clicked shut behind her. Its mouth was open and its wet tongue swung over massive canines. She screamed and turned and tried to get back inside again but her flailing hands slipped from the handle.

She squeezed her eyes shut and waited to be devoured but was yanked instead to the safety of the side passage. A growl sounded there too but, when she peeked out, there was nothing more terrifying to endure than the scrutiny of Luke's glistening quicksilver eyes.

The dog, denied its victim, started barking again.

At this proximity, the sound was deafening.

'*Not dead then?*' Luke shouted over it. He carried out a perfunctory scan of her body. '*Limbs all still attached? No obvious signs of head trauma!*' And then his eyes were back on hers, narrowed and angry. '*I suppose you remember who I am?*'

'I …' Her pulse somehow found yet another gear as she remembered exactly who he was, in disconcerting bursts. The squeeze of his hand holding hers, the tilt of his head when he concentrated, the dimples that pitted his cheeks whenever he smiled, the intensity in his eyes when they filled with desire, his heartbeat as she lay against his chest. Yes, she remembered who he was. Luke. Her best friend, her love, her *everything*. Until he'd chosen not to be. And with that thought the emotional short-circuiting finally resolved itself, settling on anger. *She* was the one entitled to it right now, not him. '*How did you know I was here?*'

'Seánie saw you on the ferry and Eric said he'd met you and your friend.' He turned to the dog. *'Shush!'*

To her relief the barking stopped.

'Were you going to come and see me?' he asked.

'No.'

He folded his arms. 'Of course not. Why would you?'

She swallowed thickly. That's right, why would she?

'Not like we're old friends or anything,' he said.

Old friends? Her heart twisted at that oh-so-flippant description. It felt almost like an insult. But fine. If that's how he wanted it. She raised her chin. 'Old friends keep in touch.'

But not a hint of shame so much as crossed his features.

She tried to go past him, to get back to the kitchen, but the dog started barking again and the sight of its flashing teeth pulled her up short. Trapped. *'Urgh!'* She spread her arms wide. *'So you found me. Congratulations! Now please go away. I didn't ask to see you.'*

'True.' He didn't move. *'So why are you back? And shush!'* he said once more.

Mercifully, the dog switched back to whimpering.

'Just to get the cottage ready for sale. Three days then I'm out of here again forever.'

His jaw dropped. 'You're *selling* it? How *could* you?'

'Easy. I tidy it, take a few photographs and leave an estate agent to do the rest.'

'But – but it's your home!'

'It stopped being that a long time ago. As you well know.'

But he tipped his head, eyes suddenly softening. 'What am I missing here, Lil?'

But that just made her fists clench. He'd forfeited his right to her pet name.

'Why are you selling?' he pressed. 'What's happened?'

'It's none of your business what I do or why I do it anymore, Luke. We're nothing to each other now.'

He flinched and stared at her for what felt like far too many heartbeats. Then he walked past her towards the dog, who started panting as if in anticipation.

Her anxiety skyrocketed as she fought the stupid impulse to pull him back to safety. 'What are you doing?'

He reached the animal and bent to pet it, mussing its face before tickling behind its ears as it leaked drool. When he finally looked back at her his expression was unnaturally still, all the animation wiped from it.

'She gets two tins for breakfast and two for dinner. She needs a long walk every day or she'll be in vile humour and don't let her off the lead for any reason. She has no interest in worrying cattle but she'll charge through any field after a magpie.'

'Why are you telling me this? I don't – I mean *no, oh no!*'

He gave a tight smile. 'Oh yes. Congratulations, Lily. You have a dog to go with your cottage.'

'No, I don't.'

'Feel free to rename her.'

'What? *Cujo?*'

'Your nana called her Pup. She was smaller once. As were we all.' He gave the dog a last pat then walked past Lily through the side passage. He made an impressive hurdle over the low wooden gate and turned right to go up the lane.

'But what will I do with her? I can't own a dog!' she called after him.

'She's not my problem anymore.'

'Yeah, that sounds about right!' *Turn your back on her too, why don't you?*

He came to a halt and spun round as his jaw clamped shut. She could almost feel the clack of his teeth and his next words were spoken through them. 'Anything I can do to speed your departure, Lily, you let me know.'

'Don't trouble yourself with *helping* me, Luke O'Callaghan,' she called back. 'Why start now?' And before he could get in another shot, she darted for the back door, yanked it open and slammed it hard behind her.

Chapter Four

Homeostasis

Luke was at the bottom of the lane before he remembered his bike. He cursed then, every oath he knew and a few he invented just for the occasion. He pictured Lily having a good laugh when she saw it lying there. Having the last laugh, as it were, to go with the last word. He'd forgotten what her laugh sounded like which was strange considering his strongest memories of her invariably had her laughing. No doubt it sounded like a cackle.

He kicked his way along the road, trying to figure out why the dull pain he'd carried in her absence had become a roaring ache in her presence. Seeing her again should have made things better not worse and he'd have given a lot to go back an hour and choose differently. If he'd just let it be, he'd at least have had his memories of her to console him but all he could see in his mind now was a mocking double of the Lily he'd loved. The evil twin – with more beauty but less heart.

He should have handled it differently, he guessed. The cycle over had given him the chance to calm down and he'd had every intention of letting her explain herself before he read her The Riot Act. But then he'd found her crying and that stupid cord that seemed to connect her tear ducts to his own had yanked, rendering him ridiculous-looking in seconds. Seeing her in distress still distressed him. Made him want to fix it. Why had she been crying? Tears of grief for her nana probably and regret she'd left it so long to come home. They hadn't been shed for him in any case. That much was clear. *We're nothing to each other now.*

With those words on repeat in his head, he made it as far as Rivers' Hostel before he became fully conscious of his surroundings, taking in the banks of colourful flowers swaying just beyond the wall. He had to hand it to Jasper, the man knew his way around a garden. Which was about the only compliment he'd ever pay him.

As if summoned, Jasper appeared around a bush and moved towards him. Tall and dapper at fifty-four in over-buttoned clothing, his face bore its usual expression of easy politeness though the eyes that flicked over Luke held their usual hint of disapproval. As if he didn't quite meet the mark.

'Good morning, Luke. Hot day for it.'

'Sure is.' He made to move on.

'You look like you could use a cold drink.'

Presumably this was a statement of opinion rather than an offer of refreshment. 'I'll get something at the bar,' Luke responded.

'Has your mother all the wedding preparations under control then?'

'Of course. It'll run smooth as clockwork. Same as always.'

'I'm sure it will.' With an easy movement, Jasper leaned his hip against the wall. 'Never seen a woman as good at getting things done her way as your mother.'

Luke nodded, unsure if this was a genuine compliment. Always hard for him to tell with Jasper.

'What has you so worked up?' Jasper asked next, chewing on a smile now.

'Nothing at all.'

'I see.' Jasper's thumb moved fleetingly over a little tuft of lichen growing from a niche in the stone. 'Well, don't beat yourself up about it. People outgrow each other. It's no one's fault.'

Luke's mind raced. He couldn't possibly know.

'Did she say she was staying long – Lily?'

He groaned silently. How had Jasper found out she was back so quickly? Had Eric stopped to tell him on his way by? Or had Lily already called on Jasper herself?

'Couldn't tell you, I'm afraid.' He turned to go.

'Do pass on my compliments if you see her again.' Jaspar pulled a stray weed from the earth and tossed it over the wall before he turned back to the hostel, moving quietly across the grass. When he reached the door though he glanced back with a grin. 'Didn't you have your bike before?' And with a low chuckle he disappeared inside.

Luke walked on around An Fáinne and up the hill until he reached the viewing point that gave every first-time visitor a wow. He slipped through the gap in a line of hawthorn trees there and followed the wheel-rutted trail up the ramparts of Sliabh Oisín, until he was looking down on the cove below. This was the windward side of the island, open to the full force of the sea and the weather fronts that lashed it in winter. It was neither an auspicious place to graze cattle nor moor a boat and, other than the occasional visitor who'd been tipped off about the fishing to be had from the rocks, it was pretty much deserted. It was a wild spot, untouched and beautiful, and the place Lily loved best on Inish Ruin.

They'd discovered it as children when they'd gone looking for mushrooms one day after school. With their heads down and eyes straining for glimpses of white, they'd covered more ground than they'd realised, shouting in delight every time they found a fresh crop. They'd raced each other down to the cove where they counted their mushrooms out onto the rocks. Luke had come up two short and Lily had given him one of hers so they'd be the same.

They'd spent the afternoon making a hut underneath a hollowed-out bush caged over by bramble vines. Lily swept the ground with a brush of ferns and made grassy beds, while Luke stockpiled large stones for a wall and twigs for firewood for when it got dark. Hunger sent them home well before dark but not before half the island had been sent out searching for them. Nana Noleen had thrown herself on Lily when she saw her in one piece while Luke got a clip around the ear from his dad for causing so much trouble.

They went back to Hook Cove, as they christened it, many times after that to work on their hut. Luke built his perimeter wall with the stones. Lily festooned the inside with long lengths of daisy chains and ever thicker mounds of grass – until the first winter storm wiped all their hard work away in a night. They didn't bother building another but went there still to play hide and seek among the banks of ferns and in the ditches under cover of the rain-drenched heathers. When they got too old for that they still went, with fishing their excuse now, rods carried lightly against their shoulders as they crossed the fields together in the early evenings. They never caught much, threw back anything they did and sometimes they didn't even bother casting a line. They just sat on the still-warm rocks as the sun slipped from sight behind the mountain and laughed and talked and listened to the sea and the sounds of the world going to sleep as the first stars appeared.

It was here Luke had first kissed her, the autumn of her sixteenth birthday, as sunlight burned the rim of the mountain and lit her from behind, turning her hair to fire. And it was here he'd tried to forget her, throwing his energies into building a house for himself in a sheltered fold on one side of the mountain.

He made his way along the last stretch of lane now as a single-storey, cedar-clad house became visible behind a copse of newly planted pines. The building was as much glass as timber. He'd wanted it to be filled with light but that meant he had to squint against the glare as he approached, fishing for the key in his back pocket as the scents of thyme and rosemary welcomed him from the garden.

He turned at the sound of the minibus approaching, creeping stealthy as a drunken rhinoceros over the ruts and bumps.

Eric pulled up, his habitual grin vanishing in the millisecond it took to get a good look at Luke. He invited himself inside for 'an old bit of a sandwich, if you're having one' and settled himself at the kitchen table while Luke buttered bread and pulled some sliced ham from the fridge.

Luke heard the rustle of paper and saw Eric nosing over his course notes.

'Physiological homeostasis,' Eric murmured. 'What in the heck is that?'

'It's the maintenance of a variable around an ideal normal value within a living system.'

'Right,' said Eric. 'And what in the heck is *that*?'

Luke smiled. 'Your body is always trying to keep things stable – like your temperature or the level of salt in your bloodstream.'

'So?'

'Glass of water with your ham sandwich?'

Eric beamed as both were set in front of him. 'Well, look at you saving lives already.'

He wolfed his food down, brushing the few escaped crumbs back onto the plate.

'I'll miss the sandwiches. You know just how much butter to put on them. Not too much that you coat your teeth, not too little that the bread sticks to the roof of your mouth.'

Luke held off his thanks, suspecting he was being buttered up himself. 'You've given the subject a lot of thought.'

'As it rightly deserves.' He pushed his chair back and tilted himself into a more comfortable position. 'Gonna tell me about it?'

'Nope.'

Eric laughed and shook his head. 'Gonna tell me about *her*?'

'Would there be any point? You'll have heard it all by now from Donie and Pat.' He sat down as Eric pushed his glass around the tabletop.

'She was your childhood sweetheart, as they say.'

'She was.'

'Then she ghosted your arse and never came back.'

Yeah, that was about the sum of it.

'I'll have to take you off that pedestal now, you know?' Eric continued. 'Whatever happened to Always the Dumper, never the Dumpee?'

'That's not my motto, Eric.'

'And to think I used to hold you in such high regard.' A gleeful tut swiftly replaced his solemn expression. 'The Playboy of Inish Ruin no more.'

It was a running joke Luke never found funny. He dated a lot, sure. There was no shortage of women showing an interest. But it never turned into anything long-term because he never wanted it to. And he was always upfront about that.

'They say the first cut is the deepest,' mused Eric. 'But then how would I know? Never been so much as scratched. I'm imagining it didn't go so well if you're back already. Could you not even get a cup of tea out of her?'

'I could barely get a civil word.'

'But was she just like you remembered?'

Was she? No and yes. Lily had changed, grown and yet, on some molecular level he didn't quite know how to explain, she was exactly the same. Still, he shook his head.

'But she was always that hot, yeah?'

'No. *Geez*, Eric, we were just kids. It was years ago.'

'Okay, okay. But now she wasn't interested in ...' he waggled his eyebrows, 'reminiscing?'

'No. She's just back to get the cottage ready for sale. A few days and she's gone again.'

'Selling, is she? *Pah!* It'll take longer than that to get it ready with the state it's in and Betty's stuff all over it. It's not like she can turf her out just before the wedding either. She'll be lucky to get that place sorted in a fortnight and I wouldn't fancy tackling that garden. She's gonna need help if she's in that much of a hurry.'

Eric was right. Lily was going to need help. More than she probably realised. If she thought she had a working lawnmower for a start she was mistaken. Or a ladder. And, sure, she'd bust a gut to clean the cottage but she had the upper-body strength of a jellyfish. How was she going to move those crates around? Or Betty's furniture? By carting it all away on her back? Knowing Lily, she'd attempt just that and do herself an injury. He tapped out a rhythm with his fingertips on the table and glanced over at his course notes as he reminded himself firmly that none of that was his problem.

'So ... you gonna offer?' said Eric. 'You know, to help her?'

'No.'

'Ah, that doesn't sound like you, man.'

Luke shrugged.

'You could even stage the cottage for her, couldn't you? Isn't that what you used to do in Dubai? What's the line? *Staged properties sell faster and for ten percent more –*'

'On average,' Luke finished for him and felt suddenly foolish.

'And maybe if you spent more time with her she might come round. Fall for you all over again.'

Luke just shook his head.

Eric studied him in silence for a moment and then said, 'You'd get closure at least.'

Closure? Luke had no idea what that would even look like for him and Lily. He imagined a wound in the vicinity of his heart that only she could see or suture. But, maybe, if she actually said goodbye to him when she left this time it would be *something*? The cue his brain had been waiting for so he could properly move on.

'Better than staying bitter,' Eric added.

'I'm not bitter,' he said instantly. 'We're just nothing to each other now.'

'At least your conscience would be clear.'

'The hell? My conscience is just fine, thank you.' But then he remembered Pup. And Lily's terror at being within ten feet of her. And her insistence she couldn't own a dog. Would Pup ever be fed or walked again?

'Well, I'm sure you know best,' said Eric.

'I do,' Luke agreed, glancing at his watch. 'Hey, are you watching the time for the next ferry?'

Eric glanced at his watch then and, with a 'feck', scrambled to his feet. He headed for the front door but paused at the threshold. 'Just ... don't not do something you'll regret.'

'*Don't not?*' Luke asked.

But, with this most confusing of advice, Eric was away.

Chapter Five

Luke&Lily4Ever

Cassandra hailed Lily from where she sat on the sofa next to Betty. 'You're not going to believe it but I'm going to be Betty's replacement bridesmaid! Isn't that great news?' Her eyes widened in appeal for Lily to agree.

Having expected to be grilled about Luke, Lily was as relieved as she was confused by this opening. And just how long was Cassandra planning on staying?

'It's another sign,' sniffed Betty, pressing a handkerchief to her eyes as she hunched forward, her other hand clutching a phone. 'Poor Gráinne has the measles. And her dress only just made up? It's Mervyn. He doesn't want me to get married again. I'm betraying him. That's what it is.'

'This has nothing to do with Mervyn,' said Cassandra firmly, though whether it had been explained to her that Mervyn was Betty's long-deceased husband Lily could only wonder. 'You're just having a case of pre-wedding jitters. Perfectly normal and, if you're looking for signs, let me tell you they're all good because just out of the blue has arrived an expert at pre-wedding jitters – that's me, by the way – and you said yourself I'm exactly the right size for that dress and it's gorgeous.' She looked expectantly at Lily.

'That's wonderful,' said Lily, 'but–'

'Yes, wonderful! And wait'll you see the design for the bouquets she's getting.' Cassandra pointed to a magazine that was open on the coffee table.

Lily sat down on Betty's other side and cast her eye over the page. 'Lovely. Will Jasper do them for you?'

'Yes,' she said with another sniff. 'He offered his services for free. Always had a soft spot for me, had Jasper.'

Lily took one of Betty's hands in her own, giving it a squeeze in the faint hope it might somehow anchor the woman to reality. 'Betty, I hope you don't mind me asking but what are you doing here?'

Betty dabbed her eyes. 'Getting married, chick.'

'Here? In this cottage?'

'No. In the church. On Thursday. If Mervyn lets me.'

'What if Lily was a bridesmaid too?' exclaimed Cassandra. 'We could find a similar dress. Wouldn't that be great?'

'Except we won't be here on Thursday,' Lily reminded her. 'We're back to London on Monday night.'

'Mervyn,' whimpered Betty.

'Well, *I* don't have to go back,' said Cassandra. 'I'm a free agent till the week after next. But couldn't you take a few more days off too, seeing as it's an emergency?'

'It would be lovely if you could be my bridesmaid,' said Betty, brightening. 'Your nana says she'd love it too.'

Lily was up off the sofa in a heartbeat. She moved to the fireplace – which was thoroughly cobwebbed – and pretended to examine the brass ornaments littered across the mantelpiece. Betty might be in a fragile state but Nana was not going to go the same way as Mervyn.

'Nana's dead,' she managed. 'You must be a little confused.'

The sofa creaked and a few moments later Betty was standing beside her. She laid a warm hand on her arm. 'I know, chick. But we still have our little chats and she's ever so helpful with the crosswords puzzles. What was it I couldn't think of the other day and she got it just like that?'

Any words of protest got stuck in Lily's throat. 'So ... she told you it would be okay to move all your stuff in?'

Betty beamed. 'Oh yes. She's fine with it. She likes Pup to have company and, with the builders discovering damp, the renovations at my place started taking forever. And I couldn't be staying at the hotel during peak season and Ned's kind of old-fashioned about us living together before we're married. So I asked your nana,' she paused here for quick glance heavenward, 'if it was okay to move in a few months ago and she very kindly said yes. I would have asked your permission *too*, Lily, but no one seemed to have your number.'

Lily raised an eyebrow. 'Nana couldn't have told you?'

Betty flushed. 'Do you know, I never even thought to ask her?'

'When will your house be ready to move back into again?' asked Cassandra.

'The builders have promised no later than a month. A week after us getting back from honeymoon at the latest.'

Lily shook her head. 'I'm sorry but we're going to need to find somewhere else for your furniture before that.'

Betty blinked in surprise. 'But my house isn't ready yet.'

'Not even one room we could use?'

'No. They seem to be working on them all at the same time. Electricians in one place, plasterers in another.'

'Then Ned's?'

'But his access road is so bad. The trailer wouldn't get anywhere near the driveway.'

'What's the hurry?' asked Cassandra. 'I hope it's not for my sake you want it tidy? I don't mind the mess.'

'Ned will put it all back nice and neat at the end of September,' said Betty, 'if that's what you're worried about?'

'That's not what I'm worried about. I'm ... I need to ...' Dammit anyway. She'd already blurted this out to Luke. She might as well tell these two. 'I'm putting the cottage up for sale, okay? And I've only got three days to do it. That's the work I've to get done while I'm here, Cass. Not a holiday,' she added, before turning to Betty. 'And I can't do it if it's full of your stuff. I'm sorry but there it is.'

Before either woman could respond, Lily darted off to the kitchen and began hunting out cleaning products. Finding a large bottle of window cleaner and some cloths, she got busy. Half an hour later all the inside panes were gleaming and she headed outside. But there was no sign of the ladder so she was restricted to the ground-floor windows only. The view looking in through these, however, was depressing enough. There wasn't a square inch of the place that didn't need something done to it to make it presentable.

She left the scullery window till last, wiping carefully around the missing pane and only then noticed Luke's bike lying by the steel gate.

He'd forgotten it when he was busy storming off. But that realisation was anything but satisfying, for the bike just meant he'd be coming back!

Ignoring the uptick of her pulse at that prospect, she propped the bike against the wall then came in by the porch and sat at the bottom of the stairs to cool off.

She was trying to recall if she'd packed sunscreen when she heard shuffling coming from the sitting room, followed a moment later by Cassandra's voice in the kitchen. 'Are you're sure you want to give me your ladybird hairclip?'

'Oh, don't you like it?'

'No, no. It's just I don't think I'm the right age for it.'

Lily had to smile. If Cassandra had just come out and said she was too old for ladybird clips, what would that make Betty?

'You're never too young for ladybirds,' said Betty, not missing a beat. 'Especially at your age when you're looking about you for a fella. Got to keep a ladybird on you then. You'll always get a kiss any day you see a ladybird. Even if it's not a red one but only one of the orange ones. Doesn't matter how many dots either. They're all good. You'll see now. First good-looking fella you see and you'll be kissing him before the day's out.'

There was a moment of silence then Lily heard a single *clip*. Presumably the thing was now in Cassandra's hair. But it was swiftly followed by one of her deep sighs. 'I wish you'd let me ask her about Luke.'

'No point,' said Betty. 'She won't tell you anything and you'll only get her back up.'

'I've never seen her lose her cool around a guy before, though.'

'Ah, well, they were always able to get under each other's skin. Luke's impulsive. Jumps before he looks. Heart of gold, now. Always the first to offer help if anyone needs it. But don't ever ask him to hang a painting for you. He'd be out with the electric drill and all those fixing bits and bobs and you'd need the painting to hide all the plaster that's come off the wall before he's finished. Lily's more cautious but just try giving her advice and she's as like to do the exact opposite just to prove she's making her own decisions. Close as a clam too.'

'So they were no good together?' asked Cassandra.

'What? Ah, no, they were an adorable little pair of ducks. Butting heads was as good as kissing to them.'

There was a rumble of tyres from the lane.

Lily sprang to her feet just as Betty's and Cassandra's heads appeared around the kitchen door. '*Phew*, just finished,' she said. She wiped her brow, feeling hopelessly self-conscious. 'Someone's here,' she added unnecessarily as the minibus screeched to a halt outside.

They all moved to the porch to see Eric alighting. 'My, don't you make a lovely welcoming committee? Cassandra, Betty and *Lily*, of course.'

Lily groaned to herself. If the minibus driver knew her name, how long before everyone knew she was back? So much for inconspicuous. 'Is there something we can help you with? We're kind of busy at the moment.'

'I was just going to invite you all to the pub tonight for a darts tournament. Islanders versus Tourists. Or you could come earlier for dinner, if you wanted? Paudie said to tell you he's looking forward to catching up.'

Well, that message was either a joke or a lie. Lily's only interactions with Luke's dad over the years had involved being on the receiving end of complaints – that she was distracting Luke from his work and that the bar was no place for 'canoodling'. Apparently 'canoodling' meant smiling at each other for they'd never as much as held hands in front of anyone.

In the drawn-out silence, Eric began to look uncomfortable. 'I can give you a lift there if–'

'We'd love to go,' said Cassandra.

'Great. What time do you want me to come get you?'

Cassandra turned to Betty. 'Is there any food for dinner?'

'It's mostly pickles,' she admitted, 'but there's a jar of onions in the fridge and I'm almost sure I saw some strawberry yogurts the other day. Might have been there a while though. No, wait, Mervyn says they're still in date.'

Cassandra turned back to Eric. 'Could you come for us at six?'

'I won't be going,' said Lily. 'But thanks anyway.'

Cassandra looked as though she might protest, then thought better of it.

With Eric's departure, Lily got on with her next task. She took all the rugs outside to beat the dust out of them but it didn't seem to make any difference. Arms burning, she tackled something lighter next with a thorough declutter of the kitchen, getting rid of anything worn-out, chipped or cracked. Cassandra and Betty pitched in to help, the one humanely removing spiders with the aid of a glass tumbler and old postcard while the other consented to have her sandwich-maker stored elsewhere before she went for a nap.

The sitting room was next. Lily ploughed through stacks of faded magazines, old board games and assorted knick-knacks with a black bag in hand until she came to a small ceramic boot out of which a cactus, somehow thriving, clung to a thimble of caked earth. She was marvelling at this hardy survivor when a toot sounded from the lane.

Cassandra and Betty came downstairs. Cassandra was wearing a pretty-as-a-petal pink top and jeans while Betty looked resplendent as a fairground gypsy in a floor-length red dress with black edging.

Eric handed them both into the minibus and Lily had just waved them off when her phone buzzed. A glance at the screen had her chest tightening. *Preston*. Feck the good signal here now anyway. She'd hoped this weekend would at least be a reprieve from her boss and his constant reminders about how bad it looked for accountants to have money troubles. How it 'didn't exactly inspire confidence'.

She put the call on silent and waited until the vibrations ended. A text followed: **Need to discuss new client. Call when you get this. Don't be late Tuesday.**

She shoved the phone back into her pocket and heard the crunch of the eviction notice this time and groaned. She had to get herself out of this mess. To get free from Preston and litigious landlords and one stupid act of kindness that had jeopardised years of hard-earned financial prudence. And the only way out was to settle her liabilities. Which meant parting with the only asset she had left: this cottage.

Unless ... Nana had also left her money? Lily went to the study and moved several suitcases to the side to access Nana's roll-top desk. Inside she found a thick wad of dusty bank statements which, after a moment's hesitation, she read. Lily had been fortunate to never have to think about

Nana's financial status growing up – beyond knowing there was enough for what was needed, and she could save for things that were wanted. But scanning the statements now, Lily noted there'd been a sizeable balance in Nana's account a decade ago which had steadily declined until all that remained now was €307.82. Enough to cover the next few utility bills? It seemed odd because Nana's income had remained steady over that period and her outgoings few. Until she spied the regular withdrawals from the ATM in Cúltrá. Whatever Nana had been spending her money on, she'd been doing it in cash.

Lily returned the statements to the desk, rolled the lid back down and, with a sigh, wandered back into the kitchen. It was cleaner than this morning but still jammed with Betty's belongings. She tried moving one of the crates but just managed to wrench her back. Frustrated, she sat down at the table and tried for calm instead. If she couldn't be productive, at least she could enjoy a moment of peace. It was so quiet after all.

And then she remembered the dog and wondered why.

She went to the back door and peered out through the glass. Cassandra had fed Pup earlier and she looked well sated still as she lay asleep beside her *Welcome* mat, one front paw crossed over the other, her snout buried in the space between.

Lily touched the door handle and Pup's ears twitched and then she opened her eyes and gave an enormous yawn that displayed every tooth in her mouth.

Lily glanced at the chain attached to the collar. Then measured its length in her mind against the distance to the door. Gathering her courage, she pressed down and pushed the door open.

Pup stood instantly, her tail wagging fast. Then she came forward – as close as the chain would allow – her eyes fixed on Lily as her eyebrows twitched expressively.

'I come in peace,' Lily whispered.

'*Woo!*' said Pup.

'Luke? Is that who you're looking for? I'm afraid you're stuck with me.'

There were more '*woos*' from Pup and much cocking of ears.

'Did he take you for your walk after dinner? Is that what–'

She got no further with that question. At the word '*walk*' the dog launched into joyous barks and started turning circles, catching her paws in the chain and smartly changing direction to unwind herself.

Lily cursed. There was no way she could bring herself to put a lead on that dog, even if she had one. 'I don't have a lead but maybe tomorrow we might find someone who–'

The word '*lead*' operated the same way as the word '*walk*'. The dog was gambolling across the yard in anticipation, throwing herself onto her back to do little shimmying back-scratches and then running circles again.

'I'm really sorry. I'll make it up to you, I promise.' Feeling the most cowardly person in the world, Lily fled inside and up the stairs to escape the disappointed howls, flinging herself onto the bottom bunk and putting her hands over her ears.

Heavy grumbling followed for several minutes, then a few pleading whimpers until, finally, silence.

With a sigh of relief, Lily rolled onto her back only to be confronted by the sight of her own handiwork on the wooden slats overhead. Dozens of fading hearts in varying colours and sizes and degrees of symmetry surrounded "*I Love Luke*" in permanent marker with "*Luke&Lily4Ever*" and "*Mrs. Lily O'Callaghan*" scrawled nearby. She reached out her hand and traced her fingers over the hearts – a secret diary she was almost mortified she could still unlock. This heart for the first time Luke had stood up for her against Katie Sullivan. This one for when he'd shared his lunch when she'd forgotten hers. That one for saying her toilet-roll caterpillar still looked great after it fell in a puddle. Those first few drawn before she was old enough to even articulate the feeling. When Love was just someone being kind to her or being her friend.

But how much more it had come to mean as they'd tumbled together like pebbles on a beach, as the years had passed over and around them, smoothing all the rough edges between them until they were finishing each other's sentences and knew what the other was thinking without words being spoken. Until every touch was like a song to make the blood thrum and the heart sing. Until they were *Luke&Lily4Ever*. As permanent as the cliffs at Trá Eilis. As inevitable as the seasons.

Until Love had actually been tested and had proved itself as durable as a sandcastle at high tide.

At that thought, Lily's fingers left the wood and fell to her right knee where they pushed up the hem of her long shorts to trace markings of a different kind on her skin, all the way up the side of her leg. Some were straight, some jagged and the years had faded them too but – like the hearts above – their trace would always remain. As a reminder. And a warning. That Love could be the costliest liability of them all.

Chapter Six

Tricky

'Lily? Sorry to wake you but I can't get the grill to come on and I promised Betty toast.'

Lily forced her eyes open and lost several lashes to dried mascara. 'What time is it?'

Cassandra was leaning over her, smiling, a large beach towel wrapped around her head. 'Half ten.'

'It can't be. I've too much to do today.'

'I know. I slept like a log too. Betty says it's the sea air. Makes you hungry as well so if you could just explain about the grill. I've been clicking the gun thing and it's giving a little flash but it won't start it up no matter where I poke it.'

Lily went to pull the covers over her head only to discover they were all beneath her. With a groan, she got up on her elbows and saw she was still in yesterday's clothes. 'Have you checked if the gas is connected?'

Cassandra's face took on a helpless expression. 'Where would I look for that exactly?'

Lily grasped the bed frame and hauled herself upright. 'I'll do it. Just let me brush my teeth first.'

'Great. I'll put the kettle on.'

Cassandra was barely down the stairs when Lily's phone started buzzing. *Sergei. Landlord.* She let it ring out, counting the vibrations as her stress levels rocketed. It was thirty-three rings before he gave up.

But then he followed with a text. As short as his attempt to call her had been long. Just the one word: **RENT**.

Then: **RENT NOW**.

The third text was a crying emoji which somehow made the first two seem a little less intimidating. It was immediately followed by a red angry-face emoji, however. Great.

She dragged herself to the bathroom and brushed her teeth before removing her clogged mascara and the rest of yesterday's make-up. She really needed a shower but there was no hot water left when she tested it.

In the kitchen Betty and Cassandra were giggling over their coffees. They wore matching towel turbans but were fully dressed and Betty fully made-up.

'Have you both had showers already?'

'Oh yes. We're up an hour,' said Cassandra brightly.

That explained where all the hot water was gone.

'Good morning!' Betty rose to greet her with a kiss on the cheek. 'Did you sleep well?'

'Out for the count. What time did you guys get in? I didn't hear you.'

'We were very quiet. Well, I was. Cassie was doing a bit of singing. Sometime after one, I think.'

'You were singing too,' said Cassandra. 'We were celebrating.'

'Ned won the darts tournament,' explained Betty. 'Imagine. And he never threw a dart in his life. Steady Neddy they were calling him. We were all waiting for his luck to run out but he was like a machine.'

'180!' said Cassandra with feeling.

'Who was there?'

'Oh, pretty much the entire island,' said Betty. 'Cassie came in last at the darts. Too busy making eyes at Eric to concentrate.'

'Oh?' Lily looked at Cassandra to see her turn scarlet. 'And how was Eric's concentration?'

'He didn't play,' said Betty. 'He was keeping score and then ...' she started laughing, catching her breath to get the words out, 'in the middle of a round ...'

'*Don't!*' Cassandra implored.

'She managed to shoot Eric in the foot with a dart!' she hooted and wiped the tears from her eyes as Cassandra muttered something about loyalty and oaths to secrecy.

'Was he okay?'

'That's the best bit,' said Betty. 'He looked down and wasn't the dart still quivering out of his shoe and he said he'd heard about Cupid's arrow but he hadn't expected anything quite so painful.'

'He was alright then? At least you didn't get him in the eye.'

'Yes, yes, he was fine,' said Betty briskly, 'only this one got all mortified and ran out of the pub.'

Cassandra tossed her shoulders with great dignity. 'I'd had a lot to drink. I might have been a little emotional.'

Lily couldn't suppress a smile. 'You? Emotional? That can't be right. So what happened then?'

'Eric went out after her. Took the dart too which brought the competition to a halt as we only had the three. He brought her back in *eventually*.' Betty lowered her voice, as though this might prevent Cassandra from hearing. 'Outside, kissing they were, the pair of them. Held up the game for five minutes. Donie could see them from the window. He gave a running commentary.'

Cassandra put her head in her hands.

'I'm surprised Luke didn't put a stop to him,' said Lily.

'Oh, he wasn't there.'

Lily waited for Betty to elaborate. Why wasn't Luke there? What was he doing instead? But Betty, Great Spiller of Secrets, had returned to her coffee.

Remembering the errand that had brought her downstairs, Lily went around the crates and to the cupboard at the side of the cooker. She gave the yellow cylinder inside a gentle shake. *Empty.* She unclipped the connector and carried the cylinder to the scullery. Behind the door was another cylinder. She gave this one a shake too. *Full.* Hauling it back to the kitchen, she chanced to glance into the yard where the chain lay in a neat pile with no dog attached.

She dropped the cylinder as she tried to get the door open in a hurry. '*Where's the dog?*'

'What's that?' called Betty.

'*The dog! The dog's gone! She got off her chain somehow. What's wrong with this lock? Whose cows are in the field beyond? Should we warn them?*'

Cassandra was by her side a moment later. 'Do you need help?'

'Just to get this stupid key to turn. It's jammed or something.'

'Yeah. It's rusty. Luke says it needs a squirt of WP-something.'

'*Luke?*'

'I told him the porch door was a problem too.'

Lily blinked. 'What? Why would you do that?'

Cassandra looked confused. 'So we can get in and out? But he says that needs a sander. And I told him you weren't sure how you'd get the mower over the grass either, seeing as it's so tall.'

Oh my God! Was nothing private? 'And?'

'He says you'll need to strim it first.'

Lily waited for several seconds. 'Is that everything?'

'Yes,' said Cassandra.

Lily exhaled.

'He'll bring a strimmer and sander later. Also, your mower isn't working and you need a ladder. He'll bring them too.'

'*Cassandra!*'

'What? I hardly dropped any hints at all. But he can't help us until after Mass. And after he's taken Pup for her walk.'

Whatever expression crossed Lily's face at that, she received a very sympathetic smile in return.

'He arrived while you were asleep and said he wasn't sure if you knew where her lead was and that you might have found walking Pup last night a bit tricky.' She paused. 'Did you know where the lead was?'

'I didn't, no,' she admitted, 'but it's not like I couldn't track one down in my own cottage.'

Lily lugged the cylinder the rest of the way and set about connecting it to the cooker. She wasn't ready for this. Luke was supposed to come back for his bike and that was all. Not be delivering strimmers and sanders he'd then have to return again to collect. *No, no and no.* Yesterday's interaction had been enough of a disaster without inviting others. She'd have to make it crystal clear when she next saw him that he was to just take his bike and go for good. And she'd stay calm and collected throughout too. Keep all the emotion out of it this time. Yes, she'd picture herself in a courtroom, she decided. A poised professional detailing her findings. *So in summary, Your Honour, and in my expert opinion, this man is a complete and utter jerk.* The connector clicked into place.

She turned on the grill and heard a telltale hiss. 'Pass me the igniter.'

'The what?'

'The gun thing you were clicking earlier.'

Cassandra handed it to her.

One carefully placed *click* and a line of inch-long blue flames travelled neatly across the back of the grill.

'Okay. Lash the bread in there and don't take your eye off it. It's faster than a toaster and it'll burn on you in a second.'

'Aren't you going to stay and have breakfast with us?'

'No. I really need a wash.'

'He probably won't be back for another half hour. You've plenty of time.'

Lily looked from Cassandra to Betty to Cassandra again. Both wore matching poker faces. 'I don't care if he's back in half a second.'

This was met with silence.

'I'm not going up to get ready because he's coming back here. I'm just making that clear.'

Betty smiled and Cassandra chewed her lip.

'I couldn't care less if he saw me in a potato sack. Why aren't you saying anything? Did you not hear what I said?'

'Yes,' said Cassandra. 'But one thing I don't understand, Lily.'

Lily waited patiently as Cassandra took a sip from her mug.

'Why would you be wearing a potato sack?'

Finding this unanswerable, Lily retreated upstairs. She stripped off and stood under the cold shower which did nothing to slow her rising heart rate. So Luke had suggested she'd find walking the dog "tricky", had he? Having a good laugh at her expense more like. He knew how scared she was of dogs. He'd been there the day Donie's cocker spaniel had gone for her. It was a week after she'd turned seven and they'd been out playing and had taken a shortcut past Donie's place when Mojo, taking this sorely amiss for some reason, had charged through a hedge and sunk his teeth into her calf. She'd let a scream that brought Donie running but not before Luke had thrown himself at the dog and locked it in a restraining hold, his head twisting and turning to dodge the snapping jaws. Donie had got his hand on the collar and dragged Mojo away to lock him into the house. He'd come back to find two children in tears.

The poor man hadn't known who to comfort first. 'Did he get you too?' he'd asked, scouring Luke from head to toe for signs of bleeding.

As crying rendered Luke inarticulate, it was left to Lily to explain – in some embarrassment for her friend's feelings – that he was only crying because she was.

'It's just the fright,' said Donie, patting him on the shoulder. 'It's like that post-traumatic stress the soldiers get after they've come out of battle. Brave lad, brave lad!'

He put a plaster on Lily and gave each of them an ice lolly before sending them on their way. Nana had taken her straight to Cúltrá for treatment and a tetanus shot and she'd had her favourite pie for dinner but the fear of the furry four-legged animal had taken hold from that day. A second nip from a visiting poodle the following summer had cemented it.

She heard faint barks now and her first thought was that she was imagining them. But they got louder and were followed by hurried footsteps and Cassandra's whisper through the door: '*Lily. He's on his way back.*'

Stern commands to herself not to rush proved ineffective. She leapt from the shower and was dried and scrambling to reach her bedroom in under thirty seconds. Every item inside her rucksack was crumpled. Vexed, she threw on a pair of jeans and her least creased blouse and let the brush fly through her hair.

She heard a rap of knuckles on the back door, went out onto the landing and cast a pleading glance through the open door of the spare bedroom, where both Betty and Cassandra were now located. Surely one of them could answer it instead? But Cassandra was busy coaxing an antique hairdryer to life while Betty was pinning curlers into her hair.

Your Honour, if I could just have a moment to prepare?

Rumpled, wet-haired and feeling at an extremely unfair disadvantage, Lily went downstairs.

Through the back door she saw Pup back on her chain and panting heavily. Luke was filling one of her bowls with water from the outside tap before setting it in front of her.

Lily took a deep breath, thrust her chin up, and opened the door.

Luke pivoted as he straightened – and the case for the prosecution collapsed with a pathetic squeak at the back of Lily's throat. The dishevelled pirate of yesterday was gone. In his place was a well-groomed Adonis in dark jeans and an expensive-looking shirt. The shade of it threw a dreamy hue into his eyes and the top two buttons were undone, leaving a glimpse of tanned, muscled chest. He'd shaved too and, as he strolled forward, she caught the scent of good eau de Cologne. Something spicy.

She gulped. If Pirate Luke was hot, this incarnation was volcanic.

It was a moment before she realised she was staring at him.

And worse that she'd been caught doing it.

'Your bike's out front,' she said.

'Good morning to you too. Here's the lead.' He pulled what looked like an oversized measuring tape from his back pocket and handed it to her. 'Are the other two inside?'

When she didn't answer, he gave a tight smile – that didn't quite ask for permission – and strolled past her into the kitchen. He glanced up at the wall clock as he went and did a quick swerve to drag one of the chairs from the table towards it. Before Lily could even begin to formulate an objection, he stood on it and retrieved a small metal crank from above the clock. He set it into the first of the three holes in the face and turned it clockwise. Then repeated this action with the other two. Inside the glass case, behind the pendulum, metal weights rose. He checked his watch next before adjusting the time on the face and finally rotating the moon dial, making a sliver of moon disappear out of sight.

'Not quite a first quarter yet.'

Lily watched with arms folded, determined to regain her composure. She knew how to get that clock working again just as well as *he* did. 'Don't pretend you know which way the moon is right now.'

He shot her a withering look. 'What? Don't you look up any more? No, I suppose you don't. Just peer down from your lofty heights instead.'

He gave the pendulum a gentle tap. It came to life with a steady *tick-tock* as it swung back and forth. '*There.*' He stepped down and pushed the chair back under the table. Then he glanced around the kitchen, taking in all the crates. 'Those must be in your way.'

'Not at all.'

But he had the effrontery to actually go towards the nearest one, as if to move it. She held out her arm to block his way. The fine hairs on it rose at the contact with his chest but she kept her eyes riveted to his face.

'*What – do – you – want?*' she said slowly.

'To – be – anywhere – else,' he replied, at the same speed. 'But there's an innocent dog in this situation and I need to know she'll be looked after.'

Lily raised an eyebrow. 'Feel free to take full custody if you're that concerned. I won't stop you.'

But he just leaned forwards, his expression hardening. 'She was your nana's dog. Thought that would mean something to you.'

She swallowed. 'Well, it doesn't. All I care about is selling the cottage.'

He looked around at all the crates again and took a step back. Lily imagined he was milliseconds from theatrically wiping his hands.

'Well, good luck with–' he started as the minibus pulled up with a loud *toot* out front.

The sound brought Cassandra and Betty downstairs, both primped once more to perfection.

A moment later, Eric was hailing Luke as he sauntered in through the front door – as casually as if he now lived here. 'Hey, man, fancy shirt. Hardly recognised you.'

'Hilarious, *man*,' said Luke, with a warning look Lily interpreted as "Don't start". 'What are you doing here?'

'Same as you, I guess.' Eric caught Cassandra's eye and they exchanged smiles. 'I'm here to offer the ladies a lift to Mass. After I help them move all those crates out of their way, of course.'

He went straight to the crate Luke had been angling for.

With a smile, Lily swept aside to make room for him. 'That so *kind* of you, Eric.'

'No trouble at all,' he assured her, as he picked it up with a straining grunt, grappling with its sharp edges.

'Mind your back!' said Betty and Cassandra simultaneously.

'I've got it,' he rasped. 'Don't worry.' Then he gave Luke a cheeky wink before he staggered off with it in the direction of the study.

'That really *is* a very fancy shirt you're wearing, Luke,' Betty remarked. 'Did your mam pick it out for you?'

He turned to her with a look of disbelief. 'No, Betty. She did not.'

'At least you're not wearing a potato sack,' said Cassandra. 'Lily said earlier–'

But Lily interjected with a coughing fit as Eric returned and asked which crate they'd like him to move next?

'The one half-blocking the fridge would be great,' said Lily sweetly, accepting the glass of water Cassandra handed her, whilst ignoring the look of incredulity Luke sent her way.

Eric tried to lift the crate, only to discover it was too heavy. After a couple of attempts, he started to drag it instead, at which point Luke finally rolled his eyes and grabbed the other side so they could walk it to its new home together.

There were low mutters exchanged between them. Lily couldn't quite make them out. But when they returned to the kitchen again, nothing further was said. They just continued to move crate after crate.

And Lily made the most of it. With the fridge now fully accessible, all the jars of pickles, along with a varied assortment of condiments, got a new home. Then she picked up Betty's wedding cake and took it to the scullery. It was cool in there and the chest freezer was empty so there was a ready-made surface on which to put it, along with all the tins of dog food. And with the kitchen table finally clear of debris, Lily was able to give it a proper wipe down and put a tablecloth over it. Then she nipped out to the lane, gathered a bunch of fuchsia branches and placed them in an earthenware jug filled with water. This went in the centre of the table and, as she pushed all the chairs back in around it, she felt the first sliver of satisfaction since she'd arrived.

'All it needs now is a few daisy chains.'

She spun in time to catch a strange expression cross Luke's face. '*What?*' she said, sharper than intended.

'Nothing,' he sighed. Here.' He pulled a scrap of paper from his shirt pocket and handed it to her. 'The number for the local estate agent.

You'll get her best rate. She'll come over to take photos whenever you're ready and have the cottage up on their website the following day.'

'Oh. I ...' That was ... helpful.

'Wouldn't it be great if you could get one of those house stagers to do a job on the place first,' said Eric loudly. 'Did you know staged properties sell faster and for ten percent more?'

'Really,' said Cassandra.

Eric nodded solemnly. 'On average.'

Betty turned to Luke. 'Didn't you used to–'

'Another life,' he said hurriedly. 'Let's get going or we'll be late for Mass.'

'Yes,' agreed Betty. 'Come on, Cassie.'

'You're going to Mass too?' asked Lily.

'Yes. I need to see how long the aisle is.' Cassandra turned to Betty. 'How many steps do you think it will take us to get down it on The Big Day?'

'Not many,' said Betty. 'It's only a little place.'

Outside, the wind had picked up, blowing mournful notes as it soughed around the eaves. It threw two sets of carefully coiffed locks into disarray. With synchronised shrieks, Betty and Cassandra tumbled into the minibus with their hands protecting their heads. Eric and Luke followed, leaving Lily standing in the doorway.

'Aren't you coming?' called Betty.

'No. Thanks.'

With a five-point turn, Eric got the minibus facing the right way and sped off, leaving Lily to review her exit strategy. Having the crates out of the kitchen was a start but what she really needed was somewhere else for all Betty's stuff to go. But where? There were only so many places furniture could be accommodated on a small island and Betty was right about the hotel not being an option right now. But what about the hostel? There were plenty of rooms there too and maybe one would be free for a few weeks? And Jasper had always said not to hesitate if she ever needed anything. Granted, that had been a decade ago. But if she still had an ally on Inish Ruin, she hoped it would be him.

So, with a series of determined yanks, Lily closed the porch door and started walking.

Chapter Seven

The Blow-in

Lily had heard of Jasper Rivers before she properly met him. He was from some county in England though no one was quite sure which. He arranged the beautiful flowers for the church each week. He ran the hostel since Mrs. Dolan had retired and had learnt flower arranging from his wife Maria who'd got cancer and was now in heaven. At seven years of age that was the sum of her knowledge but, though she passed the hostel on her way to school every day, she never saw him. Her curiosity about him was not great though for she could hardly imagine someone as old as thirty-four, no matter how clever with flowers, would prove to be in the least bit interesting.

She might never have got to know Jasper, in fact, had it not been for Katie Sullivan. Katie lived in the last house out beyond the hotel. She'd been born less than ten days before Luke and, having known him all her life, considered him her particular friend. Lily's arrival on Inish Ruin – giving Luke another object for his affections – set her back up no end. In Katie's eyes Lily had stolen Luke from her and she missed no opportunity to be mean to her.

A skirmish between them after school one day had sent Lily into hiding beneath the upturned currach near the shoreline of Jasper's garden. She'd wriggled on her belly through the small gap made by the curve of the hull and, as she lay panting under the wooden frame, heard Luke calling her name.

'*Lily! Lily!* Oh, hi. Have you seen Lily?'

Luke was answered by a voice that sounded fancy. Like someone on the news. 'I don't know. What does she look like?'

There was a pause. 'She has a patch on one eye.'

'Ah. A pirate.'

Lily stifled a laugh.

'Don't be silly. She's my friend. She has glasses.'

'A friendly, short-sighted pirate.'

There was another pause and Lily could picture the expression on Luke's face. Bothered.

'If you see her tell her I'm looking for her. It's important.'

'Indeed,' said the voice but it didn't sound like he'd made a promise and that made her want to laugh again.

That was all she heard for thirty seconds before the currach was tipped to the side and a figure who seemed to shape-shift through her blurry eyes peered down at her. 'A stowaway. Are you going to come out? He's gone.'

Lily scrambled to her feet, wiped her tears, and peered again at the face that was regarding her back just as intently.

'What happened, little pirate? Your patch has fallen off.'

She stuffed the sodden thing into the pocket of her dungarees and put her glasses back on. 'It was filling with water. My eye was drowning.'

'You were crying,' he concluded. 'Was that boy annoying you?'

'Oh no,' she assured him. 'Luke hardly ever annoys me. He's my friend.'

'So he said. But why were you hiding from him then if he's your friend? You know he passed by?'

She nodded. 'I heard you talking to him. You were funny.'

He smiled and the warmth in it made her nerves vanish.

'Was I now? Well, why didn't you come out if you knew he was here?'

Lily heaved a sigh. 'I have to hide from him when I start crying. Because ...'

'Yes?'

'Because otherwise he starts crying too. He never cries when anyone else cries,' she hurried to explain. 'He's not a cry-baby and he's really very brave. And he never cries when he hurts himself even when it's bleeding. But if *I* start crying I have to run away before he sees.' She peered up at him again, waiting for his reaction.

He had his lips pressed tightly together. He seemed to be trying not to laugh. 'What set you off crying in the first place? You look fairly tough to me.'

This was the most delightful compliment she had ever received but she felt compelled to admit she wasn't really very tough right now but that she would be one day. 'Then I'll be able to tell Katie Sullivan she can't call me names and I won't ever cry about anything.'

'Katie, *huh*? What name did she call you?'

She wasn't sure if she should tell.

He sat on the grass in front of her and crossed his legs. 'You don't have to tell me if you don't want to.'

Naturally this was all the encouragement required and she sat too.

'She called me a blow-in.' She was disappointed to see no outrage on his face so set about explaining the insult more precisely. 'It means someone who isn't born on the island and that isn't even enough because all my great-ancestors going back forever have to be born here too and then I can be an islander. Katie said her and Luke are true islanders but I'm only a blow-in.'

He scrunched up his face and she waited, hopeful for some sympathy.

'What does Luke say about this?'

'He says not to mind her because she's just being full of spite and he'll put worms in her pencil case but I don't think he will because he'd be afraid the worms would get hurt.'

'*Hmm*, well, I suppose they might,' he said. 'But in war, sometimes, you have to accept a certain amount of collateral damage.'

Lily didn't understand what this meant, but it was said with such a twinkle she guessed she was being teased. 'I'm sorry I told you if you're only going to laugh.' She got to her feet.

'I'm not laughing at you. I'm only laughing because being a blow-in makes you far more special than Katie will ever be.'

This was news to Lily. After a brief hesitation, she asked, 'How?'

He leaned forward. 'What flowers are the best?'

She looked around her at the grassy meadow. 'Buttercups,' she said decidedly. 'Do you know if you hold them under your chin and your chin goes yellow that means you like butter?'

'Isn't that marvellous?' He got back to his feet. 'But come and I'll show you some other flowers.'

Feeling not the slightest uneasiness, she followed him around the back of the hostel to where a tall glass building stood hidden from sight of the road. Inside it Lily saw table after table of the most amazing flowers she had ever seen, more beautiful than any drawing in a book. They seemed to come in every shade of the rainbow and, eyes wide, she flitted from bloom to bloom, peering into each, touching the velvety petals with her nose and drinking in the fragrances.

'Now which flowers are the best?' he asked.

'Oh these! They're much better!'

'And do you know what they all have in common?'

She shook her head.

'They're blow-ins too. This one is from Karnataka in India. This one's from Sri Lanka and this one comes all the way from the Amazon Rainforest.'

'*Wow!*' she said, not a hundred percent sure where all these places were but liking the names well enough.

He led her to a group of tall flowers at the back, all white. She told him these looked especially nice.

'I'm glad you think so. This is one of the best flowers of all. I suppose you can guess what it's called?'

She shook her head but he just waited until ... 'Li-ly?'

He nodded. 'I've never heard of a flower called Katie, have you?'

She sure hadn't. It sounded like a very stupid name for a flower.

He agreed entirely and led her back out to the garden again. At the end of the path, he whipped a single lily growing in a small pot from behind his back and held it out to her. 'You give this to your mother and tell her she gave you a great name.'

She hesitated. 'Thank you but my mammy can't have flowers right now.'

'Oh? Why not?'

'Because she's in heaven with my dad. Hey, maybe they're friends with your Maria?'

He tensed and Lily knew she'd said the wrong thing. 'Oh. I'm sorry. I didn't mean–'

'No, no. It's okay. I suppose it's ... good to think she has some company.' He crouched before her then, lines etched around his eyes. 'What happened to your parents?'

She shrugged and ran a sandalled foot over the grass, bending a few daisies' heads. 'I've had enough of telling it.'

He offered her the lily again. 'Of course. Don't explain if you don't want to.'

She gave a sigh but flashed a small smile of capitulation as she reached for it. 'A man was the wrong way on the road and Daddy tried to get out of his way but the man tried to get out of his way and that was the end. Except I was a miracle and didn't even have a scratch and Nana wanted me and that's how I got to be friends with Luke.'

'I see,' he nodded. 'I'm very sorry for your loss.'

She gave his arm a reassuring pat. 'Don't worry. We'll see them again someday and they'll be all fixed. That's what Nana says. I'll give this flower to her instead. She loves flowers.'

He got back to his feet. 'Yes, you do that. And don't cry if Katie calls you a blow-in any more, okay? Just say "Thank you for the compliment".'

She gave him a big smile and straightened her glasses. 'I'll try. But sometimes when she looks at me I forget all my words.'

'Ah. Then you'll need a weapon.'

'A – a weapon?'

He laughed. 'It's nothing scary. You already carry it.' He caught her chin and raised it up a few inches. 'There,' he said. 'Armed and dangerous. Now if Katie says something to hurt you, you just raise your chin like that and say to yourself it doesn't even hurt. Trust me, Katie will get the message.'

'I can do that.'

'And if Luke won't, I'll put the worms in her pencil case.'

'That's okay. I don't want the worms to get hurt either. It was nice to meet you, Jasper.'

'And it was nice to meet you too, Lily.'

She'd left him on a high, feeling very special, and for many years that was the feeling Jasper always engendered in her. He gave her free rein to visit his greenhouse, the only child on the island who could boast of that and, as she got older, he showed her how to cut and arrange flowers for the church. From there it was a natural step to making her own bouquets which he encouraged her to sell at the weekly market in Cúltrá. He was her mentor of sorts, interested in her concerns and full of confidence about how successful she'd be in the future.

Which perhaps explained why she felt so nervous right now, recalling the current unsuccessful state of her affairs.

She'd reached the front door and had just raised her hand to the bell when Jasper appeared around the side of the building. He pulled up sharply when he saw her, his two hands rising as if applying air-brakes to himself. Then he beamed and crossed the lawn towards her. The lines on his forehead were more pronounced now and there was more grey than brown in his hair but that only made him look as wise as she'd always imagined him to be.

She didn't wait for his greeting, just gave him a tight hug.

'Well, hello,' he said, his cheeked flushed pink as she released him. 'I was just coming from the greenhouse. Do you want to come see?'

And with that simple question and her even simpler nod, all felt as easy as ever between them. The greenhouse had doubled in size since she'd last been in it and she entered a jungle of tangled leaves and pungent scents. Jasper squeezed sideways through the gaps between the tables and she stepped slowly after him, careful not to knock any bloom until they reached the back of the building. The space here had been widened and a domed roof of tinted glass filtered light upon a spectacular array of flowering orchids that would never be cut for any bouquet.

'Oh Jasper. These ... these ... *wow*!' She made a slow circuit, naming each variety she could remember.

Jasper was quick to praise her memory but she got the feeling he was a little chuffed with himself too, as if it was a compliment to his prowess as her teacher. When she had admired and enjoyed and heard descriptions long enough, he led her back outside and down to the grassy banks of An Fáinne, to the wicker bench in its patch of oxeye daisies.

It squeaked as they sat and Lily glanced around. 'Where are all your clients today?'

'Didn't Betty tell you? She commandeered all my beds months ago for her wedding guests to stay in.'

'And ... they're paying you?'

'The guests? Yes.'

'But you have to shut up shop for the rest of the week? Before they arrive?'

He smiled. 'Well, it frees me up nicely to work on Betty's bouquets and the decorations for the church instead, doesn't it? Wilier than a fox that one. I don't mind though. A change is as good as a rest, right? So how have you been, Lily? Life's been treating you well, I hope?'

'Oh fine, yes. I've been working in London. As an accountant.'

'So I heard. Doing very well for yourself as I knew you would. Though I'd always imagined you going into something creative. Wasn't that the plan?'

It had been, yes. When she could still connect to those parts of herself that felt things deeply. Before she found a career that didn't require feeling anything at all. But she rallied. 'Oh, you'd be surprised how creative accounting can be.'

But a tinge of concern now coloured his expression. 'But you enjoy it though? The work?'

'Sure. What's not to enjoy? The pay is good and the black and white of it is sort of ... relaxing. All those checks and balances. If you follow the rules, you can't really make a mistake.'

His brow furrowed. 'And that's what's important to you now? Not making a mistake?'

A confused laugh escaped her. 'Isn't that important to everyone? Anyway, how about you? When you're not being hijacked to do wedding flowers, is business good? Any news?'

He rolled his shoulders as if to ease the stiffness out of them. 'No news really, no. I'm busier than ever thankfully. And the work still brings me joy. But nothing of consequence to report.'

She looked around her again. 'Well, the place looks great. Better than ever.'

'Thank you.' He leaned back against the arm of the bench which gave another protesting squeak. 'I hear you're just back for a flying visit.'

She cocked her head. 'How do you know that?'

'Have you not met our new Town Crier?'

Ah. 'Eric, you mean? Well, yes. I mean you're right. I have to be back at my desk by Tuesday morning.'

'Then I appreciate even more you taking the time to come visit me. Just to say hi.'

She clasped her hands together in her lap. 'Well, to be honest, Jasper, I didn't just call to say hi.'

'No? You need something?'

How she'd have loved at that moment to tell him she didn't need anything but ... 'Yes. Sorry. I'm selling the cottage but it's full of Betty's furniture. Her house is crawling with builders apparently and Ned's place – well, you know what his driveway is like – and I doubt the hotel would have a room free in summer so I was hoping you might have–'

He cut her off. 'Why are you selling?'

She bit her lip. She'd never lied to Jasper. Starting now felt wrong. 'I got stung. Stupidly. Financially. I was trying to help someone out in a hurry. Didn't do my research. But now I owe money to the worst person imaginable.'

'Who? A loan shark?'

'Worse. My boss.'

'Why? Is he violent? Some kind of criminal?'

Okay, so Preston being the worst person imaginable had maybe overstated it. Or Jasper had way too much imagination. 'No, no. I'm not in any kind of danger. Physically, at least. It's just he's a toxic ass who runs a toxic workplace but he's also extremely influential in the industry. I need to get a job elsewhere for the sake of my sanity but I have to part from him on good terms. With no professional repercussions.'

Jasper rubbed his brow for a moment. 'You need to pay off your debt to him so you can walk away?'

'Exactly. But I need the cottage spruced up first so I can sell it, which means finding somewhere else to store Betty's furniture. Just till she's back from the honeymoon. One room would do it. Two tops and I'd pay you the going rate for them after.'

'After what?'

'After I ... sell?'

'I see,' he said softly.

No doubt he did. She might as well have hung a sign round her neck saying "*Extremely Stuck for Cash*". 'So can you help me?'

'I'm really sorry, Lily, but I can't. I'm fully booked again from next week and need every room. I can't and wouldn't turn clients away without a lot of notice. Some will have booked flights.'

'No. No. Of course. I completely understand. Just thought I'd ask.' She hauled herself up and he followed suit. 'Well, I better get back to the cottage and keep going with the clear-out. It was great to see you again.'

'And you, Lily. Don't leave it another decade, okay?'

But before she could make any promises he was striding back to his greenhouse.

So she headed off herself, maintaining a brisk pace until she reached Barrett Lane where she began the slow trudge up the hill. The breeze rushing down it was welcome but her thoughts as she climbed were not. Still no home for Betty's furniture. Now what?

Betty was back from Mass, leaning out the spare bedroom window and hooking more undergarments to rope again – bras this time and a bright red blouse that flapped in the wind like a distress signal.

'Betty, we talked about this. Give me what's wet and I'll hang it in the yard for you.'

Betty's reply was drowned out by what sounded like a motorbike revving.

'*What did you say?*' Lily asked.

Betty tried again and Lily, doing her best to lip-read, was almost sure she'd said 'The washing line is gone' but that couldn't be right and what was making that noise?

Lily went to the side passage and peered down it. There was no motorbike in the side yard though – only Luke wielding a chainsaw against her garden shed!

She shot through the wooden gate and was standing beside him with her hands on her hips a moment later.

With the goggles over his eyes and a pair of bright-orange ear protectors on his head, he didn't see her. This gave her time to notice how his lovely shirt was now crumpled and streaked, the sleeves rolled up and another button undone as he gripped the chainsaw with gloved hands, the muscles in his forearms bulging. Like some sort of deranged magician, he seemed intent on slicing her shed in half.

She was not amused to see he'd cut a smiley face into one side first.

He reached a corner, clicked the kill switch and wiped his hand across his brow.

'What the hell are you doing to my shed?'

Chapter Eight

Hermit Crab

Luke spun and the chainsaw passed within inches of Lily's shins. '*Jesus!* Don't sneak up on someone with a chainsaw, Lil! What if it'd been on?' He set it on the ground then removed the goggles and ear protectors and threw them on top.

Lily was looking irate. He hadn't intended to provoke that reaction in her but it was oddly satisfying all the same.

'What am I supposed to hang my washing from now?' she demanded.

'From the line, same as always. I'll just fix the other end to a hook on the wall instead. It'll take me all of two seconds.'

But she was not to be so easily placated. She looked past him to where a lawnmower, step-ladder, strimmer and sander lay. Her foot started tapping.

'Ned dropped this lot over for you after Mass. Figured you'd need it. And, while I'm here, I thought I might as well give you a bit of a dig out.'

Her jaw dropped as she gestured to the shed. 'A dig out? Is *this* supposed to be *helping*? You're just having fun messing about with a chainsaw! Why have you destroyed my shed? That was a perfectly good shed.'

'It was in bits! The wood all rotting. Major red flag to any buyer,' he added with what he hoped was convincing authority. Technically the shed had a few more years in it but it was an eyesore that made the yard look half the size it was.

But Lily narrowed her eyes as if she knew he'd taken a liberty he shouldn't have.

'A death trap for Pup if it came down on her,' he added, appealing to any health-and-safety or animal-welfare sensibilities she might have instead.

She tensed at the mention of the dog, as if just remembering what was missing from the yard. 'Where *is* Pup?'

'I put her in the scullery for the minute,' Luke told her. 'The noise was bothering her.'

'Is that where she's supposed to live, now you've chopped up her home?'

But before he could answer there was a shriek from the cottage.

Lily's eyes went wide. 'Please tell me you took the wedding cake out of the scullery before you put the dog in?'

He imagined his expression of alarm answered that.

They both ran for the back door and Luke pulled it open to find Betty pointing a long-handled sweeping brush at the dog. If she was trying to defend her cake with it, though, she was far too late.

Pup was sprawled on the scullery floor, whimpering mournfully. On the freezer what small bit remained of the cake was gouged with tooth marks and glistening with slobber.

Lily removed the brush from Betty's shaking hands and put her arm around her as Luke crouched to deal with the perpetrator, pressing gentle fingers over her dilated belly.

'What have you done to yourself, you glutton? Have you no off-switch?'

'*Oh Betty, your cake!*' Cassandra joined them, followed closely by Eric.

'*Geez*, man,' Eric grinned over Cassandra's shoulder. 'What kind of sabotage is this?'

Lily's head whipped from Eric back to Luke. 'Sabotage?'

He held up his hands to protest his innocence. 'He's joking, Lily. That's a joke.'

'Well, you can do your comedy act somewhere else. The reunion is officially over. Get out of my cottage. Both of you.'

Eric backed up as if she'd pulled a gun and headed for the door. 'Cassandra, babe, I'll see you later, yeah?'

'*Right now,*' said Lily, rounding on Luke. '*Go somewhere. Go anywhere.*'

'Go to the shop!' cried Betty. 'I'll give you a list. If we get another cake made today we might be able to get the icing on it in time. Wait'll I find my glasses.'

'I'll get the ingredients,' said Lily, her eyes still fixed on him. 'We don't need his help.'

'It's not his fault,' said Betty. 'It's Mervyn. I told you he's not happy about the wedding but that he could do this to me is pure mean. No, don't go, Lily. I need you to stay and find the tins and weighing scales and bowls. You'll know where everything is.'

'Will the shop be open?' asked Cassandra.

'I'll call Ned and tell him it's an emergency,' said Luke. 'If he wants cake for his wedding it'll be open.'

'Of course he'll help us,' said Betty, sniffing in a manner to wrench the hardest heart. '*Ned* would never do anything like this to me. Call him, Luke, and go up and get what I need. There's the recipe card. Three lots of everything and plenty of ready-to-roll icing and if he doesn't have it–'

'I'll get it. Don't worry.'

'And take Cassandra with you,' said Betty, 'to help carry it back.'

'I'm sure I'll be able–'

'No, no,' she said firmly, cutting him off. 'Go on off now, the two of you, and you can carry it back together.'

'What about the dog?' asked Lily. The animal was still on her side, immobilised but for the heavy panting. 'Shouldn't we get her to a vet?'

'We'd have to get her on the ferry first,' Luke said, 'and I think that might be worse for her than just letting her try to digest it. Give her lots of water and get her on her feet if you can to walk about a little. I'll ring the vet and let you know if she says any different.'

Without further delay, Betty pressed shopping bags into Cassandra's hands and ushered her and Luke away.

Luke dialled the vet who okayed the plan to let Pup's digestive track have first crack at the problem. After a second call to Ned who said he'd meet them at the shop, he turned his attention to Cassandra and the unexpected opportunity to further their acquaintance which their errand presented. She was an extremely pretty girl, with a manner as engaging as it was artless but her winning attribute, he quickly discovered, was her confiding nature.

By the time they'd reached the end of Barrett Lane – and with the barest of prompting – he'd learned she was Lily's flatmate, that they never fought even though it drove Lily mad when she put empty cereal boxes back in the cupboard and it drove Cassandra mad when Lily wouldn't cry at the sad parts of movies, that she considered herself Lily's best friend – "well, maybe her only friend" – that until last week she'd worked with Lily as a receptionist at Preston Tepper Accountants in London and that she was going to start a new job in Belfast in a fortnight.

'You'll miss working together,' he guessed, when she finally drew breath.

'Oh yes. That's the worst part but I'm not going to let her get rid of me just because we won't be working or living together anymore. I think she'd be a hermit crab if she could, would Lily.'

He wasn't sure what she meant by this. 'Is it hard to get her to come out of her shell?'

'Oh no. She's not shy or anything. Loads of confidence. I just mean she'd live by herself without anyone for company.'

'Like a hermit.'

'That's what I said but she does have a bit of a shell around her, now you say it.'

Luke hadn't noticed any shell. Barbed wire maybe? 'Well, she's lucky to have someone who cares.'

'For all the good it does me when she won't let me do anything for her and she's had my back so often. Do you know I was going to give up being a receptionist until I talked to her?'

'Oh?'

'Because of my sisters. Calliope is a lawyer and Cressida is a stockbroker. All very impressive and I know they're just trying to help me be more ambitious but it just makes me feel like I'm a failure because I'm only a receptionist – but I love being a receptionist! It's the best job in the world. You get paid to be nice to people and make them feel welcome and you're so important because you're the first impression anyone gets of a company and taking messages properly can be crucial. People don't think of that but deals can be made or broken on a missed call. But my sisters don't get that.'

'And Lily does?'

'Well, she says I can do anything I set my mind to. But when I told her I was certain I didn't want to be anything but a receptionist, she said if that was the case she was happy I'd found my calling and that life was too short to waste doing something you hated. I stopped stressing about what my sisters think after that and I've never been happier. But Lily? She has people falling over themselves to get close to her but she still ends up all alone. I just don't understand how someone with so much self-confidence can have so little love, you know?'

Luke didn't know. He found it hard to imagine a world in which Lily wasn't loved. Well, unless she kept walking out on people with no warning. Yes, that might do it. Still, he was curious to understand her current situation more clearly.

'How are things for her at work? Does she have a good boss?'

Cassandra made a low sound of disgust. 'No. Preston's a manipulative prick I wouldn't trust as far as I could throw. Dangles carrots all over the place, promising promotions and bonuses. "If only everyone could just give a little more, show their commitment with even more unpaid overtime ..." And when they break their backs to impress him it's always just short of what he wanted. Maybe next time. It's all a game for his own amusement.'

Luke came to a halt and the shopping bags crumpled against him as Cassandra pulled up too late. 'Why does Lily stay working for him then?'

'Oh, she was planning on leaving months ago. But then the whole Peter thing happened and now she's trapped. I'm not supposed to know though, so don't say anything.'

'I won't,' he promised, still very much in the dark but prepared to say anything if it kept Cassandra talking.

She smiled warmly. 'I knew I could trust you.'

'Thank you,' he said faintly, wondering what had given her that idea? 'Who's Peter?'

'He was my pen-pal.'

Was? 'I'm ... sorry for your loss?'

'Oh no!' she laughed. 'He's not dead or anything. I just had to excommunicate him after all the trouble he caused.' She went on to explain – and Luke felt "explain" was a generous term for what followed – how she'd arranged for Lily to meet up with this pen-pal when she'd been attending a work conference in Chicago. This had been done with the best of intentions as she'd found out Lily's colleagues had a nasty bet going and she thought it would be better for Lily to hang out with someone nice instead of being stuck with assholes. But this Peter had been smitten and had tried to impress Lily with the strength of his devotion by throwing himself off the conference building the next day.

Luke gasped. 'He tried to kill himself?'

But Cassandra looked at him as if *he* were the one telling the ridiculous story. '*No!* How would that have got him a second date? He tied a bungee cord to the window-cleaner's rig and jumped with a massive bunch of flowers. White roses. Because red is kinda cliché, right?'

He looked at her blankly.

'He was supposed to come to a stop outside the room where they were having the conference and Lily would let him in the window and it would be a lovely scene but he ended up in the canopy over the lobby instead.'

'*In* the canopy?'

She nodded solemnly. 'Then of course he had to be hospitalised and didn't have health insurance and his family are wackos and you know they charge you over there just to cart your body away if you drop dead in the street. And, I mean, Lily couldn't just leave him without getting his back straightened out. But it cost way more than she imagined. People go, like, medically bankrupt over there all the time. It's crazy. And then she was overseas when her nana died but what could she do? She had to use all her savings and get a big loan from Preston just to get Peter sorted and herself back home, which took ages. And, of course, Preston saw his opportunity and made her agree to pay him back in overtime no hurry – which sounds generous but basically locks her in with him for years. On the plus side, though, I'd never have known about Inish Ruin but for Peter. He got it out of her about growing up here. Made her tell him stories to distract him from the pain.'

Every instinct urged caution but ... 'What did she tell him?'

'Well, he wouldn't give me any specifics but he said if I ever got the chance I was to come here. He said Lily left something important here and might need a friend to help her find it.'

He was aware of a sudden tightening in his chest which should have served as ample warning against asking anything else.

'You wondering what that might be?' Cassandra pressed. When he shook his head, she just leaned closer. 'Want to hear *my* guess?'

He assumed she was about to tell him.

'I'm thinking some old jewellery. Or a leather jacket. Something that would be vintage now maybe and worth a bit of money.'

She might have stuck a pin in him, so deflated he felt.

'*I'm kidding!*' She clasped her hands together and her eyes took on a dreamy, faraway look. 'I'm sure he meant something far more important – like her heart.'

Discovering to his annoyance he'd been hoping for just that, he took the shopping bags off Cassandra and walked on. But after a moment's consideration he couldn't help asking. 'Isn't she with anyone, then?'

'No. Not in a proper relationship at least. Lily doesn't believe in love. Says she'd rather be stabbed in the front than in the back.'

'*Huh?*'

'Yeah, I'm not sure that makes sense either. I mean, if you were going to be stabbed either way I think it would be better not to see it coming. You know, then you wouldn't have the fear bit and be tensed up and everything. She also says telling someone you love them is like handing them a loaded weapon to shoot you with.'

'*O-kay.*'

'I know. Very violent, a lot of her sayings. But, to be fair, going to nightclubs with her is like being ambushed in a wildlife documentary. The apes going apey and the wolves with their tongues hanging out. She finds it very stressful.' She glanced at him thoughtfully. 'Does that bother you?'

Yes, it bothered him. The idea of Lily being made to feel like prey made his blood boil. But he just nodded.

'Which part? That Lily doesn't believe in love or that all the men want her?'

He hesitated. 'Why does this feel like a test?'

'Because it *is* a test. You're so clever to figure that out.'

There wasn't a hint of sarcasm in this. She seemed genuinely delighted.

'It bothers me that she finds it stressful,' he said tersely. 'That's all.'

But Cassandra just smiled. Apparently this was the correct answer.

'I was her friend once,' he added, lest she get the wrong idea.

But they'd reached the shop now where Ned was waiting by the door looking like an athletic gnome: wizened of face and wiry of limb. He took the recipe card from them and started loading bags of flour and raisins onto the counter while Cassandra looked about the Portakabin in delight and took a photograph of the post office part which essentially comprised a sticker saying *An Post* at one end of the counter. There was an assorted stack of envelopes below it, a stand of postcards in front of it, and a computer just behind it.

'It must be the smallest post office in the world!' she exclaimed, taking another photograph. 'Will you take one of me in front of the sticker?'

Luke obliged, smiling at her enthusiasm. 'Don't let its size fool you. Nothing Ned can't do here that a bigger post office can. Passport applications, savings, paying bills. Isn't that right, Ned?'

'Sure is,' he said, his eyes twinkling at Cassandra. 'How are you today?'

'You've met?' Luke checked.

'Yes,' said Cassandra. 'At darts last night. When Steady Neddy here won the trophy.'

'*Arrah*, go on,' said Ned, looking pleased all the same.

It seemed the shop, like the post office, could supply anything a bigger one could and in minutes everything on Betty's card was in the bags, including the icing. It was a fair weight. Luke gave Cassandra the lightest bag and picked up the other two. Saying goodbye to Ned, they set off.

Within a minute, however, Cassandra was holding her stomach. 'I have a stitch.' She grimaced and contorted herself in an attempt to find relief from it.

'Do you want to sit down? There's a flat bit of wall over there,' he said, pointing to the side of the road.

'No. I'll be alright. I'm sure it'll ease in a minute.'

Luke took the bag from her anyway.

A minute didn't fix it. She winced again.

'Here, come on. Rest a second.'

'No, no. I'd prefer to get to the cottage and have a lie-down. I don't think it's a stitch really. It feels more like indigestion.' She grimaced. 'I'll be fine. Let's keep going. Do you want to give me that smaller bag again?'

'No. I've got it.' He kept the pace slow, watching her for signs of further pain but whatever ailed her seemed to ease and by the time they reached the bottom of Barrett Lane she was smiling again.

'You won't tell Lily I was talking about her, will you?' she said. 'I wouldn't usually because I know she hates it. Under normal circumstances I'm a model of discretion. It's just ...'

'You trust me.'

She nodded. 'Because I figured out who you really are. You're little Luko from the photograph. The one holding Lily's hand outside the school? You still need a haircut by the way and, if you don't mind me saying, I think you should go back to your given name. Luko is much more interesting than plain old Luke and you should be proud of your heritage. Is it from Italy or Spain you are originally? Lily seemed a bit confused about that.'

Lily wasn't the only one but before he could respond she was off on another tack.

'You're not really here to sabotage things for her, are you?'

'Of course not.'

'And you still love her?

'No,' he said firmly. 'I do not.'

'Are you sure?' Her eyes searched his. 'Because I was really hoping it'd be like when the hero and heroine are separated by war and they don't see each other for years and one of them has to lose an eye or a leg or be horribly maimed and the girl ends up married to the brother but she can't love him like she could the first guy. Then they meet again years later and they do whatever it takes to get back together.' Her eyes were bright with emotion as her chest heaved.

'I hate to break it to you, Cassandra, but I don't think we're in that movie.'

She sighed, a sound so plaintive he could only imagine the angel voices had suddenly faded from her head. 'Couldn't you at least try?'

'Of course. Forgive me. Is it an eye or a leg you'd prefer me to lose?'

He got an admonishing tap on the arm for that. 'I don't want you to lose either but I just can't go off to Belfast and leave her be a hermit crab for the rest of her life. Won't you help?'

She extended her right hand as if to shake on a deal.

He kept both his own firmly grasping the bag handles. 'To do what, exactly?'

'Hardly anything, I swear. Only find a way to make Lily believe in love again, make it so she stops trying to get rid of me and see if Eric is free to come to a fashion show in Belfast on the 27th of September. But you can't tell him I asked you to find out.'

He walked on. 'Right. Nothing too tricky then.'

But a glance over his shoulder showed her beaming with confidence.

'For you, Luko, a piece of cake.'

Chapter Nine

Not-relief

Lily was disinfecting the fridge when the shoppers returned. Luke was carrying all the bags and Cassandra was wreathed in smiles.

'How did you get on?' asked Betty.

'We got everything.'

Lily watched as Luke set the bags down on the kitchen table. Cassandra started to unload but Luke stopped her with a hand laid casually on the small of her back and asked her if she didn't want to have that lie-down?

She answered with a sweet smile, assuring him she was fine before adding, 'Thanks, Luko'.

Betty's eyebrows rose and Lily's pulse ticked up right along with them. What was happening here? Luke and Cassandra had been gone less than an hour but there was an unmistakable camaraderie between them now. They stood side by side, doing nothing more intimate than unloading shopping but even with their backs turned she could see the little smiles flying between them.

Luke hadn't looked at her once since he'd come through the door. Maybe he was afraid to in case she tried to turf him out again? Or maybe he was just too focused on standing beside Cassandra and making her smile like that! Pain buzzed at her like a fly she couldn't swat. No. She refused to feel jealous. Even if Cassandra looked like summer personified with her tumbling curls and pretty dress and glowing cheeks. Lily's hair might be matted, her blouse marked and even more crumpled than when she'd pulled it from her rucksack this morning but the oven was gleaming, the wall tiles free of grease and the floor mopped. That was what mattered, wasn't it? Not having Luke's attention.

She heard her name called and turned to Betty. 'Pardon?'

'Luke was just asking if Pup was outside?'

She looked again at Luke but if he'd addressed the question to her he hadn't turned around to do it. So she answered Betty instead. 'Yes. In the yard. If you're all sorted here ...' She went out of the kitchen and stood by the open back door, desperate suddenly to feel the sun on her face.

Across the yard, Pup was lying in a shady corner on a thick pile of blankets. She looked over at Lily and thumped her tail. Lily felt strangely comforted until she became aware of the wall of heat behind her and realised the wag wasn't for her at all.

Luke settled his hands either side of the door frame and looked out over her shoulder. 'How's the patient?'

'She seems much better,' she managed and waited for him to move on – to go back to the kitchen or go past her into the yard. But he stayed where he was, close enough for her to smell that cologne again and underneath it the headier scent of himself, achingly familiar.

'You've been working hard, Lily. The kitchen looks spotless.'

Someone had noticed and even though it was *him* she felt grateful.

'Your arms must be burning.'

She elbowed him reflexively. Old joke. Still not funny.

'*Geez*, your elbow got sharp!' His right hand left the door frame and wrapped around the offending joint as if to decommission it against further use. His hold was gentle but she still felt as though every digit was boring heat into her.

Don't let him touch you! The protest of her mind was instantaneous but her body rejected the command to move as that strange rush of ... not-relief coursed through her again, making her shoulders relax.

He released her but leaned closer. 'Were you very brave?' he murmured.

The warmth of his breath had her neck stretching. 'How do you mean?'

'Well, either you carried Pup outside or you dragged her somehow. That's a big deal for you, right? Getting that close to a dog?'

'I was shaking every time I got within five feet of her,' she admitted. 'Got the cold sweats and everything.'

'*Hmm*.' The sound seemed to rumble through his chest and into her own. 'How did you get her outside, then?'

'She got herself out with a bit of coaxing. I made her a nice soft bed, set out some water and left a trail of cake crumbs leading to it.'

'You gave her *more* food?'

'Only tiny bits. I don't know what motivates her other than food and w.a.l.k.s. She was happier once she got back on her feet but she was whimpering at the door to the shed. I don't think she likes what you've done to the place.'

'She'll get over it.' The rasp of his whisper brushed her ear, sending a shiver through her. And she suddenly understood that she was made of atoms – because they were all vibrating to whatever frequency Luke O'Callaghan was currently transmitting.

And then he stepped around her as if nothing had happened and headed over to give the dog a pat.

She stared after him, her mouth open, like the idiot she clearly was. What in the hell was she doing letting him affect her like that? Just so he could walk away again without a care? Where was her pride? No, forget pride. Where was her sense of self-preservation? Fool me twice or whatever that stupid saying was.

A throat cleared behind her and she turned to see Cassandra looking anxious. 'I have to cream the sugar and the butter.'

As Betty moved to turn on the oven Cassandra explained, through the medium of frantic mime, that she had no idea what creaming the butter and sugar involved.

Lily attempted to mime back the process required. Cassandra still looked puzzled so Lily took up the wooden spoon and applied herself to demonstrating the task.

'Ah, you're going to help me – that's great, Lily,' said Betty, glancing over. 'You were always a great girl for making the cakes.'

Lily groaned inwardly as she pictured the afternoon slipping away, everything on her To Do List left undone. But Cassandra immediately offered to help with any other job that needed doing. Grateful, Lily asked her to clear out any clothes that were in her wardrobe. It didn't take long and two black bags later Cassandra was on to the next task and the toys from the study filled three more.

By the time these were piled in the porch, the cake was in the oven and Lily accompanied her upstairs to clear out the books from her room. Here, however, she found herself stalled, getting no further than putting books into the bag and then taking them out again. She glanced up to see Cassandra watching.

'Why don't you keep them?'

Lily closed the book in her hand with a snap. 'No. They're for kids.'

'Doesn't mean you can't keep them. Keep a few anyway. Keep your favourites.'

'No,' she said again. 'I don't need clutter.'

'It's not clutter, Lily. It's memories of your childhood.'

Exactly why she wouldn't keep them. How many times had Nana read these to her? Until she knew them by heart? Longer? The two of them squashed together on the bunk, Nana's lilting voice spinning out the words as Lily waited for her cue to turn the pages. These books had never been passed on or boxed away. Almost as if they were just waiting here to be needed all over again.

With a press of pain at that thought, Lily put the book straight into the bag and scooped the next dozen off the shelf and put them in, too. What good were fairy tales without a happy ending? She kept going until all the books were cleared.

'There. I'll give them to the school. They can get some use out of them.'

But the line furrowing Cassandra's brow looked set to become permanent. 'Keep one book,' she urged. 'You can store it in my room so it won't clutter anything.'

'Thank you but you won't have a room in the flat next week and you won't want to be dragging books to Belfast.'

'Please, Lily.' She pulled an empty shoebox from under the bottom bunk. 'I want you to put things in here to take back to London. You can make room for one extra shoebox in your life.'

Lily just shook her head.

But the blue eyes watered as they widened. 'For me?'

Lily pressed her palms against her face. 'Fine. Okay. One shoebox.' She rummaged in the black bag, withdrew a book at random and put it in the box. 'Happy now?'

Cassandra was still frowning. 'You didn't even look to see which book it was.'

'Well? What book is it?'

She opened the lid and peered in. '*The Magic Stone*.'

'Perfect. The tale of a woman duped by a charmer. I'll treasure it.'

Revving sounded from the back garden and Cassandra looked out the window. 'Luko's started on the grass.'

Thinking of the poor dog's nerves, Lily was out the bedroom door, down the stairs and through the kitchen in a flash. When she reached the side yard, she could see Luke was already halfway across the garden, though, working his way towards the back fence, sweeping the strimmer from side to side. His shirt was off and the strimmer's thick strap was slung across one bare shoulder.

She called out to him to stop but he just kept moving further away. She guessed he couldn't hear her over the noise. Her eyes went to Pup then. The dog was still in her shady corner but now fast asleep. A pair of bright-orange ear protectors had been adjusted for size and placed over her head.

The sight drew a reluctant smile from Lily. She looked back at Luke, swinging the strimmer wildly with one hand now as he tried to swat an insect off his shoulder. He was still thoughtful then. And hard-working. And good with animals. And stupidly handsome, even more so with his shirt off now dammit. Yes, Luke O'Callaghan still ticked all the boxes. Except the one marked *Constant*.

She returned inside and checked her phone. She'd missed a call and text from Preston. She read the text. Short but sour: **Your landlord called.** *What the hell?* She was doing everything she could think of to pay Sergei the rent she owed. She'd told him her plan to get solvent again but he either hadn't believed her or hadn't understood her or just wouldn't wait. But wasn't blowing up her phone with calls and texts and issuing her an eviction notice enough? Did he really need to call her boss too?

Beyond embarrassed, Lily went to the study, closed the door behind her and dialled Preston.

He answered immediately. 'Is something wrong with your phone?'

'Hi. No. Yes. I'm on an island. The signal is terrible.'

'But you got my message about your landlord, right? That's why you're calling?'

'*Um* ... yes?'

'So you got the message I sent yesterday?'

Feck. 'Oh. Did you send a message yesterday? That's so strange. I didn't get it.'

'Very strange,' he agreed smoothly. 'As it was marked read.'

Double feck. 'So my landlord? He shouldn't have called you. I don't even know how he got your number. I'll make sure it doesn't happen again.'

'Not a good look for us, Lily,' he tutted. 'Accountants having money troubles. Doesn't exactly inspire confidence if we can't manage our own financial affairs.'

'Yes, but it's just a temporary situation. In the process of being sorted.'

His sigh was dramatic. 'I really don't want to have to start seeing you as a liability.'

Oh come on! She was the hardest worker in that place.

'Is there a danger your landlord could petition for bankruptcy against you?' he asked next.

That brought her up short. Oh God, she really hoped not. 'Could he?'

'Bankruptcy is not something I'm *personally* familiar with,' he said.

And Lily visualised throwing a coffee cup at him. Of course he wouldn't be with trust funds galore backing up any mistake *he* made.

'But if you're declared bankrupt you can't practise as an accountant,' he went on. 'If that happened I'd have to let you go. I can't imagine any other firm hiring you in those circumstances, can you?'

Lily leaned against the desk, feeling dizzy. Could she really become homeless *and* unemployable because of this debt? What was the timeline for bankruptcy proceedings? Seeing as Sergei had already issued an eviction notice, she guessed he'd move as fast as he was legally allowed.

'So I'll see you Tuesday bright and early, yes?' He was all cheery again. 'Your new client is an old friend of mine so I've promised the VIP treatment. Got himself into a bit of bother with the missus and she's trying to figure out where he's hidden the silverware, so to speak. Anyway we can have a little chat about it in advance.'

'Sure. Yes. Okay. I'll see you–'

But he'd already hung up.

With a renewed sense of urgency and the benefit of a fresh burst of adrenaline, Lily got the bathroom cleaned and was dusting everything in sight when the strimmer fell silent. Peering out a window she saw Luke working the rake now, tossing the lengths of cut grass over the fence and into the surrounding fields. It was a combination of glistening upper torso and shoulder action she could have done without seeing. But then it was back to noise again as he went over the lawn with the mower.

This was followed an hour later by the angry mosquito whine of the sander against the stuck edges of the front door. She was helping Betty lift the cake out of the oven when that sound too fell silent.

Luke came into the kitchen with his shirt mercifully back on, his hair slicked off his forehead. '*Mmm* – that smells great.'

'Yes, it does,' said Betty, 'but just make sure the dog stays away from it this time. I don't want to have to make a third.'

'No problem. But she's in the scullery right now, having another snooze. So hold off putting the cake in there for the minute.'

He turned his gaze to Lily then and all the friendliness went out of it. 'If you want the upstairs windows cleaned now, I can grab the ladder?'

'Can't you finish up for the day?' said Cassandra, coming into the kitchen from the yard. 'We'll be starting the barbecue any minute.'

'What barbecue?' Lily asked.

'Your barbecue, of course. Eric's due with supplies any second. So we don't all starve to death.'

'Oh good,' said Betty. 'Yes, enough Trojan work for today.'

Before Lily could formulate an objection there was a screech of brakes and Eric was hollering for Luke to help him carry stuff in. He disappeared out the front door to help his friend – while her own made herself scarce out the back. With the prospect of food, however, Lily was suddenly so hungry that the fact this barbecue had been arranged behind her back and without her consent was readily overlooked.

In the yard, Cassandra hauled a drum barbecue out of the coal bunker and rolled it confidently to a flat and sheltered spot against the cottage wall. Eric dumped a bag of charcoal into it and, half a bottle of lighter fluid later, he had a mighty blaze going.

Lily brought out chairs from the kitchen and the slim coffee table from the lounge. Passing Eric, she was surprised to see him already hard at work with the tongs, turning over some sausages as the flames licked about them. She wasn't a barbecue expert by any means but weren't you supposed to wait for the flames to go down before you put the meat on?

Cassandra got the portable radio going, tuning it to the liveliest station she could find while Lily brought out plates, glasses and cutlery. Aside from the sausages, Eric's supplies comprised two litres of Coke, a large bottle of rum, a six-pack of salt and vinegar crisps, a bag of jumbo-sized marshmallows, two sliced pans, a block of butter and several cartons of blackcurrant Ribena. Everything was most gratefully received and, before a sausage was even cooked, several crisp sandwiches had been assembled and devoured.

Betty came outside with a large blanket. She sat on the chair nearest the coffee table, covered her knees with it and reached for a Ribena.

She'd just slotted the straw in when Eric handed her a plate of sausages. Thanking him, she beckoned to Lily to sit beside her.

Betty took a bite of a sausage and grimaced. 'Do you want one?' She lowered her voice to a whisper. 'I wouldn't recommend it. They taste like ash. I think they're raw in the middle too. Not much of a party. Not even a little pack of jellies. Will you have a Ribena?'

'Help yourself to food,' called Eric, cheerfully blackening a marshmallow until it collapsed between the grills of the barbecue. '*Ah, feck!*' He loaded two replacements onto his skewer.

Lily came to stand beside him, grabbing a second tongs and moving some of the remaining sausages to a less fiercely burning area of the grill.

'Do you want a sausage?' he asked.

'No, thanks.'

'I hope you're hungry at least!' he called over to Luke.

Luke made his way over to join them and took one look at the sausages. 'Ah, not so much. Is Pup still in the scullery?'

'Yeah,' said Eric. 'She seems happy to be in there resting. That incident with the cake today really messed her up. She wouldn't even touch a sausage when I offered her one.'

Lily agreed this development was worrying while silently lauding the dog's belated sense of self-preservation.

'Well, I'm going back in to catch the news,' said Betty, hauling herself up from the chair with effort, 'if anyone wants to join me?'

There was an awkward silence as the other four exchanged glances.

'That's alright,' she said, shuffling past them and leaving the plate of sausages behind. 'I'll let you know if anything interesting comes on.'

With her departure, some swift alterations took place. Eric turned the radio up full blast and he and Luke carried the barbecue from the yard into the back garden. Lily and Cassandra brought the chairs and they huddled around it. A fresh bag of charcoal went on and, with another blast of lighter fluid, the flames licked up into the sky throwing tiny sparks into the swift-curling smoke.

A gentle breeze rose and the earth seemed to shiver loose the last of the day's heat, stirring the grass around them.

Eric disappeared for a minute and returned with a crate of beer. He handed a can to Luke while Cassandra and Lily's glasses were refilled with rum-laced Coke.

Cassandra and Eric were all but glued together on their side of the barbecue as Eric kept them entertained with stories of his former life as a bouncer – he was terrible at it – and Cassandra with stories of her former life as a receptionist at an accountancy firm – she was very good at it – and when they tired of laughing at each other's jokes and touching each other's hands and knees they decided they would 'stretch their legs' and 'work off those sausages' and disappeared around the side of the cottage, giggling and shushing each other as their voices faded into the distance.

This left Lily and Luke alone. Ten years ago that would have been an opportunity instantly embraced – by instantly embracing. Now she was glued to her chair, staring determinedly at the ground as Luke stared just as determinedly at the flames.

He finally spoke. 'You haven't said much this evening.'

'What is there to say?' She glanced over and saw the firelight dancing across his face, softening and then hardening its angles. It made him look younger, then older, then younger again. Flickering disconcertingly back and forth between the two versions of him as if unsure on which to settle. 'You haven't said much either.'

He turned to look at her then and, though one side of his face was now bathed fully in warmth, the expression in both eyes was cold. 'I guess there's just nothing left,' he tossed back.

She was saved from finding an answer to that by the back door opening and Betty calling into the yard. '*Lily? Cassie? You there?*'

Lily and Luke revealed themselves and headed over to her.

'I'm just letting you know I'm off to bed. Where's Cassie?'

'Gone for a walk.'

'By herself?'

Lily and Luke said nothing as Betty looked with dissatisfaction from one face to the other. 'That'll end in tears. Mark my words.' And with that ominous prediction she headed back inside.

'What does she mean?' asked Lily as soon as Betty was out of earshot. 'It'll end in tears?'

'If Cassandra knows it's just a holiday fling then it won't.'

'And if she doesn't?'

She watched as he drew a breath.

'What can I tell you? Eric's longest relationship with a woman has been a fortnight. He claims he's never been in love. It seems to me he's never out of it but it's with a different woman each time. I don't know what else to say.'

'Oh. Okay. Right. I'll give her a heads-up then before it gets serious.'

Without another word, Luke made his way out to the lane and Lily followed.

The minibus was parked by the porch door and she could see Luke had belted a black bag into each of the seats. In silhouette they looked like drunken passengers with some pressed hard against the glass whilst others listed into the foot wells.

'I hope Eric doesn't mind taking that lot away?' Lily said. 'I was hoping we could recycle the clothes and bed linen at Cúltrá and the books could go to the school. It's mostly toys after that. I don't suppose you know anyone who could use some toys?'

Luke grabbed his bike from its resting place against the wall. 'Shay's niece would probably take them. She has three under eight now. All girls.'

'Oh, that would be great and, *um*, thank you for your, *uh*, time today.'

He shrugged as if to say what else was he going to do? 'I'd have done it for anyone.'

That stung, though why she couldn't say. 'Well, I'll be out of everyone's hair just as soon as I find somewhere for Betty's furniture to go.'

There was a beat of silence and then he lifted his eyes to hers. 'Do you want my help with that?'

It was the simplest question, yet the answer came so hard. When she'd really needed Luke's help a decade ago, she'd been ignored. And she'd done everything since then to get to a place in her life where she didn't need *anyone*. But right now, she had a cottage that had to get sold. And no other options.

So, with a deep breath, she said, 'I do.'

But the admission brought no smile to his face. 'I have somewhere it can go then,' he said quietly. 'If I can get a loan of Ned's tractor and trailer, I'll move it for you tomorrow afternoon.'

'Really?' She hadn't expected him to have a ready solution. 'That would be fantastic! As long as I'm not going to be making someone's front room impassable for a month.'

He looked down again as he set the bike's pedal in place with his foot. 'They won't be in anyone's way.'

'You're sure?'

'Positive. The house isn't even furnished yet.' He reached for the handlebars.

'Wait. So it's a new place? I didn't see any new buildings on the way over. Is it up by the church or along by the old harbour?'

He hesitated before his eyes found hers once more. 'It's at Hook Cove.'

It took a few seconds to process that. Had she heard him right? Hook Cove? Not the beautiful, perfect and untouched Hook Cove. Not *their* Hook Cove? His expression had softened to a sort of watchful anxiety and she took comfort from the thought they could still be on the same page about *something*.

'Bloody planners, eh? How did they ever let that one slip through? Is the view completely destroyed?'

His expression tightened.

'Is it worse than I'm imagining? Please say it's only one storey? It's not some wacky, ultra-modern thing, right?'

His lips firmed.

'Wattle and daub?'

'It's just a house, Lily. One storey. Wood and glass. Screen planting will hide it in a few years.'

She offered a sympathetic smile. 'You're taking it well but you must have been pissed when you heard. Did anyone object when the planning application went in?'

'No.'

'Well, *I* would have.'

He closed his eyes tightly and she imagined he was picturing Hook Cove the way she remembered it, on a warm summer's evening with just the two of them sitting on the rocks to enjoy it.

'Where's the access road to it?' she asked.

He opened his eyes, his expression now hard. 'What does it matter? It's not like you're ever going to see it.'

'No, thankfully. I don't think I could bear–'

And just like that he was off, pedalling away at a furious rate, leaving her standing mid-sentence.

'*Luke, slow down! You can't see where you're going!*'

'*What's new?*' he called back as he disappeared from sight.

She waited to hear a crash but the wind rustling the bushes subsumed every other sound. She glanced up at the moon and willed it to shine a little brighter. It had just cleared the rim of Sliabh Oisín and she saw it wasn't quite a first quarter yet, just like he'd said.

His question from the morning came back to her. *Don't you look up anymore?* So she looked up now. The sky above was a vast, inky canvas and here, far from the city lights, it was thick with stars. The sight was impressive – *behold awesome Nature!* – but there was nothing significant about it really. Beyond the spectacle, it was just a lot of little dots having nothing at all to do with each other. She stood for a full minute and waited to be filled with ... something. But all she felt was cold and foolish. With a last glance, she rubbed her neck and went back inside.

Chapter Ten

Love Versus Infatuation

The day couldn't be over soon enough for Luke and the sun wasn't even up yet. A racket in his kitchen had woken him from a fitful sleep at three. It was Eric, hungry and sozzled, come to tell him how much in love he was – '*Really* in love, like first cut is the deepest, man. She gets me, you know? As much as that Spanish bird, only I know what she's saying!' He'd cleaned him out of the last of his ham and bread and then fallen asleep at the table, his forehead cushioned by a stack of tea towels.

Luke tried returning to sleep but couldn't. So he got up, made himself a coffee and wandered with it from room to empty room, looking out at the darkness from each window of his house. A house Lily couldn't even bear the thought of seeing.

Ten years ago he'd been outside with her on a night just like this one, watching the stars as the sweat cooled on their bodies. It had taken almost two years from their first kiss to work themselves up to that ultimate step. Two years of awkward fumbling and giggles. Two years of cold showers and waiting for when it would feel like the right time. In the end it had been Lily who'd bitten the bullet. She'd gone to stay with a friend in

Cork for a weekend and had seized the opportunity for anonymity to purchase condoms – three boxes of Extra Safe. She'd smuggled them back and presented them to him gift-wrapped, privately and somewhat sheepishly, on his 18th birthday. They'd made love on the flat rocks of Trá Eilis that night. The experience had been wholly uncomfortable and wildly spectacular at the same time. They'd both known it would happen again and it did, in all the lost and secret places on Inish Ruin they'd discovered as children.

Their lovemaking was like their relationship: adventurous, tempestuous and completely trusting and when they were spent they would lie in silence, no words necessary to express all that was between them. Lily would curl into him, content to let him hold her, and those moments felt like her greatest gift to him when he knew his place in the world and that it was beside her.

By the end of summer, they were down to their last box. In the throes of passion, he'd rummaged in it, cursing the clouds that were blocking the moonlight, finding one empty wrapper after another. Swept up in the moment, Lily hadn't cared to wait. She'd pulled him to her with a plea that was impossible to ignore. It had been unlike anything he'd imagined. The euphoria afterwards slow to dissipate. The experience too precious to allow for recriminations.

She'd whispered for him not to worry. She was sure it was a safe time Then she told him how amazing it had been for her.

"That's how it'll always be when we're married," he'd blurted and then held his breath.

She'd said nothing, only smiled, but it was a breathtaking smile that had seemed to him as good as a promise. But the very next day she was gone and that smile had haunted him ever since. What had it really meant? She must have known it would be their last night together. Is that why she'd let it happen like that? A sort of parting gift before she disappeared out of his life?

It was as well she was leaving today, he decided, because being around her again was starting to mess with his head. And touching her yesterday had been a big mistake. If she'd pushed him away it might have been different but her body had relaxed the way it always had. Her breathing had slowed to match his own and all the while that intoxicating scent of hers filling him. He'd had to step away before she realised the effect she still had on him.

He took his coffee outside, climbed the twenty-seven rocky steps that wended up the ridge at the back of the herb garden to come out at his own private balcony: a flat ledge of sandstone that faced east. He sat on the edge, his bare feet swinging over the two-hundred-foot drop, sipping as he looked out across the sea and admired the changing palette as the sun shimmied over the horizon. The sea this morning was mirror smooth and he watched the fishing boats pass out of Cúltrá bay one after the other, buttering the glassy surface with trails of creamy white.

He returned to the house in time to wake Eric for his first ferry run. With his fringe sticking up like a flap, he accepted the glass of water pressed into his hand with a grunt. He then made prolonged use of the bathroom, emerging looking broiled some twenty minutes later. He cast a hopeful glance at the pack of rashers Luke had just produced from the fridge and then groaned as he checked his watch.

'I'll save you some. Go on.' Luke fried the whole pack, suddenly discovering his appetite. Eggs, a few mushrooms and some tomatoes went in the pan too and he split the pile between two plates when he was done.

He'd barely taken his knife to the first rasher when the doorbell rang. Ned stood there looking smart in his summer postal uniform of blue shirt and navy shorts, the army surplus bicycle by his side looking nearly as old as himself. Ned had been cycling the lanes of Inish Ruin for most of his adult life and it showed in his toned calf muscles. He didn't look as fit as he should have, though, for he had a Father Christmas-like paunch, the result of all the tea, toast and biscuits he consumed in the line of duty. As the island's postman, he found himself in the additional, unofficial role of social worker – his morning calls an opportunity to check in on the more elderly residents who lived alone. He never declined an offer of refreshment, no matter how many cups of tea he'd already endured, and his postal run routinely took all morning. That was why the shop only opened at two. He delivered company, as well as post, and there were few on the island who underestimated his importance.

Luke knew better than to offer him anything but a glass of water.

With the heat already creeping into the day, Ned was happy to accept and came inside. 'Only an aul bill today,' he said, reaching into his satchel, 'but I've brought you the form to redirect your post, seeing as you won't be back.'

The news was out that he was going then. Donie had been quick with that. He took the paperwork from Ned's outstretched hand. 'I didn't think of that. Thanks.'

Ned knocked back the water and set the glass down as he turned to go.

'Oh,' said Luke, remembering, 'I was hoping I could borrow your tractor and trailer for a couple of hours today. I'm going to move Betty's furniture here. Eric will have the key for whenever you want to get it back.'

Ned scratched his chin. 'You can have it, no bother, but why does it have to be moved?'

'Lily's trying to sell the cottage in a rush and can't with all the extra furniture in it.'

'Oh. Right. Fair enough. Well, take it when you want it. The keys are in it. I don't suppose you know when she's leaving?'

'Today. Last ferry, according to Eric.'

'Grand so. And Seánie wants a word with her. I'll tell him he'll catch her then.' He pushed open the front door. 'Glorious day, isn't it? If we get this for the wedding we'll be blessed.' He dropped the satchel into the bike's basket and climbed on. 'I'll need the tractor back by five. Don't overfill the trailer.' And with that he cycled off.

Luke finished his breakfast, left the plate out for Eric, and headed over to the pub where the mood was buoyant. Mikey was serving tea to Donie, Pat and the two Kitty Murphys – 'Kitty the Strand' and 'Kitty the Church'. The 'Kittys' were distantly related elderly ladies whose lives mostly revolved around intense psychological analyses of the latest happenings on *Coronation Street*. They were pelting Donie and Pat with questions and, loath to interrupt what seemed to be a mutually enjoyable experience, Luke headed for the beer garden where he spied some familiar faces through the glass.

He'd no sooner stepped outside when he was rammed from behind, a blow to the knees that almost sent him flying. He rebalanced only to have his legs clasped tightly in a pair of small arms.

'*Ninja lock engaged!*'

He reached back, detached the ninja and held him dangling by two ankles in front of him.

'Ready to fight?' asked the flushed, upside-down face.

'*Born ready*,' said Luke, with all the seriousness expected when issued such a challenge by a four-year-old.

He set his opponent back on his feet. They took several paces back, bowed their respect in the approved fashion and engaged in a lengthy tussle which ended in defeat for Luke. The victor took his lap of honour, circling his fallen opponent with yells before throwing himself on top of him to bounce on his stomach.

His mother rushed over. '*Ciarán!* Leave your Uncle Luke alone. You'll hurt him.'

'I killed him. He's defeated,' he declared and turned to charge at his dad, who was just coming to join them.

His dad neatly side-stepped and Ciarán ran on down the grassy bank, tumbled to a halt and then jumped up, laughing. '*Super-lightning-shield engaged!*'

His mother gave a weary sigh. 'I don't know where he gets the energy when he never sleeps.' She gave Luke a friendly kiss on the cheek as a bundle in her arms squirmed. 'We've come for a few days' visit. Mark thought he should be here in case the groom might need resuscitating on his Big Day. Even brought an old-fashioned medical bag,' she added with a grin, 'but he didn't think to tell your mother and she's in a panic now because there's nowhere for us to stay on the island that night. Bar the sofa for Mark.'

'In fairness, I didn't expect it would be a problem, Saoirse,' Mark protested. 'When has there ever not been somewhere for us to stay before? Hello, runt,' he said, with a nod to Luke. 'I don't suppose you've managed to put any furniture in your house yet? A few beds would come in handy for Thursday.'

'Sorry but – hang on, I will actually have beds by then. I'm storing Betty's furniture there. There'll be one bed at least, maybe two.'

'No, no, it's fine,' said Saoirse quickly. 'It gives me a great excuse to stay with the kids in Cúltrá that night. It'll be pure noise here with the wedding. Hard enough to get Ciarán to sleep as it is but if we're here there won't be a hope. We'll stay at the hotel till then, though.' She shifted the bundle to her other shoulder and the bundle woke, round eyes blinking to peer up at all the faces surrounding her.

'Hello, Caoimhe,' said Luke softly. 'Did you have a lovely sleep?'

At ten months Caoimhe hadn't much to say, but making herself understood was rarely a problem. She put out her arms to Luke and he took her willingly into his own. She made herself comfortable against his chest and closed her eyes again, her warm face pressing into him to shield them further from the light.

Saoirse smiled. 'You know you'll be trapped like that for an hour. She's still refusing to nap in her cot. Cries till she's red in the face. My arms are different sizes, I swear. Look at the muscles in this one from holding her,' she demonstrated.

'You're a freak,' teased her husband.

Eithne appeared at the patio doors, looking frazzled, and beckoned Luke inside. He went, carrying his niece. She paused to straighten Caoimhe's socks before drawing him off to the empty lounge, far from prying ears at the bar.

There she halted and turned to him with a breezy smile plastered on her face. 'You're working today so?'

It didn't take a genius to figure out what she was really asking. How come you're here and not with Lily? He wondered why she could never just say her name?

'I'm here till two,' he said. 'That what's on the roster, isn't it?'

He'd been rostered to work yesterday evening as well but she didn't point that out. 'Of course. That's good then. So what's your plan for Saturday? What ferry were you thinking of getting?'

Another loaded question. Was he still leaving?

'I'll get the two o'clock.'

The tension drained out of her face. 'Great. We'll have a gang down at the pier then and give you a bit of a sendoff.'

'No need. Thanks.'

'Ah, sure we'd like to do it.'

'Didn't you like her, Mam?' he asked suddenly. 'Is that it?'

She faltered and didn't quite meet his eye. 'No, no. I liked her just fine.'

'Who?'

'What?'

'Who did you like just fine?'

She reddened and cleared her throat. 'I liked Lily just fine. But was I glad she left here all the same? Okay – I'll admit it – I was grateful to Noleen for doing whatever she did to make her go.'

Luke wasn't sure what part of that to unpack first. 'To *make* her go? Nobody *made* Lily go.'

But her expression had softened to something that looked suspiciously like pity. 'You really think she'd have left otherwise?'

'What? What do you mean?'

'She'd have stayed here forever and wasted all her potential. And you'd have stayed because she did and wasted all of yours.'

His mouth wouldn't form a response. He'd never imagined anyone could think Lily leaving him a blessing, least of all his own mother.

She seemed to take his silence as her cue to keep going though. 'I mean, what kind of a life would it have been for her otherwise? Stuck here minding Noleen into old age? Making bouquets from a garden shed? Was that to be the height of her ambition? When she could be out in the world doing anything – being anything. I'm sure Jasper felt the same. She was a bright girl with a big future but it wasn't here on Inish Ruin. Noleen loved her enough to see that and if you hadn't been so infatuated that you couldn't think of anything but what *you* wanted, you'd have wanted that for her too.'

He was flabbergasted. 'I always wanted the best for her.'

'Did you? Well, you didn't act like it. Look, I'm not saying this to be mean but you're older now so maybe you can see it more clearly – between your impulsiveness and her ...' she balled her face as if searching for the right word, 'puppy love, wasn't it only a matter of time before you ruined both your lives?'

His face heated as he understood her full meaning, but he couldn't exactly protest they'd been using protection. This was embarrassing enough.

'No one wants to hear this from a parent, I know. But I was young once too and I know what attraction looks like and ye two were fairly radioactive with it. No matter how far apart ye stood.' She averted her eyes and gave Caoimhe's back a little rub. 'You'll make a fine daddy someday, but ten years ago it would have been a disaster. And how much harder would it have been then for Lily to go to college and have a career? She'd have ended up just like me. Trapped here. And I didn't want that for her any more than I wanted it for you. You never wanted to be a publican, right?'

He shook his head.

'Well, that's how you'd have ended up if someone didn't intervene. So there we have it.' She clapped her hands together once, as if marking the end of the conversation.

'There we have what?'

'That's all there is to say. It worked out for the best. You've got your dream job in Cork now and Lily's a successful accountant in London. Living the life Noleen wanted for her. So let her go back to it with good grace. That's the difference between love and infatuation, you know? Putting what's best for the other person ahead of what's best for yourself.'

She scurried off before he could say another word, leaving him to reconcile himself to several unpalatable notions: that Lily's leaving had been for the best, that he'd endangered her prospects because he was selfish and that the life she really deserved would never have had him in it.

That's how it'll always be when we're married. Those were the words he'd said to her that night. He saw her answering smile in his mind once more but there was something wary in it now. As if she knew he was just trying to trap her – to narrow her world to just the two of them.

But if she'd wanted to be free of him so badly, couldn't she still have said goodbye?

He returned Caoimhe to her mother and worked his shift, feeling sick to his stomach. He hardly spoke to anyone, going through the motions. Two o'clock came and he roused himself to bike to Ned's for the tractor and trailer.

He'd never before doubted that his love for Lily had been something pure and special. But what if it had just been selfish infatuation? What was he supposed to do now? Feel ashamed instead of hurt? Apologise? Or just say goodbye to her with good grace and his best wishes for the future? He checked his watch to see how long until the last ferry of the day. Until Lily Barrett disappeared back out of his life again forever. Six hours until he finally got closure. Whether he was ready for it or not.

Chapter Eleven

Indigestible Mistakes

Lily's morning was extremely productive with nothing chainsawed or eaten that shouldn't have been. Having set the alarm on her phone she was up at seven, washed and dressed and pushing a bowl of dog food and another of water in Pup's direction by a quarter past. With the dog happily munching in the yard, she'd gone out the front to a cloudless day where she'd set up the ladder and cleaned the gutters and upstairs windows before moving around to do the ones at the back.

Then she brought breakfast in bed to Cassandra and Betty, dressing each tray with a small jug of flowers. But only Betty was able to appreciate it. Cassandra's stomach was paining her and she couldn't manage anything but a few sips of tea.

Eric's sausages fell under immediate suspicion. Cassandra confessed she'd eaten a good half dozen to spare his feelings. She made it down from the top bunk and locked herself in the bathroom for ten minutes. When she emerged, pale and hunched, she said she was ready to get to work but was firmly directed back to bed. A hot water bottle against her stomach and a dose of paracetamol later and she was back asleep.

Betty came downstairs and they set about covering the replacement wedding cake in marzipan. Then that was draped in a neat layer of ready-to-roll icing and trimmed. There was a lot of icing left over and, after some decidedly unsubtle hints, Lily was persuaded to spend an hour and a half shaping and colouring little leaves and ladybirds with it to decorate the top – ladybirds being 'a theme' of the wedding apparently. A wide red ribbon tied in a bow completed the cake and Betty was delighted with the result, reluctant to let Lily put it out of sight on the high shelf again.

'I enjoyed that,' Lily admitted as they had a celebratory cup of tea.

'Well, Noleen always said you were the creative one in the family. Not that she wasn't proud of you for going into accountancy.' She gave Lily's hand a reassuring squeeze. 'Always telling everyone how great you were doing. And every time you got promoted. But she missed you something terrible. If you were my granddaughter, I think I'd have insisted you come back regularly, but she was always adamant you were better off out there flying free.'

Lily opened her mouth to protest. *Flying free?* When had she ever asked Nana for that?

But Betty was in full flow. 'Trying the opposite approach after getting it wrong with your mother, I guess. Not that loving someone too much can really be getting it wrong. But Noleen was like a dragon guarding a hoard with Cora. Always so concerned with where she was and who she was with. And never wanting her to even talk to boys. Maybe it's no wonder she rebelled so badly when she went to college.' Betty sighed. 'And found the worst possible person to love instead. No insult intended to your dad, Lily, but I think we can all agree he was far too old and selfish to be the best choice for her.'

Betty went back to sipping tea and Lily could only stare at her. Not because she cared what Betty said about a dad she couldn't even remember, but because she'd never imagined the freedoms she'd taken for granted when she'd lived here might have gone against all Nana's instincts to grant her.

A bicycle bell sounded in the lane. Still thinking on this, Lily went to the door and found Ned there looking only slightly gnomier than she remembered.

'Ned, hi. Hello. Good morning.'

'Ah, 'tis yourself.'

'It is indeed.' She hoped this greeting didn't mean he'd actually forgotten her name. 'Bike's still going strong, I see.'

'Sure this thing'll outlast us all.'

'So ... will you come in for a cuppa?'

His hesitation seemed to mirror her own.

'Betty's up and dressed.' She glanced back into the kitchen but the woman had vanished. 'She's about somewhere.'

This added inducement, however, sufficed. Ned put the bike against the wall and came in with his satchel, handing her an envelope. 'Just an electricity bill. You might want to check out the other crowd. They're doing better rates at the moment. They tie you into a two-year contract but still and all it's worth it. I told Luke about it ages ago but I suppose he hasn't had the chance to get it sorted.'

'Luke? What would he have to do with it?'

'Oh, nothing.' He sat. 'Only he's been looking after all the paperwork since your nana passed. But now you're here …' He trailed off, looking uncomfortable but not half as uncomfortable as Lily felt.

At long last? Was that how that sentence was supposed to end? Of course it was. Having missed the funeral thanks to Peter's antics, she'd stalled for six months before coming back. Partly in the hope Peter's promise to find a way to pay her back would *somehow* be magically realised.

She got through the moment as best she could by asking about the upcoming nuptials, hardly hearing Ned's answers as she put the kettle on and lit the grill for toast. Nana would have fried him something 'to keep him going'. All Lily had to offer – other than toast – was a strawberry yogurt, thankfully in date. Keeping her eye on the grill, Lily turned out perfect toast to go with it two minutes later and presented it buttered and quartered.

Betty came downstairs with her make-up freshly applied. 'Ned, what a lovely surprise! Have you finished your rounds already?'

'No, no. Still going. Lily's fuelling me for the next stop.'

'Good girl,' said Betty with a smile.

'Where's young Cassie today?' he asked.

'Wait'll I tell you, Ned, she's in a terrible state. Eric made her eat a dozen poison sausages last night and she's rolling around in agony up there.'

'Ah, the poor mite. Is she taking anything for it?'

'Just paracetamol.'

'I've antacid at the shop if that might help?'

Lily heard no more. She'd reached the landing and was peering into her bedroom where Cassandra was still asleep on the top bunk, looking pale but peaceful. Puzzled, she went back downstairs.

'*You'll be opening the shop on the day of the wedding?*' Betty's voice was raised as she reached the kitchen. 'Will you be in your suit or will you change out of it after the photographs? I wouldn't like our wedding to get in the way of the shop opening now. Heaven forbid someone runs out of milk or needs a stamp!'

'No, no, love, you have it all wrong. I'll not be working. Shay's going to do it. Just till six and then he'll give the keys to Pat to take over while we're on honeymoon.'

Lily entered the kitchen in time to see Betty pout.

'I don't see why you couldn't just close it up for the few weeks,' Betty sniffed. 'You care more about that shop than you do me.'

Ned threw a glance of appeal Lily's way. 'Is this what they call wedding jitters?'

'This is not the jitters,' said Betty before she could respond. 'It's a legitimate question about how important I am to you. Let me remind you the shop won't keep you warm at night.'

'Unless he has the heater on,' Lily volunteered, and promptly clamped her errant mouth shut.

'The shop won't cook you dinners,' continued Betty, ignoring her. 'It won't kiss you after breakfast.'

'Will *you* kiss me after breakfast?' he asked hopefully, popping the last crust into his mouth and swallowing it down with tea.

'No, I won't.'

'So what do you want me to do? Do you want me to just close the shop on Thursday?'

'I don't care about the shop. You're not listening to me at all. This is about priorities and making decisions together and we're just not on the same wavelength about anything. Tell him, Lily.'

Lily looked in astonishment from Ned's placid face to Betty's cross one. 'I have no idea what you're talking about.'

'Grand so,' said Ned, brushing some crumbs off his uniform as he stood. 'Just the jitters. I'll be off.'

'You're not to go!' cried Betty. 'You can't walk out on an argument. If you loved me you'd stay and work it out. Mervyn says – ' She cut herself off but it was too late. The M word was out.

The amusement died out of Ned's expression. He said nothing but it was an awful, meaning-laden nothing that had Lily biting her lip.

Poor Betty, bearing the full brunt of it, immediately started crying.

To Lily's surprise, Ned didn't go over to comfort her. 'I do love you,' he said firmly, looping the satchel strap over his shoulder. 'You don't know how much but I won't be in competition with your dead husband for the rest of my life. Decide who you want in your future because I'm not going to share you.'

He walked to the porch and Lily followed in silence, not knowing what to say.

He climbed on his bike and set the satchel in the basket. 'I hear you're off on the last ferry today.'

'I ... yes.'

'I've something to give you before you go. I'll see you at the pier.'

'Oh, no.' The last thing she needed was someone waving her off. 'Couldn't I just stop by the shop for it?'

'Afraid not.' He looked over her shoulder and back into the cottage.

Lily glanced behind her. There was no one there but, from the kitchen, they could hear Betty's sobs turning to sniffles.

'Will you see she's alright?' he whispered. 'I have to be hard on her. It's a crutch, this Mervyn thing. And she doesn't need it anymore now she's got me.'

Lily nodded. 'If it's any consolation he's in her bad books right now. She blames him for the dog getting at the cake.'

He sighed. 'I guess it's a start. Better get going if I'm to have the shop open at all today. The tourists will be wanting their postcards.'

'Oh. Wait. Sorry, but could I delay you for one more second? I've a question to ask you in your capacity as postmaster?'

'Go ahead.'

'I can't find my Post Office Savings Book.'

'Oh?'

'I've looked everywhere but there's no sign of it. I wanted to figure out how to get my money out without it.' There wasn't exactly a fortune in there but €800 would be a lifesaver right now.

'You can't,' he said bluntly. 'There are no withdrawals without your book. You'd have to report the loss to the Post Office Savings Bank Headquarters.'

'Where's that then?'

'I don't know off the top of my head. The address will be inside your book.'

'But I can't find the book.'

She bit her lip and his expression softened.

'Look, I can find out the address of the headquarters for you but the loss has to be confirmed in writing by you before I can do anything. I'd say it'd take a few weeks to get it sorted.'

'But I'm leaving today.'

He shrugged.

'But you know I have the money in there. It'll say it on the computer surely? Could you not just give it to me?'

'That'd be against the law.'

'Only a little bit.'

'I'll pretend I didn't hear that. Thanks for the grub.' And with that he was away.

Lily returned to the kitchen to check on Betty. She'd dried her tears and was pretending to be engrossed in a crossword now, answering Lily's solicitous enquiries with one-word answers and no eye-contact. So Lily took herself off to the sitting room which was now as tidy as she could get it. She puffed up the cushions on the sofa and draped the throws more neatly over the ends but it didn't make all that much of a difference.

She glanced at her watch and cursed. She was running out of time, with the hardest job yet to tackle. Steeling herself, she grabbed a fresh roll of black bags, headed upstairs and stood, once more, outside the last bedroom door. With a deep breath, her fingers curled around the handle and she pushed.

The door opened to near darkness.

She fumbled forwards, hands outstretched towards the faintly glimmering rectangle on the far side. There she found the pull cord and heaved. The heavy curtains parted a few inches before the mechanism jammed but it was enough for a blast of sun to temporarily blind her.

Turning, she blinked away the spots as her gaze took in the room. The light spilling over her shoulder cut a narrow, dust-moted path across the woven floor mat, along the side of a hand-stitched comforter and on up to the carved wooden dressing table and, above it, the Sacred Heart of Jesus picture with its little red bulb glowing. Like a beacon it beckoned and she crossed the space to stare up at it. Hard-wired into the electrics of the cottage, there was no off-switch for it. Nor could she remember Nana ever replacing the bulb. That had always felt a little miraculous to Lily growing up. Now all she could feel was resentment that the damned thing was still glowing when the person who'd installed it was gone.

Muttering about unnecessary fire hazards, she averted her gaze from Jesus to take in the dressing table instead. A sheet of glass protected the top but underneath was a collage of photos of a growing girl with a patch on one eye. For a moment, she imagined she saw another girl with two perfect quicksilver eyes. But, as she slid her hand over the glass to remove the dust, she couldn't find her.

Her movements tipped a stack of tea-lights, though, against a single framed photograph. It was of her mother Cora, dressed all in white. Forever young and beautiful. It was strange to think she was older now than her mother had been when she died. On the night of her twenty-sixth birthday. The same night Lily's dad, a professor, had received some academic award. Lily wondered if that was the reason he'd chosen to bring his scandalously young second family to the event rather than his first? To celebrate Cora's birthday. But all she knew for sure was what Nana had told her: that he'd had one celebratory drink too many before he'd got in the car to drive them all home.

Lily yanked open the dressing-table drawer and pulled out what she could. The top layers comprised an assortment of woolly scarves and hats and shawls. But under these were an array of medicines whose names she didn't recognise in tubs and boxes and tubes, along with receipts for prescriptions, and some mindfulness colouring books. The clothes went into one black bag and everything else into another.

Next, she turned her attention to the wardrobe. Clothes went into three more bags and shoes and handbags filled a fourth. And then Lily saw it, tucked away at the very back. A naggin of vodka. Unopened. Like a giant shiny pill still waiting to be popped.

And suddenly Lily was eight again, waking in her bunk to hear the television downstairs playing too loudly. It was Cora's anniversary and, as attuned to Nana's emotional state by that stage as a seismologist to the earth's tremors, something had felt off to Lily all day. Nana had been unusually quiet and then snappy when asked if she was okay. Nana was not okay. The ground underneath her was shaking from some force Lily didn't understand.

She'd gone downstairs to find Nana on the sitting-room floor. Two of these bottles had lain beside her, empty, and her face had been streaked with tears. Frightened, Lily had tried to pull her onto the sofa but Nana had fought her off, catching her shoulder with a flailing hand that sent her tumbling.

Disjointed apologies and accusations had followed, directed to the shadows of the room; 'Just trying to keep you safe – never meant – that selfish bastard!'

'Nana?'

'*She looks just like you, baby!*' she'd wailed and her tears were flowing again.

'It's me. It's Lily,' she'd tried, keeping her distance now.

Nana had quieted, shaking her head as if there was a blanket covering it which would fall off if she could just find the right angle. 'Lily.' She'd peered at her through watery eyes. 'Don't make the same mistake as Nana and Mammy. *Promise me*.'

'I promise,' she'd said, not sure what the mistake was but knowing that was the only response.

'Or else ...'

Lily waited for her to finish the sentence, her lungs stilling, but Nana's head just sank back to the ground and she closed her eyes with a whimper.

Not knowing what else to do, Lily put a throw over her and spent the night crouched beside her, listening to her laboured breaths until the sun rose. Then she'd dragged herself upstairs to bed.

She'd been woken hours later with breakfast on a tray. Nana had affectionately called her a 'sleepy head' as she moved about the room, opening the curtains and then the window. Lily had stared at her, seeing the wan face and the bloodshot eyes. But there was no look of consciousness about her. No indication they'd seen each other since yesterday. Nana had just smiled and then left her with a bowl of porridge, a slice of buttered toast and a glass of orange juice.

Lily had slowly swallowed it down, one anxious mouthful after another. Nana's words, however, remained indigestible. *Don't make the same mistake as Nana and Mammy. Or else.* Those last two words had unsettled her more than all the rest. For they suggested what had never before occurred to Lily. That Nana's love for her might have limits she could accidentally cross.

What was the mistake she had to avoid though? She'd been frantic to figure it out. Nana had never said anything about Mammy making a mistake – except that Daddy shouldn't have been drinking the night he got behind the wheel. Was that it? That Mammy got into a car with someone who'd been drinking? Had Nana made that same mistake herself? It was hard to imagine Nana making any mistakes. But maybe when she was young? She didn't like talking about anything 'back then' and Lily had stopped asking. Maybe Nana *had* made that mistake but been lucky enough not to die. And she felt terrible now she'd never warned Mammy about it. Poor Nana. Lily would never get in a car with anyone who'd been drinking. She didn't want to die like Mammy or be upset like Nana. But most of all she didn't want to lose Nana's love.

She'd got dressed and found Nana asleep on the sofa. Lily had woken her with assurances she'd never, ever, ever get into a car with someone who'd been drinking. And Nana had beamed as if that was the answer. She'd opened her arms and Lily had lain down next to her, curled up in her warm embrace as the world had finally stopped shaking.

But she'd got it wrong.

That hadn't been the mistake.

And by the time she'd understood it was too late.

She brought the naggin to the bathroom and poured its contents down the sink, her throat bobbing to the glug, glug as it disappeared through the plug hole. She returned to Nana's room, stared at all the black bags and then sat on the bed, pulling the comforter around her.

It was warm from the sun, the cotton tender against her cheek. A scent lingered in the fibres: Nana's perfume. And Lily pressed her nails into her palms and didn't cry.

When Luke arrived at the cottage, Betty was in the kitchen eating pickles.

'Are you taking my furniture away now? Lily mentioned something earlier.'

'Yes. But I could do with a hand lifting the bed. When is Eric due over?'

Her expression darkened. 'Who knows? He's been here twice already today making a nuisance of himself. Wouldn't even say hello to me the second time. Just barged in to see Cassandra to give her some tablets he says could fix anything. He might have killed her with those sausages. I don't know how she could defend his cooking. Love is blind, with no taste buds either.'

There was no defending those sausages so Luke didn't try. 'Where's Lily?'

'Upstairs. Going through Noleen's belongings I think. Best not disturb her.'

'Of course.' He set about loading the trailer, starting with the armchair from the sitting room, then some crates, the drawers from Betty's oak sideboard and several basket loads of ornaments which were all wrapped in newspaper. He strapped them securely with rope and set off.

Getting down the lane was a precarious business but once on the main road he made good progress and reached his house without incident. He unloaded the trailer and deposited everything in the front room then returned to the cottage at top speed, ready for the next load.

As he stepped into the porch this time he heard Betty at full tilt from somewhere above. 'I remember when Mervyn died I couldn't bear to part with anything he'd worn or held or even looked at. I even got sentimental about his underpants. It took years to finally clear out all his stuff.'

With a glance up the stairs, he saw Betty at the open door to Noleen's room, talking into it, presumably to Lily. So much for not disturbing her.

Cassandra appeared from the other end of the landing with a shoebox in her hand and a hesitant expression on her face. 'Lily? Do you think you might need this?'

'*No. Thank you.*' Lily's voice was high and clipped. All business.

Cassandra retreated but Betty kept talking. 'Do you want help to go through Noleen's clothes or – oh, you've just bagged the lot?'

Luke didn't stay to hear more. He reloaded the trailer with some bedside lockers, a mound of suitcases and more dressing gowns than he'd seen in his life.

When he arrived back for a third load, he crossed paths with Lily in the study and was taken aback. She looked a lot more shook than she'd sounded: all the fight gone out of her. Her face was pale and her eyes glassy as she cleared out the roll-top desk. A wad of documents had been set to one side but everything else was being binned. They exchanged a brief – if hesitant – greeting and he wondered if he should say something to her – about things working out the way they were supposed to, perhaps? But honestly, at this point, he didn't know where to start so he just kept moving and she did too, as if in silent agreement it would be easier this way.

Two trips later and it was a quarter to five. He'd promised to return the trailer by five. Now was the moment to say goodbye to Lily with all the grace he could muster.

He found her in the sitting room, looking confused.

'Where's the armchair gone?' she said.

'Into storage. I'm mixing and matching Betty's furniture and your nana's for best effect.'

'Oh. Okay?'

'It'll look better in the photos, I promise.'

'Right.' But she was clearly unconvinced.

'I'm going now,' he told her.

She nodded and they moved together to the front door. But once outside she drifted towards the steel gate where his bike had lain previously. There she leaned her forearms on the smooth metal and looked towards the sea in the distance.

He came and stood beside her, matching her position elbow to elbow, and cast a glance at her out of the corner of his eye. Her profile was sculpture-perfect: her cheekbones high and delicate, her nose straight with lips that looked far too soft and all too kissable. It was a face he could look at for hours. A face he *had* looked at for hours. Closure, he reminded himself. 'So I'll get Eric to give me a hand shifting Betty's bed tomorrow and you can give the estate agent a shout after that.'

She turned to him, her bottom lip caught between her teeth and he watched as it was slowly raked, pinking as the blood rushed back in. 'Luke?'

'Yes?'

Her mouth seemed to form the next words in slow motion. 'About the dog ...'

The dog. Of course. He should have known. This was the part where she asked him to keep taking care of her, wasn't it?

But she caught him off guard by asking how much she owed him for six months' worth of dog food.

'I know you bought it. Could you work out a figure and let me know and I'll get the money to you as soon as I can?'

'That won't be necessary.'

'No, really. I'd like to pay for it and I was wondering if there was any way you could look after her for just a little longer? Till I can find a new owner. I'll do some research. Take out an ad, maybe? It might take a few weeks but hopefully no more than that.'

'Okay.'

Her expression was pure relief. 'Really?'

'Yeah.' He'd work something out with the islanders' help.

'Thank you.'

'You're welcome.'

He rested his chin on his hands and they both stared out to sea this time. It would be beautiful down at Trá Eilis right now, with the sun piercing that one secluded cave. And a memory of Lily pressing her lips to his neck as she sighed his name flashed across his mind. He swallowed hard. 'Some view, isn't it?'

'I'm trying to remember it.'

'I'm surprised you could forget.'

She smiled but it was a ghost of thing. 'I've been walking the lanes of Inish Ruin in my head ever since I left but I'm trying to remember it all afresh, as an adult. To make a new memory. One without all the emotion attached. Something lighter to carry so when I close my eyes all I'll see is a beautiful place I once visited where the air was warm and everything was green and black rocks ran down to a silver sea. A picture-postcard memory. Nothing more.'

He turned to stare at her. 'You're making a new memory to replace the old ones?'

'Yes.'

Lovely. The old memories. The ones *he* was in. Her constant companion on all those lanes she'd been walking in her head. Something lighter to carry? She'd as good as said she wanted to forget him. She'd just dressed it up a little fancier.

He pushed himself off the gate and started walking backwards, keeping his eyes fixed on her, his throat constricting.

She turned to watch him as her head tilted in confusion. 'What are you doing?'

'Making a new memory,' he rasped. 'One that'll be easier to carry so when I close my eyes all I'll see is a woman I once met whose name was Lily Barrett. She came here to sell a cottage. I helped her move some furniture. Then she left. *The End*.'

The End. There it was then. Closure. But whether it had a shred of grace attached to it was debatable. He turned away, not able to look at her anymore. She'd filled his days with friendship once, with happiness, with love. Now all she was capable of was giving him pain. He climbed aboard the tractor and started the engine. It rattled him in his seat which was a fine accompaniment to the rattling happening inside his chest. *Goodbye, Lil*, he thought as he pressed the accelerator, resisting a last glance in the rear-view mirror. *Goodbye* a*nd good luck*.

Chapter Twelve

Welcome Home

The minibus blasted along the lanes with its three passengers clinging to whatever supports they could find. Eric had already dropped two busloads to the pier and was now apparently trying to make up for lost time, decimating the peacefulness of the evening, beeping as he went – his method for negotiating every blind corner being to fling them into it at top speed, slam on the brakes, and trust to the banked undergrowth to keep them on tarmac.

Dressed in the best clothes she'd packed: namely dark jeans, a non-iron silky camisole top and a freshly pressed linen jacket, with her hair swept into a low chignon, Lily Barrett, accountant on the verge of solving all her financial problems, had been ready to leave for over an hour. And ready to be gone well before that. Since five to five to be precise, when Luke O'Callaghan had driven off with the last trailer-load of the day, bloodlessly wiping his hands of her. What had happened? One minute they'd been chatting peaceably and the next he was razing her to the ground with an angry look on his face. Yep, she'd been gone from Inish Ruin in all but body since then. But, as it was the body that was required behind a desk tomorrow, she was now starting to panic.

She could have saved herself this stress if she'd just walked to the pier but Cassandra had already booked Eric for the job and, at the time, Lily hadn't thought to put up any resistance. Had she known Cassandra and Betty planned to accompany her, she'd have fought harder. Had she known she might miss the last ferry because of it, she certainly would have.

Another corner taken too fast sent the rucksack flying across the seat and she exhaled with an "*Oomph!*" as the metal frame caught her in the ribs. Thankfully it was only slightly bulkier than when she'd arrived, the only additions some paperwork, a child's book and the little cactus from the dresser with its thimble of soil which she'd included for no reason she could really explain, even to herself. It weighed almost nothing to start with and, wrapped inside a paper cup and wadded with cotton wool, it still did.

They flashed past the hostel and then through the tunnel of trees. The shop and school were the next blurs and then they were going uphill, the front fender chiming off stones every few seconds. Then straight for a minute, over another slight hill, a sharp right and a dip for twenty metres and then the last level stretch of road before the steep drop at the pier. *Please God, let him slow down before we hit that drop!* There was no evidence the minibus brakes were up to much. There'd be the pier wall to stop them flying into the sea, she supposed, with a gulp. Unless he was planning some stunt-like launch onto the top deck of the ferry?

She checked her watch. It was one minute to eight. If Seánie saw them coming before his crew cast off the ropes he'd wait. She gripped the door-handle tightly and exchanged a glance with Betty, who tried to smile as she pressed her dentures back into place.

They reached the last crossroad. Straight ahead to the pier and they'd be there in thirty seconds. But with a sudden crunch of gears and a hard swing of the steering wheel to the left, they were barrelling up the hill towards the hotel and pub instead.

'*Eric? Eric!*'

'*Not to worry. It's all under control!*'

What did that mean? Lily could think of only one reason for this detour which was that he had yet another customer waiting there he'd promised to get on the last ferry. '*Did you call Seánie to tell him we'd be late?*'

'*No,*' he called back cheerfully. '*No need.*'

He pulled up with a screech outside the hotel, backed into the spot reserved for him, and turned off the engine.

Lily glanced outside in the hope that whoever was jeopardising her future would at least have the decency to be ready and waiting. There were plenty of tourists milling about but none that looked ready to go anywhere. Most were soaking up the last of the day's heat on the benches in the beer garden, sipping pints, squeezing packets of ketchup into large baskets of chips, or helping small children remove wrappers from ice lollies.

Eric hopped out of the driver's seat and came around to slide the side door open for Betty. She gathered her bag and allowed him to help her out. 'I'll just go ahead and see who's about.' She headed off into the building.

Then Eric was lifting Cassandra down from the front passenger seat. 'You sure you're up for this?' he asked. 'I can drop you back to the cottage if you'd prefer?'

'After you drop me to the pier though, right?' said Lily, still strapped into her seat, still very much ready to go. 'To get that ferry?'

Eric flushed. 'Well, no. You see the Ro-Ro's coming to do a special delivery in an hour and you'll get that back instead.'

'What's a Ro-Ro?' asked Cassandra.

'A roll-on/roll-off,' said Eric. 'It's what we use when we need to get vehicles onto the island. Kitty the Strand is getting a golf buggy delivered. A nice little two-seater thing. Plenty fast for her.'

'Oh. You have a golf course on the island?'

'A golf course? Ah, no. Sure where would it fit?'

'Are you kidding me?' Lily unfastened her seat belt and clambered out. 'I need to catch that ferry. We could still make it if we go now. Give me Seánie's number and I'll ask him to hang on.'

'Sorry. I'm only doing what I was told.' He put the keys in his jeans pocket and gave them a pat.

'You seriously won't take me?' She turned to Cassandra. 'You put him up to this?'

Cassandra drew closer to Eric, who put an arm around her shoulder. 'It was Betty's idea but you still get to catch your flight, only this way you get the chance to say goodbye to everyone before you go. It's only an extra hour. You can manage one extra hour out of your life.'

'The same way I could manage an extra shoebox in it, I suppose? *I have to go now.*'

'But you can't,' said Cassandra. 'Not yet. You left something important here, Lily, don't you see? Peter said – '

The pressure inside her head instantly doubled. '*What?*'

Cassandra looked nervous. 'Peter said, well, not said exactly but hinted that maybe you might have ... left your heart here?'

Oh my God. 'Are you actually serious right now? Peter is an idiot, Cassandra. I didn't leave my heart anywhere.' She tapped her chest with enough force to hurt. 'It's right here. Maybe it isn't all warm and fuzzy like yours but I sure as hell didn't lose it.'

'I only meant – '

'What I lost was my *home*!' she cried, startling herself as much as Cassandra. 'And no amount of shoeboxes or delays can ever give that back to me.' She grabbed her rucksack, hoisted it onto her shoulders and headed off down the road, ignoring Cassandra's pleas to come back. Through a gap in a clump of trees she spied the ferry pulling away from the pier and could have howled in frustration.

And then she rounded the bend and met a sight that knocked all the remaining stuffing out of her.

Luke emerged from a side lane with a sleeping baby in his arms.

She skidded to a halt on the gravel as the breath left her body.

He looked up, saw her, and clutched the child tighter. 'You're meant to be gone.'

No words of defence would form. Her lungs wouldn't fill. Could Luke be a ...? Why not? What did she actually know about his life now? Had she asked him a single question about it? She managed to swallow. 'Is she ... yours?'

He seemed as frozen to the spot as she was but managed a slight shake of his head. 'This is Caoimhe. Mark's little girl. My brother Mark,' he added, when she didn't respond.

She realised she'd braced to congratulate him but this reprieve, if that's what it was, left her stumbling. 'Oh, I thought ...' Well, what she'd thought was obvious. 'You – you looked the part. It was only natural to think ...'

His eyes narrowed and the anger from earlier came right back into them. 'That I'd moved on with my life? Yes, that would be only natural.'

'What's going on here?' Ned was striding up the hill towards them, the veins in his shins bulging. 'I thought you were getting the ferry?'

'So did I,' said Lily, relieved at the interruption. 'There was a bit of a misunderstanding. But the Ro-Ro's coming shortly. I'll hitch a lift back with it instead.'

Ned glanced at his watch. 'That won't be here for an hour. You'll come up for a drink first.'

Lily looked at Luke, who was still fixing her with a glare, and then back at Ned. 'I thought I'd wait at the pier.'

'All by yourself? Sure that'd be daft.'

'Well ... I'll be driving so I won't be able to have a drink.'

'Did you never hear of lemonade? Is Betty above?'

'*Um*, yeah.'

'How's her form?'

She flicked another glance at Luke. 'Good. She was practising up-styles on Cassandra earlier.'

'*Eh?*'

'Hairstyles for the wedding,' she clarified. 'You're still getting married by the looks of it.'

'That's grand so. On we go.' Ned made a little gee-up sound as if herding cattle and Lily found herself turned around and moving back up the hill with Luke on one side and Ned on the other.

'Lovely little babby,' Ned crooned, peering across at the sleeping face.

'Not so little,' said Luke, shifting her to his other arm.

'Lily'll take her off you for a minute.' Ned stopped and waited for this to happen.

'I'm good to carry her,' said Luke immediately.

'I wouldn't like to wake her,' said Lily at the same time.

'Just take her,' said Ned, rolling his eyes, 'and don't be making such a fuss. In my day the babbies'd be looked after by everyone. Passed from Billy to Jack and it didn't do them any harm. Gives them confidence, it does. They don't get clingy when they're used to being handled by different people.'

Lily had a feeling this theory might be true – for puppies, maybe? Or lambs?

'Do you want to hold her?' Luke asked stiffly.

'Of course she does,' said Ned before she could answer. 'All the women go *ga-ga* for the babbies. Here. Give me your rucksack.'

He took it from her and the child was passed into her arms. She was warm and smelled of baby powder and Luke. Lily hadn't known such a devastating combination could exist. The scent of broken dreams. But even as she fought the urge, her arms drew the small form closer against her chest.

Ned struck up a conversation with Luke about electricity rates and they strode on ahead, leaving her alone with this precious bundle. She'd never had the chance to hold a baby like this and it was both simple and overwhelming simultaneously. She felt stripped to her core, as if all the hurt and longing inside her had suddenly been exposed. But as quickly as that thought registered, physical pain intruded as she battled to ignore the strain and then the burning sensation through the muscles of her right arm and shoulder. She ever so carefully shifted the baby to her other arm and sighed in relief as she shook out the spasming muscle.

But the baby squirmed, yawned and woke. She was smiling before her eyes met Lily's and there was a split second when everything was right with her world. Then the trusting look was obliterated. She stiffened sharply. Her bottom lip trembled, her face bunched in panic and she started roaring crying.

'It's okay, it's okay. Good girl, don't cry. *Shh, shh, shh!* It's okay.' She might as well have been talking to herself. It didn't calm her, either. 'Luke!'

He came sprinting back.

'She woke up and got a fright. I'm sorry.'

'Don't worry. Hey now, Caoimhe? What's all this about? Lily's just as good at carrying as I am.'

Caoimhe wasn't buying that for a second though. She thrust her arms out to Luke, her upper body following. He took her and she quieted instantly, watching Lily warily and keeping her arms tightly looped around Luke's neck lest he be tempted to give her away again.

They walked in silence the rest of the way as Lily's pulse pounded in her ears.

Reaching the pub, she'd have loved nothing more than to just turn heel and run. Unfortunately Ned was holding her rucksack hostage somewhere inside.

She entered a step behind Luke and glanced around. The decor had changed very little. The crystal tea-light holders on the tables were new and there were a few more lobster pots on the walls, but other than that it was as she remembered it.

Paudie must have been keeping an eye out as he stepped from behind the bar and strode forward immediately, all smiles. He was a good few stone heavier and several shades redder than when she'd last seen him. A quick glance at his son seemed to give him pause. His eyes darted between them.

'There she is!' he exclaimed with his hand outstretched. 'Welcome back! How've you been? Will you have a drink?'

He was nervous, Lily realised as she shook his hand. Paudie O'Callaghan, the man she'd been so eager to impress as a child. The man who always looked on the verge of exploding. The man who'd hardly give you the time of day if you weren't a paying customer ... was nervous.

'She'll have a lemonade,' said Ned. 'Driving later,' he added, by way of apology, before heading to the beer garden to join Betty, Cassandra and Eric.

'Ah, you're not really leaving us, are you, Lil?' Paudie shot another glance at Luke.

Lil? Since when had Paudie called her Lil?

'For goodness' sake,' said Eithne as she came around the bar now too to greet her with a kiss that hit the air about an inch from her ear.

Lily gawped. The woman hadn't aged a day.

'Can't you see she's a successful businesswoman, Paudie? Look how glamorous she is! Places to see and important things to do. So, lemonade for you? Was that what I heard?'

Lily nodded as some old faces came forward to greet her next.

Donie gave a low whistle. 'Well now. You got very pretty, missy.'

He hadn't changed much either. She smiled and gave him a tentative hug. 'Looking pretty good yourself, Donie. How's the dodgy back holding up?'

'Ah, sure, you know yourself.' He shot a mischievous glance Eithne's way.

Eithne didn't acknowledge it. She twisted the top off a bottle and poured the lemonade into a glass of ice before handing it to Lily.

'Don't believe a word,' said Pat, shuffling into line to get his own hug. 'Nothing wrong with him. It's only an excuse to get out of doing anything.'

Lily glanced around. 'Where's the third amigo? Where's Tadhg?'

She'd always had a soft spot for Luke's grandad. He had many traits to endear him to children, being wholly irresponsible himself. When he wasn't providing alibis for them, he was coming up with his own madcap schemes for them to carry out. It was Tadhg who'd suggested it might be fun to add chilli to every third bottle of ketchup in the hotel to see what might happen. She should have asked about Tadhg before this, she realised.

Donie misinterpreted her hesitation. 'He's still going strong,' he assured her. 'Hearing's worse than ever, though, so speak up. He's over there.' He pointed to a quiet section near the unlit fireplace. There in a high-backed leather chair was Tadhg, looking about one hundred years old. His Dowager's Hump had deteriorated markedly. He was leaning forward, peering at something between his knees as his thick-lensed glasses slid slowly down his nose.

She went over and eased herself onto the arm of his chair. He glanced up fleetingly, gave a toothy grin, and returned his attention to the smartphone between his fingers.

He was playing a game. A game she knew. 'You've enough reds already,' she said, staring at the screen over his shoulder. 'Concentrate on the purples.'

Tadhg didn't answer. She wondered how bad his hearing had really become?

'Top left-hand corner. That bunch of purples there,' she said a little louder.

No response. But the purple dots in that corner were suddenly swiped and added to his tally.

The clock in the bottom right-hand corner ticked down.

'You could do with some blues now,' she suggested. 'Get those ones on the last line.'

Still no response but his hand drifted down to the blues at the bottom.

'*You're flying low*,' she whispered.

He dropped the phone and scrambled to check his zipper which was firmly in place. 'Jaysus, girl!' he snapped. 'Do you want to give an old man a heart attack?' As if to show how close he was to having one, he gave a wheezy cough and banged his chest.

'No. I just don't want you to pretend you can't hear me and not answer.'

'Are you kidding me? Best trick in the book. If I don't hear it, I don't have to do it. One privilege of old age. Don't tell anyone.' He glanced around. 'If you pretend to be a little *ga-ga* from time to time it helps too.' He leaned closer. 'Extra portions, you know,' he added cryptically.

He patted the chair beside him in invitation.

'Nice phone,' she complimented as she sat.

'Thanks,' he said, before his expression turned solemn. 'I'm very sorry for your loss, Lily. A fine lady, your nana. Had her crosses to bear, God knows. But always a kind word at the ready. Couldn't fool her about the hearing either but she was a good one – never let on to Eithne. I hear you're selling the cottage.'

'*Uh*, yes.'

'What does Luke have to say about that?'

'I don't know that he has anything to say about it.' But even as the words came out, her gaze travelled the room until she spotted Luke behind the bar. He no longer had Caoimhe in his arms. Instead, he was serving a cluster of women who seemed in no hurry to return to their seats, giggling as they talked to him, their voices rising.

'What's Katie Sullivan up to these days?'

Tadhg leaned back in his chair, his fingers steepling in his lap. 'Why do you ask?'

'Just ... morbid curiosity?'

Tadhg grinned, as if he understood more than she wanted him to. 'She's doing very well for herself. She's a weather girl on morning TV. Has a chef boyfriend. The pair of them have got a bit famous recently.'

'Oh.'

'Yup. Off to all the fancy parties up in Dublin, don't you know? Eithne went with Katie to one recently and a ladies' magazine sent a photographer and she got her photo in. Only they spelled her name wrong. Called her Edna O'Callaghan.' He laughed then, long and hard, until a tear ran down his face. 'Edna! She was livid.'

Lily smiled politely, more relieved than she cared to acknowledge. 'Well, good for Katie.' She saw Tadhg's eyebrow rise. 'No, seriously,' she said. 'You know she was never my favourite person but I wouldn't wish her ill.'

'I know you wouldn't. You've a good heart underneath it all.'

'Underneath *what* all?' she asked, confused now by his expression of amusement.

'The bluster.'

She wasn't sure what bluster was and had no chance to ask as a very attractive blonde-haired woman strode towards them with Caoimhe in her arms. Caoimhe's mother. She had to be. She reached them and turned first to Tadhg. 'Hello,' she said loudly. 'I see you're hogging the Guest of Honour.'

Tadhg said nothing. He only grinned and nodded and then nodded some more until the woman began to look uncomfortable.

Lily bit back a smile. Really, he was too bold. She stretched out her hand. 'Hi, I'm Lily. I'm afraid I'm the one responsible for making your daughter cry this evening.' As if on cue, Caoimhe's chin started quivering and Lily looked at her in distress. 'Oh no, I was only joking. I wasn't trying to ... Sorry. I'm Lily. Did I say that already? Maybe you should run away while you still can?'

The woman smiled and pulled over a seat so she could join them. She held the little girl's hands and let her bounce on her lap. 'Thank God you're not as intimidating as you look. I'm Saoirse and you've met Caoimhe. She's going through a clingy phase at the moment. Don't take it personally.'

Lily was prepared to overlook Caoimhe's clinginess but did she really look intimidating?

'How come you're not staying for the wedding?' Saoirse asked.

'I have work.' Lily cast a glance at Tadhg in the hope he might join in the conversation – making small talk was not her forte – but the traitor was paying no attention and was back playing his game.

'Shame to miss it. Did Luke tell you he's an usher? Himself and that minibus driver. I hear your friend is stepping in as bridesmaid. I would have thought you'd be the obvious choice when you've known Betty so long.'

Lily was taken aback by her bluntness. She'd only known this woman two seconds. '*Um*, well, the dress wouldn't fit me and Cassandra volunteered.'

'And you have work.'

'Yes.'

'Is that little Lily Barrett?' Mark joined them, giving Lily a quick shoulder hug before sitting down beside his wife.

If Lily had been afraid of Paudie, when she was younger, she'd been in awe of Mark.

Caoimhe was passed to his lap and bounced harder. 'I remember when you were barely up to my knee. How've you been?'

'Good, thanks, and you've been good too, I see. I mean congratulations. You have a daughter.'

'And a son,' said Saoirse with a smile. 'He's outside chasing some dog around in circles. He never stops.'

Lily didn't know what to say other than I hope he doesn't get bitten, which she didn't think would go down all that well. Instcad she offered to buy them all a drink.

Mark and Saoirse said they'd have Murphy's and Tadhg instantly recovered his hearing to request a Beamish – 'But don't let Eithne see.'

She stopped by Donie and Pat and added a Harp and a Budweiser to her list. There was still a crowd of women around Luke's end of the bar so she approached a young lad at the other end instead.

His eyes were like saucers as she drew closer. His hand rose to the collar of his black shirt and he gave it a gentle tug.

She placed her order, included another lemonade for herself and watched as he fumbled with the glasses and wiped a bead of sweat from his brow. The pints looked good at the end though.

Donie and Pat ambled over to help carry the drinks, loading the pints onto a tray, while the barman offered her the machine to insert her credit card. A moment later he flushed.

'*Um*, that's ... sorry ... it's declined.'

'What?'

'The card is coming up as declined.'

Oh. My. Feck! Of all the places for this to happen. Of all the times. She'd no other method of payment except to offer to do the dishes. She could ask him to try the card again – if she held out any hope the thing would work. Her credit card had been cancelled. Goodbye credit rating. She was well and truly broke.

The air was suddenly too hot. She felt Donie and Pat exchanging questioning looks, before Pat swiftly picked up the tray and carried the drinks away. Her gaze darted around, searching for a miracle. Cassandra was watching from the other side of the room and Eithne was working her way over, the woman who'd called her a successful business woman not ten minutes ago. How about this for success?

'What seems to be the problem?' Eithne asked briskly.

How to explain? How to explain?

'There's no problem.' Luke stepped up to the machine and gave it a bang with the palm of his hand as he pressed a button. It produced a printout which he tore off, folded and handed to Lily. 'Sorry about that, Lily. It's been acting up all day. The connection is loose or something.'

Oh, thank God! Lily could have wept with relief. Just a loose connection. She lifted her lemonade and took a large gulp.

Donie saluted his thanks with his pint. 'I don't trust those machines at all. Too easy to put in an extra digit and then where are you? Nearly got charged €140 for a packet of chewy toffee one time. I pressed the go button and everything. It was the girl in the shop who spotted it.'

'That was honest of her,' she managed.

'Sure she wouldn't have got to keep it anyway. It goes off into some cloud and then it lands back in a bank the next day. You don't know what you have any more in your pocket. It's all X's and O's.'

He meant ones and zeros but, as the paltry state of Lily's finances was still a secret, she heartily agreed. Shaking with relief, she finished her lemonade and excused herself to go to the bathroom, exhaling as she closed the door behind her. Just thirty minutes more and she could leave.

She looked about her, surprised to see the room had undergone a transformation since she'd last been in it. She recognised Eithne's stamp immediately, for it was a space to rival that of any high-end hotel, all cream and beige tiles with smart gold mosaic accents.

She turned on the tap and let cold water run over her hands. She'd have loved to splash her face too but that would mess up her make-up. Glancing to the mirror to check it, she did a double take at the reflection staring back. She'd undergone her own transformation since she'd last been in here. The woman in the mirror looked sleek, glossy and expensive. She was, in fact, coordinating perfectly with the decor in her beige jacket and cream camisole, with touches of gold in her ears and around her neck. But while embarrassment had softened her cheeks, the expression in her eyes was as hard as the tiles and almost as cold. 'Intimidating' Saoirse had called her. 'Unnecessarily prickly' had been Cassandra's sisters' verdict. But was she really those things? She'd spent ten years trying to be emotionally strong and financially self-sufficient. And barring one (albeit giant) mistake, she'd achieved that. She was an in-demand accountant. Supporting herself without anyone's help in London. But had something important been lost in the process? Something left behind, like Peter said? She racked her brains to remember what she'd even told Peter about Inish Ruin. She been unguarded clearly but the guy had been semi-conscious half the time, drugged up on pain meds. And Peter didn't really know her. But as she cast her eye about the room again she felt suddenly uncertain. For underneath the showy surface, this place was still what it had always been – a perfectly good, perfectly functional bathroom. Underneath the surface, was she still what she'd always been too? And was that still functional?

She pulled her phone from her pocket to check the time again and the credit-card receipt fell to the floor. She picked it up and glanced at it. At the bottom in bold was the word "**Declined**" under which she read "**Duplicate Copy**".

The letters swam in front of her eyes. Declined? That couldn't be right. Where was the word "not" in front of it? Just a loose connection? Not a loose connection. She *was* broke. Luke had just covered for her.

Cassandra burst through the door, looking anxious. 'Is your phone working?'

Lily shoved the damning slip back into her pocket. 'Yes. Why?'

'I got a call from Sergei. He says he's been calling you and you haven't been taking his calls. He says he's given you an eviction notice.'

'It's a mistake,' she said automatically.

'How could it be a mistake?'

'It just is. Don't worry. You're going to Belfast anyway so it won't matter.'

'What do you mean? It'll matter to me if you've nowhere to live. '

'I'll have somewhere to live. It'll be fine. Just a temporary problem until I sell the cottage. Don't trouble yourself about it. Go on.'

Cassandra just stared at her.

'I said go on.'

She left and Lily put her face in her hands but the door swung open again and this time Eithne stepped inside.

'There you are. Everything alright?'

'Yes. Everything is fine.'

Eithne didn't look as if she believed her. 'The Ro-Ro will arrive at nine.'

'Yes.'

'You won't want to miss it.'

They stared at each other.

Then Eithne stepped forward and gave her a swift hug. 'Thank you, Lily, and I'm sorry I had to – that things couldn't work out differently. I wish you well, okay?'

Lily nodded, not knowing what else to say, and Eithne scooted out of the bathroom as fast as she'd entered. Lily followed but hadn't made it ten paces before she was surrounded by well-wishers. Shay O'Farrell and his niece had come to thank her for the toys. Eoin and Maura Murphy had come with an invitation to dinner when she next visited, along with an update on all their children and grandchildren that had her head spinning trying to keep them straight. Josie Buckley had come with a faded photograph of Lily riding Tadhg's old donkey backwards and Bríd O'Meara with some questions about the best places to visit in London – and the tax treatment of rental income if she didn't mind explaining. They were all delighted to see her and eager to talk about Nana, to share their condolences and to reminisce. No one asked why she hadn't made it to the funeral but between the murmured remarks about 'nasty accident', 'foolish young man' and 'very unfortunate timing' it was clear Cassandra had already made excuses for her.

Paudie arrived with another lemonade. She accepted it with a cringe of embarrassment. Who was going to pick up the tab for earlier?

'We're busier than a Saturday,' he said, almost as if he knew what she was thinking. 'You're great for trade. You'll have to come back soon.'

'Oh, I ... thanks.' She took a sip.

'Pity you missed the darts,' said Shay. 'It was a good night.'

'A great night,' agreed Maura. 'Great turnout. You should make a monthly thing of it, Paudie. We could do a league. Have a women's and a men's team? Wouldn't that be an idea?'

There was general support for this. Paudie went off to check his diary and the crowd dispersed in twos and threes towards the comfort of the lounge.

Lily checked the time once more. Just a few minutes and she could start walking to the pier. But looking over she saw a dozen smiling faces all waiting for her to join them. Everyone remembered her. They'd come out specially to see her. And she was about to leave them all once more. She could visit in the future, sure. But, without a home on the island, could she ever really *belong* here again?

The question blindsided her.

No, it wasn't the question. It was the sudden longing that accompanied it.

Luke came to stand beside her. 'You ready to go?'

No. Yes. No. 'I – I just need another minute.'

She returned to Tadhg. He was still playing the game on his phone. She sat beside him once more and took in his hunched frame, his gnarled fingers, his grizzled features. This might well be the last time she ever saw him and fondness for him welled to overflowing.

'I'm heading off now, Tadhg,' she said softly. 'Not sure when I'll be able to get back.'

He put his game on pause and turned to her. 'Well, it was good to see you again. All grown up and so smart and pretty. Your nana would be proud.'

'You think?'

'Of course,' he said as Luke arrived with her rucksack. 'Sure didn't she say as much to you in her letter?'

There was a pause then, 'What letter?' Lily said at the same time as Luke.

'Noleen left you a letter,' said Tadhg. 'Or was it a message? No. A letter.'

'How do you know that?'

'Because she told me she was going to. The morning she went up to the Regional for that last "check-up" as she called it. We should have guessed something more serious was going on but she never said anything about any diagnosis. Just kept calling it check-ups. But she'd been giving things away, you know, before that. "Presents" she called them. I suppose you recognise this?' He held up his walking stick.

She shook her head.

'Used to be your Granduncle Joe's. And she gave Eithne a little cameo brooch she'd always admired – said it wasn't her colouring. And Josie got a little ceramic penguin and Kitty the Church–'

'I never got any letter,' Lily interrupted, desperate to get him back on track. 'Where did she say she'd leave it?'

'Somewhere about the cottage, I think.'

'No. I've spent the last three days cleaning the place from top to bottom, Tadhg. There was no letter.'

'Are you sure?'

'Positive.'

'Okay, wait now and I'll have a think.' He scratched his chin. 'If she'd said it to me yesterday now I'd remember no problem. Hang on. Was it …? Wait. I remember now. Yes. There was something very important she needed you to know but not to worry as she'd put it in her letter. Oh, and I was to tell you welcome home if for any reason she wasn't here when you got back.'

Lily gripped the sides of the chair. A welcome home from Nana and a letter? With her last words to her on earth? Somewhere in the cottage she was about to sell?

Eithne caught her eye from the bar, held up her watch and tapped her finger on it.

Lily nodded. *Yes. I know. It's time to go.* She looked from Luke to Tadhg and back to Eithne. 'I just need another minute.'

She got herself out of the chair and hurried to the beer garden, past Betty and Cassandra, past the picnic tables until she reached the car park. There, she pulled the phone from her pocket and dialled Preston.

He answered on the second ring. 'I presume there's no problem.'

'I'm so sorry but I need you to reschedule my meeting tomorrow. Something very important has just come up. I need a couple more days to resolve it.'

There was an ominous pause. 'You've taken twice your holiday allowance this year already without permission.'

'What happened in Chicago wasn't a holiday. You know that. I haven't taken a holiday in over a year.' She was momentarily distracted as she glimpsed the auburn-haired girl from the pier. She was sitting at one of the picnic benches beside a dark-haired boy and they were making a house out of cocktail sticks and packets of mustard. 'And I've been working six days a week for the last six months.'

'You're on holiday now, aren't you?'

'Yes. And if I could be there tomorrow I–'

'You *will* be here tomorrow. Don't make me do something you'll regret. Eight thirty.' And he hung up.

Lily looked up to see Luke standing there, her rucksack in his hands, a question in his eyes. Hot on his heels came what seemed like half the pub, their faces rife with interest. Even a few tourists ambled over to see what was happening. The auburn-haired girl looked over too, her head tilting momentarily as their eyes met.

'You're not really leaving, are you?' asked Paudie.

'I ...'

Eric pushed through the crowd, the minibus keys swinging round his finger.

Luke helped her into her rucksack, adjusting the straps so they lay flat against her shoulders. Then he stepped back, not quite meeting her eye. 'Bye, Lily.'

'Goodbye,' she murmured but her feet seemed glued to the spot.

Cassandra emerged from behind the wall of faces and embraced her. When she drew back, her eyes were moist. 'Go on. I'll see you soon.' She gave her a gentle push towards the minibus.

'The Ro-Ro's pulling up to the pier,' said Donie, craning his neck. 'If you're going, go now.'

Lily took another step. *There was something very important she needed you to know.*

'And tell Kitty to come on up and give us a good look at that buggy,' said Pat.

Ned strode forward. 'I'll come see you off so.'

'Call me when you get home,' said Cassandra.

Home. The word thrummed like a long-lost chord in Lily's chest. *I was to tell you 'welcome home'.*

'*I'm staying!*' she cried and nearly collapsed at the wave of panic that washed over her. 'Just for a few days,' she added, but no one heard that bit as a cheer went up.

Pat whistled and clinked glasses with Shay. Betty and Josie hugged her. Cassandra gave her a tearful smile and Eithne yelped as Paudie elbowed her in the ribs. Ned scratched his head and put a small padded envelope back in his pocket and Luke just headed back inside, ignoring the sly grins Donie sent his way.

It was quiet in the bar. Kitty the Strand had arrived on her new golf buggy. Lady Godiva on her steed could hardly have drawn more attention. The half of the bar that hadn't gone out to see Lily's departure had joined them to welcome this new arrival. Through the window Luke could see Kitty giving rides on it up and down the driveway.

Eric pulled up a stool in front of him.

Luke reached for the ginger ale.

'I suppose I should offer my congratulations, Playboy. Though I didn't think you had *that* in you.'

Luke glanced up but said nothing as he grabbed a glass.

'What did you do to her credit card?'

Luke scooped ice as his face flushed. 'I didn't do anything. We had a loose connection.'

'Sure, sure. A loose connection.'

Luke poured until the ginger ale frothed over the rim and said nothing.

'You don't look surprised she's staying though. Cassandra says Lily might lose her job if she doesn't show up for work tomorrow.'

Luke winced. He'd guessed Lily was in trouble from what he'd overheard of that call.

'I'm afraid to ask what you could do to her in a week. Break her heart, I suppose? That's all that's left now you've got her to stay.'

Luke held up his hands. 'Hang on a minute. I had nothing to do with that or any of the rest of it.'

'I suppose she's staying for Donie's scintillating conversation then, is she?'

'No. It's something to do with her nana.'

'Her nana who's dead?' Eric lifted a brow. 'Cassandra will have to pick up the pieces when you mess her up.'

'I'm not messing anyone up.'

'Does she know you're leaving here right after the wedding, then?'

Luke opened his mouth and gently closed it again. No. He'd said nothing to Lily about that. She hadn't asked and it hadn't mattered when she was leaving herself.

'Didn't think so,' said Eric. 'Just waiting for the right moment to break it to her? After you've got her into bed maybe or when she's told you she loves you again?' He threw him a look of disgust. 'That's not closure, man. That's revenge, plain and simple. Do me a favour and make sure I'm not around for it. I don't like to see a woman cry.' He finished his drink without another word, left a few euros on the counter, and went back outside.

Luke didn't like to see a woman cry either, especially if that woman was Lily. Through the window he caught sight of her in the passenger seat of the golf buggy. She was hanging onto the frame while Cassandra and Betty laughed from the rear-facing flip seats, trying to keep their drinks from sloshing as the buggy did a tight circle in reverse.

His dad came in with a spring in his step and a tune on his lips. He didn't say a word, just busied himself making a cocktail, something pink and orange with a generous measure of peach schnapps. Rummaging around until he found a little paper umbrella, he opened it, popped it into the drink and carried it outside. Luke saw him hand it to Lily as she stepped off the buggy. She hesitated only a moment before she took a large gulp. *Uh-oh.*

Luke glanced over his shoulder, grabbed the tequila bottle from the top shelf and hid it behind some blackcurrant cordial as he mulled over Eric's words. He was certain he had nothing to do with Lily's decision to stay but, if there was even the smallest chance she was counting on him to be around, he needed to tell her he was leaving as soon as possible. Hell, he should encourage her to leave too. Maybe if she got herself back to London by Wednesday she'd still have a job.

The crowd streamed back inside, bearing Lily with them.

Someone had given her a pint of beer.

Lily hated beer.

She drank it fast.

Luke filled pint glasses with water and set them on the counter in hope.

Cassandra bounded over and asked for two shots of tequila.

His profound apologies. They were all out.

'Two more pinky cocktails then, please.'

He set about making them, going as easy on the schnapps as he thought he could get away with. Maybe he'd just wait to see what tomorrow brought before he said anything to Lily. There was always the possibility she'd change her mind and leave anyway and spare him any explanations. Frankly, it would be a relief not to have to say goodbye to her a third time.

She was near the bar now, surrounded by a tight circle of men who were grinning at her like idiots. Cassandra squeezed her way back in and handed her the cocktail. It went the same way as the last and two of her entourage headed to the bar for the privilege of ordering her a refill.

Lily glanced over, caught his eye, and smiled.

Confused, he gave a nod in return. *Okay?*

He turned away to pull a pint for another customer but when he glanced back she was still looking his way and her expression had turned ... fond? He gulped. He'd only seen Lily get really drunk twice but it had been enough to learn the process had three distinct stages; Affectionate, Nostalgic and then Unconscious. Stage One Lily was dangerous.

Music started up through the old bar speakers. Lily chatted with her nearest admirer and exchanged a laugh with Cassandra. Donie came over and offered her his hand and gave her a twirl and a few older couples tried to make a little dance floor happen between them with intermittent cheering, clapping and foot-tapping.

As the hours ticked by, Luke tried not to keep track of Lily as she flitted from group to group. But, relaxed and smiling now, she moved so like her old carefree self his chest started to hurt, another suture coming undone. Her jacket was thrown over a chair. Her hair unravelled in stages from its bun. By midnight, she was leaning her head on Cassandra's shoulder as Eric told his "Time I accidentally knocked out another bouncer" story, her laughter at the end just as infectious as he remembered.

At half one, the Heineken ran dry. Luke made a quick trek to the basement to replace the keg. He'd disconnected the empty and was in the process of rolling it out of the way when he heard unsteady footsteps on the corridor outside.

Turning, he found Lily holding herself upright in the doorway. Her hair was now in complete disarray around her shoulders, her cheeks brighter than the cocktails she'd been knocking back and her smile ...? Sin personified was right.

'What are you doing down here?' he asked, turning away as he reached for the fresh keg and hauled it into place, his pulse quickening.

'I was looking for you.'

'*Well, you found me. Congratulations.*' He repeated her words from Saturday back to her in the hope of sobering her. 'I'm working. Go on back up.'

Ignoring that instruction, she came closer. She didn't exactly shimmy but still he was conscious of the sway of her hips in his peripheral vision and that thin strap sliding down one arm. She leaned against the wall beside him and watched as he positioned the coupler over the new keg and gave it a half turn clockwise until it clicked into position. He turned on the gas and made sure the beer was flowing before he looked her way again.

Her eyes took a second too long to find his face and then she flushed even redder. Had she been checking him out? His pulse did another uptick.

'Mikey found the tequila.'

'Oh.'

She gave him another smile but this one was tighter. 'When you look at me like that, Luke, I feel sick.'

'How am I looking at you?' he asked, wondering if she was actually about to get sick.

'Like you hate me. Like you know ...' She trailed off.

'What?'

'Everything.'

He stared at her, confused. 'I could never hate you, Lily.'

She inched closer. 'What I said earlier. At the cottage. About replacing the old memories?' She took another step. 'I didn't mean you.' She closed the gap between them and put her arms around his shoulders. He was a foot taller than her and she embraced him like a cat against a scratching post, the full length of her pressed up against him as she stood on her tiptoes. 'I could never forget you.'

A violent hiccup followed this declaration.

In other circumstances it might have been amusing.

In this circumstance it just pressed her body even more closely against his own. He kept his arms pinned to his sides and willed the rest of him not to react either.

'That's good to know. Now please go back upstairs.'

She didn't. Instead her hands slid down his chest, one coming to rest over his fast-beating heart while her head nestled under his chin. 'I can't be angry with you anymore.'

His eyes found the ceiling. 'That's very generous of you.'

The sarcasm went right over her head. The clearest sign yet that she was hammered.

'I just feel – *hic* – so sad.'

He glanced down as he felt her sigh.

'Some creep tried to feel me up.'

What? 'That's not okay. Show me who.'

He tried to lead her upstairs but she resisted.

'No, it's okay,' she said. 'Eric took care of it. He used to be a bouncer. Did you know that?'

'I did, and you did too. You're drunk, sweetheart.' The endearment slipped out of him but she didn't seem to notice.

'No, I'm not.' She hiccupped again and put her head back against his chest. 'I just wanted you to be minding me. Like old times.'

He groaned. Stage Two then. He brushed her fringe away so he could peer into her eyes. 'Feeling nostalgic, are we?'

She returned a trusting smile, her ear still pressed to his chest as if listening to his heartbeat. Another suture popped. 'I don't suppose you remember what happened the last time you were drunk in this pub?'

She shook her head.

'You spent two hours lamenting an eraser you lost when you were seven. An eraser in the shape of a sheep. Ringing any bells?'

She looked away, a slight frown between her brows. 'That was a really good eraser. I never found one I loved as much.'

'Okay but I'm not going to be your eraser tonight.'

'A sheep?' she asked, looking confused.

'No, Lily. The thing you decide to get all nostalgic about.'

She seemed to ponder this for a second and then raised her eyes once more to his. 'You gave me that eraser. At school. The first day we met. As a present.'

'A present? Is that's how you remember it? You kept staring at it on my desk and then at me and then at the eraser. I *had* to give it to you just so I could get some work done.'

Another hiccup, followed by another smile. 'Colouring?'

'Yes, Lily, colouring. Very important colouring.'

'Katie was so jealous.' The smile faded. The hand that was on his chest started playing with the middle button of his shirt. 'Do you see much of her these days?'

'Katie? Sure. Anytime she's home we catch up.'

'So – *hic* – you two got to be very good friends after I left?'

'Katie and I were always friends.'

'I thought you didn't like her.'

'No. I just didn't like when she was mean to you for no reason.'

'Oh.'

'Why does that upset you?' He felt her fingers move to another button and realised she had undone the first.

'I just thought – *hic* – we felt the same about everything back then.'

It was said so plaintively he couldn't help but brush her cheek with a consoling stroke of his thumb. 'I thought we did too.'

But she shifted at his touch and raised her face to his, lips parted. It would be the work of a moment to close the gap between them. She'd be soft and yielding and his hand would slide into her hair and he knew he'd be punch-drunk in a heartbeat on feelings only she'd ever brought him. The blood pounded in his ears, keeping time with the mantra of her name in his head. She leaned closer still, her breath a hot, sweet caress that tasted of ...

He stepped back. Swallowed hard. 'No,' he rasped. 'I can't.' *Not like this.* Because all her sweetness was just peach schnapps edged with tequila. Because all he'd really taste if he kissed this woman again was heartbreak.

From somewhere above, Cassandra called Lily's name. He took another step back.

'*She's here!*' he called and then turned and walked away, passing a wide-eyed Cassandra on the stairs.

A minute later both women emerged, one hanging off the other, arms linked. Eric met them with Lily's jacket and rucksack and steered them both towards the exit.

Back behind the counter Luke watched them leave, waiting to see if Lily would turn around for a last look his way. But a crowd gathered in behind them and he lost sight of her before she'd even reached the door.

His dad joined him, carrying a tray of empty beer glasses. 'Busy night,' he remarked, opening the dishwasher and starting to load it.

'*Uhuh.*'

'You packed for Cork yet?'

'No.'

Paudie just nodded but Luke could tell he was pleased. 'You practically ran the bar tonight,' was his next sally.

'It's not rocket science. Mikey could do it if you gave him half a chance.'

'Ah, but it wouldn't be the same as my own flesh and blood. We could rename the place for you. "Luke's". What do you think?'

'Catchy. How long did it take to come up with it?'

'Okay, whatever. You could rename it yourself. Or get Lily to do it for you. I can see her now greeting all the customers and taking orders. Just as professional as your mam ever was. That's what makes these places work, you know. A good team at the top. Be a good life for her too. No more money troubles with you looking after her.'

'She doesn't have money troubles,' he said instantly.

'Then why isn't her credit card working? There's nothing wrong with that machine. Probably why she's selling Noleen's cottage too. So sad. She could keep it if she stayed with you. Keep it to pass down.'

He didn't add the words 'to your children'. Presumably he felt he'd laid it on thick enough already.

He turned on the dishwasher and, with the parting suggestion Luke might want to check his shirt, left him with his troubled thoughts and two buttons to close over his chest.

Chapter Thirteen

Cerberus

Lily's first semi-conscious thought on waking the next morning was that she'd died from alcohol poisoning and that the grey, wet world she was standing in must be Limbo. She had a fleeting recollection of meeting Cerberus. He'd turfed her out of a cosy heaven. She'd been warm and now she was cold. Well, at least she hadn't gone to the other place was her second semi-conscious thought. Though a bit of heat might be ...

Lily turned around to see Cerberus peering out a window at her, three large black heads sniffing the air.

Lily squinted, rubbed her eyes and squinted again. No wait. Not three heads. One head. One *familiar* head. Pup was in the sitting room and Lily ... was in the back garden. *How the heck?*

She moved forward as Pup backed up, excited apparently to see what Lily would do next.

What Lily did next was push closed the window she'd evidently just climbed out of.

She heard Pup whimper on the other side of it before she clambered onto the sofa and settled herself with a "*Humph*". She buried her snout into the quilt that lay in a tangle on it, doing her best to look cute and non-threatening. Lily wasn't fooled as she registered the drool cooling on her ankle and shuddered. It might have started as a lick but Pup was probably just tenderising it. All the better to sink her teeth into later. No, her instincts – unconscious or otherwise – had been spot on. If you wake to find yourself being prepped for breakfast, you escape through the nearest available exit. Even if that exit is a window. And she wouldn't be returning until Pup was safely incarcerated elsewhere. But who was to do this incarcerating? She glanced up and saw the bedroom curtains were all closed, Betty and Cassandra surely still out for the count. What time was it? She couldn't guess with the mist. A quarter past sometime since dawn.

She took stock of her situation as effectively as a severely dehydrated brain would allow. She was still dressed in yesterday's 'going-away' outfit, now thoroughly rumpled, but wearing someone's slippers. Red with black dots? Her dishevelled state was the least of her problems though. She was broke, a hair's-breath from eviction and just hours from pissing off her only source of income.

But Nana had left her a letter and that couldn't be walked away from. And a 'welcome home' too which felt almost as precious. But now doubt was creeping in, dragging reservations in its wake. Tadhg's memory hadn't seemed the most reliable, had it? And the horrible thought that maybe Nana hadn't been of soundest mind at the end occurred to her. Could illness have affected her thinking? What if she was going to write a letter and then forgot? She'd have to ask Luke to see if he'd seen any sign – *Luke!*

She slapped her face into her hands as she suddenly recalled what else she'd done last night, and groaned. She'd all but thrown herself at him. Angling for a kiss as he kept trying to politely extricate himself from her grasp. And he'd had to resort to plain old '*No*' in the end because she just wouldn't take a hint. Why had she done it? She'd been pickled, yes, but she couldn't blame it entirely on alcohol, could she? Not when she'd spent the night fighting the impulse to go to him. To share something funny or get his opinion on some bit of gossip or just have him look at her once more as if she was the sun rather than a raincloud blocking it.

What should she do if she saw him today? Apologise? Plead temporary insanity? Or pretend she didn't remember doing anything and pray he'd be chivalrous enough to do the same? Yes. That one. Definitely.

She shivered as a breeze picked up. She needed to find shelter urgently and the only dry spot she could think of that wouldn't require waking anyone was the cave on Trá Mhór. Head pounding, she headed down the lane and turned left, walking as fast as she could safely manage as the mist thickened.

She felt rather than saw she'd arrived when a thin layer of sand underfoot alerted her to the turnoff. The sea sounded too loud as she faced it, making her way along a crumbling boardwalk which led through a stretch of grass-knitted dunes. She heard laughter from within them: young and carefree. It was followed by dull thuds, then a tumble of shifting sand and the next moment a girl appeared at full tilt, her hair a flash of auburn through the misty grey ahead. She was followed a moment later by a dark-haired boy. They didn't see her as they crossed the boardwalk and disappeared into the dunes on the opposite side, their trailing giggles subsumed by crashing waves. Lily kept going to the end of the boardwalk. Here the dunes flattened and she reached the hard, open sands beyond. She turned left and traversed the beach to reach the black wall of cliff on the far side. For several minutes she searched its length for the cave entrance, getting colder and wetter and more frustrated with herself before she realised it had at some point been sealed up behind fallen boulders.

This was followed by the even more frustrating realisation that she'd have been just as cold and wet inside it as she was standing here.

Shivering forcefully now, there was nothing for it but to head back to the cottage and ring the doorbell. She took a different return route though with a shortcut through the fields. It was a choice quickly regretted, however, as she stumbled over lumpy terrain, dodging waist-high thistles every few strides, the slippers now sodden. She came to a metal wire blocking the way at knee height. The yellow notice hanging from it warned it was electrified. Hopping over would be easy enough but it meant there were cattle in there and probably a bull, which she'd rather not run into blind.

She turned right instead, following the wire in the expectation it would turn uphill at some point so she could go around it.

Luke had half expected to hear Lily had left on the first ferry the next day. Half expected, half hoped. Whatever nostalgic figary had got into her last night, the sobering light of day would have her thinking the better of it and she'd leave. That's what she did best after all and it would be the best thing that could happen to him. Another sleepless night trying to get his feelings in order had made that much clear. She needed to go back to London and he needed to get to Cork – to take up the job he'd trained so long and hard for. Lily sticking around right now had him questioning his priorities and he didn't like it one bit. She was messing with his homeostasis. Impeding optimal functioning.

But the memory of her pressed against him was like a live wire that kept sparking in his brain. And an internal debate about whether he should have kissed her and damn the consequences was already on round three. She'd said she could never forget him. But even if that was true, what difference did it make? Thinking of him fondly while living in perfect equanimity four hundred miles away was hardly a compliment. And she hadn't come back because she'd missed him, he reminded himself. Just to tie up a financial loose end. Just to leave again. Which was what he needed to do himself. So when eleven o'clock came and went with still no word of her getting the ferry, Luke set out for Barrett Cottage to confess his imminent departure and encourage her own.

A sea mist had rolled in with the morning, shrouding the landscape – concealing, revealing and concealing it again, like one of his charcoal sketches being randomly smudged out and redrawn. He heard the minibus approach and hopped up the bank as it rolled by. Eric didn't see him, his nose pressed to the windscreen as the campers onboard huddled, their disillusioned faces peering out through condensation.

He reached the cottage and tapped on the back door. Cassandra opened it with a finger to her lips and drew him inside.

Betty was nursing a mug of tea at the kitchen table. At her elbow was a dish of Turkish Delight.

'Good morning,' Cassandra whispered. 'We're celebrating. Have you come to take Pup for a walk?'

He hadn't but it was as good an excuse as any to be here. 'Sure,' he whispered back, 'but maybe in a few minutes when I've dried out. How are you feeling today, Cass?' He peeled off his jacket and took a seat beside her.

'Much better, thanks. The tablets Eric gave me worked a treat.'

'Good, good.'

There was a long pause, which neither lady seemed in any rush to fill.

'Why are we whispering?' he asked at last.

Cassandra nodded towards the closed sitting room door. 'Lily's asleep.'

'Ah.' He reached over and helped himself to a piece of Turkish Delight. 'And why are we celebrating?'

'Because she's fixed, Luko. Hermit-less at last. You saw how she was at the pub, reconnecting with everyone and making new friends. She even gave Eric a hug when we got back here. It was so cute. She told him if he broke my heart she'd break his nose.'

Luke smiled. 'Yes. Very cute. But that's just Lily drunk.'

'What do you mean it's just her drunk?'

'I mean, it doesn't mean anything.'

Cassandra *tsk*ed as if he was a complete idiot. 'It means *everything*. Lily is never more herself than when she's drunk. It's the only time the shell comes off and you know exactly how she feels. Didn't she go looking for you when that asshole hit on her?'

'Yes but–'

'And what did she say?'

'That she ... wanted me to mind her.'

'There!' said Cassandra, beaming. 'See how much she trusts you? That's huge.'

Was it?

Cassandra's hands were now squeezed together. 'And what else? Did she tell you how she was feeling?'

Luke tried to remember what Lily had said between the hiccups. *I just feel ... so sad.* Yes, that was the word she'd used: sad. And then she'd told him she'd been groped. But would she have felt sad about that? Upset and angry certainly. But *sad*? Still he wasn't about to lay Lily's innermost emotions out for these two to pick over.

'No. She didn't.'

Cassandra's face fell. 'Oh. Well, hopefully next time. But she was really happy once she got back here, wasn't she, Betty? Putting flowers in all the bedrooms and then she had this big ceremony of hanging her clothes in the wardrobe, all the time singing some herby song.'

'*Scarborough Fair*,' said Betty. 'And she still only knows the first verse.'

Cassandra's brow knitted thoughtfully. 'I'd never heard Lily sing before.'

'Count yourself blessed,' said Betty. 'The child hasn't a note in her head. And I swear she thinks she's in perfect pitch. Definitely something wrong with her ears.'

'That was always her song when she was flower-arranging,' said Luke, feeling a touch of nostalgia himself. He thought he'd like to hear Lily sing again. Once maybe. A brief rendition.

'The poor thing was evicted last night, imagine, and never let on,' continued Betty. 'That landlord fellow shouldn't have told you,

Cassie. She mightn't have paid the rent but she's still entitled to her confidentiality.'

Luke was shocked. Lily had been evicted? 'I'm glad you think that, Betty,' he said stiffly. 'But you really shouldn't be telling people Lily's business, Cass.'

'I only told Betty. She's like her grand-aunt.'

'And I'm a model of discretion,' Betty added. 'Oh, don't look at me like that. Do you really think I'd tell anyone?'

He folded his arms. 'You just told *me*.'

'*Ah, pah!* But you're already in on it.'

'In on what?'

Cassandra and Betty exchanged surprised glances. 'Aren't you and Lily going to have a go of things again, now she's staying?'

'No.'

'What do you mean no?' said Cassandra. 'What about everything we talked about?'

'What about it? This is not a movie. I can't just whip out a violin and make a happy-ever-after just because you want one.'

'*Shhh,*' said Betty, her head nodding towards the door. 'It should be a surprise when you tell her you're still in love with her.'

'Yes,' agreed Cassandra.

Luke pointed a finger at Betty. 'You, stop encouraging her. It's getting ridiculous ye are. Where's the dog and I'll take her for that walk?'

There was a long pause. 'She's in the sitting room too.'

Luke's eyes widened. No wonder they didn't want Lily to wake up. She'd have a heart attack if she found herself trapped in a room with Pup. He pushed out of his seat. 'Why did you let her in there?'

Cassandra's shoulders rose. 'Because Lily needs to break away from all her fears.'

With a shake of his head, Luke headed for the sitting room, opening the door as quietly as he could. It was dark inside but in the corner he could just make out the sofa and a form huddled under a quilt. He looked around and patted his side but no dog came trotting over from the shadows.

'Pup,' he whispered. 'Come here.'

There was an answering *thump, thump*. He crept closer and heard a whine from under the quilt. He lifted the material to reveal Pup who was panting happily. He glanced around the rest of the room in confusion. The curtain moved, shafting light across the floor as it swung in gently. The window was open a fraction but the garden outside was devoid of life.

'Eh, Betty? Cass? Where's Lily?'

The two ambled in and looked around. 'That's strange,' said Betty.

'Very strange,' agreed Cassandra, lifting the quilt for a last check before folding it back neatly beside the dog. 'She definitely didn't come out through the kitchen. Unless ...? When I went to the bathroom that time?'

'No. I was here the whole time.'

'Strange.'

'Very strange.'

Luke tapped his foot. 'Yes, it's strange. We've established that but where is she?'

'Gone somewhere,' said Cassandra. 'Will I check upstairs?'

'*Li-ly!*' screeched Betty and waited. 'Maybe give her a call?'

'No. Her phone is here.' Cassandra examined it and then recoiled, 'Oh, I hope she didn't see this!' She held it out to Luke and Betty.

It was a photo message of Preston Tepper headed paper, with the words "**You're fired**" on it. 'I'm deleting it,' she said. 'He can send her an email like a normal person. But where is she? Oh, I know. Pup, come here. Good doggie. Smell the phone.' She held the screen out and made a sniffing sound to demonstrate what was required. '*Find Lily. Seek.*'

Pup gave Cassandra's fingers a lick. '*Eeeew!*' She disappeared into the kitchen and they heard the tap running.

When she returned she had Eric with her. 'Hey, lads. What's the story?'

'Lily's missing,' Luke told him. 'I think she climbed out the window.'

'That's strange.'

'Isn't it though?' said Betty.

'What was wrong with the door?'

'What does it matter?' said Luke with rising frustration. 'People, *focus*. She has no phone. It's cold and wet outside.'

'Ah, it's not that wet,' said Eric. 'Just a bit damp.'

'She's in a fragile state.'

Betty rubbed her temples. 'Aren't we all this morning?'

'She's in a fragile state *emotionally*.'

But it was only after he said it that his blood ran cold. *I just feel so sad?* Regardless of her drunken happiness last night, Lily was all alone in the world with no one to look out for her. Well, except for a friendship with a fruitcake who thought setting a dog on her was a good idea. She was out of credit, evicted, and now fired. How much more would it take to push her over the edge? She wasn't five minutes from a cliff if she wanted to throw herself off one. Heck, she could fall off one without trying in this mist.

'Well, whose fault is that?' said Eric. 'She'd have been in London by now if not for you.'

'For the second time, I had nothing to do with that.'

'Maybe she just went for a walk to clear her head?' said Cassandra. 'I'm sure she'll be back any moment.'

Everyone fell silent, even Pup, as they waited for this prediction to come true.

'I'm going to look for her,' said Luke. 'Who's with me?'

Three sets of shoulders shrugged.

'Fine. I'll go myself.'

'Do, so,' said Betty.

'Pup. Get up off that sofa. You can help,' said Luke.

Pup whined and Eric crouched to pat her stomach. 'Ah, leave her be. It's miserable out there.'

'It was "just a bit damp" a second ago. Come on, Pup. Where's your lead?'

The dog somersaulted to her feet and *whooshed* out to the kitchen to bark frantically at the back door. Luke found her lead and clipped it to her collar but before he could pick up the other end she gave an excited bark and darted away and off through the open front door instead.

Luke followed and lunged, trying to grab a hold of the bouncing, trailing lead but Pup nipped sharply left, wriggled underneath the bars of the gate and dashed across a field before disappearing from sight into the mist.

Luke cursed and gave chase. Thirty seconds later he heard a bloodcurdling scream and veered towards the sound, hurdling over an electrified cattle wire, and sprinted diagonally across a lumpy field to find Lily on her hands and knees at a cliff edge, desperately fending off Pup's attempts to lick her face.

The dog was having another go at finishing her off as she clung white-knuckled to the anchorage of a grassy tuft.

'*Heel!*' Luke's booming command carried over the crash of the waves below.

Pup obeyed by halting her attack and sitting on her haunches to scratch herself vigorously.

Lily got back to her feet and almost fell over the electric wire before limping uphill as fast as she could. If there was a bull in this field she'd take her chances.

When Luke caught up with her, Pup was with him, her lead wrapped firmly around his wrist. 'Why were you by the cliff, Lil?'

'*Trying – go round – bull!*' She could hardly speak for lack of oxygen.

He caught her elbow, forcing her to stop. 'Swear that's the only reason.'

The concern in his voice caught her off guard. Did he think she'd been trying to do herself in? Last night had been super-embarrassing but still.

'*I swear.*'

He searched her face as though trying to spot a lie. 'There's no bull in the field. You could have gone through.'

'*Couldn't see – mist.*'

'Okay but what was wrong with the lane?'

She put her hands on her knees to get her breathing back under control. '*I was coming – from the beach. Thought – it would be quicker.*' She felt a wet tongue on her hand and screeched as she stumbled away from Pup again.

'It's okay – I have her. She's only licking you. She wouldn't hurt you.'

'No. Just tenderise me softly and then herd me to my death.'

He said nothing but a small smile suddenly rose on his lips.

With an indignant sniff, she hobbled on, but her progress slowed as her breaths became laboured once more. The adrenaline was wearing off. Dizzy, she came to a complete stop.

'Do you want me to carry you?'

A glance showed him still smiling, feck him. So glad her terror was entertaining. 'No. I just need a minute and I want to ask you something anyway.' She spied a moss-covered boulder and eased herself onto it while Luke tied Pup's lead to an old fence post and came and sat beside her.

She should have found a bigger boulder. The heat of him zipped all the way from her ankle to her shoulder. One of his hands rested on his knee. She remembered that same hand brushing her cheek and for a moment felt as if she was back at the cliff edge, exposed once more to the elements.

She heard him swallow and turned to look at him. Her gaze fell to his lips which he suddenly wet with the briefest slide of his tongue. Oh God. Was he remembering last night too?

'Nice slippers.'

Apparently not.

'You wanted to talk?'

'Yes. Yes.' She cleared her throat, determined to be as normal and sane now as she could manage, which meant finding something else to stare at. Gosh, wasn't that blade of grass long? 'So I've, *um*, been thinking about what Tadhg said last night about Nana leaving me a letter and, you know, the welcome home? And before I start ripping the cottage apart I was hoping you could be completely honest with me. Don't sugarcoat anything.'

'O-kay?'

She looked to him again. His face was so close she could almost count his eyelashes. And that scar cutting through his eyebrow was sexy as – *focus!* 'Is there any sign you ever saw that Nana wasn't quite ... herself?'

He searched her face for several long seconds. 'Well, not recently. But then she did let you go all those years ago. And that certainly didn't seem to be straight-thinking to me.'

His choice of words confused her. 'Let me go? You make it sound like I had a choice.'

He came to his feet as smartly as if he'd sat on a thorn at that, and moved several paces away. Then he ran his hands through the damp mess of his hair. All of a sudden, he didn't look so well.

'Are you actually saying,' he said, 'that you got *sent* away?'

'*Um*, well, yeah.' Because that was obvious.

But he returned to crouch in front of her, his gaze so intense she leaned back.

'Because staying here wasn't going to be enough of a life for you?' he said. 'Or because *I* wasn't going to be enough for you?'

What in the hell kind of questions were those?

But he was already rushing on. 'I know I was impulsive. Making plans for us. As if you didn't have any dreams of your own. But I'd never have stood in the way of anything you wanted to do with your life.'

Now she was even more lost. 'I know.'

'Then what did I do to deserve it? Just tell me that! To go without even a goodbye. And leave it to your nana to say you were gone.'

'That's not–'

'And me telling her it had to be a mistake? That we'd been talking about getting married, for Christ's sake!'

Her jaw dropped. 'What did she say to that?'

He shook his head as if that was beside the point. 'She didn't believe me. Said how could we be getting married when all we ever did was squabble? And we were far too young to be getting so serious anyway. So, thanks for leaving me to look like a fool. For not having the decency to break up with me to my face.'

But it was Lily's turn now to get to her feet. This wasn't right. Luke was rewriting history. 'If I'd wanted us broken up, Luke, why would I call you again and again? You were the one who didn't–'

'Call me? I never got any phone call,' he said, before his eyes suddenly widened.

And something turned over in Lily's stomach in that moment. Something cold and horrible and spiked. Dread, searching for the most tender spot to bed down.

'I called you,' she repeated faintly.

But the space of a few more heartbeats was all it took for her to wonder how she could ever have imagined he'd just ignore her? Even if he'd moved on with someone else? She took a step away as black etched in at the sides of her vision. Then she bent, her hands falling once more to her knees as she remembered to breathe before she sat back heavily on the boulder.

'Lily?'

His voice sounded far away.

'Lily.'

She looked up and met Luke O'Callaghan's stare anew across six feet of grass and ten years of disillusionment.

He edged closer, hands raised now as if she was an animal at risk of bolting. He crouched once more and his gaze scoured hers more softly this time. 'You didn't want to leave?'

'*No*,' she rasped. '*Why would I have wanted that?*'

'Because it was a chance to go to a fantastic school where you'd be with all these better people and have every facility and opportunity and be in line for scholarships and, and ... everything?'

'Better people, Luke?'

He looked away for a moment, just long enough for her to see his Adam's apple bob. When he looked back there were a dozen questions in his eyes but he just asked one, 'How did it happen then?'

She wasn't sure where exactly to start but went with, 'Nana.'

He nodded.

'She organised an early ferry. Just me and Seánie. His neighbour met me in Cúltrá and she drove me straight to the school. But I was certain you'd get the whole story when you called to the cottage at lunchtime. That you'd be able to reassure Nana. Explain how it wasn't the same for us as it had been for her or Mam. I mean, you weren't going to abandon me. You weren't twice my age and already married.'

'Hang on. What?'

'I thought she'd come to her senses. Realise she'd overreacted.'

'Overreacted to what? I don't understand.'

'To us having sex, Luke. She caught us that night. Her bedroom door was open when I snuck in. The room was empty. I thought at first she'd just gone to the kitchen for a glass of water. So I legged it to my bed. But then I heard the front door open and she came straight upstairs, panting like anything, and stopped at my door. She was fully dressed and pale as a ghost. And she just whispered "Oh, Lily," like her heart was broken.' Her voice cracked as Nana's face flashed in her memory, with an accompanying pulse of guilt. 'She went back down to the study then and locked the door. I thought I'd be able to talk to her in the morning. Apologise for sneaking around behind her back. But as soon as I woke she told me I was going to boarding school in Dublin for my last year of schooling. The principal was an old friend and had made a space for me and to please not argue and if I ever loved her I was to do as she asked. I was too shocked to speak, let alone argue. She could hardly look me in the eye.'

Luke was leaning back now, his brow furrowing harder by the second. 'You think she sent you away because we were having sex?'

'Yes.' Because she'd grasped too late what her eight-year-old self had been too immature to understand. The one mistake she'd promised not to make? It wasn't getting in a car with a drunk after all. That was just a horrible consequence. It was sex outside of marriage that had ruined both Nana and her mother's lives. 'But I honestly thought I'd be gone a day at most. After you'd had the chance to explain how things were between us. But instead there was complete radio silence.'

'And?'

'And I kept trying to contact Nana. Every chance I could. But she wouldn't answer the phone. So then I called you – at the only number I had for you – but your mam always answered. And I was so embarrassed. I didn't know what Nana had told everyone about why I was gone. So I just hung up.'

His expression turned so stark she shrank from it.

'That was it? You just gave up?' When she hesitated, he threw his hands in the air. 'Come on! Don't you think I've been tortured enough with this?'

'I didn't know you'd been tortured at all. I was the one sent away and ignored, not you.'

But he was back on his feet and pacing now, wearing a muddy path through the wet grass. 'Why didn't you just come home?'

'I'd no money except what was in my Post Office savings book. And I'd left that behind me.'

She could almost see the steam coming out of his ears.

'Christ, Lily! If the roles had been reversed there's nothing I wouldn't have done to get back to you. I'd have hitchhiked if I had to.'

She flinched.

'Well?'

Her heart started to race. *Tell him something. Just not that.* 'I ... I did speak to your mam. In the end.'

That halted him in his tracks.

'Twice.'

The colour slowly leached from his face. 'What did she say?'

'The first time? That you were out and she'd let you know I'd called. I gave her the number for the school. Told her it was urgent I speak to you.'

He raised a hand to his forehead. 'And the second?'

'She was all surprise you hadn't called but said you were doing a line with Katie Sullivan now and you maybe hadn't had a minute to yourself. She was very apologetic but said she'd be sure to let you know I'd called again.'

Clearly Eithne hadn't passed on either message. But as Luke's hand fell, his ire was directed wholly at herself.

'*That's* why you were asking about me and Katie last night? Oh my God! You believed what she said. How could you?'

She guessed they weren't pretending not to remember last night then? 'The same way you could believe I'd just up and leave you, I suppose. That's why you've been so mad at me, isn't it? Why you've been looking at me the way you have?'

She got to her feet and started back towards the cottage as Luke untied Pup's lead and quickly followed.

'What else was I to think? That your nana had spirited you away against your will? I don't understand how you could have let yourself get put on the ferry in the first place.'

'Because I didn't think it would be forever, did I? And what else was I supposed to do in that moment? Chain myself to the bunk bed? Nana didn't want me around anymore and I had nobody else.'

'You had *me*.'

Her heart clenched to hear the disappointment in his voice. She'd have taken an expletive-laden rebuke over it any day. But he didn't understand. How could he? He had a mam and dad, three brothers and a grandad to love him. All she'd had was Nana and she'd been terrified of losing her. In that moment, doing what she asked had seemed the only way to keep her.

Luke strode ahead now, away from her, towards the gate.

'Luke. Be fair. *Wait!*'

He gave no sign of complying but Pup dropped smartly to the ground, effectively halting him in his tracks.

He hauled on the lead in vain as Lily caught up with them. 'I'm sorry,' she said but she wasn't sure what exactly she was apologising for. That he'd been hurt? That he didn't understand?

'I'm sorry too,' he said, but it sounded more like 'I'm done with this conversation'. He tried to get the dog off the ground again. 'Pup, come!'

Pup looked to her, as if for guidance.

'*Wait*,' she said.

With a thump of her tail, Pup put her head straight back down on the ground.

Luke groaned. 'Unbelievable. Trust the females to stick together.'

'I really am sorry.'

'Fine,' he said, 'but I've had ten years of not knowing why you left or how I was to blame. Of getting into fights and messing up exams. I spent five years in Dubai selling overpriced mansions of all things just to get far enough away from thinking about it. And when that didn't work–' He shook his head. 'And the only consolation I had all that time was that *your choice* had made you happier somehow. But now you're telling me you didn't have a choice. That you were just what? Too embarrassed to stand up for us to your nana and come home?'

She bit her lip. That wasn't how it was.

'And she didn't send you away because she caught us having sex. Just so you know.'

'She did, Luke.'

'No. Because right after she said we were too young to be getting so serious I–' He halted abruptly as if having second thoughts.

'Yes?'

'I ... might have promised we wouldn't have sex anymore till after we were married.' He held up his hands at her gasp. 'It wasn't my finest moment. You were gone and I panicked. My thinking was she'd know how serious we were about each other that way. That she'd appreciate the grand gesture.'

'And did she?'

'Not exactly. Honestly, she just looked shocked. But she definitely didn't know about us having sex *before* I blurted that out so that can't have been the reason she sent you away.'

Lily's hands slid down her face and formed a gesture of prayer against her chin. She stared hard at the grass while Pup turned Luke in a circle, following a scent.

'Well?'

'That was the reason, Luke. It had to be.'

But he was adamant it wasn't. He told her what he thought had really happened. Her nana and his mother – by design or coincidence – had wanted them separated for their own good. Her nana so Lily wouldn't be tied to a life on Inish Ruin through loving *her* and his mother so *he* wouldn't be tied to a life on Inish Ruin through loving Lily.

'But how could that be for my good?' she asked.

They reached the side passage and halted as one. 'Because she didn't want you wasting your potential, I guess. Or maybe she thought you could find someone better than me, given the chance. I don't know.'

Lily tried to process this as Luke reattached Pup to the chain in the yard and then returned to her side.

'Well?'

'No,' she said. 'I'd swear she had no plans for me going anywhere. We were working on all these ideas to expand my flower business. To get a bigger shed for me to work out of. Something happened to change her mind that night. If it wasn't us having sex it was something else.'

'What?'

'I don't know.' She shivered and rubbed her arms. 'But now I really need to find that letter.'

Chapter Fourteen

Do Not Bend Envelope

Lily headed for the back door but Luke didn't follow straight away. He needed a moment to dig himself out from the emotional rubble first. Six hours ago he'd had every intention of ridding himself of Lily Barrett once and for all. At dawn she was the girl who'd just walked out on him when a better offer came along. But by noon she'd somehow become a victim of forces beyond her control. She hadn't walked, she'd been pushed. But while that might explain her leaving him in the lurch, her lack of effort at returning seemed poor recompense. She'd been lied to by his mother, yes, but *she'd believed that lie*. That he'd just move on with Katie. She'd given up on him – on them – with barely a fight. *She just let it happen*. That was the thought tormenting him now.

His phone buzzed in his back pocket. A text message from Gráinne, asking if he could call? Last time he'd seen her was three weeks ago when they'd broken up. Well, when he'd broken them up, telling her it'd been lovely and that she was lovely but that the relationship had run its course and he hoped they could still be friends. She hadn't done what some of his previous girlfriends had, which was to ask if he wanted to be friends with benefits instead? That idea always left him cold. But Gráinne had said nothing, just nodded, but with that little furrow in her brow he'd seen when she was tending patients in Accident and Emergency. As if she was doing a mental triage of his wellbeing.

He took a few steps back into the yard and dialled her number. It was answered after two rings.

'Luke. Hi. Thanks for calling back.'

'Sure. No problem. Everything alright?'

There was a brief pause. 'Everything is fine. Except I've been a bit unwell. Nothing serious,' she rushed on before he could respond. 'Thought I was coming down with the measles. One of the junior doctors here fancies himself the budding dermatologist and put the wind up me but it turned out to be nothing.'

'Well, that's good.' Inside the cottage, he heard Lily being greeted by Cassandra, Eric and then Betty from the sitting room.

'Ah, there she is!'

'Right as rain!'

'I'm glad we didn't think to worry about you, chick, or we'd have been nervous wrecks. Search parties galore setting off.'

He strained to hear what Lily was saying in return. Something something, Luke, something.

'I don't know if you know,' Gráinne continued, 'but I actually rang Betty the other day to say I couldn't be her bridesmaid. Thinking I was infectious and all.'

'Oh?' He hadn't known Betty had asked her to be a bridesmaid. Had Gráinne told him that?

Eric was laughing in the sitting room. Lily said something that sounded playful. He remembered what Cassandra had said about Lily giving Eric a hug. Saw a mental image of it. Didn't like it.

Gráinne was still saying something about being a bridesmaid. That Betty had found a replacement but she'd still like to come as a guest? If he didn't think it would be awkward?

Eric was talking again. Telling a joke Luke recognised as one of his flirty ones. Lily let out a peal of laughter and now it was Eric's voice in his head. *She was always that hot, though, yeah?*

'I never told Betty we were a couple so I know it wouldn't bother her either way, but I thought it would be a good opportunity for us to talk. To see if it's what you really...'

And now Eric was starting on another well-tested joke. And Luke had lost track of what Gráinne was saying to him. 'I'm sorry, what?'

'I'm asking you if it's worth my while still coming?'

'To the wedding?'

Lily was laughing again and Luke started walking into the cottage, impatient suddenly to clap eyes on her again.

'Yes.'

'Of course.' He didn't know why she needed his permission.

'Great, great. I'm looking forward to it.'

'Okay. I'll see you then.'

'Yes. See you then, Luke. Bye.'

He reached the sitting-room doorway. The laughter stopped as his eyes sought out Lily. She was cocooned on the sofa beside Cassandra. A large throw blanket was wrapped around her body with just her toes peeking out. Her hair was a bedraggled mess, the tip of her nose was as pink as her cheeks and she looked completely and utterly ... beautiful.

She glanced over, her eyes bright, and saw him standing there. She hesitated a moment and then made room for him beside her.

It was an invitation of a sort. Or a peace offering? But his legs wouldn't move, his mind seized with a rush of conflicting emotions. So he stayed where he was, leaning against the jamb, as Eric, Betty and Cassandra exchanged glances between them.

'The mist's going,' Eric finally said, peering out the window as a sunny day finally emerged from behind the last wisps. 'Another busy afternoon, I guess,' he added with a sigh.

'It's such a shame you have to work every day,' said Cassandra. 'Maybe you should think about getting someone to fill in once or twice a week? Give yourself a chance to do a few other things. We could put an ad up in the pub and see if anyone was interested? Or maybe you'd know, Luke, if anyone wants some part-time work?'

'I don't. Not off the top of my head.'

'Well, not to worry.' Cassandra gave Eric a reassuring smile as he sat on the arm of the sofa beside her. 'I can find out for you. What days would you like off? I suppose it can't be the weekends because that's when you're busiest but what about Mondays and Tuesdays?'

There was a sudden shift of tension in Eric. '*Um*, that's alright, thanks,' but he was looking at her as if she was sprouting a second head.

'It's no trouble,' she assured him. 'And if I'm going to be staying it'd be nice to have a bit more time so we could do things off the island. Go on a few day trips, you know?'

The strained silence was broken by Lily. 'But your new job starts on the 17th.'

'Yes, but I don't have to accept it. I thought it might be nicer if I stayed here now, seeing as you're staying.'

Lily's eyes widened. 'But you were so excited to get that job.'

'It's just a job.'

'It's not *just a job*, Cassandra. It's *the* job. You went through two interviews for it. And then you ran around the flat singing *9 to 5* for days.'

'And then I sang *Islands in the Stream*.'

'So?'

'*Islands in the Stream*. It was a sign. That I'd actually decide to live on an island. Isn't it amazing how the brain works?'

'Amazing,' agreed Betty.

'But – but what about all the famous people you were going to meet? And all your plans to be a fashionista and, and – and everything?'

Cassandra just shrugged. 'What does it matter? It felt like the right thing then and staying feels like the right thing now. What can I say? I'm not like you, Lily. I don't need a risk analysis for every decision. And I'll give you rent, but I'll probably need a new bed. The bunks are cute but they aren't all that comfortable.'

'How would you pay rent without a job?' asked Luke, curious about how far this plan had actually been worked out.

Cassandra brightened instantly. 'Oh, that's all sorted. I'm going to be helping your mum with the new wellness spa we're putting into the hotel. We've great ideas. Yoga on the lawn at dawn. Seaweed wraps and sea-salt scrubs. All very high-end and classy. I'm going to be the receptionist.'

That wiped the smile right off Luke's face. 'Dad'll have a heart attack when he finds out.'

'*So* ...' Eric finally got a word out, a choked whisper of a thing.

'So,' said Cassandra, sliding her arm around his waist, 'I'll be staying. Isn't that great?'

'*Great*,' he squeaked. He looked at his watch but Luke had the distinct impression he didn't actually see what time it displayed. 'Next ferry. See you.'

He made a brisk exit and Luke exchanged a glance with Lily. Had she warned Cassandra about Eric?

The slight shake of her head said no.

'*I can come with you!*' Cassandra called after him but he was already gone. She didn't seem unduly concerned though, just disappointed. 'I was hoping he'd have time today to show me the Inish ruin.'

'The what?'

'The Inish ruin. *The* ruin. The one the island is named after.'

All three stared at her.

'*What?*'

'Nothing,' said Betty, her cheeks rounding.

'There is a ruin, isn't there? Otherwise it's a stupid name for this place. Why are you all smiling?'

'There *are* ruins,' Luke admitted, 'but nothing you'd make a day trip for.'

'The name is *Inis Rua* really,' explained Lily, 'from the Irish for red but it got anglicised to Ruin way back when, which sounds good but means nothing.'

Cassandra's nose wrinkled. 'So it should be Red Island?'

'For the ferns in late autumn,' said Betty.

'And the hair colour of the heathen natives,' added Luke, with a glance to Lily who was no longer smiling.

'It looks red from the mainland in autumn,' she told Cassandra. 'Especially in the early mornings.'

Cassandra pursed her lips as she contemplated this. 'I think I prefer Ruin Island. It has a bit more character to it. I suppose I'll just have to go somewhere else to see proper ruins. So, Lily, what's the plan for today then?'

This innocent question, though, threw Lily into a fluster. 'Oh *um*, well,' she began, her eyes sliding to Luke's, looking uncertain. 'I was going to ask for Luke's help with this thing first, *um,* that we were talking about earlier. Because he might be able to help me figure out this *um* ...'

'Thing?' he supplied. He looked to see what Betty and Cassandra would make of Lily's sudden rambling but apparently they understood perfectly, exchanging wide smiles before finding pressing business for themselves elsewhere.

'Not at all suspicious,' he assured her.

Her cheeks flushed but she said nothing as she led him through the kitchen – past Betty and Cassandra, who started a random conversation about jam – into the hall and on to the study. There she sat down in front of the roll-top desk and pushed up the lid. It clattered and rattled as it disappeared into its frame. She looked to him again but still said nothing.

Was he supposed to be a mind reader?

'Now might be a good time to tell me about the "thing"?' he said.

The flush deepened. 'I just wanted to pick your brains as to where Nana's letter might be. Without anyone listening in. It's obviously nowhere obvious.'

'Obviously.'

She looked back towards the desk and ran her hand over its top. 'This is where she would have written it.'

He examined the desk with its myriad compartments, cubby holes and impractically small drawers. Could the letter be hidden in one of them? He pulled out the first drawer and Lily pulled out a second and then a third and fourth but other than a cheque stub, a few elastic bands, a pea-sized ball of Blu Tack and a shed-load of dust they were empty.

'Ned told me you looked after all Nana's paperwork after …' She swallowed.

'If you've a problem with that I'm sorry but post kept arriving for her and I was afraid something important would get missed.'

She shook her head. 'No, I, that's … I appreciate it. I really do. It shouldn't have fallen to you. I should have been here sooner to deal with it.'

'Then why weren't you?' It came out harsher than he'd intended and he could see she felt it when her head dipped.

'When I heard she'd passed I was … stuck. In a situation. In America. I didn't feel I could leave until it was sorted.' She took a deep breath. 'And then having missed the funeral I just kept putting off coming back here. Finding reasons. Denial, I suppose. Told myself I couldn't take the time off work but I think I just wanted to keep pretending Nana was still alive. Like if I didn't see this place,' she glanced around the room, 'without her in it …'

He wanted to say something consoling but before he could draw a breath she was brushing the dust from her fingertips.

'What if Nana's letter was in here but someone stole it?'

'That seems unlikely.'

'But there's a broken windowpane in the scullery. Someone could stick their hand through it and lift the latch. You could climb in there easily. Here, I'll show you.'

But he halted her departure with a hand on her arm. 'Is this going to become a thing for you? Climbing through windows?'

'No. But I'm just saying it's possible.'

'Technically, yes. But when do we ever have break-ins here? I mean hardly anyone even locks their doors. Except in the summer. And why would anyone steal a letter?'

'I don't know.'

He didn't either. Honestly, it sounded like she was grasping at straws. 'Is there anywhere in the cottage you haven't checked? The attic maybe?'

'No. I was up there yesterday.'

He rubbed his face, trying to think. 'I don't suppose your nana had a safe?'

'No.'

'Any loose floorboards?'

'Not that I–'

But she was interrupted by the sound of the doorbell.

It was Ned, in his wet-weather uniform this time, but still looking cheery as they opened the door. He handed Lily a **Do Not Bend** envelope which just bore her name and the word *Private* across the top. 'Special delivery,' he said. 'From Seánie. He says it's urgent.'

Lily asked if he'd like to come in and Betty and Cassandra, joining them at the door, added their entreaties. But he was apparently under pressure and promised he'd see them all later.

They watched him cycle away.

Then three faces turned to Lily expectantly and the envelope in her hand.

'It's marked private,' she said.

'Yes,' said Betty, but made no move to leave.

'So I'll just go open it ...'

'Do,' said Betty.

'... somewhere private.'

'Oh. Well. Of course,' said Betty stiffy and turned to go back to the kitchen. 'It's all very hush-hush and private, Cassie. Don't be nosy. Come on and help me with the crossword.'

With a smile at Lily, Cassandra followed.

'I'll leave you to it, so,' said Luke but was surprised when she stopped him with a finger to her lips, wide eyes and a nod back to the study.

He followed her there and watched as she sat back on the chair, while he found a perch for himself on the edge of the desk. 'Why am I here?' he asked.

'Because this has to be Nana's letter, Luke!' she whispered. 'Just dropped into our laps. Don't you see? She must have left it with Seánie for me.' She flipped the envelope over, peeled open the flap with care, tipped it on its side and emptied out its contents.

But there was no letter from Noleen inside. Instead there was an official-looking document, stapled in one corner and headed: **LAST WILL AND TESTAMENT OF NOLEEN MARY BARRETT.**

Lily went pale. 'Oh my God! She did make a will!'

Luke leaned forward and attempted to read it upside down. **I,** *Noleen Mary Barrett,* **presently of Inish Ruin, Co. Cork, Ireland, hereby revoke all former testamentary dispositions made by me and declare this to be my last Will and Testament.**

'Didn't you know there was a will?' he asked.

'No! I called all the solicitors in the area a month after the funeral. Nana hadn't been to any of them. And I called Josie and asked her to check if there was any sign of a will lying around here and she said no, and that no one she'd talked to had heard Nana mention getting one done and, without any instructions or information otherwise, I just assumed she'd died without one.' She looked up at him. 'As her next of kin, I applied to the Probate Office and it's up to me to ... well ... settle the estate.'

'But you get the cottage, right?'

'As her only surviving relative, then yes. Without a will, everything comes to me.'

'But if she's written a will?'

Lily's eyes widened. 'Then she could have bequeathed the cottage to Dogs Trust for all I know. And it'll be up to whoever she's named as Executor to see her wishes carried out.'

'Who's the Executor then?'

They both turned back to the document. Lily flipped over the first page. There was a section halfway down titled **APPOINTMENT** and *Seán Patrick Murphy of Cúltrá, Co. Cork* jumped out as the **Sole Executor.**

The island's ferryman was Noleen's Executor? His 'powers' filled the rest of the page and some of the one after.

Lily looked confused but they kept scanning the document together until they hit a section in capitals marked **DISPOSITION OF ESTATE** and a few paragraphs beneath this was the following: *I direct my Executor to divide my estate, which comprises the cottage on Inish Ruin and all its contents, as follows: To my granddaughter Lily Barrett of Islington, London, and to my neighbour Luke O'Callaghan of Inish Ruin, Co. Cork, – to be shared equally between them.*

Luke's breath caught. Noleen had bequeathed him half the cottage? *Oh shit.*

Chapter Fifteen

Oh Shit

Lily stared in disbelief and then turned to Luke.

His eyes were wide as saucers. 'I don't want it, Lily. I don't know why she did that.'

She glanced back at the will, reading it all the way to the end now hoping for some miracle paragraph that would somehow undo what came before. The 'Just Kidding Clause', perhaps?

'Maybe she wasn't of sound mind after all?' he suggested.

Lily shook her head. 'No. One of the witnesses is a GP in Cúltrá and the other is a priest. And surely neither would have signed if they had concerns about Nana's mental capacity?'

She didn't know if she wanted to scream or cry as she reran all her financial calculations through her head, now halving the value of the asset that had previously been enough to save her hide.

'Just rip it up,' said Luke. 'No one has to know except Seánie, and he probably won't care. Rip it up and then you'll get to keep all of it.'

'But this is what Nana wanted. For you to have half.'

'Then I'll refuse to take it. There has to be a way of doing that legally, right?'

'I don't know but no, Luke, no. I wouldn't ask it of you.' But everything felt suddenly hopeless. How long would it even take to settle the estate now with Seánie as Executor? Not fast enough to avoid eviction, if the process had to start all over again. If Seánie was even prepared to take on the role or had any idea of how to go about it?

Luke's phone buzzed into the silence. A quick glance at it left him frowning. 'Sorry, Lily, I've got to go. There's a problem with some supplies from the wedding caterers that needs fixing right away. Best not mention it to Betty.' But, as he stood to leave, his eyes scanned her face, concern creeping into his expression. 'We'll sort this out, okay? I'm not taking any part of your cottage. Whatever a piece of paper says.'

She waited until she heard the front door close behind him then took a deep breath and went to the kitchen. Betty and Cassandra both looked up as she entered but neither made any allusion to whatever might or might not have been in the envelope. For that much, at least, she was thankful. The less people who knew the situation the better, at least until she had her facts straight.

She made tea for them all, washed hers down with yogurt and a side of mixed pickles and, when she was done, put on some fresh clothes, threw a light summer jacket over her shoulders and walked out of the cottage alone. She needed to talk to Seánie and the next ferry was due in less than twenty minutes.

Thoughts plagued her on the way to the pier. They, like the cottage, were now divided equally between two people: Nana and Luke. Why had Nana done that with her will? Because she hadn't believed Lily deserving enough to have it all was her first and most painful thought. Because she'd disappointed Nana by breaking her promise and sleeping with Luke and this was some sort of punishment. But then Lily remembered what Luke had said about Nana's reaction when he'd let that information slip. That Nana hadn't seemed to realise she and Luke were more than just friends. That she'd been shocked. Yes, that was the word he'd used. *Shocked*. Not disappointed. Or angry. Certainly not angry with Luke, if she'd left him half a cottage! But then, who else was there to leave the cottage to if Nana didn't want Lily to have it all? When Granduncle Joe had died, Lily had become the last surviving bud on Nana's family branch. And Luke had always got on so well with Nana. Had often helped her with jobs while Lily lived here – and had no doubt been there for her umpteen times when Lily hadn't. Likely without ever being asked. He'd looked after her post and her dog after her death, hadn't he? Why *wouldn't* Nana leave Luke half the cottage? But by that logic ... why not leave it all to him then? Why split it between her and Luke – and force the two of them together again to sort it out? Her granddaughter and the best man they both knew? For after their earlier conversation in the field, Lily was now in a better position to acknowledge Luke's goodness than ever.

For he hadn't ignored her phone calls home.

He hadn't just turned his back on her when she'd needed him.

He hadn't just moved on with Katie Sullivan.

And it was such a relief to lay down all she'd been carrying against him, to have him restored to the man she'd loved – warm-hearted, faithful and a better person than she'd ever be. But other, more unpleasant, feelings were now making themselves known, chief amongst them regret. For how she'd treated him since she'd come back, for the hurt he'd suffered but, more acute even than that, for how sunk in his esteem she was now. His look of disappointment when he'd said "You just gave up?" felt seared into her brain.

But what if she told him the truth? That she hadn't just given up on getting back to him? That she'd tried? But what would that accomplish now except to distress him? No. It was enough that she had to live with the consequences of that night without making him carry the burden of it too.

The ferry was just pulling into the harbour when she arrived at the pier. Only a handful of tourists were on it. They appeared to be couples mostly and one group of friends who seemed to have come on a whim, unsure what they planned to do there.

A young crewman was tying off the ropes as Lily tried to catch Seánie's eye.

He was in the cabin.

She waved.

He looked uncertain but waved back, his head tipping to the side as if not quite sure what it meant. He rolled down the window and leaned out. 'Hello there,' he said in his soft voice. 'Good to see you again.'

'Good to see you too, Seánie. Have you got a second? To talk about ... something.'

His expression turned uncertain. '*Um*, well, now?' He glanced down, his eyes tracking the last of the disembarking passengers. Then he looked at his watch.

Lily looked at hers. He wasn't due to depart for ten minutes. He had time.

He turned off the engine which gave a couple of coughing *lub-dubs* before it fell silent. Lily became aware of the splash of water against the hull and the wind whispering through the life preserver to her right, tapping its yellow strings against the orange plastic of the ring.

Seánie's crewman was looking at her. He was a gangly teenager in weather-worn jeans and an even more weather-worn jacket.

She gave him a nod.

He winked back.

Seriously? With a sigh, she turned away to stare at anything else. There was a little piece of seaweed that floated beyond the bow and the small film of diesel that coloured a smooth patch of water in a rainbow slick.

Seánie climbed down from the cabin. He ambled over to her across the deck, then climbed the few stone steps up to the pier to join her. '*Give us a minute, Jonah!*' he called back.

Without acknowledging him, the teenager headed off to the opposite side of the boat, where he pulled a set of small white headphones from his pocket and started messing with his phone.

Seánie shifted slightly from one foot to the other, as if correcting his balance in high seas. 'I nearly missed you the other day. With the mighty sunglasses.'

Lily felt a sharp tug of embarrassment, verging on shame. She should really have said hello to him. There was no excuse. 'Oh. Yeah. It was just a ... really bright day. I'm sorry.'

His nod was accepting, as if that was a perfectly reasonable explanation, and he pulled an open packet of Iced Caramels from his pocket and offered it to her.

'Oh. Thanks.' She loved these. She reached in, rummaged around until she found a pink one, and drew it out.

Seánie was smiling when she looked back at him. 'You know the white ones taste exactly the same?'

She smiled back as she pulled off the clear wrapper. 'Not convinced.' She popped the sweet into her mouth.

Seánie pulled out a white one himself and started unwrapping it. 'I'm very sorry for your loss, Lily. Your nana was ...' he blushed, 'a very special lady. I hope you know how much ...' another shift of balance 'she meant to ...' and looked away, 'well, everyone. And how much she loved you. She'd have done anything for you.'

Except ask me to come home, thought Lily. Or tell me she was sick. 'She gave you – ' She had to pause a moment herself to work the caramel off a tooth with her tongue.

Seánie tipped forward, balancing on his toes as he waited.

'That envelope to give to me?' she finished.

Seánie came back onto his heels. 'She did, surely.'

'Do you know what was in it?'

He gave a slow nod, while chewing. 'Her will. She asked me to give it to you as soon as you came back. Though I'm thinking she thought that'd be for the funeral.'

It was definitely shame Lily was feeling now. Embarrassment had long faded. 'I ... couldn't make it.'

There was another accepting tilt of the head from Seánie.

'And ... I suppose you know she named you as Executor?'

'I do.'

'And you're happy to act in that capacity?'

'I'll do my best in any capacity that's needed, lass, of course. We can have a sit down of a Sunday if you like maybe and figure it all out. With your head for numbers, it'll be no bother, I'm sure. There's certainly a lot of forms that need filling. I know that much.'

'And you know she wanted Luke to have half the cottage?'

Seánie offered her the packet again but she declined. 'Yes. She came up with that at the last minute. And I told her it was daft, but she said you'd have her reasoning in her letter.'

'So there really *is* a letter? Tadhg mentioned one but I didn't come across it. Do you know where it is? And what was in it?'

He went bright-red now and glanced over his shoulder in the direction of Jonah, who was still flicking through something on his phone, and then over her shoulder.

'Seánie?' she prompted.

'I couldn't say for sure. Ah look!' He sounded relieved. 'Last-minute-dot-com.'

Lily followed his gaze. Two women were running down the hill towards them in flip-flops, holding sunhats to their heads while their free hands clutched bulky canvas bags.

Jonah moved over to help them board.

Lily glanced again at her watch. Out of time.

Seánie stepped back. 'I'm sure the letter will turn up soon. Noleen would have made sure you got it.'

She waited where she was until Seánie was back in the cabin and the engine running once more before she began a slow trudge up the hill. Another Iced Caramel had somehow found its way into her pocket, a white one this time. It did taste the same and she chewed on it as she mulled over what Seánie had said. *Nana would have made sure she got it. Got it. Not found it.* So if the letter wasn't some*where*, maybe it was with some*one*?

Cassandra was playing games with Pup in the sitting room when she arrived back. With a look of concern, Betty whispered there'd been no sighting of Eric since earlier. Thinking to take Cassandra's mind off this desertion, Lily immediately offered to take her to visit Trá Eilis, but she said she wasn't in the mood. Lily guessed she just didn't want to go in case Eric came back, and worried for her. This is what love could do to the unwary, she reminded herself. Cause pain.

Eric didn't call again. Nor did Luke.

And the rest of the day dragged.

Ned arrived back at dinnertime but Cassandra said she'd lost her appetite and to go ahead and eat without her. So it was just Ned, Lily and Betty who sat down to baked potatoes, crisps and mixed pickles. Other than the dog food, four tea bags, a bottle of vanilla essence and the few slices of bread set aside for breakfast, the cupboards were once again bare.

They ate in silence, listening to Cassandra's instructions from the room next door and the dog's boisterous replies. The warmth of the evening and the comfort of a full belly made Lily drowsy. She got up and opened the window by the sink, admiring the view over the fields blushed orange by the setting sun.

'The air is so fresh here,' said Cassandra from somewhere behind her.

'You should smell it in winter.' Lily breathed deep as though inhaling the recollection. 'In the mornings. At the beach. So clean it smells of absolutely nothing.' She turned to find Ned, Betty and Cassandra watching her. Then she spotted Pup advancing across the kitchen floor on her belly, her front paws pulling her along. In any other dog, it might have suggested humility. In Pup, it looked more like stalking prey. Her eyes flicked up to meet Lily's and she froze. When Lily said nothing, she edged forwards a little more until she was right below her. As Lily held her breath, Pup put her head ever so gently on her runner.

'Isn't that strange?' said Betty. 'I wonder if you smell like Noleen? What do you think, Ned? Or would she sound like her, maybe? She definitely thinks you're her owner.'

'She does, doesn't she?' said Cassandra. 'Even though you keep rejecting her. Poor Pup. You just want to be friends. Look, she's saying "Love me, Lily. I don't ask for much. Just a few nice pats and the odd tin of food and a bit of a walk whenever you're in the mood".'

Lily looked down at the mottled fur-ball leaking drool. 'Did you teach her to do that?'

'Me? No. She did that all by herself.'

Pup raised two soulful eyes and gave a tentative wag of her tail.

'Give her a pat,' said Ned. 'Tell her she's a good girl.'

The tail wagged harder and Lily swallowed. 'Good girl,' she said curtly.

'And a pat,' urged Betty.

'Maybe later.'

'Ah, give her a pat, why don't you?' said Ned. 'What are you afraid of? She's gentle as a lamb.'

'Allegedly.'

'She is. Aren't you, Pup? You're a gentle little thing.'

The gentle little thing was crushing her foot. Lily bent slightly and touched the furry head with her fingertips. 'There you are,' she said, straightening swiftly. 'Off my foot now. Off you go.'

'She's highly trained,' said Cassandra, even as the dog ignored this request and settled her head more comfortably. 'What do you want her to do first?'

'To get off my foot would be great.'

Cassandra pulled a piece of paper from her pocket and scanned it. 'Then we need her to roll over. *Pup*,' she said. '*Paw*.'

To the room's surprise, Pup rolled onto her back.

'Good girl. Now *sit*.'

Pup got up off the ground and went towards Cassandra.

'*Come!*' she cried and Pup promptly sat.

Cassandra checked her sheet. 'Ah yes. You'll like this one. *Pup, roll over*.'

Pup immediately lifted her right paw and Cassandra shook it. 'Isn't that cute?'

Bizarre rather than cute would have been Lily's word.

'I can't figure out how to get her to lie down but that's a pretty good start, right?'

Remembering the morning's adventures, Lily came to peer at the dog over Cassandra's shoulder. '*Wait*,' she said softly.

Pup dropped smartly as Cassandra clapped her hands in delight.

'You're a very strange dog,' Lily told her. 'You've the commands all wonky.'

At that, Pup scrambled to her feet and tried to come to heel as Lily edged quickly away.

'Would you look at that?' said Cassandra, reaching for a pencil. 'Wonky, eh? No wonder I couldn't figure that one out.'

Lily stepped around Pup and lowered herself into a kitchen chair, putting another chair beside her to block Pup from getting any closer. 'So let me get this straight. If you want her to sit, you say come. If you want her to come, you say sit. If you want the paw, it's roll over and if you want her to roll over you say paw?'

'And if you want her to come to heel you say wonky,' said Cassandra.

'Clear as mud,' said Betty. 'Do you think Noleen taught her that?'

'No,' said Lily, glancing at the animal who was on her back now, offering her belly up to Ned's ministrations. 'I think she's just doing it for kicks. Wait and see. It'll be like trying to crack the Enigma Code. All the commands will reset in the morning.'

But despite her scepticism, Lily found herself more relaxed around the dog, now there was at least the prospect of having some control over her. Pup was ordered to '*wait*' every time she came near her and, though she whimpered in protest, she did as she was told. In fact, she was as good as gold, bothering no one as she lay on the rug by the empty hearth while they watched a movie.

In consideration of Ned, a war epic was chosen. Cassandra and Betty hid behind cushions during the fighting and, when the love interest died, wept shamelessly. At some point between the explosions and heroism and the incessant heart-tugging of the violins, Pup edged her way over to Lily and put her head on her knee. Engrossed in the movie, Lily was patting her before she realised what she was about, surprised to discover ears that were warm and pliant and as soft as velvet. It felt ... nice. Even if her knee was getting damp. 'Alright,' she whispered, 'I'll try take you for a you-know-what tomorrow. But you can't go getting any ideas, okay? I'm not going to be your owner. Just so we're clear.'

And Pup thumped her tail as if she understood perfectly and wouldn't dream of making presumptions.

Chapter Sixteen

Rapunzel

The issue with the suppliers had been sorted with a few angry phone calls. After that Luke had returned to his house to find an email from the team he'd be working with at the ambulance service. It had schedules and equipment lists and contact details but his excitement was muted, even as he turned again to his course notes: **Scene Safety when Dealing with Narcotic Overdoses, The Different Types of Hypoxia, Joint Injuries and Dislocations**. But nothing new was going in. The sun was low when he finally gave up, grabbed his sketch pad and charcoals and headed up to the sandstone ledge to try to capture the view. But with his mind racing faster than his hand the result was a mess. The view inside his own head was the one he needed to pin down.

So he flipped to a fresh sheet, closed his eyes and saw Lily. Not as she was now but as she'd been that last night they'd been together. She hadn't planned on leaving him after all. Her smile in that moment had been a 'yes'. A promise in answer to his own. And with that certainty restored, he sketched the image and it became crystal clear in his mind once more, with all the force of his teenage feelings reattached.

But when he opened his eyes, the result on the page was more scary Picasso than serene Da Vinci.

So he flipped to another sheet and wrote instead. All the things he'd learned since breakfast: That Lily had been sent to boarding school against her wishes. That she thought it was because she'd disappointed her nana. That his mother had convinced her he'd moved on by lying to her about Katie.

He reread that last one a few times before he was in motion once more.

The pub was only half full when he arrived but there was no sign of his mother. His dad, however, was busy serving Donie, Eric and Pat at the bar. Pat was levering a beer mat under Eric's left elbow. Donie was pushing one under his right as Eric stared into the dregs of his glass as though the mystery of the universe was being resolved at the bottom.

Luke joined his dad behind the counter and from habit rolled up his sleeves and washed his hands.

Paudie was busy putting the head on a pint of stout.

'Did you know?' whispered Luke.

He paused and looked at him, assessing.

'That Lily rang here years ago? That she talked to–'

Paudie gave a quick nod and put a finger up to stall him. He passed the glass to a waiting hand and moved to the other side of the bar as Luke followed.

'She told me this morning. Guessed it was only a matter of time before Lily told you now she's staying. Making up that story about you and Katie being an item? Completely out of order. She knows where I stand on it.'

Luke glanced over to see Pat and Donie with their ears cocked. Eric slumped lower on his stool between them, the better to peer into his glass.

Luke turned his back to them again. 'She admitted it then?'

'Sure did. Proud as a peacock too. A mother's first duty is the welfare of her sons. As much as said this place wasn't good enough for ye. My home, her home and four lads raised as good as you like in it. Nothing ye didn't have that ye needed. Never wanted for anything. Good schooling. Good manners. No. Not good enough for her is what she really meant. I asked her why she stayed if she hated it so much and what does she say?'

'I don't know.'

'Says she'll like it just fine when she's running a wellness spa out of it. A spa, I ask you? Is it mad in the head she is? There'll be no spa here. We'd be a laughingstock. Who'd come all this way just to get their bits waxed?'

Luke's attention was caught by Eric who listed and then straightened himself with a jolt. Luke suddenly realised the stout had been for him. For a man whose liquid intake comprised ginger ale and the occasional light beer, stout was hitting the hard stuff.

'You alright there?' he asked, peering at him through the taps.

Eric lifted his head languidly. 'Yeah, I'm grand.'

'Why are you drinking that?'

He took a large gulp and winced. 'Don't know, man. Awful stuff.'

Luke turned to his dad who held up six fingers. Six pints already? 'Why do you keep ordering it, then?'

Eric wiped a line of foam from his mouth with the back of his hand. 'Because it's delicious.'

Luke scratched his head. 'Are you not heading over to the cottage to see Cass?'

Eric gave a little shiver and his head rolled slightly, as if too heavy for his neck to quite manage. 'Ah, I'm *coooooling* me jets on that.'

'You're cooling your jets? You mean you're breaking up with her?'

'*Shh!*' he said loudly. 'That's between me and me buddies here.' He gave Donie a good whack on the back but missed Pat by several inches and sliced the air instead. '*Whoa!*'

Pat's hand shot out to steady him and Eric laughed as he rolled back onto the seat.

'I thought you were mad about her?' Luke reminded him. 'Thought she was heaven. Better even than that Spanish girl?'

Eric smiled fondly and belched. 'Twice as better.'

'First cut, you said.'

'*Shh!*' Eric said even louder and attempted a cross face through a silly smile. He leaned forward and whispered as though only Luke could hear him. 'That is expeckily the problem. Plan all shot to bits, man. Head for the hills.'

'Once a woman tries to get her hooks in ya, you've gotta run,' agreed Donie. 'Don't let yourself be caught.'

'Ah, I don't know,' said Pat with a wistful sigh. 'Might be nice to have someone hookin' you – even if they were trying to run your life.'

'Is this because she was trying to get you to take a bit of time off?' said Luke. 'Because you've been floating that idea yourself for months.'

'That's right, that's right. I remember you saying that,' said Pat. 'You was having a pain in your head with all the driving around.'

'Maybe he did say that,' said Donie quickly, 'but he doesn't need a woman to go bossing him into it.'

'She wasn't bossing,' said Eric. 'I don't mind that. It's the staying part that's …' and he mumbled a few words Luke couldn't make out.

'What's that?'

Eric went back to staring at his glass.

'You're breaking up with her because she's going to *stay*? Are you mad? Finally a woman stays and it's the one you like the best. What could be better?'

Eric shook his head. 'You don't understand the plan, man. *Ha!* That rhymes.'

'What plan?' asked Paudie, giving up the pretence of not listening.

'The plan. *The* plan. The knowing-it's-only-for-a-while plan. The enjoy-it-while-you-can plan that ends in the have-a-good-life-and-no-hard-feelings plan. She's wrecking the plan and it's all your fault!'

'Me?' said Luke.

'If you hadn't tricked Lily into staying, Cass'd be going too.' His eyes widened with sudden hope. 'You can fix this. Give up your plot for revenge. Get Lily to go. Repent your evil ways. *Repent, I say!*' He held up one finger as though to add something momentous, then slumped back on his stool and took another swig of his drink.

The lounge door swung open. They turned to see Eithne holding it wide for Tadhg to hobble through. It was unclear who had wrangled whom downstairs to the bar that evening for neither looked too pleased to be there. Eithne's usual impatience at Tadhg's lack of pace was noticeably absent though. She kept herself a step behind, using him as a shield as they crossed the room. When they finally reached the bar, her eyes went from her husband to her son and back to her husband again.

'He knows,' Paudie told her, his tone grim.

Tadhg turned to Luke. 'Your mother wants a word with you.'

'You can tell her I'll never speak to her again.'

He got a poke in the shins from the end of Tadhg's walking stick. 'Good. You'll be able to listen for once. *Come on,*' he added in a tone that brooked no refusal. 'I'm not getting any younger.' He led the way to a quiet corner by the fireplace and pointed Luke into one chair and Eithne into another. He took the one between them, groaning loudly as he sat. With a nod to Eithne to start, he leaned back and closed his eyes.

Eithne straightened out the pleats of her skirt. Then she clasped her hands in her lap and examined her nails.

'You're sorry,' prompted Tadhg, eyes still closed.

'Yes,' she said, without looking up. 'But you'd have to be a parent yourself to really understand what it is to worry about your children and want them to achieve their full potential in life.'

'That's your defence? You wanted me to achieve my potential? By letting me get my heart broken? It's a wonder I survived your tender mercies.'

'Ah Luke. Please.'

'Please what? Do you even care what happened to Lily? She thought she'd been rejected. Abandoned even. Between Noleen not answering any of her calls and you not passing them on.'

'But how could I have known it would be that important, Luke? I mean, one little call.'

'Two,' he growled. 'When she actually spoke to you. But you must have realised she'd hung up on you several times before that.'

His mother faltered. 'I – I'm sure I don't remember any of that.'

'Do you remember telling Lily I was dating Katie Sullivan?'

She held up her hand. 'Now I might have said you were *hanging out* with Katie. But that would have been true enough, wouldn't it?'

He put his head in his hands. She wasn't going to admit she'd deliberately interfered. Not to him at least.

'I am sorry,' she said at last, 'if I said something I shouldn't have. But I can't undo it now. You're not to hate me.' And with that she got to her feet and walked away.

Tadhg waited ten seconds before he leaned in. 'She's not the best at apologies, is she?'

'No.' Luke righted himself. 'But there's something else I want to talk to *you* about, if you could take your detective hat out of retirement for a minute?'

Tadhg was all ears, delighted to be asked.

'Lily says the night before she was sent away, her nana came home all upset.'

'Oh?'

'She thinks whatever happened that night was the reason she was sent packing.'

Tadhg assumed his thinking position with his hands clasped and knees spread. 'So ...?'

'So where did Noleen go that night?'

'The pub. Where else is there to go here for company?'

'Except ...?'

Tadhg pursed his lips and thought. 'Except Noleen never came to the pub without Lily.'

'Correct. And she'd hardly have gone calling on Betty in the dark.'

Tadhg's fingers tapped for a minute. 'No,' he conceded. 'That does seem unlikely.'

'So where else? The night before Lily turned eighteen? When Lily was supposedly asleep in bed?'

Tadhg raised an eyebrow. 'Supposedly?'

'Actually asleep then. That's not the important bit.'

Tadhg grinned. 'You tell me. You clearly have a working theory.'

'What if she went to get a surprise for Lily's birthday?'

'Okay? And what kind of surprise would she need to get at night?'

'Flowers?'

There was a beat and then all enthusiasm vanished out of Tadhg's expression. 'I might have guessed you'd find a way to drag *him* into it.'

But Luke carried on undaunted. 'Hear me out. She went to get Lily a special bouquet or something for her birthday and went to Jasper's. It's the only answer.'

'It's *not*.'

'We need to interrogate Jasper about this. See what they talked about.'

'*We* don't need to interrogate anyone,' Tadhg said firmly. 'I'm long retired and you're ... well, not exactly his favourite person.'

'But–'

'If you'll hear me out just this once, Luke, I'll explain a very important principle of policing to you.'

'Go on.'

'A man can't be under suspicion just because you don't like him.'

Luke groaned. 'But what do we even know about him after all his years here? Always everything so secretive with him. Even his name sounds made up.'

'It's just the nature of his business. All that client confidentiality.'

'Do a background check.'

'Are you cracked? He arranges flowers for the church. He donates money to the Tidy Islands competition. He's spent years helping people suffering from alcohol addiction.'

'You mean he's above suspicion?'

'I mean what exactly is there to be suspicious about?'

That brought Luke up short. What was there exactly? What was Jasper's crime other than keeping to himself and ... making it clear he thought Lily was far too good for Luke? And hadn't he suspected that himself on more than one occasion?

With a defeated sigh he leaned back in the chair, turned his face to the empty hearth and tried to let his mind drift. It wouldn't though. Like a compass finding north it went straight to Lily, wondering what she was doing right now and if the morning's revelations were messing with her feelings the way they were messing with his?

Tadhg regained his attention at last with a soft tap of his stick. 'Why don't you just tell her you're still in love with her?'

'What diff–' he started. Then, 'Who says I am?'

'You do, you dope. Every time you look at her or talk about her or stare longingly at the sea when it's a certain shade of greeny-brown.'

'I've never done that,' he protested before he caught the teasing twinkle in his grandad's eye. 'Besides, even if I did still have feelings for her, who's to say she'd feel them back? She's a different person now. She's changed.'

'No, she's not. Just a bit more bluster.'

'It doesn't matter. Love is not a candle you can just relight.'

This pearl of wisdom, though, sent Tadhg into a kink. 'Where did you get that one?' he laughed. 'Love *is* a candle. It's one of those relighting ones they put on the kiddies' cakes. Love is like a boomerang. No wait, wait. Love is like a fluffy kitten–'

'Okay, okay, whatever. I can't just get Lily to love me again.'

'Course you can. Just do what you did last time.'

Luke could only shake his head in bemusement now. 'I didn't *do* anything last time. It just happened.'

'Fate?'

The twinkle was back in Tadhg's eyes. Luke didn't trust it one bit. Too like the flash of a lure.

'Maybe?'

Tadhg laughed again, delighted with himself now. 'Mush, you are. Pure mush. There's hope for you yet. Women love mush. Mush and persistence. That's the magic combo.' He cricked his head towards the bar, still smiling. 'What about Prince Charming? What happened to his fairy tale?'

Luke watched as Pat caught a listing Eric and set him back on his stool for a second time. 'Rapunzel let down her hair and he's discovered he's afraid of heights.'

'*Huh?*'

'Cassandra told him she's staying and now he's freaking out.'

Tadhg tutted. 'What a coward.' He hauled himself up and out of the seat with a series of low groans. 'I'll say this for you, my lad. You've never been that.' He laid a hand on his shoulder. 'Next time you see Lily just ask her where she thinks ye'd be right now if she hadn't been sent away? See what happens.' And with a parting grin he excused himself to join his friends at the bar.

Chapter Seventeen

Wonky

Lily was on the road at noon the following day with the lead in her hand and the dog trotting neatly beside her. She was relieved to have escaped some of the pre-wedding tension at the cottage. With just a day to go there seemed a dozen critical details had yet to be decided. But, as it had become clear Lily knew even less about wedding planning than she did about dogs, she'd been excused for half an hour.

She was in just as much trouble financially as she'd been yesterday and, to add to her woes, she was exhausted. For the first time since she'd come back her sleep had been fitful: full of dreams of Luke, invariably shirtless. His arm around her as he whispered her name. Holding a baby while singing to it softly. Facing off against a hippo while armed with a strimmer? That one had been weird. But nonetheless her spirits, at this moment, were high. She was chuffed in fact at her own daring to be out alone walking a dog. Not just walking but *training*. Every time Pup veered off Lily said "*Wonky*" and, when Pup returned to her side, she immediately said "*Heel*" and reinforced this amended command with a small piece of the toast she'd taken the precaution of bringing with her.

After a while she just had to say "Heel" to bring Pup back in line and her confidence soared. This dog business was a cinch.

Shay passed in his tractor and Lily raised a hand in greeting. And then, coming around a bend in the distance she spied Bríd with what Lily initially mistook for a sheep trotting beside her, but which turned out to be a large white dog with a big wide head and an expression of dopey delight on its face. The animal was not on any lead, nor under instruction to stay by Bríd's side it seemed as, after a momentary halt on seeing Pup, it charged towards them with its tail doing circles, breaking to a halt at the last second to sniff Pup nose to nose, as Lily held her breath and moved to keep Pup between her and it.

'*Cooper! Be a good boy!*' called Bríd, just at the moment it – he – was having the impertinence to try to sniff Pup's behind.

Lily was pleased to see Pup put a swift end to that by promptly sitting down. Cooper's response was to instantly abase himself on his belly, as if to show Pup how harmless he was, before just as abruptly racing off in one direction only to turn and race back in the other. He kept going, doing wild, elliptical laps as Bríd finally reached them, excused the madness with the word '*zoomies*', and explained she was on her way to help Kitty the Church fix herself lunch. Apparently the poor woman had injured her shoulder trying to help a bullock out of a ditch. Pup did Lily proud while this injury was discussed. She neither moved nor barked the whole time, content to have Lily playing with her ears even as the white blur kept circling.

Sending her best wishes to Kitty, Lily said goodbye to Bríd and watched in relief as Cooper went with her. Then Lily praised Pup for being 'a very good girl compared to that mad yolk' and they walked on and were just passing the shop when Lily's phone rang. It was a number she didn't recognise but, in a moment of unaccountable optimism, she answered it. 'Hello?'

'Are you actually trying to end your career?'

Her stomach lurched. 'Preston?'

'When I fire someone I expect them to at least *try* to negotiate their way out of it. I've rearranged your meeting for ten o'clock on Friday. The client is being very accommodating. I'll see you in my office at nine.'

Lily tried to process this. She'd been fired? When had that happened?

'He saw your photo on the website and now he'll only deal with you. *Quelle surprise!*'

Her hackles rose at that. As if all the qualifications listed underneath her photograph had no bearing whatsoever. 'Which put you in a difficult position when you'd fired me, I suppose?'

'Not at all,' he said airily. 'If you get back here and do your job we'll forget about that. I hate to remind you,' he added, in a tone which suggested just the opposite, 'there's the small matter of fifty thousand pounds you still owe me. I don't want to take you to court for it, Lily, but if you quit – and I have to say that feels like what's happening here – then you have no way of paying it back. And, if you have no way to pay it back, I'll have you declared bankrupt myself. No one will hire you as an accountant ever again.'

Panic bubbled to life inside her as the harsh realities of her situation came crashing back. Could he really get her declared bankrupt? 'I'm not quitting, Preston. I never said that.'

'Then why aren't you here?'

'Because I inherited a property. I'm trying to figure out what to do with it.'

'Well, I'd have thought that was beyond obvious.' There was a long pause, then, 'Describe it. You said you were on an island?'

'Yes. Off the coast of Cork. It's just a cottage.'

'How many bedrooms?'

'Three.'

'Land?'

'Half an acre.'

'Overlooked?'

'No.'

'Do you have a photograph?'

'Yes?'

'Send it to me with the exact location. I'll be back to you in ten. Make sure you answer.'

Lily tapped into her phone's album, selected the only photo she'd taken, and sent it along with the address. What was Preston playing at? He had a property portfolio to boast about but he wouldn't be interested in something as humble as a little cottage surely?

Eight minutes later he was back. 'What's your expectation price-wise?'

Lily took the figure she had in mind, added a hefty chunk and stated it with confidence. 'Four hundred and fifty thousand.'

Preston didn't even baulk. 'Sterling or Euros?'

'Euros.'

'Perfect. The Eddingtons will take it off your hands.'

'Who?'

'Tania and Geoffrey. Friends of mine. They'll think that's a bargain. They've been looking for a cutesy Irish bolt-hole to modernise for ages. Were outbid on two last year. You get to fix your finances and I'll get my money back and we'll move on. You're welcome.'

Lily was stunned. A quick sale at a great price. Exactly what she'd dreamed of a week ago but ... 'When you say modernise?'

'The usual. They'll leave the front intact and tear out the guts and back. Extend and redo. Plenty of scope with half an acre. Particularly as it's not overlooked.'

'But, but I couldn't just let the place be destroyed. It was my childhood home. No. Thank you, Preston, but I'll find someone who loves it as it is.'

'Not in the hurry you're in, you won't!' he snapped.

He was right, of course. Whatever about settling the will, it could take months to find another buyer even if she listed the property tomorrow. With no guarantee of getting such a great price either.

'Your landlord called again by the way.'

Feck!

Preston let a deep sigh, as if this was all very distressing to him. 'What I don't understand is how you can be so fastidious with other people's money but so soft with your own.'

'That's not true.'

'No? An idiot you barely knew bungee-jumped out of a building to impress you and instead of running a mile you paid his medical bills.'

Okay, yes, that maybe hadn't been the smartest call from a strictly financial point of view.

'Leaving you broke, on the verge of eviction, absent without permission and owing me money. With a property you won't sell to bail yourself out? I try to be understanding, Lily, I really do. But it feels like I'm all that stands between you and financial Armageddon right about now. Am I right?'

Lily felt an imaginary noose tightening around her neck.

'And I'm sure running away feels like the answer but we have to be grown-ups. Accept reality. And the reality is you can't afford to be precious about this cottage, can you?'

She swallowed. 'No.'

There was another silence before Preston spoke again, his tone now conciliatory. 'I appreciate things have been difficult but I need you to come back to work. And when you sell the cottage and your debt to me is repaid, we can look at giving you a raise – tied to some extra responsibilities. Put you into a position to rent something better. Closer to work. A place you won't have to share with anyone. How does that sound?'

A week ago she might have said great. But now? 'Okay.'

'Okay. Good. So I'll see you back here the day after tomorrow.'

The line went dead and Lily felt ill. She knew it was her own fault she was in this mess but couldn't help feeling as if Preston had trapped her into an escape route of his own design. She could have her financial freedom from him eventually but the price was letting Nana's cottage be destroyed. She'd get more than it was worth on paper, sure, but at the cost of a piece of her soul.

And then she remembered Luke and that it was his cottage now too. How would he feel about selling it only for it to be gutted?

And she couldn't sell it without his agreement. Hope and despair made for confusing companions as they walked on, Pup whimpering sympathetically now as Lily absently flipped the lock switch on the handle of the lead forward and back and then forward again.

They'd just reached the viewing point when a cackle of magpies sounded in the distance. Pup halted, her tail quivering, then dashed out of sight through a gap between two gnarly hawthorns. The line of the lead lengthened with a whizzing sound and, before Lily had even thought to brace herself, it snapped taut again and she was being yanked along behind, through the gap and into an overgrown field. Lily was surprised to see there was a new road here, well, a dirt track at least, that headed in the direction of Hook Cove. But it wasn't the moment to explore it when she was scrambling to keep herself upright as she lost sight of Pup in a dense tangle of tall ferns. They smacked her legs hard and repeatedly as she struggled in Pup's wake. '*Wonky! Wonky! You stupid mutt!*' There was only the crash of foliage though until a line of gorse suddenly loomed and Lily finally caught sight of Pup again at full throttle, heading for a narrow gap between two large bushes. She never broke stride as she ran through them, fitting perfectly.

Lily, however, was not so fortunate. If she'd had the chance to turn sideways she might have made it but she was clinging to the lead with both hands and met the gap head on, her arms and shoulders snagging painfully on each side. The resulting abrupt halt tore the breath from her lungs and the lead from her hands. Pinioned, she could only watch as Pup continued on with the lead trailing, several magpies bursting into flight before her. '*Wait!*' she yelled.

'Lily?' Luke appeared along the dirt track, carrying a bulging paper bag in his arms.

Like a missile re-engaging its target, Pup swerved sharply and charged towards him. She launched herself at him, barking wildly. The bag flew right as he was sent left but Luke was back on his feet in seconds and continuing towards Lily as she carefully detached herself from the gorse, trying to avoid any tears to the fabric of her blouse. Pup circled, bounding joyously, then leapt at Luke from the other side. It was like a sequence from last night's movie: the hero advancing through enemy lines, soldiering on as he was blasted repeatedly from every angle. When he finally reached Lily's side she didn't know whether to offer sympathy or applause. Pup circled for one more assault and Lily shouted "*Wait!*" again and the next moment they were horizontal as Pup jumped Luke from behind, felling them both in one move.

Sandwiched between the hardness of Luke's body and the ground, Lily was aware of several things simultaneously. The heat of him seeping into her bones. His musky scent filling her nostrils. The minty breath that tickled her lips. And that Luke's face framed by blue sky was still the most gorgeous sight she'd ever seen.

'Hi,' he said with a smile that would have left her breathless had she any air left to lose.

She tried to say something back but only managed a whimper before he was pushing himself up off her.

But he halted mid-rise and a sharp inhale was followed by, 'Lily?'

She lifted her head, only to see him staring at her right leg, where her baggy shorts had ridden all the way up. High enough to reveal ...

She scrambled off the ground and turned away from him, brushing the shorts down and fixing her blouse which had been pulled out of the waistband.

'What happened to your leg, Lil?'

'Nothing,' she said automatically. Which was the most stupid answer she could have given him. She might as well have waved a flag in his direction with the words, '*Something to see here*' written on it.

Sure enough he took a step closer, his expression of concern intensifying. 'What happened to you? That's a serious scar.'

'Yes. I broke my leg. It was serious. Now it's not.'

'How did you break it?'

But the lie she habitually spun about a paragliding accident just wouldn't come out. 'I was just ... in the wrong place at the wrong time.'

'Meaning?'

'Nothing.' She went to turn away from him again but in a blink his arm slid around her waist, preventing her, and his splayed hand pressed her to him as his chin rested on the top of her head. He was ... holding her. It was as unexpected as it was confusing.

'What are you doing, Luke?'

She felt him swallow hard.

'*Trying to mind you?*' he rasped.

'What?'

'You started this. Just go with it.'

'But the dog,' she said, faintly, even as her cheek pressed against his chest and she heard the comforting beat of his heart through the brush of shirt fabric.

'Is fine. Are your eyes closed?'

'Yes,' she lied as she cringed. This was way less awkward when drunk.

'Good,' he said. 'Now tell me what happened.'

'Are you trying to hypnotise it out of me?'

He just sighed. 'What happened, Lily?'

'*Why?*' she choked.

'Because my imagination is conjuring the worst scenarios right now and if I don't know what happened to you I'm going to need to find something to punch.'

Her mind fell silent as she absorbed that, though her heart started to race as if desperate to get to his. 'I was hit by a van, okay? It was my own fault. I stepped into the road.'

He tensed at that. 'Were you feeling sad?'

It took her a moment before she realised what he was asking. If she'd done it deliberately. If she'd been suicidal. 'No, no. It was just an accident. I was careless. I just made a stupid mistake.'

She felt him take a few deep breaths. 'Okay. A mistake. And when did it happen?'

'*Um*, a good long while ago.'

'I guessed that from how much the scar is healed. But how old is it exactly?'

The words 'fifteen weeks' were on her tongue. She grappled them back.

His other hand came up and started stroking her head, smoothing down the length of her hair only to repeat the action again. It was distracting and relaxing in equal measure. She could see why Pup liked it.

'Should I start wagging my tail?'

His hand stilled. '*Fuck.* Sorry.' He released her and stepped back but his eyes found hers again and stayed. 'Does Cassandra know this happened to you?'

She wasn't sure why that mattered? 'She's seen the scars, yes.'

'Did your nana know?'

She hesitated for just a beat. 'The Principal was informed I'd been in a traffic accident and passed that on to her, yes.'

He studied her. 'The Principal? So this happened while you were at that school?'

Her heart started to race again and not in a pleasant way. Her chin rose, though, and she gave what she hoped was a flippant shrug. 'A bummer, right? No one wanted me on their team for Sports Day. Oh well.'

But Luke's eyes flared and he gripped her chin between his thumb and forefinger. 'Why do you do that?'

'Do what?' she said.

'*That?*' he repeated, still gripping her chin. 'Pretending you don't care. That nothing hurts you?'

'Because nothing does.'

He leaned closer, his eyes never leaving hers. And though he said nothing, she heard the word *liar* clear as day.

Her face heated. She pulled her chin free and looked for Pup. She was heading towards the paper bag which had split apart to reveal a pile of groceries. '*Pup, come!*' she called, using the excuse to put some distance between her and Luke's X-ray vision. 'No, not come. What was it? *Rollover?* No. *Sit. Sit!*'

A glance back to Luke showed him looking concerned all over again. 'Did you bang your head when we fell?'

'No – I – never mind.'

But the next second he was sprinting past her, grabbing the dog's lead just before Pup got her maws on a packet of sliced ham. He reached for a loaf of bread next and then a carton of milk before Lily snapped herself out of it long enough to rescue a block of butter, two tins of beans, a cucumber and several tomatoes. The ripped bag was as good as useless now so she just scrunched it into a ball and put it in her pocket.

Luke returned to her side where he swapped Pup's lead for the rest of the groceries, until they were stacked into a precarious pyramid in his arms. 'Well, lunch is saved anyway,' he said.

'Lunch?' she rasped.

'Aren't you running low on supplies?'

'*Huh?*'

'At the cottage?'

'This is for the cottage?' she managed. 'You were bringing food for the people at the cottage?' She sounded like an idiot but the realisation that all Luke's disappointment in her yesterday hadn't kept him away today hit like a ton of bricks. He'd deliberately sought her out again. To make sure she was fed. To ... mind her. Because even after everything he still cared.

And a risk analysis opened in her mind. **Title: Luke O'Callaghan. Probabilities against Impact Levels**, with a range from **Insignificant to Catastrophic.**

'Lil?'

She looked to him and gulped. 'Yeah?'

There was a trace of a smile around his lips again. 'Are you sure you didn't hit your head?'

She managed an insignificant nod. Her heart, however, gave one catastrophic flutter.

'So will we go?'

Chapter Eighteen

Thistle Seed

When Luke had decided to bring whatever food he had left in his cupboards to the cottage, he hadn't expected to meet Lily on the way there. Or have her pinned beneath him minutes later. And he certainly hadn't expected to see evidence of a traumatic injury to her leg. Or find her so cagey about discussing it.

In the wrong place at the wrong time? And the Principal had to be *informed*? And something about the formality of that word made him wonder in what exact scenario Lily had found herself beside a road while at boarding school? For only two immediately came to mind. She'd either been on a school tour or she hadn't. And if she hadn't, she'd been travelling without money, seeing as she'd left her Post Office savings book behind. He hadn't missed that odd flinch of hers yesterday when he'd mentioned hitchhiking. All while telling her there was nothing *he* wouldn't have done to get back to her. And now he felt like an ass. Because if she had tried to hitchhike back to him, she'd ended up with a broken leg for her troubles.

He mulled it over as they reached the road together, walking in silence as Lily chewed on her lip. He decided to try to pick up where they'd left off yesterday. 'I don't suppose you'd any luck finding your nana's letter, in the end?'

'No,' Lily addressed the path, 'but I now know for sure that there *is* a letter. Seánie confirmed it and said it was going to explain all about the will.'

'But he'd no idea where it might be?'

'No.' She went back to chewing her lip.

'Well, I've been trying to make sense of some things overnight. I mean about your nana sending you away in the first place. And I was wondering what she actually said to you that morning when you were getting on the ferry? Did she really say she was disappointed in you?'

'No. But she didn't have to, Luke. She just stood at the end of the pier and never even waved. Like I was a blow-in just blowing out again.'

It was said lightly but he could hear the hurt behind it loud and clear. 'You were never a blow-in, Lil.'

She turned away, hiding her expression as she made a show of fussing over the dog. But her shoulders had tightened. 'Jasper says I am. He means it as a compliment but maybe he's right, you know? Maybe I never really belonged here.'

Bloody Jasper. Always messing with Lily's insecurities by insisting she was *different*. The way Jasper liked to imagine himself different, Luke supposed. Different as in *better,* naturally.

Luke set down the groceries, darted off and made several jumps, his arm swiping the air before returning to her side clutching a thistle seed.

He held it out to her, the seed part lifting and falling uselessly as its fluffy wings were held in the pinch of his fingertips.

'Where did this come from?'

Lily raised her eyes to his at last but with a look that expressed concern for his faculties. 'I don't know. Some field?'

'Which field?' he pressed. 'Tell me the exact one.'

'I don't know. It could have come from any field.'

He held it up to examine it more closely as sunlight bounced off his watch and scattered tiny rainbows across her face. 'It could have come from the mainland, right?'

'It could have come from anywhere, I guess. If the wind carried it far enough.'

'A blow-in, you might say?'

She hesitated. 'Yes?'

'But if it lands in a good place it'll grow. That's all it takes. A good place, a bit of rain and some sunshine, and then it belongs.'

He brought the seed to his lips, gave a strong puff and set it loose. It went about two feet before drifting back to earth to land on his shoe. He could see Lily trying not to smile. Not quite the uplifting moment he'd been counting on.

'You landed in a good place,' he ploughed on, his face heating. 'You were fed and watered and loved and you grew. It doesn't matter where you came from. Do you understand what I'm trying to say?'

She raised an eyebrow. 'I understand you're trying to compare me to a thistle.'

'You? A thistle? More like a rose, Lil. Out of season,' he added, which just made her laugh.

The sound warmed him. He bent to retrieve the supplies.

Lily waited till he'd rejoined her then gave Pup's lead a tug and they moved forward together once more.

'It's a nice thought, Luke, but even if I could belong here again it's just not feasible and ... there's an offer on the cottage. A good one. We should really accept.'

He was astonished. 'But it's not even on the market yet.'

'I know but a friend of my boss wants to buy it.'

A friend of ... ? 'The asshole that fired you?'

She cocked her head in confusion. 'How do you know I was fired?'

He pictured Cassandra deleting that message. '*Umm* ...'

'Well, I'm not fired. At least not anymore. But this friend has plans to gut the cottage. To just leave the front wall standing. But I can't afford to wait for another buyer to come along who loves it the way it is.' She sighed. 'I know it's stupid. I'm just being sentimental. It's only a building.'

'It's not stupid. It was a home, Lil. Your home. You're entitled to be sentimental about it. But is there no way you could keep it?'

'Not unless I win the lottery. Even if I hadn't any other debts, just inheriting the cottage makes me liable to inheritance tax. As a grown-up granddaughter I don't get much of an exemption. You're liable too, by the way, now you're inheriting half.'

He was about to protest again that he had no intention of inheriting anything, when another option suddenly occurred to him. 'What if I did take half and then bought out your half?'

'What do you mean?'

'I mean, I'll buy your share of the cottage and keep it safe for you. You can buy it back from me at a later date when you get yourself sorted.'

She gasped. 'I couldn't possibly ask you to do that.'

'Why not?'

'Because it could be years before I'd be in a position to buy it back. If ever. And in the meantime you'd have an inheritance tax bill to pay and how would you even afford it?'

He shrugged. 'I have some savings left from working in Dubai and an asset I could part with that I'm, *uh*, not expecting to need in the future.'

'Really?'

'Yes. Really.'

But she was shaking her head again. 'I don't know, Luke. You'd have to get independent financial advice. I couldn't – not with a vested interest – and what would you even do with the cottage?'

He shrugged. 'Rent it out? Use it as a B&B?'

She scratched her forehead. 'I suppose it would be good for you to have somewhere else to live besides the hotel. A bit of space to call your own?'

He thought about his house at Hook Cove but just smiled. 'Sure. So, you'll think about it?'

'Yes. Okay. But only if you do too.'

That resolved as far as was possible, he asked how Cassandra was doing then and inadvertently stepped on a landmine.

'She's miserable, Luke. Where *does* that person you call a friend hide himself when he's not driving the bus?'

'Ah, he's not hiding. He's just trying to work out a few things.'

'Like what? Deciding if he's interested in her again? He did *all* the chasing. Then as soon as she shows the first sign of interest he bolts.'

'The first sign? She told him she's staying here. For him. For good. They've barely known each other a few days. And he *is* interested. I've never heard him go on so much about a woman. She just caught him off guard.'

She was silent for a moment and then, 'I just don't understand how it got so serious between them *and* so screwed up so quickly.'

He couldn't help but smile. 'You know, you're very protective for someone she's convinced wants rid of her. She's very fond of you, you know?'

But he watched her just shrug that off.

'Cassandra is fond of everyone. Her only failing. But you don't need to worry about her. She has a family that dotes on her. She makes friends at the drop of a hat. I don't know how many times she's been asked to be a bridesmaid. She just doesn't see how great she is and you can tell her till you're blue in the face–' She drew a breath. 'I just don't understand how someone with so much love in their life can have so little self-confidence.'

Recalling Cassandra's take on Lily, he was smiling again.

'What?'

'Nothing.'

'She doesn't need Eric knocking the little self-confidence she does have.'

'I know, I know. That's the furthest thing from his mind, I swear. I think he's the one with the self-confidence issue really but I *oooooh*–' He yawned so hard his jaw cracked. 'Sorry. I can't seem to sleep at all since you're back.'

'Really? That's weird. I've been sleeping like a log. Sweet dreams all the way.'

'Oh? Was I in any?'

It had been asked in jest but to his surprise Lily went bright red. 'No.'

He tipped his head as he examined her. '*My, what big eyes you've got!* Sure I wasn't in at least *one*?'

'Why yes,' she said, recovering fast. 'Now I remember I had a dream about the most annoying person in the world and you were in it.'

He leaned closer, delighted. 'So what exactly was I doing in this dream?'

'I think you're missing the point of that particular insult.'

He laughed and put an arm around her neck in a mock headlock, the other balancing the groceries precariously. 'Your eyes are all bloodshot. Are you sure you're sleeping well?'

'Perfectly.' She shrugged him off but her smile was back, along with the sparkle in her eyes. 'I think I'm just allergic to the dog.'

He glanced at the animal trotting neatly beside her. 'It doesn't look that way. How did you get her to do that?'

'Bribery.'

Pup looked up at Lily adoringly.

'There's no point looking at me now like butter wouldn't melt. You lost all credibility after that bank of ferns. I'm on to you.'

They walked in comfortable silence after that, taking turns with Pup's lead and the groceries. Lily made no effort to hide her delight when Pup paid no heed to any of Luke's commands and kept trying to walk by her side.

It made him happy to see her so relaxed around a dog, though. Maybe there was method to Cassandra's madness after all?

They made quick progress around An Fáinne and through the tunnel of trees but as they approached the hostel they heard a distinctive clatter.

Luke shot her a look that asked her to please be nice to his friend.

Her replying glance was one that made no promises.

Eric slammed on the brakes, his haggard face looking pitiful through the rolled-down window. 'You're needed at the cottage. The wedding rehearsal is cancelled. Father Daly has the mumps. He's getting a replacement but he won't be here till tomorrow so there mightn't even be a wedding at this stage. Betty's in a state. Mervyn's getting the blame. Ned's looking anxious.'

Lily's hands went to her hips. 'And how's Cassandra? How's she doing?'

'Fine. I think.'

'Happy to see you, was she?'

He winced. 'Ah, not so much. She's pretending I don't exist this morning.'

'Good,' said Lily and strode off with Pup.

But Eric detained Luke with an urgent grasp on his arm. 'Have you told her you're leaving yet?' he whispered.

'No. I'll get to it.'

'I really feel sick, you know?'

Luke gave his friend a look of sympathy. 'Well, you shouldn't have drunk so much last night, should you?'

'It's not that, it's Cassie. It's all wrong.' He tapped his chest. 'Here. You have to get her to go back to London with Lily. I can't cope with her looking through me like that again. Fix it, man, or I will. I'm so far off the plan now it's not even funny.'

He sped off, leaving Luke with a sprint to catch Lily.

He reached her just as Betty emerged from the porch, wringing her hands.

'Well? Did you hear? This whole wedding is cursed. No priest now.' She headed back inside but Lily didn't follow. Instead, she took a few steps back and stared up at the cottage, her eyes roving over the facade. Then she moved to the porch and hauled up the wisteria that was lying in a tangled heap in front of it. She reattached it to the cable ties nailed around the frame. They held for a moment before dumping the branches back across the doormat.

He was about to ask what she was doing when Betty stuck her head out the door again and glanced between them.

'Would you check how Jasper's getting on with the wedding flowers, Lily? With the way today's going he's probably in some kind of trouble.'

'Oh, *um*, sure. Yes. I can do that. Let me just grab a sandwich first.'

Lily brought Pup inside and came back a moment later to take the groceries from Luke. She was gone less than two minutes after that before she reemerged, munching. 'Thanks for the food, Luke, and, *num*, sorry to rush off. I don't suppose you could hold the fort here while I'm gone?'

He heard 'wait for me' in that but perhaps it was just wishful thinking. Still, he nodded and watched once more as she strode away.

'What do they talk about, do you think?'

Luke clutched his chest. He hadn't realised Betty was standing behind him. 'Who?'

'Lily and Jasper. An odd little duo. Noleen had her issues about it.'

'Really?' This was news. 'Since when?'

'Since always, I think, as a kind of a niggle. But then of course you went and put the cat among the pigeons that night at the pub and he was off the Christmas list after that for sure.'

'What are you talking about?'

'When you tried to get him barred because you said the way he was looking at Lily was all wrong.'

Ah yes. An incident he'd much rather have forgotten. It had been the week before Lily turned eighteen and had proven a humiliating lesson in picking his fights and his moment. Unable to explain exactly what Jasper's crime had been – other than to set his eyes on Lily in a way that didn't seemed to Luke to be that of a mentor towards a student – he'd been on shaky ground from the start. Never mind the fact Lily herself was roundly defending Jasper, while Jasper somehow managed to look the picture of innocence. His dad had told him to apologise to Jasper at once. He had but with his teeth gritted. Jasper was not only *not* barred but had passed the whole incident off with great dignity, insisting he held no grudge and making magnanimous excuses for 'young hotheads'.

'I've always maintained he's a good egg, Jasper,' continued Betty. 'Just very, very private. But of course that's the worst sin you can have living here. Trying to keep things to yourself. Seems suspicious to some. I was forever telling Noleen that.'

She returned inside just as the minibus arrived, rolling to a torturous stop.

'Have you told her you're leaving yet?' Eric asked, climbing out.

'No. I said I'll get to it.' Determined to finally make it inside the cottage, he left Eric to follow him or not.

In the sitting room Cassandra was poring over wedding plans. 'The way you have the seating is perfect now, Betty,' she was saying as he came in. 'Everyone has a view of the top table and almost everything else is sorted. Eithne has the food and drink all ready, I'll be doing your make-up, we'll have a replica priest tomorrow and it'll all be wonderful, you'll see. And I haven't given up on the idea of finding a dress for Lily to wear so she can be a bridesmaid too. Something red to match mine.'

'I don't think I've anything suitable,' said Betty, 'but maybe Eithne? She's more the right size. Will you ask her when you're over at the hotel, Eric? You're heading that way for the next ferry, right?'

Eric glanced at his watch. 'Well, not for another while but ...' He looked at Cassandra who'd yet to take her eyes from her papers, though her face was beetroot. 'If anyone wanted to come along we could maybe wait at the bar? Have a drink and a sandwich and – and a chat?'

No one said anything.

'*Ca – ssie?*' asked Eric, his voice breaking. 'How about you?'

'No, thank you,' she said, shuffling the pages randomly.

'Why not?'

She looked up at last, her little chin raised higher than usual. 'Because you don't go where you're not wanted.' She turned back to Betty as Eric backed out of the room.

Half a minute later the minibus was away.

Luke used the time to do a quick staging of the cottage. Betty's neat two-seater and armchair were a much better combination in the sitting room and he rearranged the placement so neither was blocking the window. He fixed the ornaments on the mantelpiece – by removing half of them – and then replaced the dusty painting above it with a mirror from the scullery and re-dressed the sofa by rearranging the throws and cushions. He'd swapped out the chairs in the kitchen for Betty's already but left Lily's floral arrangement on the table where it looked perfect. The ugly net curtains at each side of the kitchen window went next as they only hid the view. He screwed tight the hinges on several drooping cupboards, switched around the ornaments in the bathroom, dressed Lily's now empty bookcase with some wicker storage boxes he found and beat a beach-full of sand out of all the rugs. The only thing left was to remove the double bed from the study but this would have to wait until he had the trailer again and someone to help with lifting.

He returned to the living room at the same time as Betty. 'Have you seen my bolero anywhere, Cassie?'

She shook her head. 'No. Sorry. I haven't.'

'Well, I need it. It's part of my going-away outfit.'

'Of course. So where did you last see it?'

'It was in the study. On a suitcase. I knew exactly where it was and then *he*,' she said, turning to glare at Luke, 'took it all away.'

'I was under instructions to take everything away,' he protested. 'I didn't know your wedding stuff was in there. But I'll get it. No problem.'

'Okay. Good. It's satin and it's crimson.'

'Right,' said Luke. 'And tell me what a bolero is?'

But Betty suddenly heaved in a breath, went bright red and put her hand to her chest. 'For the love of God!'

And Luke speedily backed up. 'Okay. Don't worry. I'll get it.'

'Yes. And be quick, won't you?' pleaded Betty. 'Before anything else for this wedding goes wrong. I swear I'm about to have palpitations.'

As Cassandra's entreaty was added to Betty's, before Luke knew what was happening he was being hustled out the front door and back down the lane.

Chapter Nineteen

Daisy Chains

The trip to the hostel felt shorter than it had before. Lily wasn't quite sure how to account for it, except that her steps and her heart both felt a few pounds lighter. And a little smile seemed to have affixed itself to her face.

She knocked and Jasper shouted for her to let herself in.

He was in his kitchen hemmed in by flowers. Two rows deep in humble plastic buckets were exquisite red peonies and roses interspersed with bundles of assorted foliage. On the table were some pale-green succulents in little pots – looking like smooth but fleshy flowers, tinged pink at the edges. Next to these were dishes already fitted out with floral foam. A huge roll of black ribbon and floral tape lay by Jasper's elbow.

He was dethorning the roses, feeding the stems through his fingers as a small knife hit target after target. *Snip, snip, snip*. The air was so thick with fragrance Lily almost expected it to offer resistance as she picked her way through to a seat across the table. 'I've come to help. Betty thought you might be swamped.'

'Thanks but I'm fine.'

She plucked a rose from the nearest bucket anyway, let the water drip from the stem, and looked about her for a knife. There was one at the end of the table. Its handle was ergonomic but the blade wickedly sharp as she discovered when she ran it over the first thorn and promptly sliced herself.

‘That’s not for playing with.’

‘I wasn’t *playing* with it. It’s just sharper than it looks.’

‘So it’s the knife’s fault?’ With a grunt, Jasper extricated himself from his flowery den, fetched the first aid kit and handed it to her.

She rummaged inside, found a plaster and stuck it on. Then she searched for the knife again but it had mysteriously vanished. ‘Seriously? I can help. You’ve a lot to get through.’ She looked about for something else she could do. ‘I could take the excess leaves off the peonies?’

‘I’m going to leave that till later.’

‘I could get the succulents ready. I remember how to do them.’

He snipped several more thorns as he made her wait. ‘Use the twenty-two-gauge wire and make sure the stems are good and strong.’

Lily reached for the nearest little pot and teased the succulent from its soil bed, careful to keep its short, stubby root intact. After a quick wash at the sink, she carefully pushed a length of wire through the root and, with the help of a wooden stake and some floral tape, created an artificial stem for it: starting at the root and working the tape around it, the wire and the stake, binding them all together as she stretched and twisted her way to the bottom. When she was finished, the succulent had a long and perfectly straight stem and was ready to go into a bouquet. ‘Will that do?’

Jasper glanced over and nodded. ‘Very nice.’

He went back to working through his thorns while Lily prepared five more succulents as the tune of 'Scarborough Fair' started up in her head. She'd forgotten how much she enjoyed working with flowers – the colours, the scents, the softness against her fingertips. So different from running calculations and checking balances.

Jasper finished removing the thorns and they started together on the damaged guard petals. When that was done they broke for tea and then Jasper suggested, without much subtlety, that it was probably time for her to go.

He walked her to the doorstep but she detained him there by asking if she could just get his thoughts on something first.

'Of course.'

'There's someone interested in buying the cottage. It'd be a quick sale at a great price.'

'That's good news, isn't it?'

'Yes, but I'm racking my brains to see if there's any way I could keep it instead.' A way other than using Luke's money. 'And I know I couldn't exactly commute between here and London but maybe I could set up an accountancy practice here? Well, not here, here. But in the local area? Or offer my services online, seeing as we've gone all high-speed now? But if I'm declared bankrupt that won't be a runner–'

'*Bankrupt?*'

'No bank would touch me but maybe I could make bouquets again as a second job? Or give up food. I could become one of those forager people that live off the land. Seaweed is supposed to be very beneficial, right?'

He rubbed his forehead. 'This is just a first draft of your ideas, I hope?'

'What if selling turns out to be a terrible mistake? What if I blow out of here and never land anywhere good again?'

Jasper was silent for a moment. 'What does Luke have to say about it?'

She hesitated. 'Why does that matter?'

He looked over her shoulder, his gaze sweeping his garden. 'Because I can't help wondering if it's because he's going away that you're now considering staying or because he's had a change of heart himself about leaving?'

That took a moment to untangle. 'What do you mean he's going away?'

'Because ... Cork?'

'Cork?'

Jasper looked back to her, his confusion apparent. 'He's been commuting to Cork these last few years. He's about to start living there full-time. Did he not tell you?'

Lily took a small step back as her chest tightened. 'No. He never said a word.'

'But has he been suggesting you should stay?'

'Well, not in so many words.'

'So what put the thought of staying into your head then?'

Lily looked out at the garden herself now and caught sight of a drifting thistle seed. And the ground beneath her slowly shifted. What story exactly had she started telling herself off the back of their earlier conversation? Luke had said something nice about her not being a blow-in and she'd jumped on right ahead to imagining he wanted her to stay. And he'd brought her some food so she'd jumped on to imagine he must still care about her. As if he couldn't just bring it because he was a thoughtful guy. Or say something nice because he was just kind.

'Why would Luke encourage you to stay if he's not going to be around?' Jasper insisted.

'I don't know. He probably didn't.'

Jasper's brow furrowed. 'Well, don't make any big decisions until you find out what he's at.'

No. She certainly wouldn't. Not when it would have such major financial repercussions for her. Of course, Luke wouldn't have known the full extent of those when he was throwing about his random weed analogies. Or guessed he was making her long for something that might never add up on paper.

'He's leaving for good the day after the wedding,' Jasper added, for good measure.

That soon? Why hadn't Luke mentioned it? *And why would I stay here without him?* That thought delivered the most unsettling jolt yet. When had she started imagining needing Luke back in her life? The answer was an image of him standing in the cottage kitchen with a piratical swipe of black across his cheek. Her stomach dipped.

Jasper was rubbing the back of his neck now. 'You should probably know, Lily, that he's got himself a bit of a reputation these last few years. The Playboy of Inish Ruin. He's not exactly the person you remember.'

That made Lily angry but not at Luke. 'Well, I'm sure I'm not the person he remembers, either. I haven't exactly been living as a nun.'

But Jasper just shook his head ruefully, as if she'd overwatered one of his saplings. 'And still the impulse to defend him.'

'He doesn't need any defending. So he's had a girlfriend or three in the last decade? So what?'

'That's not what I'm saying.'

'Then what? That he has a girlfriend now?'

Jasper was silent.

'Well ... does he?' The question sounded pathetic but she had to know.

Jasper drew a deep breath in through his nose. 'Last I heard her name is Gráinne Cassidy. And she's a nurse. At the Regional.'

Lily was momentarily stunned. Luke had a girlfriend. Well ... of course he had. He was *him*. The only real shock was that it hadn't occurred to her sooner. No wonder he'd refused to kiss her at the pub. He'd someone waiting for him in Cork. A nurse. Someone as good and kind and helpful as himself. Everyone knew nurses were angels in disguise. Gráinne. Even her name sounded lovely. And all Lily really was to Luke now was one of his many ex's. The one who'd caused him the most grief at that. *Don't you think I've been tortured enough?* Luke had moved on. *Only natural*, as he'd said himself. And all she'd been doing these last few days, apparently, was making a complete and utter fool of herself. A dreaming-of-him-with-his-shirt-off fool no less. *Urgh, Love*. As sneaky as it was dangerous. You give it an inch ...

'He's coming this way,' said Jasper. 'Ten seconds.'

Lily glimpsed a dark form moving swiftly beyond a gap in the bordering hedgerow and all the knots inside her tightened right back up. But it was okay, she told herself sternly. Because Luke didn't need to know easily he'd burrowed his way back into her heart. She could be cool and calm and collected around him again. No need to incriminate herself any further. What was it they did in all those courtroom dramas? Plead the Fifth?

But there was no time for further planning as Luke passed Jasper's garden gate, did a quick double-take when he spotted them and skidded sharply to a halt. And then he was calling her name.

The scene caught Luke off guard as disconcertingly picturesque. Lily and Jasper were framed in the doorway of Jasper's hostel, surrounded by jasmine as they stared into each other's eyes. They turned to him but made no move to break apart.

'Hello, Luke,' said Jasper, sounding resigned. 'Hot day for it.'

'Lily,' he repeated, ignoring him.

She gave a smile that didn't quite reach her eyes. 'Hi, Luke. I'm busy right now. Did you need something?'

'No. I ... well ... yes, actually. I have to find part of Betty's going-away outfit that's gone missing. A bolero.'

'Oh. It was in the study. On one of the suitcases. It'll be wherever you put the rest of her stuff.'

'Yes. Right,' he said, caught between asking her to come with him to help identify it and risk looking hapless versus the advantage of having a nifty excuse to remove her from Jasper's side.

His expression clearly gave something of his struggle away though, for she said. 'It's crimson and it's satin. You'll know it when you see it. I'm just helping Jasper with the flowers here so ...'

Jasper held the door open for her to come back inside.

She went to move.

'I'm sorry,' he blurted, 'but Betty's in a panic for it. Talking about palpitations.'

Jasper scoffed but Lily's brow furrowed. 'Really?'

'Please?' he said, hoping she'd understand the question without him actually having to ask it.

She stared at him for five seconds then turned back to Jasper. 'I'll be back as soon as I can.'

He let out a sigh. 'No, it's fine. Go help Betty. Make sure there's actually going to be a wedding so all our flowers don't go to waste.' Then he gave her a gentle nudge towards the path before he slipped back inside.

The gravel path from Jasper's door to his gate crunched with Lily's every step and Luke scanned her face as she drew closer, noting a wariness in her expression that hadn't been there earlier.

'Is something wrong?' he asked.

'No. Nothing.' She gave him another quick, tight smile.

'You're sure?'

'*Mhuh.*'

He turned away and started towards the tunnel of trees and she fell into step beside him. But whatever playful energy had buzzed between them earlier had somehow changed polarity, its force now repelling. The breeze picked up at their backs and the branches overhead groaned and squeaked, scratching against each other and sending little pieces of lichen falling.

'Did something happen?' he tried again.

'No. Why do you ask?'

'I just thought ... '

But the ferns by the roadside hissed like a jeering crowd, leaving him even more unsettled.

'So ... where are we going?' she asked, after a minute. 'Where did you put Betty's stuff?'

'It's, *um*, probably just easier to show you.'

She accepted that with a shrug and was back to being silent.

They reached the shop and school and strode on until the viewing point where they passed through the gap in the hawthorn trees and onto the dirt track as it wound its way in a slow climb around the side of Sliabh Oisín.

Lily's pace picked up, enthusiastic, he imagined, to be exploring something new. Whispering grasses replaced the noisy ferns until they reached the highest point where the wind rose to greet them in a mighty roar, bringing them both to an abrupt stop.

Below, the waters in Hook Cove could at last be seen – vivid against the black rocks as the rocks were against the sweet-yellow of the gorse and surrounding purple of the heathers. And beyond it all lay a burnished mirror of tranquil sea.

He looked at Lily. Her expression seemed almost fierce as the wind whipped her hair in a wild fury. Her gaze slowly panned the scene from left to right until a line furrowed her brow. She'd seen it then. His house.

'That is where you put all Betty's stuff?'

'The trees will hide it in a few years,' he said.

'*Hmm.*'

'It's still a beautiful view.'

She made no further comment as they headed downhill towards it. She'd set her heart against the place. He knew that much. No one likes when their 'perfect' gets messed with. He tried to tell himself it didn't matter what she thought of his house. In the absence of approval he'd get an unvarnished opinion at least. But still ...

They both had to shield their eyes simultaneously against the glare from the windows on the last stretch. But when Lily's hand fell her frown faded, replaced by a look of confusion instead.

He searched his pockets for the key while she continued to stare up at the building, her gaze sweeping the garden briefly before returning to it.

'*Hmm*,' she said again.

A sound he was beginning to find frustratingly uninformative. 'So what do you think?'

'I think I'm even more pissed now.' But there was a flicker of warmth back in her tone.

'Oh?'

She turned to him, an edge of a smile to her lips. 'Hello? Log cabin meets Elven bungalow? Like what the hell?'

'So you *like* it?'

Her smile widened. 'Are you kidding? Wooden beams? Big old windows? And I've never seen cladding done that way. It's so intricate. Almost art.'

'Probably handmade,' he ventured, suppressing his delight.

'For sure.'

He got the front door open and she followed him inside with an eager step. 'Who did you say the owner was?'

'Oh, *um* ...'

He steered her towards the front room but she stopped by a charcoal sketch on the wall. 'This is one of yours, isn't it?'

'Yes,' he admitted and held his breath.

'Do you remember we built a hut like this once? You wanted to fortify it in case of Vikings and all I wanted was to make it pretty.'

A vision of grassy beds and daisy chains flitted through his mind. 'Betty's stuff is this way. What's a bolero anyway?'

For a moment she looked disappointed. 'It's a short jacket-type thing. Spanish originally. Rounded here and open at the front. Sort of like a fancy shrug.'

'Ah. Like a shrug!' Whatever the hell *that* was?

They reached the front room and she glanced around at the four white walls and then at the mass of Betty's belongings. But instead of moving towards them she went straight to the nearest window and looked out. 'He's done a lovely job on the garden. Must be big into his herbs. Most people would concentrate on the inside first.'

'Yes.'

'Are the other rooms as bare as this one?'

'Pretty much.'

'He's not a chef, is he?'

'No. But he makes a good sandwich. Do you want us to search a suitcase each?' He clicked the lock on the nearest one which burst open in a riot of red and black.

'I'd love to know where he got that bench. Great taste.'

'Oh. *Uh–*'

'So how come you have the keys? Do you water the plants or something?'

'I water the plants, yes.'

Her cross examination apparently complete, she joined him and they each went through a suitcase without success. The search of the second two proved similarly unfruitful but Lily's third yielded up the bolero – satin, crimson and heavily wrinkled.

'We'll need a bag to put it in,' she said. 'This way to the kitchen?' She didn't wait for confirmation and found the room easily when she turned left at the end of the hall.

Luke scrambled to get in front of her, scanning the room for any of his belongings that might give the game away but, bar the few dishes by the sink and some crumbs on the table, it was clean and unremarkable. At least he thought so.

Lily, however, was all delight. '*Wow!* Is this kitchen handmade?'

'Well, there's a cabinetmaker in–'

'And the table and chairs are the same design as the bench. And look at the back garden! *Ooh!* Where do those steps lead? No. Don't tell me!' She got the sliding door open and was off up the rocky steps, taking them two at a time.

This place was incredible. A dream home. And the view from this sandstone ledge? Lily couldn't imagine what lunatic had given permission for it, if indeed anyone in a position of responsibility had. It was a death trap. A crazy, beautiful, ingenious one. If you had children, it would have to be completely fenced off. But she was sitting on it, her legs swinging, when she heard Luke approach and turned. He was holding a paper bag. Presumably the bolero was in it but Lily was in no rush now to leave.

'If this was my house, I'd have breakfast here every morning,' she told him. 'I'd watch the sunrise with a coffee and a packet of biscuits. *Every* morning.'

She didn't know what to make of his expression. Pleased yet hesitant. 'I can picture it,' he said. 'The light pinking your face. The breeze chasing through strands of your hair.'

It sounded almost romantic. She held her breath.

'The chipmunk cheeks as you devour too many Hobnobs.'

And let it out.

He came and sat beside her and they looked out to sea together in silence.

Lily tried to ignore the delicious scent of him wafting over. And the deeply confusing impulse to rest her head on his shoulder.

She heard him draw a deep breath. 'Lily?'

'Yeah.'

'Where do you think we'd be right now if you hadn't been sent away?'

She stiffened, her gaze fixing on a gull as it took flight from the cliff below. '*Uh*, on Inish Ruin, I suppose?'

It wasn't what he was really asking but perhaps it would suffice.

He shifted on the ledge beside her. 'But do you think we'd have made it as a couple?'

The gull was making a low sweep over the water, with just the occasional beat of its wings. On the horizon beyond a dark line of cloud was gathering. Why was Luke asking her this? It felt like a trap. And she was suddenly grateful to Jasper for explaining his situation in Cork to her. God knows what she might have said to embarrass herself otherwise.

'Well, we had a lot of growing up still to do,' she tried, her voice sounding steady at least. 'People don't always grow together.'

'But don't you think we would have?' he pressed. 'That we'd be married by now? A couple of nippers even?'

She couldn't look at him. Instead she looked down at the waves lapping the cliff base as her chest tightened once more. Reminiscing about old times was one thing. What-iffing a future that wasn't going to happen was something else. As pointless as it was painful. What was to be gained by it?

'Lily?'

'What, Luke?' she said. 'What do want me to say? That we could have been happy?'

His voice was soft. 'Maybe?'

She faced him at last and found his earnest expression disconcerting. 'Or maybe we couldn't be. Maybe …' she swallowed, 'maybe everything was just meant to go wrong?' She got back on her feet and stepped away from the ledge. 'Maybe we'd have ended up miserable. Or divorced. Or one of us up for attempted murder.'

'You probably.'

She halted, unable to help weighing the odds of that. Which of them would have killed the other? And then she laughed, though it sounded as bleak to her own ears as the cries of the gull. 'Me definitely. So a lucky escape all round.'

He made no reply but she heard him following her down the steps.

She felt almost relieved. As if the book between them, their fairy tale that wasn't, had finally been closed.

She followed the wending, pebble-lined path through the garden leading back to the front door. She glanced through the pane here and saw Luke's sketch on the wall again. She halted for a last look. Yes, it was exactly like the hut they'd built as children. She stepped closer and could just make out a flash of colour now amidst the charcoal grey. A faint string of green with white dashes and little dots of yellow.

Her breath stilled. *All it needs now is a few daisy chains.* She glanced back to Luke. His face, usually so expressive, now gave nothing away but a terrible certainty crept slowly over her. This was *his* house. This house she'd disparaged before she'd even seen it. This house she'd said she'd have lodged a planning objection against. This beautiful house he'd clearly poured his heart and soul and creativity into designing. *Probably handmade?* Of course it was handmade. Maybe even by him.

And the answer to his question of where they'd be right now if she hadn't been sent away was suddenly obvious. They'd have been right here. In their favourite place. In this house built on their childhood memories. But would they have been happy?

Yes, her heart whispered and her mind had no rebuttal to offer.

But this must be the asset he was prepared to part with to buy out her share of the cottage. The asset he no longer needed. And why didn't he need it? Because he had another home now somewhere else. With someone else.

She forced her legs into motion and walked on. 'I think we should sell the cottage after all,' she called over her shoulder.

'Oh?'

'It makes the most sense financially. We'll split the proceeds.'

'I don't want your money, Lily.'

'I'm going to book a flight back to London for after the wedding. But thanks anyway for the offer. I really appreciate it.'

'You can take some more time to think about it.'

'No, no. Thanks. I, *uh*, hear you're leaving for Cork soon,' she added, in a swerve that was far from smooth. 'Jasper mentioned it.'

She heard him mutter something.

Then, 'Yeah. I kept meaning to tell you and getting sidetracked. I'm starting a new job there on Saturday.'

'That's great. Is it in a pub?'

'No. I'm going to be a paramedic.'

She halted and slowly turned to face him. Luke was going to be a paramedic? Why had she never thought of that profession for him? It was perfect!

'Oh my God. You'll be *amazing* at that, Luke. I'm picturing lots of high-speed ambulancing and endless precarious rescues. And I suppose you hadn't really any interest in bomb disposal?' And then she laughed, because everything was changing and it was easier than crying.

But he just looked at her as if she'd lost the plot.

Still she bombarded him with questions as they headed back towards the road – about the training he'd done, what he was most excited about, the challenges he'd be facing. His zeal for the work glowed bright in the heat of her enthusiasm but every question seemed to put further distance between them and that house and the life that might have been.

At the gap in the hedge she took the paper bag from his hands to indicate she'd make her way on from here alone. 'I'll get this back to

Betty. Hopefully that's the last of the wedding drama. Provided we get a priest. I hear you've been roped into being an usher. Hard luck on that.'

His smile seemed to weigh heavy though. And suddenly it felt as if they were both just acting. Reciting lines. Struggling to remember what came next.

'Don't feel sorry for me just yet,' he managed. 'Apparently Cassandra hasn't given up on some plan to turn you into a second bridesmaid?'

'Oh no. Really?' She started walking backwards, away from him.

'Yeah. And Betty's on board. And what the bride wants the bride gets, so you'll have to suck it up. Just try not to raise too many heart-rates whatever outfit they put you in. There'll be old people at this thing. A bridesmaid has a sacred duty not to kill anyone. You know that, right?'

'Yes, that's Mervyn's job, isn't it? If there's lightning forecast I'm not attending.'

'He'll be aiming for the groom, though. Surely you'll be safe enough?'

'Depends how good his aim is.'

The distance between them continued to lengthen, Lily's footsteps unerring over remembered terrain. She was almost at the bend now that would take her from his sight.

'I'm happy for you, Luke,' she managed. 'And I hope ... I hope Cork is everything you deserve.'

She raised her fingers in goodbye before he vanished from her view.

'*Lily!*' he called after her.

She came back a few steps to peer around the bend again. 'Yeah?'

'You're going to be okay, right? Do you need help with anything else before I leave?'

'No. Thanks. I'm all set.'

And she was, wasn't she? Set to go back to London. To a boss who didn't appreciate her. To colleagues who were assholes. To an empty flat from which she was due to be evicted. To leave Nana's cottage to a stranger who'd take a wrecking ball to it. To leave Luke to a stranger and take a wrecking ball to herself?

And on that dismal thought she walked on.

Chapter Twenty

Mervyn

Betty was leaning against the front wall of the cottage with a cigarette dangling from her lips. The sight stopped Lily in her tracks. 'Betty, you don't smoke.'

'No, chick. Not for twenty-seven years.' She took a long drag. 'But still and all it takes the edge off.'

No smoke came out with the words. Lily peered closer and saw the cigarette wasn't lit. She stepped over the fallen wisteria and watched in fascination as Betty tapped the cigarette with her finger as though knocking a head of ash.

'Rough day?' she hazarded.

'Yes. You?' She looked past her up the lane. 'No Luke?'

'No.' There was no Luke. Nor would be again. 'We've both ... moved on.'

Betty sighed, murmured something that sounded suspiciously like 'idiots', then dug into the pocket of her dress, pulled out a faded and flattened cigarette box and offered it to her.

Lily peeped into it and saw a cigarette among the crumpled silver paper. 'Ah, you've only the one left.'

'That's alright. I'm giving them up tonight.'

Lily drew out the cigarette and rolled it between her fingers. Half the tobacco fell out. She put it to her lips and then took it away again. 'Do I need a light?'

Betty held up a fist, flicked her thumbnail against her forefinger as though striking a lighter and put her thumb to the end of the cigarette.

After a moment Lily put it to her lips again, then puffed out past it.

'First time?' asked Betty, taking another drag herself.

'Should I be coughing?'

'Maybe a little. Wheeze if you can manage. It's so long ago I forget what it's really like.' She tapped her cigarette again and resettled it between her fingers. 'Well, no, that's a lie. I remember perfectly. Some things you can't forget once they've been in your system. Mervyn was forever at me to give these up.'

Lily was silent, not sure whether she should steer the conversation away from Mervyn or not. Betty seemed calm though and maybe it was important for her to talk about him the evening before she married someone else?

'If he was alive he'd be hounding me still,' she continued. 'I was mad for them, you know? But when he died I just stopped.'

Lily nodded tentatively.

'I'm sorry you never met him. I think you would have liked him.' She flicked the cigarette into the fuchsia bushes and then, to Lily's dismay, started to cry.

'Oh Betty. No. It's okay.' She tried to give her a hug but Betty's back was pressed so hard to the wall it was impossible.

'I did love him,' she whispered. 'Even though I give out about him.'

'Of course you did.'

'As much as I love Ned, but he left me all alone and I missed him so much.'

'But he's still with you. You talk to him all the time, right?'

Betty gave her a baleful look, her lower lip trembling. 'But he doesn't talk back. I don't hear him. I don't hear anything.' She dissolved into tears again. 'I'm just a crazy old lady going around talking to herself. I was so lonely. And it was a comfort to imagine he could hear me and then I started to imagine what he'd say and then to imagine that he said it and then I – I just couldn't stop.'

'So you don't hear anything? Not even ...?'

Betty shook her head as the tears kept flowing. 'Your nana doesn't talk to me either. I just invited myself to stay here. She didn't say it was okay or anything.'

Lily felt a pang but now wasn't the moment to dwell on it. 'But she'd have wanted you to stay. I know she would have.'

Betty managed a nod. 'And I *have* got better at the crosswords since I've been here.'

'Well, there, see?'

'But what if Ned dies too? I don't want to be pretending to talk to him as well. I couldn't bear it.'

Aware she was out of her depth Lily glanced towards the porch door, praying for Cassandra to make an appearance. No such miracle.

'I didn't mean to love anybody else after Mervyn. I didn't want to have to go through all that again.'

'But you had to be brave, Betty. You had to love again.'

She blinked watery eyes at her. 'Why?'

'Because if you hadn't you'd have only ended up like, like ...' Lily sought frantically for a suitable analogy, 'like a hermit crab. Scuttling around. Safe but all alone. That's no good, right?'

Betty was silent for a moment. 'But if you come out of your shell again you might get hurt.'

Lily nodded.

'And that's a scary thought, isn't it, chick?'

And suddenly Lily wasn't sure who was counselling whom. 'All I know is you've got a good man who loves you with all his heart. Why would you want to miss out on that?'

Betty got herself back upright and smiled at her kindly. 'Why, indeed? I'd have to be an idiot.' She straightened her skirt and tucked in a loose hem of her blouse. 'Ned does love me, doesn't he? I don't understand why when he could have his pick. Kitty the Strand has been making eyes at him forever.' She patted her tears. 'Father Halpin rang while you were out and we had a long chat, me and him and Ned. He sounds like a lovely man. He promised he'll be here tomorrow.'

Lily clasped her hands together. 'So the wedding can still go ahead? That's great news and I have your bolero. It just needs a quick press and if there's anything else that needs doing before tomorrow I'm here to do it. Just tell me whatever you need.'

'You're a good girl but I think it's all under control.' She leaned closer then lowered her voice. 'You won't tell Ned I was upset?'

'Of course not.'

'And I do actually need you to do something. Will you keep an eye on Cassie? She's looking peaky again.'

'Sure. Where is she?'

'Inside. Beating Ned at Scrabble.'

Lily paused. 'How do you know she's beating him?'

'Because she's a whizz. No one can match her. She makes words between words and everything.'

Sure enough Ned and Cassandra were at the kitchen table, a Scrabble board between them. Cassandra was preoccupied arranging tiles so Lily got a good long look at her: *Pale face? Check. Circles under her eyes? Check. Look of recent upset?* She was going to murder Eric.

But her attention was shortly drawn from Cassandra to the kitchen itself. It looked different. Better. Way better. The cupboard doors were back in line. And the whole place looked ... brighter? 'What happened in here?'

'Luke did his re-arranging thing. Everywhere.'

Lily did a slow circuit of the cottage and saw every room had been improved. There was less clutter yet the place felt homier somehow and bigger. Smart yet still quaint. She could imagine seeing photos of it online and wanting it. And then she visualised the sitting room being bulldozed and felt her stomach churn.

She returned to the kitchen and sat at the table. She needed to book a flight to London for tomorrow night – which meant a working credit card which she no longer had. Logging on to eBay, she reduced the price of her only designer bag by forty percent. It was sold thirty minutes later and she could then bring herself to borrow Cassandra's card knowing she could at least pay her back. She got a seat on the last flight available as Cassandra and Ned paused their game to discuss Lily's bridesmaid dress options.

They went through the clothes they'd got from Eithne but there was nothing dressy enough to pass as a bridesmaid's outfit.

'Does it have to be red?' Lily asked, remembering the black ribbon on Jasper's table. 'What about black? It's still in keeping with your ladybird theme. Red and black.'

Betty thought about it. 'I guess it could work. It's not like ye were going to be matching exactly anyway. Maybe it would be better if they were completely different.'

'Complementary.'

'Eithne didn't give us anything in black though,' said Cassandra.

'No, but there might be something else.'

With that sparse explanation Lily dashed upstairs, heart thudding. Nana's black silk cocktail dress. Simple, strapless and elegant. The one she'd bought on an impulse in a charity shop one time but had never worn. She reached the bedroom and flung open the wardrobe. Two dozen wire hangers chimed and Lily stared in startled dismay at the empty space. She'd forgotten. She'd thrown the dress out the same way she'd thrown everything out. *How could I have done that? I could have kept that dress. I could have kept lots of things.* She rocked on her heels and sat on the bed, then laid her head on the comforter. But it didn't smell of Nana's perfume any more since she'd washed it. She was losing things she hadn't even thought to keep. She closed her eyes and searched for the memory of Nana's scent but came up empty.

She returned downstairs where the sight of three expectant faces sank her further. 'I'm sorry. There was a dress – before – I'm sorry.' She sat down and put her head on the table and closed her eyes. *Another mistake. A stupid, stupid mistake.*

Pup came padding over to drool consolingly on her knee. A cup of tea was placed by her elbow. Ned and Cassandra finished their game. Ned congratulated Cassandra.

A chair squeaked. She heard the back door opening and then the sound of the bolt being worked at the coal bunker.

Lily raised her head to see Cassandra coming back inside, lugging a black plastic bag over her shoulder. She put it on the floor and gave it a tentative nudge in her direction.

'What's this?'

Cassandra twisted her fingers nervously. 'Don't be mad but I hid a few things away. Just in case you changed your mind.'

Lily stared at her. 'You did not.'

'I'm sorry. I just thought you might–'

But the rest of the sentence was smothered as Lily flung her arms around her and gave her a big hug. 'You little dote!' Pup barked and wagged her tail furiously as Lily planted three rapid kisses on the top of Cassandra's head, released her with a laugh and tore open the bag. A bazaar of items fell out including some of Nana's best clothes: the blue dress she'd worn to Lily's confirmation, the cream-and-grey dress she often wore to Mass, the linen smock worn for comfort in summer, a dented trilby that had been Granduncle Joe's and a cream cashmere cardigan that was soft as a whisper against her skin. The scent of vanilla and lavender was on it and she inhaled so deeply it almost stuck to her face. *Nana.* She wrapped it round her shoulders and kept looking, unearthing more treasures until there, at the bottom of the pile, was the cocktail dress.

Glancing up she saw Cassandra's eyes were moist. 'Try it on.'

Lily took her time changing in the scullery. She emerged, hands fiddling with the clasp at the back. 'I just need a bit of help.'

Cassandra obliged then stood back with Betty and Ned to admire.

'Perfect,' said Betty.

'Very pretty,' added Ned. 'Give us a twirl, so.'

Lily obliged, blushing profusely.

'You can wear my black strappies with it,' offered Cassandra as Lily cleared a lump in her throat. 'As we're the same size.'

'Thanks.'

'Well, then.' Ned stood and turned to Betty. 'Now that's sorted I'm going to leave you all in peace to do whatever else you need to do. Promise me you'll be there tomorrow?'

'I promise,' said Betty solemnly.

He raised her hand and kissed her knuckles, which made her giggle. 'No matter what happens or who might tell you otherwise?' He glanced upwards to indicate the direction from which he expected trouble to arise.

'You won't have to worry about Mervyn anymore,' said Lily, cocking her head as though listening hard. 'He's just told me he'll rest in peace now someone else will be looking after Betty for him.'

Betty shot her a questioning look.

She returned an encouraging smile.

'That's right,' said Betty. 'I won't be hearing from him anymore. He wishes us well.'

'That's very chivalrous,' said Cassandra.

'Yes,' sighed Betty. 'He was always good like that.'

'Right so,' said Ned. Evidently Mervyn's peaceful slumber couldn't start soon enough. 'Until tomorrow.'

Betty went to the porch to see him off then headed upstairs for a quick 'forty winks'.

While she slept, Lily got the bolero and the black dress ironed and then lost innumerable games of Scrabble to Cassandra.

Cassandra got up to get them glasses of water at the sink. 'Do you think I'd have time to see Trá Eilis before we leave tomorrow?'

Before *we* leave? 'You're coming with me then?'

'Yeah, I'm going to book the same flight. And take that job in Belfast after all. Just changed my mind.'

'Cass? What happened with Eric?'

She waited for her to turn around, but she just kept looking out the window.

'It doesn't look like the wellness spa is going to be a runner. Eithne can't convince Paudie it's a good idea.'

'Eric's an idiot. Just an immature oaf who can't handle an actual relationship.'

She sniffed. 'I'm not even thinking about it.'

'Good. Really? You're not? No. Of course you're not. Sure you only knew him two minutes. Why would you be?'

Cassandra finally turned, her colour high. 'How long did it take Juliet to fall for Romeo, do you think?'

'I'm sorry, what?'

'Or Meg Ryan to fall for Tom Hanks.'

'*Um*, they're not together, Cass. They're just actors.'

'Okay. Well, their characters then.'

'I'm ... I don't know. What are you trying to say?'

She sighed. 'That I felt it. That love-at-first-sight thing. Just like in the old movies. I've been waiting all my life to feel it and then I did and it was amazing and everything was brighter in the world but it was all pretend for him and now I've been disillusioned and I can't ever be re-illusioned. Even if I meet someone else, I'm never going to have that faith I had before that everything will work out. So that's the best I'm ever going to feel and I felt it for less than a week.'

Lily was too shocked for a moment to say anything. Cassandra was crushed. How was she still functioning? Her very calmness was unnerving. This was Miss Heart-on-her-Sleeve. Miss Emotion. 'Are you alright?'

'Yeah. Other than this last bit of stomach upset, I'm fine.'

'No. No, you're not. Why aren't you crying?'

Cassandra looked surprised. 'I thought you'd be pleased I've taken some leaves out of your books.'

'And ... which leaves would those be exactly?'

Cassandra counted them off on her fingers. '*Don't go where you're not wanted. Crying is pointless. Better in than out. Be an island.*'

Lily gulped.

'You were right. Love wasn't worth the trouble. So I'm just going to push all the feelings down like you do from now on. I'm sure I'll feel better once I get the hang of it. How long did it take you not to care?'

Lily stared at Cassandra in horror. There was no accusation in the question. She genuinely wanted to know.

Betty returned to the kitchen, her face a picture of calm but her hair looking like she'd been plugged into a socket. There was microwave food for dinner. Ned had brought supplies. Cassandra nibbled half-heartedly on her own portion, pushing it away after a half dozen bites saying she hadn't much of an appetite. Lily, almost ready to pass out with hunger by then, devoured her own meal and what remained of Cassandra's without a second thought.

The rest of the evening passed quietly. Cassandra went to bed early in the hope a good night's sleep would restore her. Betty followed half an hour later.

Lily opened the kitchen window and looked out. The night was muggy now, the sky to the west a blanket of brown undulating away as far as the eye could see. Until it was lit by a sudden pulse of light. Lily counted to thirty before she heard the faint rumble of thunder. She closed the window and made her way to Nana's room for the best view of the approaching storm. Flash after flash, the landscape flickered in and out of view as the gap between lightning and thunder shortened: twelve seconds, eight seconds. Then it was straight overhead, the rain pelting down hard enough to make the corrugated roof of the coal shed vibrate. It continued for several minutes until the gap slowly lengthened once more and, with a few last grumbles, passed away. The rain took longer to peter out but eventually softened to a drizzle that skimmed the pane.

'Yes, Mervyn. Get that all out of your system and be done with it. She'll always love you. But everyone deserves a second chance. And some sunshine for the wedding if you can swing it.'

She went to the door but halted at the threshold, peering back into the room. 'Nana?' she whispered. She stretched all her senses out into the darkness. Trying to find a trace or some lingering connection.

'Lily?'

'Christ!'

Betty was standing right behind her with a glass of water in her hand. 'Sorry, chick.'

Lily sagged, gasping to catch her breath against the doorframe.

'Noleen always did love her storms,' she said. 'Bit of drama to liven things up.'

Lily could only nod as Betty shuffled on. But when she glanced back into Nana's room she could have sworn she heard the echo of a laugh as she closed the door softly behind her.

Chapter Twenty-One

Bride on the Right

'Wake up, chick. You've slept the whole morning.'

Lily opened her eyes and screamed.

'Ah, it's only me again,' said Betty crossly. 'It's a face mask. I'm getting married in three hours.'

Lily couldn't move, her eyes riveted to the green sludge.

'I've made you a sandwich for lunch. Up now, eat it and get dressed. Eithne's coming soon to do hair.'

'I'm getting up,' she promised.

She waited until Betty had gone downstairs before turning her head on the pillow to look out the window. All credit to Mervyn, he'd done well. It was a day of blue, green and straw-coloured perfection with the sky unblemished and the woozy lines of hedgerows looking lush. The tall grasses in the surrounding fields barely moved but the air through the open window was crisp and clean.

A bee knocked against the glass, head-butting it three times before it flew off, narrowly avoiding a web slung across one corner. A thistle seed hadn't been so lucky though. It fluttered against its sterile resting place – all its potential thwarted by one capricious puff of wind.

Lily tried not to draw unwelcome analogies to herself.

And failed.

With a sigh, she got out of bed, ate the sandwich and then endured another cold shower but Nana's dress felt heavenly against her skin after. She applied makeup, packed her rucksack and took it and herself to the kitchen. There she found Cassandra looking like a Valentine's Day goddess in a flowing red-chiffon gown with softly coiling straps and a sweetheart neckline. But her face was pinched and she was pacing.

'What's wrong?'

'Nothing.'

'You look like you're in pain. Why don't you sit down?'

'I'm not getting this dress crumpled.'

'But you're uncomfortable.'

'It's this stomach ache,' she groaned. 'It keeps shifting around. I didn't want to take the last of Eric's stupid medicine but I'm going to have to.'

'Yes,' said Betty, sweeping into the room, her skin restored to glowing pink. 'You should always finish the course. Any doctor will tell you that.'

'Is it antibiotics he gave you?' Lily asked, confused. 'That doesn't sound right. Not for a stomach upset.'

'Ah, I don't know what he gave me. I threw out the packet.' She opened her palm, displaying a pair of colourful capsules. 'I suppose it'd only be silly pride not to take them.'

'We won't tell him,' promised Betty, handing her a glass of water so she could knock them back.

Lily watched as she started pacing again. 'I think you might need to see a doctor, Cass. I know it's not a good time but–'

'No, no. I'll be fine. I'm not missing this wedding.'

'Alright,' said Lily, 'but as soon as we're back in London I'm taking you to see one. Maybe you have an ulcer.'

'Sure. Okay. Now who's that?' she snapped as the doorbell rang.

Lily answered it to find a blonde-haired and soft-featured woman in her twenties standing there. She was wearing a stunning figure-hugging silver-sequined dress, and had a gold-wrapped parcel in her hands. How she'd made it up the hill in four-inch heels without breaking a sweat, Lily had no idea.

'Hello,' she said. 'Sorry to disturb your morning. Just wondering if there's any chance I can say a quick hello to the bride?'

Betty ambled up behind Lily and shrieked, '*Gráinne? Ah, darling!* Come in, come in! Aren't you a picture? How are you feeling?'

'I'm absolutely fine, Betty. False alarm. Sorry for upsetting everything at the last minute.'

'You upset nothing,' said Betty, drawing her into the kitchen. 'And I've made a new friend out of it. *Cassie?* And this is Lily. Noleen's granddaughter. Did you ever meet Noleen?'

'I don't think so, no.'

'Ah well, I'll show you a picture of her inside. *Cassie?*' she called again.

Cassandra appeared from the living room. 'Hello?'

'This is my grandniece, Gráinne Cassidy. My original bridesmaid I was telling you about. She's a nurse up at the Regional.'

Gráinne reached out to clasp Cassandra's hand. 'Thank you so much for stepping in. And the dress looks lovely on you. A perfect fit.'

'Do you think so?' Cassandra's answering smile was already forming. 'I feel like it's a little pulled at the straps.'

'Where?'

Cassandra turned around and twisted to one side.

'It looks just fine from here. But what way are you planning to do your hair? Will you have it up or leave some hanging down the back?'

They headed into the living room together as they discussed this, Betty beaming as she trailed after them.

Lily scrambled to catch her balance. *This* was Gráinne Cassidy? Betty's *grandniece* Gráinne and Luke's *girlfriend* Gráinne were one and the same? Luke's very *attractive* girlfriend moreover. If Lily had imagined what she might look like – and she was not proud to admit she had – it was never like *that*. But Betty obviously didn't know about her relationship with Luke. Was it some kind of secret?

The three women were laughing in the sitting room now. Gráinne was offering to help with something. Well, of course she was. Wasn't she just like Luke. No wonder he'd fallen for her. They were clearly a perfect match.

Spirits lowered by that thought, she made her way inside to join them, smiling at everything that was said though she barely followed any of it with her head too full and her heart too sore. Ten minutes passed, or maybe it was only five, until Gráinne got up from the sofa.

'I better let you go and get your hair done.' She gave Betty a kiss on the cheek, Cassandra's hand another encouraging squeeze and told Lily it was lovely to have met her.

Then she was gone, but there was no time for reflection as Jasper arrived a moment later with the bouquets. They were works of art in crimson and green with black ribbon and he accepted the effusive squeals of the bride and bridesmaid with a smile but wouldn't stay to be thanked beyond that. He was needed at the church.

They'd hardly caught their breath when the doorbell rang again. It was Eithne this time, looking very glamorous in her shell-pink dress and matching jacket. She was armed with curling tongs, a wallet of diamante accessories and a large can of hairspray.

Cassandra hustled Betty upstairs to do her make-up and Eithne suggested she curl Lily's hair in the kitchen while they waited for them to return. Lily, who hadn't decided if she cared more or less about her appearance now, having met Gráinne, hesitated. But imagining it would be preferable to Eithne and her looking across the table at each other in awkward silence, she agreed.

Eithne ran a brush through it and gave it a spray with heat-protecting mist. 'You've such thick hair. It's in very good condition.'

'Thank you.' Maybe awkward silence would have been better?

Eithne sectioned a piece and wound it around the tong, holding it for a count of ten before she let it unwind and reached for another. 'I just wanted to say, Lily, while I have a chance that I'm sorry for ... you know ... when you rang that time. Not passing on the message.'

Oh no. Trapped. Having *this* conversation. 'It's fine,' she said through her teeth.

'No. No, it's not. I shouldn't have done it. But my intentions ... it wasn't to hurt you. I really want you to know that. I just didn't think you were ...'

'Good enough for your son?'

Eithne hesitated a moment too long. 'No, no. It was just getting a bit too serious.' She wrapped another section. 'Ye were very young and I was afraid ye'd just hold each other back if anything ... untoward happened. But hasn't it worked out for the best? You've your great career now and Luke's found his passion for being a paramedic. He's so excited to start working in Cork too. And now he can have it all. A satisfying career and a family too.'

'A – a family?' She turned her head and saw Eithne gazing absently out the window, smiling as if at a thought. Still squeezing the tongs.

'Well, wouldn't he make a great dad? You should see him with Ciarán and Caoimhe. He's a natural. Changed their nappies as babies and everything.'

While this didn't seem something deserving of a trophy exactly, still Lily couldn't help but agree. Yes, Luke would make a great dad. The best.

'So I just wanted to say,' continued Eithne, 'that whatever resentment you might feel against me, please don't hold it against Luke. Let it be in the past.'

'Mrs. O'Callaghan?'

'Eithne, please.'

'You're burning my hair!'

'Oh! Oh, hell! No, no, it's okay.' She blew repeatedly across the strands as if that would somehow fix it. 'You'd hardly notice.'

Lily made to rise.

'No, stay,' said Eithne. 'I have to finish. Otherwise it'll be lopsided.'

With the smell of burnt hair in her nostrils, Lily stayed, springing from the chair when the last strand was released. Without a glance in a mirror, she said she was needed at the church, grabbed her rucksack and fled.

Five minutes later she'd found Jasper who was adjusting flowers at the end of a pew. He grinned when he saw her. 'What's with the curls?'

Her hand went to her hair. 'Is it bad?'

'Maybe just try to flatten it all out a bit.'

Lily did the best she could, pulling the strands with her fingers as she peered around the church. With its thick walls it was always cool in here but the sun had warmed it with colour at least, the stained-glass bathing the space in gentle hues. And the flowers of course looked stunning.

She praised Jasper on a job well done and he surprised her by asking if she wanted to visit her nana.

She tossed her rucksack behind the last pew and followed him out of the church, around the side and up a short flight of steps that led to the graveyard beyond. Here dozens of headstones listed generation after generation of the same families. But the newest one in the far corner bore just one name: *Noleen Barrett.*

A lump rose in Lily's throat, raw and rough-edged. She'd managed to convince herself she felt nothing when Nana had passed. Imagined because she'd grieved their lost closeness at eighteen, what remained of their relationship afterwards hadn't really mattered. But faced with this stark finality, recorded in polished granite, it hurt. When all the words she could have said now lay useless on her tongue. *I miss you, Nana. I love you. I want to come home. Please ask me to come home.* She bowed her head and hugged herself before reading the inscription again, taking note this time of what followed the name: *Mother, grandmother, first love and friend.*

First love? That was odd. Then she remembered Jasper was still standing behind her. 'Who organised the headstone?'

'Seánie.'

'Oh.' Well, that was ... good of him? Her eyes went to the wreath that rested against the base. 'Thank you for the flowers.'

'You're welcome. It was a lovely ceremony by all accounts.'

'You missed it too, then? The funeral?'

She turned to see him falter.

'I – you don't go where you're not wanted.'

'That was one of Nana's sayings.'

'Yes,' he said softly.

Just then the minibus arrived, rattling like a coin box as it pulled up to the nearest kerb. Eric climbed out, his shirt collar open above a lurid red waistcoat. He released his passengers – Josie with a bundle of Mass booklets, Father Halpin, all smiles, and Tadhg who hobbled inside out of the gathering heat.

Eric made his way over to them as Jasper excused himself.

'Is she here?' Eric looked almost fearful as he glanced around.

Lily bristled. This man had crushed the romantic dreams of the softest, sweetest person she knew and he was acting as if she might do *him* harm? 'She's helping Betty with her make-up,' she said tersely.

'Is it true she's leaving today?'

'That's what she says, yes.'

He nodded as if to himself. 'Right, right, right. *Fuck*.'

'Excuse me?'

'*Fuck,*' he repeated firmly, turned on his heel and disappeared inside the church.

This cleared Lily's line of sight all the way down the hill to the tunnel of trees. From its shadowed mouth a trickle emerged, gradually becoming a steady stream of brightly bedecked women intermingled with men in blacks and browns, jackets slung over their shoulders. She saw Pat leading the way, guffawing at something Donie was telling him.

She stepped down and waited to meet them at the church door and got a wolf whistle for her troubles.

'There's a sight for sore eyes,' said Donie. 'If I was a few decades younger I'd give Luke a run for his money.'

'Don't mind him,' said Pat. 'He started the celebrations early.' He gave the 'drink, drink' gesture behind Donie's back.

Donie wasn't looking to be excused, however. 'I don't have to be drunk to compliment a fine-looking woman. Why would she take offence?'

'You're doing the music today?' asked Lily, nodding towards Pat's guitar case.

'I am.'

'Who's singing?'

Donie cut in. 'That was supposed to be Josie but I don't see any sign of her so you'll have to do it.'

'God no,' murmured Pat. Meeting Lily's eye, he hastily added, 'I mean *um*, that *um*, God will know what to do.'

'Oh,' said Lily, confused. 'Well, I'm not a professional singer by any means but Josie's already here so not to worry.'

'Ah well,' said Donie, 'it would have been interesting. *What?*' he barked as Pat elbowed him sharply and pushed him inside.

Eric stuck his head out with a phone to his ear and signalled frantically to the sauntering crowd to get a move on. '*The bride is on her way!*'

'Says who?' asked Shay.

'The bride. This way, this way, please! Move it along there, folks! No stopping in the porch!'

Lily checked her watch. This bride was going to be bang on time. All credit to Cassandra who was proving far more than just an expert on pre-wedding jitters.

Without thinking, she made haste to get inside herself too, forgetting she was supposed to be waiting outside, but collided with Luke just inside the entrance. Her pulse leapt and that lovely surge of not-relief rushed through her once more as her eyes soaked him in. Holy moly, but he looked fine in a suit! Even with the lurid waistcoat. Like a suave croupier in a Bond film. A croupier that kicks James Bond's ass.

She spied Gráinne chatting to Bríd near the top of the church, her dress sparkling prettily in the light, and tried to step back to get outside again but was instead jostled further forward by the incoming crowd. Her next attempt to go sideways first and then reverse was blocked by Luke's arm as he passed someone a Mass booklet over her shoulder. 'Here you go,' he said. 'Bride on the left, groom on the right.'

She tried the other side but was again checked and forced to wait as first one passing guest and then another blocked her escape.

'Hi,' said Luke, as he handed someone else a booklet. 'Welcome. Bride on the right, groom on the left.'

'*Other way round*,' Lily whispered.

'Bride on the left. Sorry. Yes, the left. Best Man on the right.'

'Concentrate.'

He looked down at her and his smile fluttered her insides. 'You make it difficult.'

That means nothing. It means nothing. But the butterflies were having a party in there and her heart started pounding and she could almost imagine the tinkling of bells. No wait. Those hadn't been imagined. The sound was coming from the golf buggy which pulled up outside festooned with white ribbons and bearing the bride and bridesmaid.

Cassandra looked even more stunning now, with an angelic-looking half-up half-down hairstyle comprising elaborate twists and plaits. Lily finally managed to make it back outside and Cassandra handed her a bouquet, giggling as the photographer posed them to the right of the buggy.

The bride herself was angled sideways on the passenger seat, her legs dangling to show off a pair of sparkling courts under swathes of ivory duchess satin. The bodice held her poker straight and, across her shoulders, was the most delicate lace Lily had ever seen. There wasn't a touch of red or black in sight – bar the giant bouquet, of course – but as she climbed down Lily spied just one ladybird clip positioned fetchingly behind a curl.

Glancing back in through the open porch entrance Lily saw Luke, with his back to her now, helping his grandad into the last pew before sitting down beside him. She breathed a sigh of relief. Her and Luke's book might be closed but her body had yet to get the memo. She made her way inside again for a quick peep up the aisle. At the altar the priest was chatting with Ned. Paudie was standing beside him, checking the pocket of his waistcoat with a look of sudden panic followed by relief. Receiving a signal from Eric, Pat started up on the guitar with 'Jesu, Joy of Man's Desiring' and there was a scuff and rustle as everyone in the pews stood to look.

Lily pulled back out in time to allow the photographer to go past her.

He walked backwards down the aisle, clicking away, as Cassandra, with a reassuring beam at Lily, started forwards clutching her bouquet, charmingly framed in a spilling arch of light just inside the door.

From halfway down, Lily heard someone groan. It sounded like Eric.

Lily followed Cassandra in then and they began their slow walk, their dresses as dissimilar in design as in colour but, with the help of the bouquets, perfectly coordinated. They reached the altar and stepped to the left and turned as the bride finally made her entrance.

Betty was an absolute joy to behold, lit up with such happiness she had everyone smiling back in turn.

'Would you look at that!' Lily heard Josie whisper from a row away.

'I know,' sighed Maura. 'What every bride hopes for.'

'Ah, poor Ned, bless him. I think he's going to cry.'

Chapter Twenty-Two

Bomb Disposal

Luke settled back to watch the ceremony but found it impossible to concentrate. Whatever Lily's bomb-disposal comment from yesterday had been about, today it really did feel as if he'd been tasked with averting a disaster – with no instructions and the highest stakes. His future happiness was the bomb in this messed-up analogy, about to be blown up unless he could somehow decode Lily's heart fast enough to save it.

But he'd asked Tadhg's question about where she thought they'd be right now if she hadn't been sent away and her answer had been enough to flatten all his hopes. If she couldn't even picture a hypothetical future between them – that didn't involve one of them murdering the other – what hope for an actual one?

But this couldn't be the last day he ever saw her. He couldn't bear the thought that for the rest of his life she'd exist only as a memory again, fading in clarity as the days passed. He groaned to himself. Bombs and memories. That's where his brain was at while the congregation laughed around him.

Gráinne glanced his way from a few pews ahead. She smiled, her eyes bright and her cheeks flushed, and he gave her a smile and a nod in return. But her gaze stayed on him just a few seconds longer. There was the briefest flutter of lashes and he felt an inkling of unease. There was something in that look he hoped he'd misinterpreted. Maybe it was just the occasion of being at a wedding? Romance in the air? He looked towards Lily in the first pew, hoping she might be similarly afflicted. She didn't turn around.

So he straightened and tried again to pay attention. Father Halpin was doing a fine job, telling anecdotes about Betty and Ned as if he'd known them for years. Mervyn got a brief mention – everyone held their breath – but Betty just smiled and squeezed Ned's hand. Ned, in fact, was the one going to pieces. He got all choked up as he said his vows and dropped the ring en route to Betty's finger. It clinked and rolled too fast for Cassandra to catch and it was left to Bríd in the third row to return it to the man's shaking hands.

The bride and groom kissed to enthusiastic applause. Then they disappeared briefly into the sacristy to sign the register after which they re-emerged and exited the church as a receiving line formed, bottle-necking at the door.

Luke scanned the crowds and saw Lily just before she ducked out of sight into the sacristy, which he knew led to a second exit. Via that shortcut she'd be out onto the lane again in five seconds, while he was stuck in the aisle agreeing it was a lovely ceremony over and over again.

When he finally made it outside, the photographer was balanced precariously on the far wall, directing everyone along the side of the church for a group shot.

Then it was off to the hotel for the guests. Luke led the way with Eric, leaving Betty, Ned, Paudie, Cassandra, Lily and Gráinne behind for more photographs. Luke thought it as well the ushers had been deemed dispensable, for Eric hadn't managed a genuine smile all morning. It didn't take a genius to figure out why.

'You heard Cass is leaving,' he surmised.

'Yeah. So?'

'Thought you'd be pleased. Back to the plan for you, right?'

Eric gave him a cold stare. 'Like you're any better, asshole.'

'Asshole? Well, you're an idiot.'

'You're a bigger idiot!'

'Ah lads, please,' said Pat. 'This isn't dignified.'

'Yes,' agreed Donie. 'I never heard such namby-pamby insults. You want to get stuck in proper if you're going to bother at all. One of ye should be a dirtbag at least. The other could be scum. Use some imagination.'

This advice had the fortunate result of shutting both men up till they reached the hotel where they parted. Luke went to the bar to help his dad with the drinks and Eric went to the beer garden to brood.

It was only when the bridal party arrived that Eric returned inside. His hopeful expression was obliterated, however, on finding Cassandra flanked by two male guests in their twenties. Under a barrage of compliments, she was blushing enough to ignite jealousy in the most indifferent lover. In Eric, the effect was profound. A look of desperate resolve hardened his features and he started forward.

Paudie pushed Luke out from behind the bar to prevent things coming to blows right in front of them.

'I thought there'd be no one at this thing.' The first admirer leaned in and winked at Cassandra as though sharing some fantastic secret.

'Here all by yourself?' asked the other. 'That's terrible. We can't have that.'

'Well, yes. I mean no. My friend is here too.'

Cassandra flushed harder and bit her lip. 'And she's genuinely gorgeous. Like top-model beautiful.'

Both men straightened with interest. 'Where is she?' asked the first.

Cassandra turned, spotted Eric approaching and paled. 'Over there,' she squeaked. 'In black.'

Luke followed their gaze and sure enough Lily was there, tucked almost out of sight into an alcove. Saoirse was beside her with Caoimhe clinging to her neck, both mother and daughter looking overheated. Saoirse had a carryall over her shoulder and a harried expression on her face. Luke guessed the kids had had enough of wedding excitement and she was planning an early exit to catch the ferry. Lily was trying to help her, by the looks of it, crouching down and gesturing to Ciarán who was grinning cheekily from under a table, with some kind of canapé sticking out of his mouth. Meanwhile, Jasper sat across from them, smiling benignly but doing nothing useful.

The two men were continuing their attentions to Cassandra. 'So what drink did you say you wanted?'

'I'll get it,' said Eric, pushing past Luke to address Paudie. 'A peach schnapps with ice for Cassandra.'

Both men stiffened and then smiled harder.

'What did you want to drink, babe?' one asked.

Cassandra spluttered as though this was the hardest question she'd ever been asked. 'I–I'd *um*, I *oh*, I don't know. I'm not thirsty right now.' She edged away. 'I have to go to the ladies'.'

'We'll catch up with you later, yeah?' said the first.

'Save me the first dance!' said the other.

She didn't make it five paces before Eric intercepted her. 'Can I just talk to you for one second?' he pleaded.

She shook her head.

'I was thinking I'd ask Shay if he'd do the ferry runs for me on Mondays. See if I can get a little free time after all.'

Cassandra blinked hard and then raised her chin. 'I'm happy for you.'

'I'm sorry for freaking out about you staying.'

'I'm over it. It was nothing, us. A few kisses. Hardly worth mentioning.' She turned once more to go.

'*You should stay!*' he cried.

She spun around, her face lit with hope. 'Why?'

Luke watched Eric take a step back and fumble. 'So we could do a bit of sightseeing?'

Cassandra's shoulders slumped and she walked away, disappearing into the ladies' seconds later.

'What are you looking at?' Eric demanded as he brushed past Luke on his way back towards the beer garden. Then he halted, veered course, and tried to order a whiskey at the bar.

'Not a chance,' Paudie told him flatly.

Eric's jaw dropped. 'Did you not hear me? I want a whiskey.'

'I did hear you,' said Paudie. 'And the answer is no.'

'I can get whatever I want. I'll pay for it. Here.' He pulled a €20 note from his pocket and slapped it on the counter.

'Still no,' said Paudie. 'Have a ginger ale.'

'It's a whiskey or nothing. I'll go to Cúltrá for me drinks in future if you won't serve me.'

Paudie's smile turned sympathetic. 'A whiskey won't help you. A clear head is what you need, trust me. Women like us even less when we're stupid. Here. We'll make it a double. On the house.'

With a growl of frustration Eric stormed off. Out the door this time. Destination unknown.

At half six they were called for dinner and Luke found himself seated at the top table next to Father Halpin. Betty had placed Lily at a nearby table beside Jasper and though Luke was close enough to see every forkful that slipped between her lips, he was too far away to catch any of the conversation passing between them.

Eric returned from whatever cave he'd been in and sat at the other end of the top table. He cast frequent glances at Cassandra who'd got the place of honour beside Betty but his expression gradually changed from pained to concerned. Luke wasn't long in understanding why. Cassandra's laughs and giggles were all gone. She hardly touched her food. As the meal went on, she starting looking more and more uncomfortable. Her posture went from stiff to rigid. Whenever Betty addressed a remark to her she smiled and answered cheerfully but as soon as Betty turned away she was back to grimacing.

As the shadows lengthened Paudie stood up, tapped his champagne glass, and the speeches started. Ned's was extremely romantic, Betty's effusively grateful, and Paudie's had them all laughing and clapping but Luke noticed Lily wasn't paying attention anymore either. Her gaze was likewise locked on Cassandra, a worry line deepening between her brows.

Ned and Betty stood up to cut the cake. Half the room moved to get a photograph and Cassandra hurried for the bathroom.

Lily was on her feet the next instant to follow her in but burst back out twenty seconds later, her face wild with fright, and ran to Luke. 'Get Mark quick! Something's wrong with Cassandra. She's on the floor. She's been sick. She says everything hurts.'

By the time Mark had grabbed his medical bag, a small crowd had gathered round the stricken bridesmaid. A hand towel was balled under her head and Lily was on her knees beside her, holding her hand and trying to reassure her as she bucked with pain.

'Oh, Cassie!' cried Betty. 'What happened?'

'Everyone out, please,' said Mark. 'Let's give her some privacy.'

With Luke's help, the bathroom was cleared, leaving just Lily, Luke and Mark behind.

Mark crouched. 'How long have you had this pain?' He took Cassandra's wrist and checked his watch as he got her heart-rate.

'About a week,' she gasped. 'On and off. But never – *this* – *bad*.'

'Where is it most sore?'

'Here,' said Cassandra, touching a spot below and to the right of her belly button, 'but it was up higher before and then it moved.'

'Can you describe the pain? Is it sharp? Dull?'

'Sharp,' she gasped, higher-pitched than ever. '*Very sharp*.'

Mark secured a thermometer under her arm and kept talking. 'And before?'

'Less sharp. More like indigestion.'

'We thought she had indigestion,' said Lily. 'Or food poisoning. She ate some under-cooked sausages a few days ago.'

'It wasn't the sausages,' said Cassandra, her grip tightening around Lily's fingers. 'The pain was there before.'

'She had a stitch on Sunday when we went to get the cake ingredients,' Luke remembered.

'And she's been off her food,' said Lily.

'Any chance you could be pregnant?' asked Mark.

Cassandra blanched. 'No. Why?'

'Just trying to rule out possibilities. Any medical conditions?'

She shook her head.

'Recent surgery?'

'No.'

'Allergies?'

'I don't like peanuts.'

'You're allergic to them?'

'No.'

'Taking any medication?'

'Yes,' said Lily. 'She's been taking pills Eric gave her for days now. She took the last of them this morning.'

'What was the medication?'

'I don't know the name,' said Cassandra. 'It was on the box. Black writing.' That was all she managed before she was writhing again, her eyes streaming.

'Get Eric,' said Mark. 'Find out what he gave her.'

Eric was pacing just outside and fell on Luke like an expectant father. 'How is she? Is she alright? Betty says she can't move.'

'We don't know for sure what's wrong with her yet. Mark's examining her. We need to know what medicine she's been taking?'

Eric looked at him blankly.

'You gave her medicine a few days ago? After the barbecue. For indigestion.'

His eyes went wide. 'She was only supposed to take two of those. They're not for indigestion. They're painkillers. Very strong.'

'Come in and tell Mark what they're called.'

'I don't remember,' he said, following Luke in.

The sight of Cassandra on the floor drew him to a shocked halt.

'*Oh Jesus!*'

Mark was palpating Cassandra's abdomen through her dress.

She cried out frantically.

'I know,' he soothed. 'Tight and tender. Especially here? And when I take my hand away?'

She yelped.

'Okay.' He turned to Eric. 'What did you give her?'

Eric didn't answer because he wasn't paying attention. 'Oh Cassie, I'm sorry. I'm so sorry.' He slumped to his knees beside her.

'You didn't do anything,' she panted, her face clenching as she cried out again and tried to turn sideways.

'*Eric!*' said Mark. '*I need to know what she was taking.*'

'Just painkillers,' said Eric. 'I've had them lying around for ages.'

'Where did you get them?' asked Luke, as Mark removed the thermometer from under Cassandra's arm and checked it.

'They gave them to me at the hospital. After I had me tonsils out. I didn't use them all. Did they do this to her?'

'No,' said Mark, getting to his feet, 'but I'm guessing they've been masking the pain nicely.' He whipped out his phone and dialled 999. 'Ambulance service, please.' There was a brief wait as everyone looked at each other wide-eyed and then he was talking again. 'Hello, I'm calling from Inish Ruin. I have a patient with suspected acute appendicitis. I've no access to analgesics and moving her is not an option.' There was a pause. 'Yes, we'll definitely need a helicopter.' There was another wait, longer this time. 'O'Callaghan's Hotel. Field to the side. No overhead wires. Yes. Yes. We'll be ready. Thank you.' He hung up and came back to Cassandra and smiled reassuringly. 'Help is on the way. Hang in there.'

'*That's it?*' cried Eric. '*Hang in there? Can't you give her something?*' and he promptly burst into tears.

Luke and Lily exchanged a glance.

Donie, Pat, Betty and Gráinne tiptoed in to get an update. Gráinne asked if she could be of any assistance.

Donie let out a low whistle. 'It's nice in here. Very fancy. Why don't we get flowers in our bathroom?'

'*Get out!*' shouted Eric. '*Leave her alone!*'

'You're in here,' said Donie, 'so we're allowed too.'

'Why is he crying?' asked Betty, glancing over at Lily, who could only shrug.

'Post-traumatic stress,' said Donie. 'He's reliving some previous injury.'

'No, he's not, you twit,' said Pat. 'He's in love, isn't he? When someone you love hurts, you cry. Everyone knows that.'

'*What?*' spat Donie. 'You've been watching too many chick flicks. Real men don't cry. Not unless their commanding officer risks his life to pull them out of enemy territory getting severely injured in the process and then only one tear – quickly brushed away – and no one mentions it again. This,' he said, pointing to Eric as if he was some unnatural aberration, 'is not right and I'm not having it. *On your feet, soldier!*'

Betty flicked Donie in the head with her finger.

'*Ow! Hey – that hurt!*'

'Don't make me twist your ears! Then we'll see how long you take to cry. *Out!*' She hustled Donie and Pat outside and they heard her ordering everyone else to have a slice of cake.

When she returned, Cassandra was still writhing but it was Eric not Lily holding her hand now and no one was suggesting he leave, least of all the patient who was managing somehow, between groans of agony, to comfort him. There was nothing for Gráinne to do except offer reassurances.

The helicopter landed thirty torturously long minutes later, sending greenery flying. Two paramedics strode from it carrying a stretcher and several bags of medical kit. A line of guests directed them to the bathroom where Mark gave a brief history and watched as they set up an IV line with antibiotics and morphine before they moved Cassandra onto the stretcher. As they lifted it Eric, through the tactic of feigned deafness, remained firmly attached to her side, effectively stealing Lily's place beside her friend in the helicopter. A look at Cassandra showed no objection to this substitution though and Luke guessed it was more beneficial, time being of the essence, to include Eric than have a protracted fight trying to leave him behind. With another blast that sent guests scurrying, the helicopter took off and headed north into the last hour of daylight.

Luke came back inside to find Lily standing by the door, staring uncertainly at two rucksacks on the floor as the band started up in a far corner. 'You okay?'

'I feel so guilty, Luke. Poor Cass. She asked me what side her appendix was on the day we arrived. I should have realised what was happening.'

'How could you have? We none of us guessed. But she'll be fine, you'll see. They'll have that appendix whipped out of her in no time.'

'And what about Eric?' She managed a weak smile. 'You think he'll survive?'

He shook his head. 'I'm afraid that one might be touch and go. First cut, you know. Extremely serious. Never guaranteed a recovery.'

He hoped she might understand what else he was trying to say but she just sighed. 'He won't know what hit him. I give it a month before they're moving in together. Two before he's painting the minibus pink.' She glanced at her watch and then tensed. 'Oh, for the love of – '

'You've missed the last ferry again, haven't you?'

She groaned.

'I can give you a lift across in Dad's boat?'

She considered it for just a moment. 'Thanks but even if I left now I'd still miss the flight. Damn it. Excuse me. I have to phone work.' She walked away to a quieter corner of the room, pulled out her phone and dialled.

As Luke stood watching her, Gráinne approached him. 'Hi. Well, that was dramatic. The poor girl.'

'I know,' he said. 'But, look, thanks very much for the help.'

'Ah, I didn't do anything. You and your brother had it covered.'

He watched as Lily's expression changed. Clearly, her boss was not taking the news well.

'So, the band is kicking off,' said Gráinne. 'Can I grab a dance with you?'

He glanced down at her, conscious suddenly that she had looped her arm through his as the sequins of her dress rubbed against him.

'I don't think that's the best idea, do you?'

Her playful expression fell. 'But I've been waiting to get you for five minutes to myself all day. To have that talk. Remember?'

'What talk?'

Her cheeks flushed and she removed her arm. 'Luke. You agreed that my coming to the wedding was a good idea. That we'd have an opportunity to talk – to re-consider our break-up.'

Luke couldn't remember any such thing but she clearly believed he had.

'We have something good together,' she went on. 'It's easy and it's natural. You don't get that in every relationship. Where you feel you can be yourself. I mean, you feel you can be yourself with me, right?'

'Sure but–'

'So maybe we should have a second think about breaking up. Nothing's gone wrong. We haven't fought. We haven't done anything to each other. And we have so much in common. I mean, we understand what makes the other tick.'

He glanced back to Lily. She was still on the call but had gone pale.

'It's just this bad habit you've got yourself into,' Gráinne continued, 'of only doing short-term relationships. But I don't know what you're so afraid of? Just give us another few months. Give us a year. See for yourself that it's something you can do. Something you'd be great at.'

He looked back to Gráinne as her words sank in. She was right, they had plenty in common. And she was a good person. He thought it unlikely she'd ever walk away from him if he made her a commitment. She'd never break his heart. But then how could she, when it was already broken?

'I wouldn't be great at it, Gráinne. I'm sorry.'

'You would, Luke.'

'I wouldn't because I don't have a whole heart to give you.'

She stared at him and that little crease was back between her brows again. Her mental triage. 'Who?' was all she said at last.

His gaze drifted back to Lily. The phone was still pressed to her ear. Her face was flushed now, her eyes wide as if enduring something unpleasant.

'Does she know?' she asked.

Know what, he wondered? That he still loved her or that she'd broken him for anyone else? 'I don't know,' he admitted.

'Does she even care?'

He didn't say anything as Gráinne stared at him, then back at Lily. And an expression crossed her face, the likes of which Luke imagined might be reserved for a tumour proving particularly resistant to treatment. Then she abruptly headed for the bar, where she pulled up a chair in front of Mikey.

Luke turned back in time to see Lily standing rigid with the phone now hanging limp from her hand. He made his way over to her.

'Hey, you okay?'

'No. I'm finished,' she said in a whisper.

'What?'

'I'm fired, Luke. For good this time. He's going to sue me as well. I'll never work as an accountant again.'

'But that's ridiculous. Just because you missed another ferry? Did you tell him about Cassandra?'

'Yes.'

'And?'

'He said the removal of a vestigial organ hardly counts as a medical emergency.'

'Hardly counts? You can die from a ruptured appendix! What a prick! But why is he going to sue you?'

'Because I owe him a lot of money, Luke, and he's knows I can't afford to pay him back if I don't sell the cottage.'

He blinked. 'But you said there was a buyer for it?'

'There is. I just ... I just couldn't let them have it. Not to gut it.'

'Okay. Okay. Well, don't panic. We'll figure this out.'

Jasper ambled over. 'You okay, Lily?'

'I – I'm fine. Thanks, Jasper. Just worrying about Cassandra.'

'That's understandable but they'll have that appendix whipped out of her in no time.'

'That's what Luke says.'

Jasper's lips pursed. 'Well, I'm sure he'd know. It's a shame his expertise didn't spot the problem sooner though.'

Luke didn't bother rising to the bait but found Lily defending him instead. 'Eric had Cassandra on strong pain meds, unbeknownst to everyone. They masked all her symptoms.'

Jasper looked between them and then raised his hands. 'I'll leave you to it.' And he headed off to the mens' on the other side of the room.

'Are you going to try to find another buyer for the cottage then?' Luke asked, drawing her gaze back to him.

'I don't know. Maybe not, if I can find a way to keep it.'

'Really? Then ... would that mean you'd be staying in it? I mean, coming back here to live. For good?'

She nodded.

Luke's mind raced. 'But that's ...' Lily was actually going to *stay*? Was he a fool to let hope rise so quickly in him? Could he relight the candle between them if he had proximity enough to at least try? There were fewer miles between here and Cork than London certainly. But still there were miles. Unless he stayed too? Ran the pub? *It'd be a good life for her.* Perhaps. But how much did he want to be a paramedic? As much as he wanted Lily back if he could get her?

'Well, we should have a drink to celebrate that, shouldn't we? Or do you fancy a dance?' he said.

They looked at the dance floor together. It was heaving with uncoordinated bodies doing a movement that seemed to alternate between a rugby scrum and a can-can.

'It doesn't look entirely safe,' Lily murmured.

'No,' he agreed. 'So will you have something?' He nodded to the bar.

'Thanks but I'm not really in the mood to celebrate. What with Cassandra and ... well, blowing up my career. Do you think Betty would mind if I still skipped out of the wedding early as planned?' She glanced at the rucksacks by her feet again. 'And I should probably get Cass's stuff back to the cottage.'

Luke instantly scooped up the larger rucksack and slung it over his shoulder. The thing weighed a ton. 'Good idea. I'm sure that's where she'll be expecting to stay once she's recovered. Until she talks Eric into letting her move in with him, anyway.'

But Lily took a step back. 'Oh no, I didn't mean for – to drag you from ...' She glanced around the room as if looking for someone. She cleared her throat and started again. 'I don't need any help, thanks.'

'Really? You reckon you can carry them both at the same time?'

Her eyes made the briefest dart to the rucksack and then back to him. 'No?'

'Planning on making two trips?'

A swallow. Another no, then.

'So what's the problem?'

'*Um*, there's no problem, I suppose, if you're ... sure no one will mind?'

'Can't see why anyone would?'

'Well, okay then. Thanks.' She reached for her own rucksack and, without further ado, they slipped out of the building in silence.

Chapter Twenty-Three

Ruined

A solitary cloud passed high overhead – a slow-drifting island, its edges bright-rimmed against the dimming sky.

Lily tracked it as she tallied the various calamities of the evening:

Cassandra borne off in an air ambulance? *Check.*

Preston set on destroying her career? *Check.*

Being alone again with Luke when she'd expected at least one large body of water between them? *Double check.*

She tried to focus her attention on her senses: hearing again the forgotten rhythm of their footsteps on the tarmac, the occasional tumble of a loose pebble, the warmth of the air against her skin as she spied the sea in the distance and breathed its salty tang. But none of these was quite distraction enough to forget that Luke O'Callaghan was making her atoms vibrate once more to whatever damn frequency he transmitted.

She tried to picture the dynamic between himself and Gráinne, imagining Gráinne was far easier to get along with than herself. She'd be softer, probably. Less prickly, certainly. But did she make Luke happy? Did she know how lucky she was to have him?

She willed so hard for Luke to say something then, *anything* to trip her out of this unhelpful train of thought. But he remained silent as they passed through the tunnel of trees, seemingly lost in his own contemplations.

A group of four approached them. There were two women whose faces Lily didn't recognise and two children whose faces she did – the auburn-haired girl and her dark-haired friend. The young ones reached them first. They were whispering conspiratorially and Lily noticed the girl carried a bright-blue delphinium which she recognised as one of Jasper's hybrids. Had she plucked it herself or had the boy got it for her? Seeing the embarrassed smile on her face, Lily guessed it was the latter.

The women passed with nods of greeting and then they were alone again.

They reached the hostel and stopped briefly. The flowers in the garden stood perfectly still as if posing for a painting, while a wood-pigeon cycled through its five-coo-melody, hidden somewhere within a gnarly oak beyond. The lights in the building were out. It would be a couple of hours yet before Jasper left the reception to receive his overnight guests. But even in his absence she could sense tension rising in Luke. But still, he said nothing, just led them onwards and then up Barrett Lane until they finally reached the cottage.

Lily's rucksack hit the ground by the porch and she took a few steps back to stare up at it. The flaking paint still showed. And there was no light inside shining a welcome. But still something felt *different* about the place.

She moved to the front door and examined the support ties around the frame, pressing a few that had come loose back into the timber with her thumb. Then she picked up the wisteria and eased the trailing stems gently onto them.

A glance over her shoulder showed Luke with his fingers crossed. But after a minute the ties were still holding. She retrieved the key from her rucksack and inserted it into the lock. It turned easily. The door opened with the gentlest push. The air inside was fresh. All she could smell were the leftover strawberries from breakfast. All she could hear was the wall clock in the kitchen beating steadily.

She took the deepest breath then turned to Luke who beamed as if he could actually feel her happiness and she couldn't resist putting her arm around him and giving him a hug. It felt like *home*. Had she finally found it again at long, long last?

Pup started barking and Luke went outside to feed her. By the time he returned, dusk had fallen and he set about lighting some tealights as if knowing the moment was a fragile one for her, too delicate for the harsh touch of a light bulb.

She expected him to head back to the reception then where Gráinne was surely waiting. She told him she was going to have a bath, expecting him to take his leave. But he just raised an eyebrow as if to ask if there was room to share. And she blushed because the thought of them naked together once more suddenly made the blood sing in her veins. And then she blushed because she was making a fool of herself all over again. And then she blushed because, while she was busy blushing, Luke had taken three steps towards her and pulled her into his arms.

He kissed her with all the fierce passion she remembered from their youth and a degree of skill she did not. *Holy Mother of ...!* Her toes curled, her mind went to mush, while her body hoisted the white flag to sensation. The feeling of his fingers tangling in her hair. The hardness of his chest, the warmth of his lips and the soft, beckoning slide of his tongue. She lost all concept of time, only knew it was much too soon when he released her, his breath shaky.

He ran a hand through his hair. '*Damn*,' he said and shook his head at her, one cheek dimpling.

'I thought you couldn't,' she whispered.

His gaze heated. 'Oh, I definitely can.'

'But what about Gráinne?'

He stared at her in surprise. 'We're not ... no. Not for weeks. It's only you.'

Her heart soared at that. She made to kiss him back but he stopped her with a hand cupping her cheek.

'Not if you want that bath. Kiss me again, Lil, and I won't be able to let you go.'

She waited then for the fear to return, for her head to start running risk calculations. But there was nothing except a feeling of rightness in her heart. So she just nodded shyly and went upstairs.

The water from the tap was close to scalding and, as Lily only seemed capable of extremes of feeling right now, she laughed as she reached for the cold tap to even it out. She added a few drops of bath oil and started humming as the smell of chamomile and lemon balm filled the room. The humming turned to singing. Some random bit of a tune. She heard Pup start howling in the yard. Ah, so cute. She was trying to sing along. Suddenly the radio in the kitchen was turned on to a classical station. At maximum volume. *Romantic*. She shivered to herself in anticipation and was just about to lower herself into the bath when her phone pinged with a text message. Thinking it might be news of Cassandra she halted, got back out, and reached for where she'd left it balancing on the edge of the sink. It was from a number she didn't recognise. And lately those had meant nothing but trouble. Requests for payment. But underneath this phone number the message just showed **Attachment: 1 Photo**.

Lily clicked to open it, stared at the image and blinked a few times before tapping on it again to expand it. It was a photograph of a couple in an embrace. A man and a woman. Someone had photographed them kissing. The man was instantly recognisable as Luke. The woman in his arms had her back to the camera so Lily couldn't see her face. But if her blonde hair hadn't given away her identity, the silver-sequined dress that clung to her body certainly did. And something squeezed so tight in Lily's gut she dropped the phone to the floor and clutched the sides of the sink with her hands, before resting her head against the cold porcelain rim as a wave of nausea rushed over her. The phone pinged again by her foot and she sagged low enough to flip it upright to see the screen. It was another message from the same number. And she didn't even have to click it to read its opening line. **Just thought you should know ...** And when she did click it, the follow-up read **... how happy I can make him**.

Gráinne had sent this to her? Lily didn't know if that made it better or worse than if it had come from a stranger. She must have got her number somehow and sent this as a ... what? Gloat? Warning? No, as evidence. Proof she and Luke were still together. That they'd been together *today*. Someone had caught the moment on camera. Who, she wondered? A friend of Gráinne's at the wedding? Or one of Betty's family? Gráinne must have seen Lily leaving the hotel with Luke and thought ... Lily gulped ... suspected maybe that she and Luke might ...

But she'd asked Luke outright about his relationship with Gráinne. And he'd said it was over – that now it was only *her*.

But that had been a lie. Here was proof. But what game was Luke playing? Keeping Gráinne sweet with kisses in case Lily didn't respond to his advances the way she had downstairs? Hedging his bets? What sort of person did that? But Jasper had said Luke had got himself a reputation. What had he called him? *The Playboy of Inish Ruin?* That he wasn't the person Lily remembered anymore. No. He certainly wasn't. She didn't know who *this* Luke was at all. And a Risk Analysis opened in her mind once more. **Title: Luke O'Callaghan. Probabilities against Impact Levels**, with the range now adjusted from **Safety** to **Heartbreak**.

She got back in the bath. But, once in, she wondered if she was in fact suffering from shock. She should probably be doing something else right now other than having a bath but she didn't quite know what. The bath was comforting and cocooning whilst everything inside her felt unmoored and adrift.

She went through the motions of washing, buffing her skin until it gleamed. Then buffing it some more until it started to go red.

The melody through the floorboards changed. Another classical piece. 'Spring' by Vivaldi. She remembered a joke someone had told her about how Vivaldi was so good they couldn't believe he got cancelled after only four seasons. It had been funny at the time. She shampooed her hair, rinsed, then she put a dollop of conditioner on the burnt bit, even though she knew it wouldn't do anything to fix it. Things that were burnt were never the same again after. They just stayed burnt. She counted off an imprecise three minutes in her head then disappeared under the water to rinse again. But there was so much product in the bath now, it was impossible. She went under again, swishing vigorously and getting water up her nose for her troubles. Coughing, she sat up and reached for a towel. But she was still coughing when she took the towel away and could suddenly smell *smoke*.

She scrambled out of the bath, wrapped the towel around her and opened the door to be greeted with a cloud of it on the landing.

Lily's eyes instantly started to sting.

'*Luke!*' She rasped. But he didn't answer. And whatever tumult of feelings she had towards him right now, fear for his safety trumped them all. If a fire had broken out downstairs he could be trapped or injured right now. He could be dying as she stood here vacillating! She ran down the stairs, clutching her phone, and rounded the corner into the kitchen. Only to find there was no smoke in here at all. But there was no Luke either. She ran on to the sitting room where her relief at finding him in perfect health was instantly obliterated on seeing him add a bucket of coal to an already blazing fire ...

He beamed as he saw her and crossed the room instantly, running an admiring glance over her face, before his palm met his chest with a dramatic thump. 'God, you're so beautiful, Lily. I swear you'll give me a heart attack.'

'Not if you *kill me* first, I won't!' she cried, tightening the towel. 'There's smoke filling the whole upstairs!'

He stood stock-still in confusion as she ran back into the kitchen, filled the largest bucket she could find with water, ran back in and tossed it all on the fire – which was extinguished with one anticlimactic *pooomph* of smoke and a pitiful sizzle of steam.

Then Lily returned to the bottom of the stairs and looked up – into a dense cloud of noxious grey which was now descending.

The radio was knocked off and then Luke was standing beside her, looking up too.

'Holy shit,' he said. 'How on earth ...? The chimney must be –' But Pup's high-pitched barks cut him off and he turned to Lily. 'Best get outside, Lil. And get Pup away from the yard too. If the fire's got into the chimney breast itself this mightn't be over yet.' He grabbed the bucket from her hands. 'I'm going to try douse it where it goes up through the cottage.'

'Is that the right thing to do?'

'Not a clue. But you'll be safer outside. Away from the smoke.'

'But what about you?'

'I'll be after you in a minute. *Go*.'

Lily ran to the yard, catching her bare foot on a loose stone, and looked back up to see Nana's bedroom window. And the mass of thick smoke behind it.

She turned back to face Pup, who bared her teeth as Lily approached, clearly unimpressed with the night's proceedings. But Lily didn't have the luxury of being afraid of her right now so she just told her to stop it. Sharply. '*I mean it*,' she warned.

The growling stopped and Pup whimpered and then sat as Lily came closer.

'We can't stay here. It's not safe.'

Pup cocked her head and twitched her brows.

'I'm taking off your chain now and if you snap at me I won't take you for any more walks.'

This threat was treated with a bark of delight and Lily guessed something crucial had been lost in translation.

She unhooked the chain but Pup stayed sitting, her tail tapping the ground and looking at her expectantly.

'You go out the front and wait for me in the lane.' When Pup didn't move, she tugged on her collar and dragged her down the side passage, almost losing hold of her towel in the process, opened the gate and pushed her out. '*Now stay there, like a good girl!*' She closed the gate again and ran back inside to find the kitchen now all smokey.

'*Luke!*' She followed the sound of coughing and found him at the bottom of the stairs, clutching a fresh bucket of water.

'I'm making headway,' he rasped. 'I think we're alright.' Then he coughed again, as though ejecting a lung, and dropped to his knees.

Lily grabbed him by the arm and half-dragged him back outside.

In the lane they slumped onto the grass, Luke still coughing between heaving pants. He was black from head to toe, his clothes riddled with smoke.

But Pup had vanished. Lily called her again and again in vain. She ran to retrieve her rucksack from where she'd left it by the porch door but fell on it heavily, hurting her wrist. But there were clothes inside so she threw on underpants, a bra and shorts. Reaching for a T-shirt, though, her fingers found the cactus.

It was squashed through the middle, fatally wounded.

Irrational anger rose inside her, muddled with pain. '*I didn't ask you to light a fire, did I?*' she called over her shoulder. She put the T-shirt on and returned to Luke who was back on his feet and staring at the cottage, an expression of awe on his face as the remaining smoke looped out from the eaves, like the strangest crown.

'I'm sorry, Lil. I've no idea how it happened. I checked the draught first and everything. Lit a piece of paper. The smoke went up.'

'Well, it didn't come out the chimney. It went everywhere else.'

She stared again at the cottage and thought of everything inside now coated with soot. Nana's dress that she'd been wearing. The cardigan that smelled of her ... oh no. Cass had suggested they split the contents of the black bag of Nana's clothes between their rucksacks for the plane. And that cardigan had not been in hers. *No!* She looked around, hoping against hope.

'Where did you leave Cassandra's rucksack?'

Luke rubbed his forehead, smudging a streak of black. 'On the sofa in the sitting room.'

Lily covered her face with her hands. She'd never get that smell back so. She felt tears threaten and all the knots inside her clenched tight to hold the weakening emotion in check. *She would not cry*. So anger was all that was left. And there was an all too convenient target for it.

Luke reached for her hand. 'Come on. We don't have to stay here. We'll go to Hook Cove. Figure out a plan.'

She pulled away though and balled her hands to fists. 'I want to stay here. At my cottage. *Alone*.'

'Ah, Lil. Don't do that.'

He tried to put his arm around her but she wrenched free. 'Go back to the hotel, Luke. *To Gráinne*. I'm sure she'll be more than happy to see you.'

His jaw went slack. '*What?*'

But her chin rose. 'It's been fun. A trip down Memory Lane. Best of luck in Cork.'

'*What?*' he said again. 'No. Look, I know you're upset. But come on! We can get the cottage cleaned up good as new. Repaint everything. It's unfortunate but it's not the end of the world. It's not the end of ... us. I mean, I didn't do this on purpose.'

'Tried to set fire to the cottage? No. No, I don't think you did *that* on purpose.'

'Then *what*?'

She pulled up her phone, opened the text message from Gráinne and showed him the photograph.

He cocked his head as he squinted at it. 'Where did you get that?'

She raised an eyebrow. 'You're not going to claim it's not you, then?'

He stared at her. 'Why would I? It's clearly me. And my question was: where did you get it?'

She hesitated. 'From a concerned party. So you can see how our business together is now concluded.'

'*Our business? Fuck sake, Lily!* You obviously know I was dating Gráinne or you wouldn't have asked me about her earlier. What exactly am I supposed to have done wrong now?'

'Well, if that isn't obvious, there's hardly any point in me explaining.'

His eyes narrowed. 'Humour me, all the same. *Explain it. Go on.*'

She swallowed. 'Fine. Okay. If I have to spell it out. *Exhibit A.*' She pointed to Gráinne's dress.

'And?' he said, looking confused now.

'She's wearing it *today*, Luke. Meaning you two aren't done. Meaning you and I aren't anything.'

He took the phone from her. Stared at the photograph. Tapped into it and then turned it back to face her. 'And that's the date and timestamp.'

Lily stared at it. It was from 1.06 in the morning. Five weeks ago.

'We were at her friend's wedding together. She wore the same dress. And, furthermore, I'll draw your attention to *Exhibit B*.' He zoomed into the photograph. To the shirt he was wearing in it. And raised an eyebrow. 'What's missing from this picture, detective?'

Lily looked at him, looked at the stupid lurid red waistcoat he was still wearing over his shirt and back to the photograph. No waistcoat. *Oh God*.

Luke brushed down said waistcoat, straightened the cuffs on his shirt and then started walking away from her down the lane.

'Luke, I'm – I'm sorry. I ... *Please*.'

He halted in his tracks, his shoulders rising and falling, before slowly turning to face her. 'The candle never went out for me, Lily.'

'What?'

'I've always loved you. I think I always will, as inconvenient as that is. But I can't be with someone who believes the worst of me *every chance she gets*. First Katie and now this? If you can't trust me, even knowing me as well as you do, I don't think you can ever really love me. And you know what?' He swallowed. 'I think I deserve better than that.'

With a look of pain then he turned and walked away and Lily was left with all the satisfaction of knowing that everything now was ruined. And that *she* was the one who'd ruined it.

Chapter Twenty-Four

The Tenderest Parts

The cottage didn't burst into flames with Luke's departure, though a part of Lily thought she might deserve it if it did. Instead, the smoking crown dissipated, trailing off into the air to become a faint wispy plume. The final slap in the face was the rain that rolled in half an hour later and tamped down any remaining trace of smoke, as Lily sheltered in the coal bunker. Then the rain too died away and the clouds rolled back, leaving the night sky clear and cold.

Lily went to the back door of the cottage and heard the kitchen clock ticking away inside. *We have a pulse.* She tried the light switch, surprised when nothing happened. Could the smoke have knocked out the electricity? She activated the torch on her phone instead and entered. She shone the beam of light around the kitchen but could see no obvious damage, though the air was acrid. She could taste it on her tongue.

She continued on to the sitting room and retrieved Cassandra's rucksack from the sofa. She brought it outside and put it into the relative freshness of the coal bunker before returning to the sitting room to see if anything else needed salvaging tonight. But everything she touched was coated in soot and, in the end, she just stared at the mess for a minute before making her way to the hall.

There, she shone her light up the staircase. No smoke lingered on the landing above but somehow everything still looked grey as Lily climbed slowly.

Nana's door was open and on the far side of her bedroom, where the plastered chimney breast took a wedge out of an otherwise perfect rectangle, there was a smear of black on the wall. Moving closer to examine it, Lily saw that the plaster had cracked here, revealing the stonework behind. It was wet to the touch too. From one of Luke's buckets of water, presumably. But nothing else in the room was damaged or burnt, thankfully. Although everything stank.

Lily pushed aside the heavy curtains and opened the window, shivering as the air whispered past her and on out into the night.

Lily grabbed the curtains and draped as much of their fabric as possible outside the window, causing a shower of soot which covered her hands and arms in the process. And then, not knowing what else to do, she sat on the floor, where she noticed the Sacred Heart picture resting against the skirting board in front of her. There were a few dents to the frame but otherwise it was fine. It was even the right way up. Lily tried to figure out how it could have got there for it had travelled some distance from its usual spot on the wall. She could only guess it had come loose from its fixings somehow, dropped the few inches onto the projecting ledge that held the light bulb and then tumbled clockwise to come to a halt by the window.

It had made for the nearest exit in an emergency.

Well, Lily could understand that instinct. 'Guess you weren't the fire hazard after all.'

She straightened out her legs and her right foot knocked the base. The picture tipped instantly and whacked her hard on the shin. She went to push it upright, cursing the sting, only to find herself eye to eye with Jesus. And surrounded by mess, with her leg hurting, her mind replaced His face with another almost exactly like it. On the wall of a hospital. Where she'd woken with her leg in plaster. Woken to discover that pieces of her – both seen and unseen – had been shattered.

A baby. Fifteen weeks. No bigger than her palm. Too small to survive the impact she'd had such trouble remembering. But the memories came flooding back now. Of the cold seeping through her boots. The flakes falling small but so fast they spun in her eyes. The squeak of compressing snow underfoot. Every step taking her further from that school and closer to home. Back to Nana. Back to Luke. Because she was pregnant. Because she needed their help. Because she needed *them*. The road and path blurring into an unnavigable expanse of white. The blare of an engine rounding a bend, headlights blinding. Realising she was *in* the road. The squeal of brakes. Swerving and then ...

That room.

That bleak awful quiet.

And that serene face staring back at her from the wall.

Then the doctor coming in and asking who she'd like them to contact to let them know what had happened?

And Lily had sobbed then because there was no one. No one who'd pick up anyway. And even if she could reach them, what could she tell them now? When her mistake had cost Luke their baby? Or Nana? Who already had one terrible anniversary to bear. Would she really give her another? That involved the loss of another child?

No. Because she was eighteen and it was her choice. Her business. To tell or not.

So instead, the principal was informed she'd been in a traffic accident and nothing more. And a fortnight later she'd gone back to school to finish healing in public and to grieve in secret until grief had turned to bitterness which had nowhere to go but in. Until all the soft and tender parts of her had calcified, leaving only the hard shell of Lily Barrett in their place.

By the time Nana reached her at the school, Lily had become numb, feeling no connection anymore to the voice on the other end of the line. She asked no questions about their friends or neighbours. She asked nothing about Luke, who was shrouded along with their daughter now in the darkest crypt of her heart. She was fine. Getting some physio on her leg soon and would be back in action before she knew it. School was great. But she really needed to get some homework done. She'd talk to her again when it was a better time.

But it had never been a better time. Not really. Not to say the unsayable. Only to keep pretending.

The wetness on her cheeks registered before Lily realised she was crying, hard enough that it quickly became gaping jags of weeping. She cried for her baby and the life she would never lead. She cried for Nana who wasn't there anymore to comfort her. She cried for Cassandra, for the trauma she was going through right now. She even cried for the cactus. Then she cried because she was crying for a cactus and there were bigger problems in the world to cry about. So she had a good long sob about climate change and by that stage her head hurt so much from crying she just cried in self-pity.

Then her phone rang.

It was a number she didn't recognise. Someone looking for money probably or ringing to give out to her and that made her cry all over again.

It rang a second time. She answered and waited for whoever it was to speak first in case she needed to hang up.

'Hello? Lily?'

'Cass?'

There was a groan. 'Yes, it's me. Calling from Eric's phone. Just to let you know I'm fine. Still alive. Well, I feel awful but the nurse said it's the anaesthetic wearing off. Kind of a sicky feeling. They took out my appendix. It hadn't burst so that was lucky. Eric was amazing. He stayed with me for as long as they let him. He's gone to a B&B now but he says he wants me to move in with him! Not to the B&B but to his place on Inish Ruin. He said I knocked him off his feet and he just didn't know which way was up. I drove him to stout. Isn't that romantic? I don't know what I'm going to do for money if the spa won't be going ahead but I'll figure something out.' She gave a happy sigh and then another groan. 'I really feel sick. So what did I miss?'

Lily looked about her at the soot-laden mess of her childhood home. 'Nothing much.'

'Did you catch the last ferry?'

'No.'

'I guessed you wouldn't. Did you dance with Luko then? He was really hoping to have a dance with you.'

'No.'

'Ah you dope, Lily! I'm sorry to have to say that to you but you *are* a dope. Why didn't you dance with him? He's crazy about you. And you could be so happy if you just gave him a chance. He's like your little hermit-crab buddy.'

Lily's chin wobbled as she remembered their kiss in the kitchen. That feeling of rightness in her heart. Of belonging somewhere again. A fat tear fell.

'Can I say something to you?' continued Cassandra. 'As a friend.'

'Sh-sure.'

'I don't think the no-feelings thing is working out for you. I've tried it and I'd have to say it's more trouble than it's worth.'

Another tear fell and then another and Lily reached for the hem of her T-shirt to stem the flow. '*O-kay*,' she choked.

'So I want you to do something for me. I want you to cry. Just once and see how you feel after. I know it's hard for you but I want you to think of something really, really sad. Go somewhere no one can see you,' she added, 'and just see does it make things any clearer. Will you do that for me?'

Lily turned the phone away so Cassandra wouldn't hear her sobs.

'Lily? You still there?'

'*Ahum*.'

There was a long pause and then a whispered, 'What's happened?'

Lily held her breath as long as she could before ... 'I was pregnant.'

'Oh. *Oh!* When?'

'When I was eighteen. And I lost her. And it was my fault.'

She heard Cassandra's inhale. 'How was it your fault?'

'Because I made a stupid mistake. I stepped into the road and got hit. That's how I really got that scar on my leg.'

'Oh, Lily, I'm so sorry.'

'It was my fault,' Lily said again.

But Cassandra was silent now.

'Cass?'

Still nothing. And Lily swallowed around a ball in her throat and went to hang up. 'Okay, so I'll just–'

'No, wait,' said Cassandra at last. 'Just wait a minute.' Then: 'What was her name?'

'I don't ...?'

'What did you name her, Lily?' she insisted.

Lily shook her head, even though Cassandra couldn't see it. 'She was just fifteen weeks.'

But Cassandra was silent once more. Waiting. As if knowing there was more.

'Emma,' said Lily, at last. 'Her name was Emma.'

'Ah. That's a really lovely name. And what did she look like, Emma?'

Lily closed her eyes and took a shuddering breath as she imagined her daughter. Not the tiny body she'd held in her hands but the girl she would have been. 'She had auburn hair like mine and eyes like Luke's.'

'Of course,' said Cassandra. 'She was a beauty then.'

'Yeah. She was perfect.'

There was a sniff on Cassandra's end of the line. 'What else, Lily?'

Lily drew another breath as she felt something loosen in her chest. 'And she loved living here on Inish Ruin. And she really loved her dad.'

'Well, of course she did,' said Cassandra with feeling 'He probably spoilt her rotten.'

'Yeah.' She smiled. 'We'd fight about that a lot.'

'I'll bet.'

'And she loved when her grand-nana read to her most of all.'

'Oh yeah? What was her favourite book? No wait, don't tell me. Let me guess. *The Magic Stone?*'

Lily laughed at that through her tears. 'No. The guy in that's an asshole. But she liked all the rest.'

'That's good.'

'Yeah. Yeah, it is.'

There was another long silence interspersed with sniffs at both ends now.

'I'm very sorry I didn't get to meet her, Lily,' said Cassandra at last, and Lily could hear the wobble in her voice.

'I'm very sorry too.'

'Well ... I better go and get some sleep now, if that's okay? Eric's coming back to the hospital first thing and hopefully I'll be out of here and back there again soon. Oh, and if you get a chance, could you ask Shay if he'd do the minibus for him tomorrow? Or Pat if Shay isn't free?'

'Sure.'

'And Lily?'

'Yeah?'

'I love you.'

'I love you, too,' she said and ended the call.

In the darkness, Lily leaned her head back to look up at the sky through the window. But as she raised a watery gaze this time, the stars went from solitary dots to tiny crosses of light, reaching out with shiny beams towards each other, covering the sky in a golden web. She stared at the sight in wonder before two blinks washed it away, but the night didn't seem quite so cold anymore nor did she feel quite so alone.

She hugged herself then and tried to make sense of everything that had happened but her brain was preoccupied with physical discomfort now. Her head thumped, her eyes stung and her throat was coated in soot particles. Plus her leg was cramping. She shifted to one side to ease it out, reaching a hand back to steady herself, and felt a small lump on the floor behind, where the curtains usually hung. Her fingers closed around it. The shape felt oddly familiar. It was smooth and flat top and bottom but around the edges she could feel six rounded bumps and one pointed one. She held it up and in the moonlight picked out the unmistakable outline of a sheep eraser. She felt a moment of joy even as a stray tear rose, remembering who'd given this to her. *Luke*. Who was alive and well and still the same good soul he'd been at four years old. Always trying to make her happy. Always trying to do right by her. Always trying to protect her, even from herself.

She squinted to make out the sheep's face. Its expression was faded but the little side smirk was still visible. It told her she was an idiot. Well, she told herself that and it didn't disagree. She'd convinced herself she was better off without love. But, in truth, wasn't she just too scared to take another chance on it? Only seeing the risks? Bracing in case it might be taken away from her again if she disappointed someone? Or made a mistake? But everyone was afraid of losing love, right? But not everyone was such a *coward*. Betty had known the deepest of losses but she was still brave enough to give love another go. And Cassandra put her heart on the line every day for anyone to break if they wanted. And Luke? He'd spent a decade believing she'd just abandoned him. But he hadn't shut himself off from his feelings because of it. Not like she had. He'd been angry, confused and hurt, yes. But he'd still *felt*. He'd still loved. He still loved. *Her*. And she still loved *him*. Everything she felt when she was with him: safety, happiness, attraction – even the occasional bout of annoyance – what was that but love? She *loved* Luke O'Callaghan. He was her hermit-crab buddy and with belated clarity she realised that telling him that was worth *any* risk.

She needed to find him. To apologise for being such a coward. For lashing out instead of trusting him. To tell him he *did* deserve better than that. And to do it in a hurry before he left Inish Ruin for good. She needed his phone number. She didn't have it. The pub would though and she knew *that* number. She grabbed her phone, pressed it several times. The battery was dead. She shook it in the vain hope an emergency situation would spark some sort of emergency back-up. No such luck.

She got herself back downstairs, retrieved the charger from her rucksack and went to plug it in by the microwave. Then she thought 'safety first' and retrieved some old wellington boots and the long-handled yard brush from the scullery. She put the boots on her feet, connected the charger to her phone and settled the plug so it was just tipping the socket. Then she picked up the broom, put one end against the plug and pushed. The plug slid smartly into the socket – and nothing happened. *Woman not electrocuted. Phone not charging*. Then she slapped her forehead. Of course phone not charging! Because the power was out. Which was why she was doing this in the dark!

Now what? Now she'd just have to find the next nearest place with working electricity.

She ran down the lane as fast as she could in the wellies, all the way to Jasper's. The lights were still out in the hostel though, which didn't seem right at this hour. She knocked on the front door.

Candlelight flickered down the hallway. 'Come in and welcome. I'm afraid the power's out.' She stepped inside and Jasper's eyes widened as they took her in. 'Lily? What on earth?'

She found she couldn't speak as she made her way towards him, tears threatening again. What was wrong with her? Could she not turn the damn tap off now?

He ushered her into the kitchen, made her sit and asked her to please tell him what was wrong.

She did her best, inarticulately, to explain what had happened and then to confess she was the most cowardly person in the world.

'How do you figure that?'

He handed her a glass of water along with a tea towel which she used to dab her eyes.

'Because I push anyone that tries to love me away before they get the chance to hurt me.'

Jasper pursed his lips. 'Well, that doesn't seem true. What about your friend?'

'Cassandra? She's like a little sister to me.' Her chin started to wobble. 'And I was just going to let her go off to Belfast and never see her again!'

Jasper started to look uncomfortable. 'O-kay. But that sounds like something you could fix. What about Luke?'

'I accused him of something horrible,' she sniffed. 'And right after he nearly killed himself trying to stop the cottage from burning down too.'

'But it didn't burn down,' he double-checked.

'No. Just smoke damaged.'

But she put her head on the table and folded her arms around it.

'Ah, come now. Chin up. I'll get you a biscuit.'

Jasper made his way to the dresser, where a second candle was burning, and pulled out a tin shaped like a flowerpot.

Lily raised her head. 'Did I push Nana away too?'

'Of course you didn't,' he said, returning with it.

She popped off the lid. 'Then why did she send me away?'

It had been a rhetorical question but Jasper stiffened, then walked to the sink and opened the window in front of it. In the dim light, the sweet-musk of jasmine filled the room, along with the faintest hint of seaweed. 'What do you want to know?'

Lily stared at him in astonishment. 'Whatever you can tell me.'

He cleared his throat and drew a deep breath. 'Your nana wasn't my biggest fan.'

'Really? She never said anything.'

'She didn't have to, Lily. When a person isn't relaxed around you, you know it. You feel it. Well, that was your nana and me. She didn't warm to me for some reason and, in return, it was hard for me to warm to her.'

'Oh. I'm ... really sorry to hear that.'

'It doesn't matter now,' he said. 'We were always civil. But she'd asked me, a week before your birthday, if there was a rare or exotic orchid I could recommend for her to give you. She said you'd asked for a new shed to do your flower-arranging from – and that it was on order – but she wanted to have something special to give you on the day itself. I said I knew just the one you'd love and that I'd get it for her. But there was a delay. I was let down. And I only got my hands on it the night before.' He shifted his weight. 'But in the meantime, Luke had his little ... outburst at the pub about me looking at you "the wrong way". And it seemed to trigger her.'

'Trigger?'

'When she arrived to collect the orchid, she demanded to know what my intentions were towards you? What exactly I was *doing with you*?'

Lily's jaw dropped. 'What you ...? *Oh my God*. Oh, Jasper, I'm so sorry.'

He held up a hand. 'Given your mother's unfortunate history with an older man, I suppose I could understand how she might go to imagining the worst. But she implied I must have been taking advantage of you, Lily. That I must have been brainwashing you if you'd defend me even against Luke. As if you thought it was okay for me to see you,' he swallowed, 'in that way. And hadn't I had you alone with me out of sight of everyone in the greenhouse *for years*. Trying to make you feel special with gifts of seeds and flowers. As if I'd been ...' He shuddered, apparently unable to finish the sentence.

Lily was horrified. 'But it was *never* like that between us.'

'Of course not.' He turned his back and looked out the window again, but not before Lily caught the sudden flash of pink across his cheeks. 'But ... you got to be so lovely and that night at the pub the thought *did* occur to me that you'd be all grown up soon. It was the most idle, passing notion,' he hurried on, 'but Luke caught it and took exception and your nana trusted his judgement over my word apparently and, well, it ended with your nana standing in this kitchen and glaring as if I was some kind of terrible threat to you that needed urgent stamping out. She called me selfish and ... well ... worse. Said I'd only ruin your life. I was taken aback and I didn't know what to say in my own defence except that I cared about you very sincerely and would never hurt you. But that just seemed to make everything worse. Maybe if I'd said I didn't care about you at all it might have been better. But she said if I really cared about you, I wouldn't ever see you again.' He ran his hands over his eyes for a moment, and the expression left in their wake was pain. 'I blew the lid at that, Lily. I don't remember exactly what I said but it wasn't ... I shouldn't have ...' He turned to face her again, his eyes filling with remorse. 'I tried to take it back. I told her I didn't mean it but she just left. Without the orchid. And did something drastic.'

'Sent me to boarding school,' Lily whispered.

'Yes.'

'To get me away from you?'

He nodded.

Lily stared at him for a long time, letting that sink in. Nana had sent her away rather than risk her suffering her mother's fate by getting entangled with an older man. Why hadn't she just told her that, though? Because she didn't think Lily would believe her? That she was too far under Jasper's thrall to see him clearly? Whatever her reasoning, though, one thing was certain. Nana hadn't sent her away out of disappointment. Only misguided love.

Lily got up off the chair and crossed the room.

Jasper braced as if expecting her anger but she just took his hand in hers. 'I'm sorry Nana got the wrong end of the stick about you, Jasper.

That was terrible. And I'm really sorry I got sent away. But I don't regret any of the time I spent with you. Either as my teacher or my friend. You were one of the best parts of growing up here for me. I want you to know that.'

His eyes moistened. 'Lily, it was always my pleasure.'

She smiled. 'But now I have to find Luke.' She was headed for the door the next second.

'I suppose you do.'

'And ask him to give me another chance.'

'Won't be a problem.'

She reached the door and stopped for a final look back. 'Jasper?'

'Yeah?'

'You know he's good for me, right?'

Jasper sighed. 'I know he makes you happy, Lily. But honestly he gives me high blood pressure. I never know what he's going to do next.'

She grinned. 'Isn't it great?'

He shook his head but, with a resigned smile, let her go.

Chapter Twenty-Five

Relightable Candle

Luke had showered and changed but the smell of smoke still lingered in his nostrils. The taste of disappointment in his mouth was just as harsh. *Lily.* What did he have to do to prove himself to her? What would *ever* be enough? They'd lost ten years because she'd been so quick to believe he'd just moved on with Katie. And now she was throwing a photograph of Gráinne in his face? Ready to give up on them all over again? Whatever happened to giving someone the benefit of the doubt before you rushed to condemn? Wasn't that what you were *supposed* to do for the people you loved? Except Lily didn't love him, clearly, and that there was closure with a capital C.

So he packed his suitcases with the last of his belongings and wheeled them down to the pier, tucking them under some loose tarpaulin in case it rained before morning. He had planned on getting the ferry tomorrow afternoon but now he was getting the first. He wanted to be gone before anyone was the wiser. No fanfare. No looks of disappointment from his dad. He was done.

He dragged himself back to the hotel where his mother looked relieved to see him. 'There you are! I've been looking for you everywhere.'

'What's wrong?'

'Have you had a drink?'

'*Um*. I had a beer about three hours ago. Why?'

'Saoirse's been on the phone and she's worried about Caoimhe. She's running a very high temperature and she'd really like to get Mark back to Cúltrá to check on her. And they're staying in that awful guesthouse next to the fishmonger's.'

'Okay,' said Luke, struggling to see the connection.

'And your dad's had a few too many.'

'Grand. So you want me to run Mark over to Cúltrá in Dad's boat? No problem.'

'Yes. And your ex has been downing shots since you left. And is now dead to the world on the couch upstairs. Where Mark was supposed to be staying.'

'Then I guess it's as well he's not staying now?' suggested Luke.

He'd be having words with Gráinne about the photograph she'd sent Lily – he'd recognised her number. But not while she was drunk or unconscious, obviously.

'So is Mark ready to go now?'

'Yes. I'll tell him. No, wait.' She searched his face. 'Did you talk to Lily? Did she tell you I apologised about the phone calls?'

'No.'

'Ah, I might have known she wouldn't,' she said, looking peeved. 'Not after I burnt her hair.'

'You did what?'

'It was an accident. I was trying to style it. I wouldn't have thought she'd be so unforgiving though.'

'Yeah, well, she gets tetchy about people burning things on her. Where's Mark and we'll get going.'

Mark was there in an instant with his bags and they made their way down to the small cove below the hotel where Paudie's boat was moored. It was a modest, third-hand cruiser with plenty of poke.

Luke was handing Mark a life jacket when Tadhg came down the wooden jetty as fast as his walking stick and two bowed legs would allow. 'Room for one more?' He accepted Mark's help to climb aboard and a life jacket too which he had to put on sitting down as he was panting so hard.

'What's up?' asked Luke.

'Nothing.'

'O-kay then.' Luke started up the engine and untied the ropes, listening with satisfaction to the eager growl that turned into a steady purr. He reversed and turned the boat towards the bay.

They were all silent for the crossing, the combination of the movement and the night air lulling everyone to contemplation.

As they reached the pier at Cúltrá they found it deserted. Luke tied off the boat so Mark could disembark. With a parting 'Thanks, bro' he was off and they watched him jog up the hill of the pier towards the main street and the largest guesthouse.

Tadhg hadn't left the boat and Luke eyed him curiously as he climbed back aboard. He got the engine started and when they'd left the harbour behind them Tadhg ambled forward and hoisted himself onto the seat beside him.

'So, Lily missed the ferry again,' he opened. 'Does that mean she's staying?'

Honestly, Luke had no idea anymore so just shrugged.

Tadhg seemed to take this as a positive. 'Love was a relightable candle after all then, *eh*?'

'No. More like a fire that almost burned down a cottage.'

Tadhg held up a hand in protest. 'Ah now, I don't need to hear that. Keep your private business to yourself.'

'No, seriously. I almost burnt down her cottage.'

Tadhg shuddered. 'Go back to the love is a candle thing. Leave a bit of mystery to it for the love of God!'

'Grandad, I lit a fire in the grate. The whole upstairs of the cottage filled with smoke!'

Tadhg suddenly paled as his eyes widened. 'Oh, there might be a wheeshy problem with the chimney in Barrett Cottage.'

Luke took a long, hard look at Tadhg's face. 'What *about* the chimney?'

'*Um*, Noleen thought it might be cracked. I was to tell Lily not to light a fire until she got it properly assessed.'

'And when did she tell you this?'

Tadhg bit his lip. 'The same day she gave me the walking stick?'

Luke groaned. 'Was that the actual message you were supposed to give Lily?'

'It might have been. I'm sure she said something about welcoming her home too.'

There was no point in recriminations, even if Luke had the heart for them. 'Why so keen to come aboard?' he asked instead.

But Tadhg was now looking chastened. 'Because I enjoy going fast,' he said quietly, 'and I don't get to do it much anymore.'

Needing no further prompt, Luke opened up the throttle and floored it, smiling at his grandad's sudden whoops as he clung to the rail with one hand, the other spread wide to catch the breeze. In half the time of the outbound journey they pulled up to the jetty in a motion which sent a massive wake crashing against the surrounding rocks.

'Now *that's* what I call mooring,' Tadhg said, with the twinkle back in his wind-brightened eyes.

Luke helped him back onto the jetty and they made their way at a far more sedate pace back to the hotel.

Tadhg hobbled inside but Luke just glanced in the door. It was clear the guests weren't going anywhere soon. The professional entertainment might have ended but the amateurs were just getting warmed up. The karaoke machine was being connected up by the low stage and a queue was forming by Betty and Ned who seemed to have been charged with writing down names and song choices. In the meantime the old sound system was playing a slow song at full volume.

He spied his mam and dad at the edge of the dance floor. Her hands were on his shoulders and his were around her waist. As he watched, his dad took one of her hands, kissed it and then gave her a spin, smiling as she returned to him flustered and beaming.

It was disconcerting seeing them like that. Disconcerting but sweet. He wanted that for himself so badly, he realised. Commitment. And connection. And *trust*. But maybe it didn't have to have whiskey hair or lips that were begging to be kissed or eyes that couldn't decide if they were green or brown. Maybe he'd just woven a fiction for himself all these years that Lily needed him to wait for her when she clearly hadn't.

Yes, her nana's cottage had smoke damage but it was insured. He knew that because he'd paid the renewal bill himself. And Lily was a grown woman. She'd figure it out.

He backed out of the pub and made his way to the furthest picnic bench in the beer garden where he sat for a few minutes before he tipped his head to look up at the stars. He'd loved stargazing as a child, inventing new constellations with Lily as they lay on their backs on the grass together. But that had just been a game for foolish children. Beyond the spectacle it was just a lot of little dots having nothing at all to do with each other.

When Lily reached the end of Jasper's gravel path, she found Pup waiting for her by the gate. Her tail was wagging fast.

'You're looking very pleased with yourself,' Lily said, instantly suspicious. 'What have you been up to?'

As Pup offered no insight other than to cock her head, Lily took it upon herself to explain how she had to go find Luke urgently and that she didn't have time to w.a.l.k. her back to the cottage and she didn't have the l.e.a.d. so Pup could either a) return to the cottage by herself – Pup's eyebrows twitched expectantly – or b) come with her but only if she promised to be good. Pup offered her paw so they shook on this option and set off.

It was a struggle to keep her feet in the boots at any speed and Lily was forced to adopt a kind of hop-jog technique Pup found very exciting, bounding along beside her and giving the occasional approving bark. She had a stitch by the time she reached the viewing point where she halted to catch her breath. Where was Luke? At his house or at the hotel? She prayed the house. It would be so much easier to apologise without an audience. She slipped through the opening in the hawthorn trees and retraced the route she'd taken the day before, reaching the place without incident. There were no lights on but she rang the doorbell all the same.

She heard a crunch and turned to see Pup chomping down on a thyme bush. She made a dash to get it out of her mouth but came out of a boot instead. She got her foot back in and went to straighten the doormat, which had been kicked out of place, but spied an envelope that had been hidden underneath it. The word '*Eric*' was written on it.

She opened it without scruple.

Inside was a key and a scrap of paper which she could just about read in the moonlight.

Decided to leave early. Hope everything works out for you. You know how to reach me.

Luke.

He'd decided to leave early? Like how early? Right now early? Already left early? Luke's dad had a boat and could give him a lift, she remembered. He could leave the island any time he liked! *You know how to reach me.* Well, Eric might. But *she* didn't. And if she tried to ring Eric's phone right now to get Luke's number, she'd just wake a post-op Cassandra. Not that she could even do that much because her phone was still out of power. She was starting to panic.

'Come on, Pup. We've got to get to the hotel.'

Pup rose obediently, bringing a large thyme branch with her.

They reached the road again but it was slow going as Pup kept stopping every twenty seconds to lie down and have a chew. Lily had to keep taking the branch to hold it out to the side as she walked, with Pup jumping to try to take it back. Pup would get it back, lie down for another chew and then they'd repeat the process. High-stakes drama for Pup. A pain in the ass for Lily.

When she got the stick back for the thirtieth time Pup finally had enough and ran off with it into a field. Defeated, Lily left her to it and headed up the hill.

She heard the music well before she'd even reached the car park.

A couple kissing in the minibus's shadow didn't notice her passing but, as she drew closer to the main door, she was spotted by two lads leaning against the wall. They were smoking a joint between them, their expressions alternating between super-tense and panned out with each puff.

They watched her approach. Their eyes raked her and she'd just grasped the door handle when the first drawled, 'Just how many packets a day you on, darlin'?'

'Might wanna switch to Extra Light,' suggested the other.

And both broke their hearts laughing.

Maintaining what little dignity she had left Lily sniffed, turned away, and went around the back of the building to a single door that opened near the far side of the bar, where she slipped in unnoticed.

The wedding party was all gathered by a low stage at the opposite end of the room. Swathes of tables had been rearranged around it. She scanned the place for Luke but there was no sign of him.

The bar itself was deserted but for that young barman who'd served her before. The one who'd told her that her credit card was declined. Happy memories. Mikey, wasn't it?

As she approached, he did the same little nervous gesture with his collar he had before. He didn't laugh at her though. She didn't know how when she glimpsed herself in the mirrored glass behind him. She looked like an extra from a disaster movie with the whites of her eyes startling against her sooty face. How could Jasper have let her leave his house like this? She could picture him laughing his arse off right now.

'Hey, Mikey. Luke around?' she asked as casually as she could manage.

'He's left for Cúltrá.'

'When?'

'About half an hour ago.'

Half an hour? She'd missed him by a measly thirty minutes? She really wanted to cry but apparently there were no available fluids left. She climbed onto a bar stool and her wellington boots fell to the floor. A moment for hard liquor if ever there was one. Sadly, hard liquor had to be paid for. 'Can I have some water?'

'Sure. Still or sparking?'

Lily looked down at her rumpled outfit and then back at Mikey, wondering what prosperity he was seeing that she wasn't. 'Tap, please. Your finest.'

Mikey's lips quirked. He pulled out a glass, scooped a few ice cubes and filled it with tap water. Then he added a splash of lime cordial, a slice of lemon, a paper umbrella and a straw and tentatively pushed the glass towards her.

'No olives?'

He ducked his head this time to smile, his cheeks reddening. 'Sorry. All out.'

She took a sip. 'Cheers.'

He passed her a paper napkin next.

She looked at him for a second in mock confusion. 'Have I something ... on my face?'

He burst out laughing. He was a good-looking kid when he wasn't petrified.

She went through a dozen napkins without getting all the soot off. Mikey wet a few more with tap water and directed her to the bits that were left.

He still hadn't asked her what had happened to her. He was just being professional and helpful. Looking after his customer.

'You're a good barman, you know?'

He instantly looked nervous again. 'No, I'm not.'

'Why do you say that?'

'Because I keep making mistakes.' He glanced towards the dance floor.

She followed his line of sight and saw Paudie laughing with Ned.

'Do you keep making the same ones?'

'Well ... no.'

'So you're still learning how to be a barman. You're a trainee, right?'

'Yeah.'

'So you're gonna make mistakes. That's how you'll learn.'

'Paudie doesn't think I have what it takes. Says I'll never be as good as Luke.'

Paudie was an ass. 'Well, of course he'd say that. He's his son and he's going to be biased about him and Luke's been pulling pints in here since he was old enough to reach the taps. He's had years more practice than you. But you have to understand if Paudie isn't giving out about something he's miserable. Some people meditate for inner peace, Paudie gives out. It's not fair but it works for him. Try not to take it personally.'

'Oh. Okay. Thanks.'

She leaned in and lowered her voice. 'Do you want to hear a secret?'

'*Um*, sure.'

'I've been afraid to make a mistake for ten years. But I just realised that sometimes being afraid *is* the mistake. Do you know what I mean?'

Mikey nodded and Lily felt really good for a moment. How a mystic might feel, she imagined, imparting wisdom.

'Can I tell you something too?' he said.

'Of course.'

'I don't really know what you mean. But thanks for trying.'

Their sanctuary was about to be breached. A man in his twenties was sidling their way. Oily-faced. Too much hair gel. Looking hungry for company. Lily turned back to Mikey. 'Thanks for the chat.'

She slid swiftly off the bar stool, picked up the wellington boots and made her way back towards the exit.

She'd nearly reached it and was just passing a pair of high-backed chairs when a walking stick blocked her path. 'Hey, missy. Where are you off to?'

She looked down to see Tadhg grinning up at her, his chin adorned with cake crumbs.

'Tadhg, I – I'll catch you tomorrow, okay?'

The walking stick didn't move but the grin faded. 'Sit down for a minute.'

'I really can't.'

'Go on. One minute. I could be dead tomorrow.'

She blinked. 'Really? That's what you're going with? Emotional blackmail.'

He shrugged. 'Might happen. No guarantees at my age.' He patted the seat beside him. 'Come on. Tell Grandad Tadhg all about it.'

She sat reluctantly.

'You had a bit of trouble this evening,' he started. 'With the cottage.'

'You could say that.'

'That was my fault. I was to warn you the chimney might be cracked. I forgot. I'm sorry.'

She took a deep breath through her nose and let it out of her mouth. 'I suppose there's no point giving out to you about it.'

'No,' he agreed amicably. 'Not when I could be dead tomorrow.' He gave the back of her hand a little pat. 'I'm glad we could sort that out.'

After waiting for what felt an extremely patient amount of time for him to say something else, Lily stood up. 'Well, great talking to you.'

That roused him. 'You came here for Luke, yes?'

'I did.'

'Then why are you leaving without him?'

'Because it's too late for anything else.' She fished in her pocket and pulled out the sheep eraser and handed it to him. 'Could you give that to him whenever you see him next? Tell him ... tell him I'm sorry I didn't deserve him.'

Tadhg promptly handed it back. 'Tell him that yourself, coward.'

'What?'

'You heard me.'

A tear rose suddenly and tracked down her cheek. Great. She was hydrated again. 'I'm trying to be brave now,' she said, as her chin gave a wobble.

'Then tell him that to his face. Don't disappear again and leave him guessing. You've haunted him long enough.'

Donie bounded over. 'Lily! The very person we need to start off the karaoke.'

'What? No,' she said, brushing the wetness away.

'But it's Betty and Ned's big day and I know they'd love you to sing them a song. Think of it as a wedding present. Seeing as you didn't give them one,' he added with one of his sly grins.

Her eyes narrowed. 'How would you know if I gave them a present or not?'

'Because I told Betty I'd keep track of all the presents so she could write her thank-you cards properly after.'

'Nosy parker,' said Lily, folding her arms. 'The free use of my cottage and the making and decorating of a wedding cake and – and my emotional support during a time of recent crisis were my gifts to her.'

'What about Ned?' challenged Donie.

Lily felt her cheeks heat. 'I gave him toast. Two slices.'

'Come on, Lily. Just one little song. Don't be such a coward.'

She looked at him and then back at Tadhg. What was this? Gang Up on Lily Day? First Tadhg calling her a coward. Now Donie. Only *she* got to call herself that.

'Fine,' she said.

'Really?' said Donie and Tadhg together, the first looking delighted, the other aghast.

'I've never done karaoke though so I'm not exactly sure how it works. Actually, I don't think I know all the words to any song. Maybe I shouldn't–'

Donie patted her shoulder and pushed her back into the room and towards the stage. 'Sure all the words come up on the screen. You can't go wrong. Just follow them along.'

'Okay, I guess.' Everything was already a disaster. Job gone. Cottage currently uninhabitable. Luke lost. How much of a difference could one song make? Three minutes and it'd be over. 'What song should I sing?'

'Any song you like. If it isn't in the machine, Pat can accompany you on the guitar and you can make up the words even. Or look them up on your phone in advance.'

'My phone's out of power.'

'Have mine,' he said, with a quick but expansive smile, pulling it from his pocket and handing it to her.

'I did always like 'Scarborough Fair'. I don't know if that's a good song for a wedding though?'

'Perfect, perfect. I'll let Pat know.' And with another beam of delight he hurried off.

Lily scrambled to look up the lyrics. There were more verses than she remembered. In fact the only one she knew without looking at the phone was the first. All in all a bad choice but she couldn't think of another at short notice. She was standing behind the stage and Donie was already talking to Pat. Pat was shaking his head vigorously and hope rose. Maybe he didn't know the chords? But, no, the next second Donie handed her a microphone and picked up another himself. He clambered up on the stage and cleared his throat. The music stopped and all eyes turned to him.

'Ladies and gentlemen. We have a very special first singer to the stage for the evening. Miss Lily Barrett, come on up here!'

She forced her legs to move. As she stepped up, she heard gasps and then more than a few laughs. She knew she looked a mess but the lights in her eyes were a mercy. She couldn't make out anyone's expression beyond the first row. The only people she could really see clearly were Betty and Ned, Eithne and Paudie, Tadhg, who'd moved to a seat beside him, and Pat with his guitar at the ready.

'First, Lily would like to make a little speech to the Bride and Groom,' said Donie.

'*Wait. What?*'

'And she's very sorry she didn't get you a wedding present,' he added, before he skipped off the stage, leaving her facing an expectant crowd while contemplating ways to murder him.

'*Um*, hi, everyone.'

'Hi, chick,' said Betty. 'You okay?'

'I'm fine. Yeah. *Phew.* It's hot under these lights.'

'*Smokin'*,' said a voice from somewhere at the back.

Another laugh rippled around the room.

Feck, this was embarrassing. She lifted the microphone again. 'So just to let you all know Cassandra rang from the hospital and she's going to be fine. She's sorry to be missing this but she's looking forward to being back here as soon as she's recovered.'

'That's great news,' said Ned. 'A big relief.'

There were murmurs of agreement all round.

'Well, there were some lovely speeches earlier. I'm sure you don't want another one.'

'*Oh, but we do!*' said Donie as Pat reached over with his free hand and smacked him on the arm.

'So I'll just say how happy I am for you both and that your love is truly an inspiration.' There. Short but sweet.

'*How so?*' prompted Donie as Pat made a second futile attempt to block his mouth.

She glared at him. 'Because,' she said through gritted teeth, 'it just is. So I'll ask you to raise your glasses, please, to Betty and Ned!'

'Betty and Ned!' Everyone cheered.

'And, while we're at it, to all the other loving couples in the room too. Shay and Josie, Eithne and Paudie, not forgetting the greatest love story never told – Donie and Pat –'

That got a laugh, except from Donie who glowered.

'Tadhg and his new phone,' she continued, on a roll.

Another laugh.

'*You and Luke!*' Tadhg shot back.

There was a loaded silence. Lily swallowed hard. Yes, she and Luke could have been a great love story, she guessed, if she hadn't been such a coward and, for the umpteenth time that evening, the tears welled up.

'Sorry. Don't mind me,' she said, wiping them away. 'This just keeps happening.'

'Lily?' She straightened and squinted once more against the lights. A figure was approaching. She heard chairs being moved out of the way and then Luke was standing there, ten feet away, his eyes bright under dark furrowed brows and his hair all windswept. The person she most wanted to see in all the world.

'You alright there?' he asked, cocking his head.

She smiled at him through her tears. 'Yes. Just having a breakdown.' Then, remembering, she wiped her tears frantically. 'Oh no. Don't look at me. Close your eyes.'

'It's alright,' he said. 'I won't cry.'

On instinct though, she squeezed her eyes closed anyway. 'I thought you were gone to Cúltrá.'

'I was. I came back.'

Hope rushed to fill Lily's chest. Did that mean she was already forgiven? 'For *me*?' she asked, tentatively.

'*Uh*, no,' he said. 'Because my dad needed his boat back?'

'Oh. Right.' *Crap. And cringe. With everyone in the room listening.* She squeezed her eyes shut tighter than ever.

'Yeah ... so are you going to come down from there?' he asked next.

'I can't. I have to sing a song first. Oh, but I found your sheep eraser.' She pulled it out of her pocket and held it out on her flattened palm. But he didn't take it from her.

Instead, there was a pause. And then ... 'Are you *really* going to give it back?'

She unscrewed one eye and then, seeing Luke wasn't actually crying, the other. She glanced around at all the expectant faces and felt herself flush. 'Well,' she swallowed. 'It belonged to you first, didn't it?'

'It did,' he agreed. 'And then I gave it to a girl.'

She wasn't sure what he was saying. 'So ... you *don't* want it back then?'

Luke hesitated, glanced around the room himself and took a few steps closer, his voice lowering. 'Do you *really* want to give it back to me, Lily?'

The look in his eyes was deadly earnest all of a sudden. And Lily's heart gave an extra hard thump.

She shook her head and swallowed again. 'No.'

He took another step closer. 'Why?'

And Lily's pulse went from hammering in her chest to hammering in her throat. 'Because ... I never found one I loved as much.'

He smiled then, his dimples showing. 'Then try holding onto it a bit tighter next time. So you never lose it again.' And then he beamed.

And she beamed back.

And Donie groaned. 'For feck's sake. That was some messed-up analogy.'

'Ah, Donie,' said Pat. 'It's a wedding. They're allowed. But fair play for picking up on the subtleties.'

'Subtleties? Nothing subtle about that,' said Donie. 'They're talking about an eraser. And what's that another word for? A rubber. And what's that code for? It's the sheep bit that disturbs me.'

Pat closed his eyes and shook his head.

'*Don't mind them, Lily!*' called Ned. '*Anything else while you're on a roll?*'

Lily looked to Luke to double-check.

He just shrugged, though he was still beaming.

'No. No, I think that's it.'

'Well, thank God,' said Donie. 'I was going to barf. Hit it, Pat!'

Pat obliged with the opening bars of 'Scarborough Fair' and Lily scrambled to find the lyrics on the phone again, surprised and delighted as Luke jumped straight up beside her.

Chapter Twenty-Six

Evaluating Heart Rhythm

It was truly horrible and he had no way to save Lily or anyone else from it other than to try drown her out as they shared the microphone. To give her fair dues, she sang from the heart and looked at him with such an expression of love in her eyes, in between glances at the lyrics on the phone, that it only doubled the pity that all that emotion had to go through such an instrument to come out. A choking crow would have been more melodic and, though he'd withstood her tears earlier, his eyes welled in pain now, trying so hard not to wince, trying to keep her gaze locked on him so she wouldn't notice anyone else. From his peripheral vision he saw Donie fairly bursting with glee, Pat stoically playing on beside him while his shoulders shook. His mother had her fingers pressed discreetly to her ears while Betty and Ned were heroically nodding and smiling in encouragement, their hands clasped together just a little tighter than looked comfortable. His dad was in hysterics though. He was shaking, his face redder than ever, slapping his leg as he rocked forward and back.

Just one more verse to go. Thank God. Then he was going to take Lily back to Hook Cove, kiss her until she forgot her name and finish what they'd started earlier.

Paudie slapped his leg once more but then stood straight up out of his chair with a look of fright on his face. His hand went to his heart and the next second he dropped like a stone, hitting the chair on his way to the floor.

Eithne screamed. Pat stopped playing. A final wrong note came out of Lily's mouth and the entire room stood and stared.

After a moment of shock, Luke jumped off the stage and ran, shouting for Mikey to get the AED and Lily to call 999. He cleared the space around his dad, pushing back the table and chairs and knelt beside him.

Unresponsive. Check.

Airway clear. Check.

Not breathing. Check.

No pulse. Check.

He pulled off his dad's tie and ripped open the waistcoat and shirt and then started chest compressions with the rhythm of 'Staying Alive' in his head to get the pacing right.

Mikey flew up beside him, AED in his hand. 'Got it.'

'Open it.' Luke stopped the compressions to give two rescue breaths before restarting them for another thirty seconds.

Mikey set the case on the floor and flipped the lid. The defibrillator started talking, a calm female voice prompting them to '*call for help*' and '*remove all clothing from the patient's chest*'. Next it instructed them to apply two adhesive-backed pads with trailing wires to Paudie's bare chest.

Mikey followed the pictures on the pads to get the placement right as Luke kept going with CPR.

He heard his mother's panicked voice behind him. 'Mark? Oh Mark, your dad's having a heart attack. He just keeled over. He's on the floor. Come back quickly!'

There was a pause as his mother listened.

'Yes, yes, he's here. He's working on him. I'll put you on speaker to him.'

His brother's exasperated tones came through instantly. 'Do *not* put me on speaker. Luke doesn't need me telling him what to do in the middle of an emergency. He's the specialist at this. He's got it, Mam.'

Eithne said nothing.

'Am I on speaker?'

'Yes,' admitted Eithne.

'Sorry, Luke. If you can hear me I know you're doing everything you can.' And with that he hung up.

'We can't get the air ambulance back,' said Lily, Donie's mobile in her hand. 'They said they'll have to send a team on the lifeboat instead.'

'Okay,' said Luke. 'Pat, go to the pier. Direct them in.'

Pat took the phone from Lily's hand and dashed off.

'Evaluating heart rhythm,' said the machine.

Luke stopped compressions and held up his hands as the room held its breath.

'Stand by. Preparing to shock.'

'Stand clear,' said Luke at the same time as the machine.

'Do not touch the patient. Delivering shock'

There was a series of warning beeps and then a 'thump' and Paudie's body shifted slightly. *'Shock delivered. Provide chest compressions.'*

Luke started compressions again, his elbows locked, pushing from the shoulders.

'It didn't work!' cried Eithne. 'Why didn't it work?'

'Sometimes it takes several shocks,' Luke gasped.

Betty put her arm around Eithne, who turned into her and shook as she cried.

Everyone else in the room drew closer until a thick ring of people surrounded them. Some had their heads bowed, lips moving in prayer. Others watched silently, hands clasped together or balled under chins. Lily was on her knees beside Mikey on Paudie's other side, rocking to the rhythm of Luke's compressions, her hands clasped in the same fashion as his own, as if she could somehow add her strength to his.

He wished she could. His muscles were burning.

'Evaluating heart rhythm.'

Luke stopped compressions and once more held up his hands. As everyone leaned back, he sent his own prayer upwards. *Please God, let this work.* He'd resuscitated a gagillion practice dummies without a hitch but though knowledge was clearly power in this situation, a little ignorance would have been bliss. Unfortunately he knew all too well the statistics for getting a human heart restarted after a sudden cardiac arrest. That he was battling those odds with his dad as his first real patient was terrifying.

'Stand by.'

'Preparing to shock.'

'Stand clear.'

'Do not touch the patient.'

'Delivering shock.'

Another series of beeps and then another 'thump' as Paudie's body shifted again.

'Shock delivered.'

'Provide chest compressions.'

Luke started compressions again as a deeper silence fell, broken only by the sound of his mother's frightened sobs. He fought to keep his own emotions at bay. His dad was coming back from this. He was coming back and no matter how long it took for rescue to come he'd keep going. Another two breaths. More compressions.

And then suddenly Paudie's eyelids flicked and he gasped as Luke took his hands off him. '*Dad! It's okay. You're okay. Stay calm.*'

Paudie floundered, his colour changing from blotchy-white through red and back again as he coughed and groaned and tried to roll to one side. Ned grabbed a cushion and tried to get it under his head but the man was having none of it and tried to sit only to be pushed back by Eithne, who fairly flattened him under a relieved embrace.

Luke attempted to calm his own racing heart with a few deep breaths, his hands on his knees as he told Mikey to get some aspirin and a glass of water.

Paudie allowed himself to be propped up by Eithne as Luke checked him over. Given the circumstances, the man was doing well. He was lucid, knew everyone's name and was complaining loudly which was pretty close to normal. There was no guarantee he wouldn't have a second episode though and he was in considerable pain from the compressions. Luke hoped it was only bruising and not a broken sternum or fractured rib. He hadn't felt anything break but there were no guarantees. The sooner they could get him to a hospital the better. Paudie managed to swallow the aspirin as Mikey held the glass to help him wash it down. Remembering they'd left Mark on tenterhooks, Luke called him back to tell him their dad was still alive. Mark sounded exhausted. Caoimhe was crying in the background while Ciarán was shouting about dinosaurs.

'Well done, runt. Knew you could do it,' was all the praise he was at leisure to bestow, along with instructions to give aspirin and a last-second assurance that Caoimhe was fine.

Luke thanked him and promised to call him with an update tomorrow.

He pocketed his phone and turned only to have Lily squeeze him fiercely round the middle. She pulled back and looked at him with such a glow of admiration he felt ten feet tall.

'Any word on the lifeboat?' he called to Donie who was standing by the open door.

'Five minutes,' he called back.

He crouched beside his dad whose head was now nestled in his mother's lap. His breathing seemed more comfortable and his colour had improved.

His mam clasped his hand. 'Thank God you were here, Luke.'

'Yeah, son,' said Paudie. 'I'd have been a goner otherwise.'

'I didn't even know we had one of those electrocution thingies,' continued Eithne.

'The AED? It's been on the wall for three years.'

'Oh, that explains it. I try not to look too closely at the walls. All those lobster pots.'

'They give the place charm,' said Paudie.

'They smell,' said Eithne, her mouth curling into a fond smile as she looked down at him, her eyes still red from crying.

'Of the sea?'

'No. Of dead lobsters.' She looked to Luke again, the emotion in her voice rising even as the volume dipped. 'You can't go to Cork, Luke. We need you here. Your dad needs you. This could happen again. He has to slow down. You have to stay and run this place.'

His heart dropped along with the ground under him. 'But ... I have to go. This is my – this is what I've been training for. It's what I want to do with my life.'

'I know and I'm sorry, Luke. It's not fair. But sometimes when you're the youngest you have to make sacrifices for your family. Take care of them as they get older, the way they've taken care of you.'

Stunned, he looked from his mother's pleading face to his dad's shaken one and saw all his plans for the future crumble to nothing. How could he say no after what had just happened? And a new future spread out before him, clear as could be. A future where he was trapped inside the four walls of this pub, the numbing sameness of every day wearing him down to nothing. No challenges. No one to help. No lives to save except for his dad's. He was the last to leave the nest but suddenly it was too late to fly free.

He felt warmth to his right and the next second Lily dropped to her knees beside him.

'*Are you two for real?*' she said.

Eithne stiffened. 'This doesn't concern you, Lily Barrett. We wouldn't be in this mess if it wasn't for you and your squawking. Sending everyone's blood pressure into orbit. You're the real one to blame here.'

'What's she talking about?' Lily murmured to Luke.

'You sang a few notes off key, that's all.'

'No, I didn't.'

'No, you didn't,' agreed Paudie. 'You sang them *all* off key. I laughed so hard it gave me a heart attack.'

Lily's jaw dropped. '*I* gave you a heart attack? Nothing to do with your diet being 90% chips? Or the fact I've never once seen you exercise? Or that you're incapable of calming yourself down without shouting at someone?'

Paudie went an alarming shade of red.

'Sweetheart,' Luke interjected, 'he's just had a heart attack. Maybe you could give out to him another day?'

'*No.* They're not being fair to you.' She looked from Paudie to Eithne. 'Did you not see what Luke just did? Well, you didn't,' she excused Paudie, 'but *you* did, Eithne. He was incredible. He saved his life. And instead of just being proud of him you want to stop him from doing that for others? All he's ever wanted is to help people. That's who he is. And you want to take that away from him? *No.*'

'What do you care?' said Eithne. 'You'd get to be with him here and live in that fine house at the Cove we all know he built for you.'

Her eyes flashed to Luke who gave an apologetic smile.

'Don't you want that?' continued Eithne. 'To be with him?'

'I do,' she said, not taking her eyes off him. 'But too well to ask him to give up what makes him happy.'

'You think he'll be happy when I die of a heart attack,' said Paudie, 'and he's not here to save me?'

Lily shook her head. 'Nobody wants you dying of a heart attack. But you have an AED and a very able first aider to hand in Mikey.'

'I trained him myself last year,' said Luke.

'See? And there'll be enough doctors at the hospital that you can ask one of them to give you a plan to get yourself in better health so you won't be at risk of having another attack.'

'*Exercise!*' spat Paudie as if it was a dirty word.

'Yes, a bit of exercise wouldn't do you any harm but it doesn't have to be boot camp either. It could just be ...' her eyes suddenly lit and her gaze shifted purposefully to Eithne, 'yoga on the lawn at dawn. It's probably less about exercise and more about ...' She raised an eyebrow and waited for the woman to catch on.

'*Wellness*,' Eithne finished the sentence for her, the word uttered with just a hint of reverence as a small smile curved one side of her mouth.

'Seaweed wraps and sea-salt scrubs,' continued Lily. 'You might even enjoy it.'

'Little schemer,' said Paudie, his eyes narrowing. A quick glance at his wife seemed to confirm his worst fears. 'Charge up that machine again, Luke, and send me back. She'll be trying to convince me a back wax is good for cholesterol next.'

But Luke just smiled.

'I *am* proud of you, son,' said Paudie, his eyes suddenly welling. 'So proud. I hope you know that.' He glared then at Lily, as if his emotional state was her fault too.

Luke laid a reassuring hand on his shoulder.

'*They're here!*' shouted Donie as a team of medics arrived carrying a stretcher and equipment.

They got Paudie's vitals checked and manoeuvred him gently onto the stretcher and put an oxygen mask on him before he could complain any further. He was hoisted aloft and, with an accompanying procession of family and friends, brought down to the pier where the lifeboat was waiting.

Luke had a quick word with the captain while the medics secured his dad on the vessel. He retrieved his suitcases from under the tarpaulin and tossed them aboard. Then he turned to the waiting crowd and found his mother. 'I'll go with him. I'll call you when he's settled at the hospital. And after that–'

'You're going to Cork. To be a wonderful paramedic.'

'Thanks, Mam.'

He looked around for Lily. She was on board the lifeboat with Betty, handing out slices of wedding cake to the crew. Luke called her name and she disembarked and came to him.

He tried to pull her off to the side but there was no privacy available. All he could do was lower his voice.

'I have to go.'

'I know. I'll keep an eye on your mam. Make sure she's okay.'

He wasn't sure how pleased his mother would be by that but knew the offer was kindly made. 'Thank you for ...' He trailed off because he didn't quite know how to finish that sentence. For believing in me? For standing up for me? For saving me? 'I don't know when I'll get a chance to come back.'

She smiled. 'That's okay. Go do what you have to.'

His chest tightened. It wasn't a dismissal but it wasn't exactly a promise she'd wait for him either. Surely he hadn't just got her back only to lose her again? Not after everything. 'Lil?'

Thirty pairs of attentive ears surrounded them.

'Yeah?'

'*My* Lil?' he asked, his heart in his mouth.

She nodded.

'*Sooo* ... can I get your number?'

She laughed and he handed her his phone so she could type it into his contacts.

The captain cleared his throat, ready to cast off.

Luke checked his pockets: keys, wallet, phone. He was leaving Inish Ruin with all the essentials bar one. 'I'll call you,' he promised.

'I know you will,' she said, and her eyes were full of stars.

Chapter Twenty-Seven

Whatever it Takes

Lily moved into the house at Hook Cove and rang Luke every morning from the sandstone balcony, her legs swinging. His happiness was clear to hear though it was mixed through with plentiful yawns of tiredness. He'd hardly had a second of downtime but was loving the work. No two days were the same. The crew he was working with were all sound and time was flying – which was as well as he was counting the seconds until he could get back to her.

Lily's news for him in return was more mixed. On the plus side, Pup had taken to her new lodgings with aplomb, though her appetite had gone through the roof. On the minus side, Preston started legal proceedings for his fifty thousand pounds and made sure the matter was as public as he could manage. Lily would probably never work at a top accounting firm again, though it wouldn't go to court as Peter, of all people, came through at the last minute. His fall from the conference centre had been caught on camera by a film crew who'd been shooting an ad nearby. And the 'tragic love story' behind the fall, as Peter had told it anyway, had been enough to catch the interest of a Hollywood producer who'd secured a two-year option on the story in return for the whopping $60,000. Which, when converted to sterling, had been enough to save Lily's hide. And she hadn't, in fact, needed to go back to London at all as Sergei, understanding 'on the brink of bankruptcy' enough to be willing to negotiate, agreed to sell off what remained of her furniture, jewellery and belongings to clear the remaining back rent she owed.

As for the cottage, there was good news and bad. It was insured and the smoke damage would be addressed. But then it would have to be sold. No matter how many times Lily ran the calculations, there was no other way to cover their inheritance tax bill without selling it or Luke's house. He'd left the choice to her ultimately. Said he was willing to sell it if that's what she wanted but, though she'd shed a few tears for the cottage, she couldn't let him do it. It was her mess to fix after all and, besides, between Luke and Cassandra, all the islanders and even Pup, she was feeling blessed with such an abundance of assets these days as made its loss seem a lot more bearable. And she'd make sure it ended up in good hands.

She worked part-time at Jasper's for some income, while making plans to set up her own floristry business, and took over minibus duties from Eric on Mondays and Tuesdays, to Cassandra's delight. She served drinks in the pub too at weekends where Eithne updated her about plans for the spa, its final dimensions and price-tag fluctuating by the minute. But, while she kept herself busy and solvent, it felt as if her reunion with Luke would never come.

But it did come. And when it did it was ... *well* ... adventurous. And as they lay curled around each other after, panting and glowing on a stray patch of grass between two concealing banks of heather, Lily finally told him what had happened the day she'd tried to hitchhike home.

He was as heartbroken as she'd feared he would be, but for her as much as himself. For the blame she'd needlessly carried all those years. But they could share in the knowledge now that they'd made a little life between them once. A little life called Emma. And though it had been cut short, they'd carry her with them always.

But they needed to look to the future too and figure out a plan for themselves. Getting back to Inish Ruin two days out of every twenty was all Luke could manage at present. Would that be enough to sustain a relationship when they'd already spent so many years apart? But he understood how important it was for Lily to be on Inish Ruin. She'd been adrift for so long in the world, after all, and now she needed to be at home.

Lily had thought about that. Of how she'd longed for Barrett Cottage to feel like home again. But that had only happened once, just before it got smoked. But she'd experienced that feeling in Hook Cove since the moment she'd arrived. The feeling of being *exactly* where she was supposed to be. Looking at Luke, his gaze warmer even than the arms that were wrapped around her, she understood what the two experiences had in common – namely himself. So she told him she could be as happy in Cork as anywhere ... as long as she was with him.

He'd asked her to say that again.

She'd obliged and was rewarded with a kiss so full of feeling it curled her toes.

Would she be willing to move to Cork before Christmas?

She'd be willing to go the next day.

But willing or not, in the end she couldn't leave the island until the first week of January when the goofy-looking brown-and-white fur balls known as Pup's pups got their final vaccinations. They barked and whimpered on the pier, making little howling sounds to each other from inside their luxuriously appointed cage as Cooper stopped his 'zoomies' long enough to sniff them intermittently, wagging proudly, before heading off on another lap. Pup stayed beside them, though, with her head on Lily's foot as a broken umbrella did its best to shelter them both.

There were high swells that day and Seánie was taking the long route to reach them, the ferry hugging the coastline for shelter before making a dash across the open sea to reach the island.

Cassandra pushed through the crowds with Eric in tow, her umbrella held high. 'I'm so excited for you both but I'm really going to miss you.'

'But you'll see us all the time,' said Lily. 'We'll be back and forth. And you're coming to stay with us on Monday, right?'

'Yes. But it won't be the same as just calling in whenever I have something to tell you. Speaking of which, I meant to say if you and Luke ever have another baby and you need, you know, a godmother or whatever, you can always ask me. And Eric would love to be a godfather. Be great practice for when we have our own. Isn't that right, sweet pea?'

Everyone looked at Eric. The man had coped with having an actual relationship. He'd coped with being sweet pea'd but, besotted though he was, it had never occurred to him he'd have any business with Cassandra's womb. He stood dumb-stuck as his beloved gently explained, while winking at them all theatrically behind his back, that they'd probably just have the one child but they could think about having two if he really wanted.

A gargled protest issued from Eric's throat.

Okay, three, but she definitely drew the line at that.

Luke said the ferry was there.

Eric looked as if he was considering getting on it.

'I don't mean right away,' Cassandra assured him as she slid her hand into his with a smile that made Lily want to laugh. 'It might be nice to get married first.'

'Of course,' he squeaked.

Luke and Lily picked up the puppy cage and Pup's lead respectively and pushed through the crowds to board. They were handshaked and hugged all along the way. Tadhg patted their heads affectionately and wished them the best of luck. Jasper shook Luke's hand and told him to take good care of Lily or else. Donie and Pat gave them bags of nachos for the journey. Betty kissed them both.

Ned strode over last and placed a small, padded envelope in Lily's free hand. 'There,' he said, with a sigh of relief. 'Most difficult delivery ever. From your nana.'

Lily's jaw dropped. 'From *Nana?* What – what's in it?'

'It's marked confidential,' said Ned, looking a little affronted, as if his professionalism as a postman was being questioned. '*And* private,' he added, 'But she said you'd be glad to see it and if I could hold off giving it to you until you were heading away again it would be best. Which you kept not doing, by the way.' He stepped back and put his arm around Betty, who just gaped at him, her expression incredulous.

Lily stared at the envelope as Luke guided her down the steps and onto the ferry.

'*You'll catch your death, Luke!*' Eithne called. '*Where's your coat?*'

'*I don't know. Somewhere.*'

'*It's not good for your lungs going around without a coat. You're not Superman, you know?*'

'Relax,' said Paudie, beside her. 'Lily'll look after him. Stop fussing. Bad for your blood pressure.'

'Don't you start with all that relax business again,' said Eithne. 'You're driving me insane. How will she look after him? She has only a thin jacket on herself. Not a lick of sense between the pair of them.'

Seánie started up the engine. Pup and the puppies were stowed in the cabin. The ferry reversed and turned and Lily and Luke moved to the stern to wave to everyone on the pier and then to wave them away on home before they were all soaked.

The ferry bobbed and dipped till they cleared the shelter of the harbour. Then it pitched and heaved. Lukc gripped the handrail either side of her to keep her in place and they watched as the pier gradually emptied. The minibus was first up the hill. Next was Shay's tractor. The golf buggy followed and then it was the turn of the walkers, trailing slowly, hooded figures in green and black until there was just one person left: a small figure by the end wall, getting smaller by the second.

'Who's that?' asked Lily, squinting through the rain.

'I don't see anyone.'

The sun broke free from the clouds. A rainbow formed, spanning the gap between the mainland and the island. It touched the pier and Lily's heart sped in her chest.

She raised her hand in greeting.

She could have sworn the figure by the wall did the same.

'Lily?'

Afraid to even blink, she thrust the envelope at him. 'Open it. Quick.'

Paper ripped. 'It's your Post Office savings book.' She heard pages flipping, then a long, low whistle. '*Um*, there's a rake load of money in it. And a letter.'

'Read it!'

He did so. Aloud.

'*My darling Lily,*

Please find enclosed your Post Office savings book. I've been squirreling away cash for you as you'll see. But I just found out it might count against you when it comes to calculating your inheritance tax. Which doesn't seem fair. I haven't mentioned it to Seánie who's stressed enough about being an Executor. Nor Ned, who's as by-the-book as it gets. My thinking is it's probably best to keep it to yourself. If this reaches you after everything is settled, all the better.

I'm sure it was a surprise to read the will. That I left half the cottage to Luke? But in doing right by you when you were younger, I fear I did wrong by him. I hadn't imagination enough back then to realise a first love could be anything but what my own had been – a calm and peaceful thing. But by bringing you two together again in settling my will, I'm hoping to make amends. My guess is that Luke will refuse to take a cent anyway but I imagine ye'll have at least one good squabble about it. More hopefully! And maybe get the chance to rekindle your spark?

And finally, can I ask you to look out for Seánie for me? I never told you but he was my first love. Though other relationships separated us over the years, we stayed friends. I wish it hadn't taken my illness for him to tell me he was still in love with me but he's never been the best at expressing himself. More the silent type. Unlike Luke, who's prone to tell a person more than they ever needed to know! How ye ever kept your dalliancing a secret so long is beyond me.

My greatest wish for you, Lily, has always been that you don't make the same mistake as your mam and I and give your heart to a man who doesn't deserve it. But, with Luke by your side, I don't think there'd be any danger of that. He told me once he wanted to marry you. Know he'd have my blessing and you'd have it too, my most darling girl, with all the love in my heart.

Nana x

PS Keep Pup if you can. She'd never bite you. Drool on you for Ireland now but never bite.

PPS In case Tadhg forgets, there seems to be a problem with the chimney. Best get it assessed before winter.'

The rainbow had vanished and the figure on the pier along with it. Lily felt warm tears on her cheeks. Nana had never stopped loving her. It was only the streak of determination they shared, tangled with misguided love and pride, which had kept them apart. But she had faith they'd see each other again someday and make it all right. That they'd laugh and hold each other once more and all would be well. But until then, Lily had a life to live and people to love. So she wiped the tears away and turned to Luke, meeting his concerned expression with the most reassuring smile she could muster.

'So, now what?'

He slipped his arm more tightly around her, spacing his legs to balance them as the ferry caught a rolling swell. 'I'm thinking, if we're very lucky, happily ever after?'

She cocked an eyebrow. 'And if we're not?'

'Death by disgruntled spouse for me. Eight to ten with good behaviour for you.'

She smiled. 'That assumes you have me for a spouse first, though.'

His cheeks dimpled and his quicksilver eyes shone irrepressibly. 'It does, doesn't it?'

She felt her own eyes widen. 'Luke O'Callaghan, don't you dare propose! *On a pitching ferry. While I'm soaking wet.*'

'I've seen you in worse states. All I ever think when I look at you is rose – out of season. So I would like to propose now, even if you do look like a drowned rat, but unfortunately I'm under strict instructions from Cassandra to be far more romantic.'

'Well, thank goodness for that,' she said, burying her head in his chest.

He rubbed her back, warming her. 'So here's the plan instead. First, I'm going to go off to war and get horribly maimed. You'll get married to my brother while I'm gone – you can take your pick between Conor or James, I suppose – and then years later I'll return home, lame and half-blind and you'll realise you can't love them the way you love me. And then we do whatever it takes to be together.'

She laughed, the sound muffled against his jumper.

'Or we could just skip the messy bit and get married now. But I'm easy, either way.' He pulled back and waited until she looked up at him. 'Seriously though. What do you say? Even your nana is telling us to get married. From the afterlife, no less.'

'She's not *telling* us to get married. Just that we'd have her blessing if we wanted to.'

His head shake was all affection. 'This is no time for accuracy, Lil. It's perfectly clear if you read between the lines. Go on.' He got down on one knee, clinging precariously to the rail beside him. '*Marry me. I dare you.*' When she didn't reply he attempted a casual shrug. 'I mightn't ask again.'

'I give it a fortnight but why do you even *want* to get married? You know I love you. It's not like I'm going anywhere.'

'Sure you won't come to your senses at some point?'

'I have no plans to,' she promised with a straight face. 'I do solemnly swear.'

He got up off his knees and put her in a mock headlock for that. 'Will you marry me or won't you?'

'*Yes!*'

He released her and eyed her with suspicion. 'Yes you will or yes you won't?'

'Yes, Luko. I will,' she beamed. 'Now, what do you have to say about that?'

His smile of triumph said plenty – before Seánie tooted the horn in celebration and made them both jump.

Luke drew her to him swiftly for a kiss to seal the deal. 'Thought as much.'

The End